DAVID EBSWORTH is the pen name of writer negotiator and workers' representative fo General Workers' Union. He was born in L Wrexham, North Wales, with his wife Ann since 1981.

Following his retirement, Dave began to write historical fiction in 2009 and has subsequently published ten novels: political thrillers set against the history of the 1745 Jacobite rebellion, the 1879 Anglo-Zulu War, the Battle of Waterloo, warlord rivalry in Sixth Century Britain, and the Spanish Civil War. His sixth book, *Until the Curtain Falls* returned to that same Spanish conflict, following the story of journalist Jack Telford, and is published in Spanish under the title *Hasta Que Caiga el Telón*. Jack Telford, as it happens, is also the main protagonist in a separate novella, *The Lisbon Labyrinth*.

Dave's *Yale Trilogy* tells the story of intrigue and mayhem around nabob, philanthropist (and slave-trader) Elihu Yale – who gave his name to Yale University – but told through the eyes of his much-maligned and largely forgotten wife, Catherine.

Each of Dave's novels has been critically acclaimed by the Historical Novel Society and been awarded the coveted B.R.A.G. Medallion for independent authors.

The previous and tenth novel is the third of his stories about Jack Telford and takes Jack into the turmoil of the Second World War but through a series of real-life episodes, which are truly stranger than fiction.

For more information on the author and his work, visit his website at www.davidebsworth.com.

Also by David Ebsworth

The Jacobites' Apprentice
A story of the 1745 Rebellion.

The Jack Telford Series
Political thrillers set towards the end of the Spanish Civil War and beyond.

The Assassin's Mark

Until the Curtain Falls
(published in Spanish as *Hasta Que Caiga el Telón*)

A Betrayal of Heroes
(published in 2021)

The Lisbon Labyrinth
(an e-book novella, set during the 1974 Portuguese Revolution)

The Kraals of Ulundi: A Novel of the Zulu War

The Last Campaign of Marianne Tambour: A Novel of Waterloo

The Song-Sayer's Lament
Another political thriller but this time set in the time we know as the
Dark Ages, 6th Century post-Roman Britain

The Yale Trilogy
Set in old Madras, London and northern England between 1672 and 1721

The Doubtful Diaries of Wicked Mistress Yale

Mistress Yale's Diaries, The Glorious Return

Wicked Mistress Yale, The Parting Glass

To Sue, Lots of Love!

The
HOUSE
on
HUNTER
STREET

DAVID EBSWORTH

Best Wishes from Dave

SilverWood

Published in 2022 by SilverWood Books

SilverWood Books Ltd
14 Small Street, Bristol, BS1 1DE, United Kingdom
www.silverwoodbooks.co.uk

ISBN 978-1-80042-223-0 (paperback)

British Library Cataloguing in Publication Data
A CIP catalogue record for this book is available from the British Library

Page design and typesetting by SilverWood Books

Dedicated to the memory of Eric Scott Lynch

Author's Note

This is a work of fiction. Its historical background derives from the turbulent events in Liverpool during 1911. Like so many historical events, these are still frequently the subject of fierce debate – and particularly those surrounding the transport strikes which took place during that fateful summer. To a lesser extent, there is also some dispute about the city's reaction to the Votes for Women campaigns running alongside the strikes. And one element of the historical events – the strike by West African Kru seamen which preceded the more widespread disputes – is almost entirely unresearched and rarely even mentioned.

For readers who would like to know more about the background, I've included some additional explanations in the acknowledgements at the end.

As usual, where I have knowingly tweaked the history, I've detailed those distortions in the separate notes at the back of the book. Also as usual, any other examples of the events, or the characters, being inaccurately portrayed are errors on my part. But perhaps more than any of my other novels, in this case I need to stress that I deliberately wrote the events as I imagined they would have been viewed by the three very different fictional characters through whom the story is told – by Cari Maddox, by Tom Priddy and by Amos Gartee. To make the point, sometimes the same event is portrayed entirely differently, depending on the perspective of the beholder. They are the perspectives of my fictional characters – rather than my own.

So, yes, this is a disclaimer! And, therefore, I should make a point about Amos Gartee's part in the story. About language, as well. It's impossible to relate this aspect of 1911 without touching on the issue of racism. Even "liberal" contemporary accounts use terminology in relation to the African seamen which, today, is unacceptable. But it would have been stupid, in my personal opinion, not to have reflected some of those attitudes in the language of the book. Hence some of the characters will use terms like "Darkies" or "monkey boats", and similar. And even the word "Krooboys" – in which the element "boys" would have been used to imply that Africans were somehow inferior to European men. Offensive, yes.

Then, just to make things even more difficult, I needed to deal as realistically as I was able with Amos Gartee's own voice, and those of his fellow-strikers. The research for this was complicated, and I may well have got the end result completely wrong. The Kru, of course, have their own languages – part of an entire family of languages prevalent, at least in the early 1900s, throughout that area of Liberia, Sierra Leone and the Ivory Coast. And within each language, a mass of dialects. In the case of Nana Kru, in Liberia, the language known as Daloa Bété, or simply Bété. And where I couldn't find the vocabulary I needed, I borrowed words from neighbouring tongues – and hence my use of *poto* for "white."

In addition, there was – and still is – a form of vernacular creole Liberian English, known as Liberian *Kreyol* (also in the West Indies) or sometimes *Kolokwa*. In neighbouring Sierra Leone, this is *Krio*, still hugely widespread. So, it's *Kreyol* which Amos uses most often when he's speaking English – though it's a massively simplified form of this vernacular, to make it easier for contemporary readers in English. I just hope it works – and apologies if it doesn't.

David Ebsworth
May 2022

THE HOUSE ON HUNTER STREET

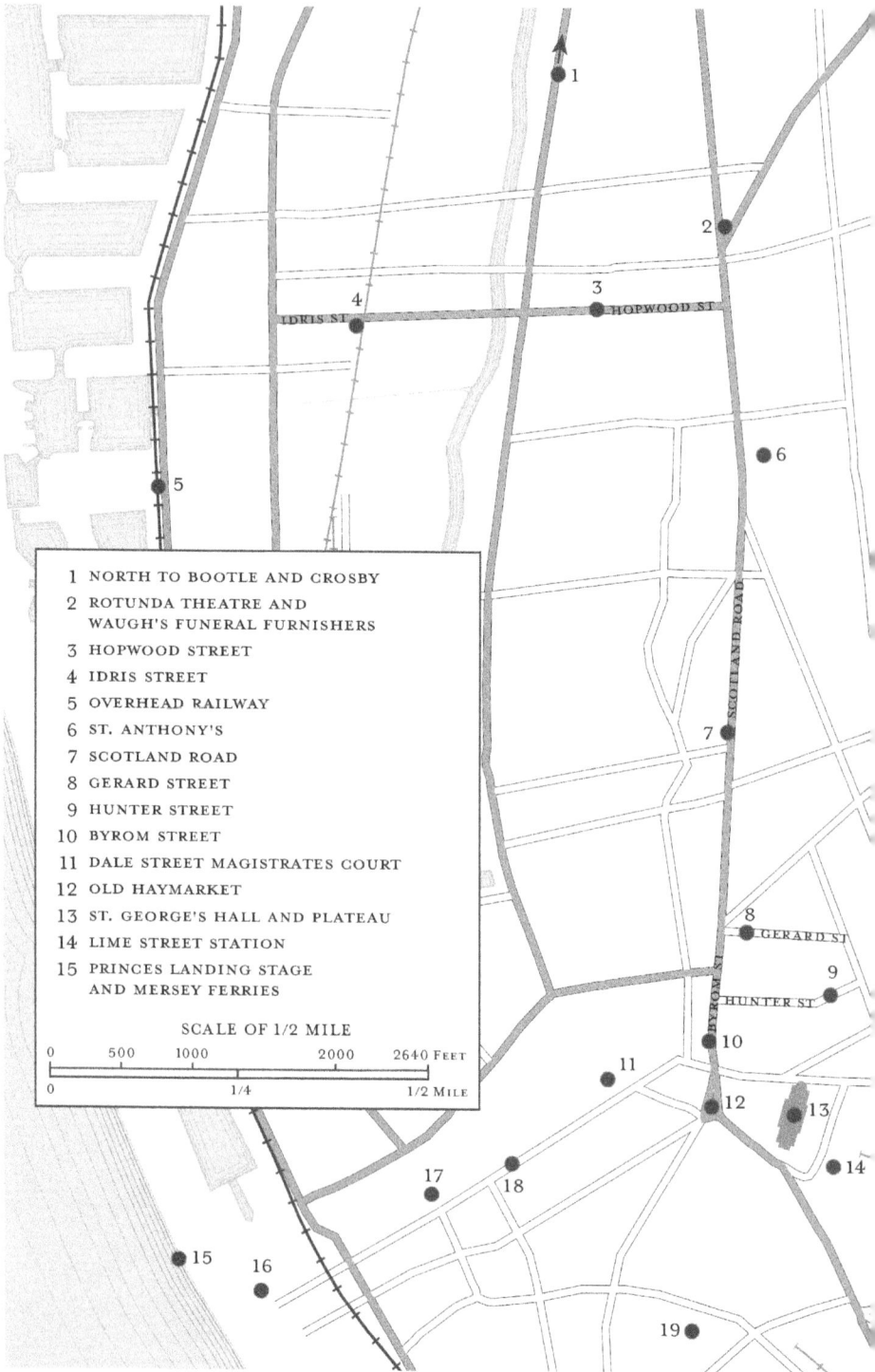

1   NORTH TO BOOTLE AND CROSBY

2   ROTUNDA THEATRE AND
     WAUGH'S FUNERAL FURNISHERS

3   HOPWOOD STREET

4   IDRIS STREET

5   OVERHEAD RAILWAY

6   ST. ANTHONY'S

7   SCOTLAND ROAD

8   GERARD STREET

9   HUNTER STREET

10   BYROM STREET

11   DALE STREET MAGISTRATES COURT

12   OLD HAYMARKET

13   ST. GEORGE'S HALL AND PLATEAU

14   LIME STREET STATION

15   PRINCES LANDING STAGE
      AND MERSEY FERRIES

SCALE OF 1/2 MILE

0   500   1000   2000   2640 FEET

0   1/4   1/2 MILE

IDRIS ST

HOPWOOD ST

SCOTLAND ROAD

GERARD ST

HUNTER ST

BYROM ST

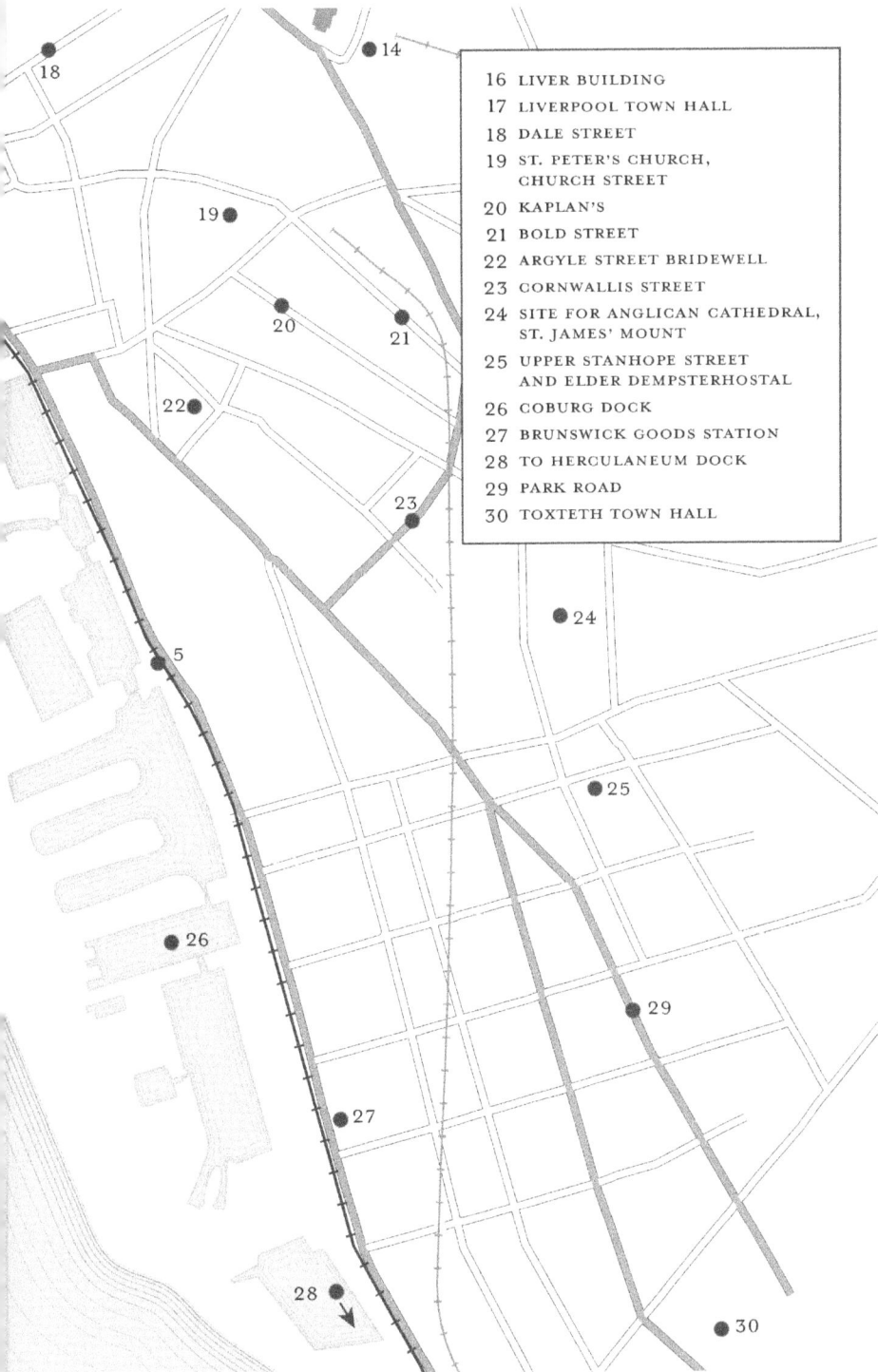

16 LIVER BUILDING
17 LIVERPOOL TOWN HALL
18 DALE STREET
19 ST. PETER'S CHURCH,
   CHURCH STREET
20 KAPLAN'S
21 BOLD STREET
22 ARGYLE STREET BRIDEWELL
23 CORNWALLIS STREET
24 SITE FOR ANGLICAN CATHEDRAL,
   ST. JAMES' MOUNT
25 UPPER STANHOPE STREET
   AND ELDER DEMPSTERHOSTAL
26 COBURG DOCK
27 BRUNSWICK GOODS STATION
28 TO HERCULANEUM DOCK
29 PARK ROAD
30 TOXTETH TOWN HALL

Chapter One

Sunday 2nd April 1911

11.15am

Like Pastor Jenkins, he had heard the word revolution whispered on the streets.

The city was a patchwork quilt of skin colours and creeds. Sin on every corner. A puzzling place, but one in which Tom Priddy had been forced to find his way, to track down his prey.

Thus, he had followed them today – the old man and the two girls. Followed, as he'd done many times since his arrival in Liverpool. Watching and learning. Biding his time.

One girl, a couple of years younger than him, of course. Thin as the runner beans straggling up their sticks in the gardens of the Llewellyn Hotel when he was a boy. The other, shorter, pleasantly rounded. Both of them in their Sunday best, grey hems showing beneath the dun-coloured coat skirts.

The old man? A Humpty Dumpty, stocky as the eldest daughter was slim, his build closer to the younger girl.

Tom had followed them, as often before, to the grand Victoria Chapel on Crosshall Street, where they'd met with other members of the family. He sat himself, camouflaged in the shadows at the back, and listened to the outraged words of Pastor Jenkins. Romans, thirteen: two.

'Whosoever therefore resisteth the power,' the preacher had roared, 'resisteth the ordinance of God: and they that resist shall receive to themselves damnation.'

And yes, Pastor Jenkins had heard men speak of revolution. Had there not been signs aplenty?

The murderous Jewish anarchist, Peter the Painter, on the run from London, and sighted here, in their very midst. The threat of a seamen's strike to disrupt the summer's Coronation. Strikes already spreading – the boiler scalers and so many others. The Wallasey carters. Heathen Africans on strike at the Harrington Dock. And even – women.

Such sadness in the pastor's voice that Tom Priddy believed the poor fellow's heart must surely break.

Women at the sugar works on Falkner Street. Women – on strike! And now, another woman, one of those suffragettes, had brought shame on the city – attacked Secretary of State for War Haldane at Lime Street Station. Votes for women, indeed. Where would it all end? Was this any way to commence a new century? He prayed that tonight, Census night, the women of this city would obey the law, not be pushed over the edge into recklessness.

A closing hymn. *The Lord's My Shepherd.*

Indeed, He was, though Tom was careful to mouth the words quietly, for his singing voice tended to turn heads, and he could ill afford to draw attention to himself.

'*My table Thou hast furnished, in presence of my foes.*'

Yes, quite. His Lord Jesus had led him here, approved Tom Priddy's plans for revenge – even though the plans themselves still lacked refinement.

He'd thought about it as he followed them back to the Hunter Street house. Most of it occupied the two floors above the Weights and Measures Office, at numbers one to five, the front door at number seven, and then around the corner into Dawson Place. The old man, and the thin beanpole of a girl had gone inside. But the second girl, the shorter dumpling, had parted company with them on the doorsteps.

Tom Priddy couldn't hear what they'd said but she'd made some gesture, pointing up the street, as if she intended to visit a friend or neighbour. Indeed, she had done so, emerged minutes later with a man from an alleyway up the road. With this fair-haired and square-headed fellow in tow, she'd doubled back, careful not to be seen, headed off towards the tram terminus at the Old Haymarket.

Interesting. Just one more riddle, he supposed. Perhaps time would provide the answers. Time – and his Lord Jesus.

For now, he'd have to wait a while, build up his courage. Tolerate the raucous noises, the stink of sour ale from the boozer at his back. The Byrom. Wouldn't be allowed back home, of course. No Sunday opening in Wales. God's own country – though he guessed he might never see it again.

11.30am

Census night. And she would strike a blow. Cari thrilled at the thought of it, glad to be distracted from her guilt. A guilt she dispelled, as so often when she tackled her demons, with a line she might work, later, into another of her poems.

The Census circumstances make no sense.

The line amused her, though the mirth quickly vanished. Up to her elbows in carrot and spud peelings.

Sometimes, alone in the place, she could almost swear she heard him. The baby, Pryce, still there. It was her guilt, she knew, which bound him to their gloomy house on Hunter Street. A conundrum. A sense of the babe's retaliation for her wickedness.

His christening gown hung to this day, seventeen years later, in her tada's bedroom closet – next to a last reminder of their mam. The occasional Sunday frock, rose pink.

Here on the shelves of the confined kitchen, more of the reliquaries to help harbour the child's spirit. Reminders none of them had quite been able to discard despite the time they'd stood there. Two prow-shaped babies' drinking bottles. Soothing syrups. The emerald flask of children's cordial. And the collection of powders and pills which had so spectacularly failed to save a sacrificial Pryce.

Treatments for an unassuming fever before the Medical Officer finally understood that smallpox was back in the city. Merely a short-lived taste of the explosive epidemic six years later, but sufficient to claim the babe. And enough to almost take Cari's youngest sister, Wyn – Winifred – as well.

Cari, senior of three daughters and one surviving son, had tried to fill her mother's shoes ever since. When their mam had died – and far worse after Pryce had followed her – there'd been her tada's years with the demon drink. Long, long before his temperance days.

15

Memories. How old was she, back then? Nine? Ten? She could recall to this day how her tada's feet had dragged and stumbled on the risers during the tear-drenched task of helping and hauling him up the stairs to his bed. And how many times had he lashed out at her in the process? She couldn't remember. Chose not to remember. Family, see? It's what you did with family. Choose not to remember. In any case, there'd always been the younger ones to worry about.

She glanced around from the white stone kitchen sink.

'You'll be home, then?' she shouted to her tada. 'When they come to collect the forms tomorrow?'

Census night. Prospect of breaking the law. Later. For the fight. For the vote. For the cause.

11.35am

Blood was, of course, literally thicker than water, Tom Priddy decided. Every fool knew *that* was true. Just spend a few days in the Preparation Room with Old Clamp. He'd learned a lot from Old Clamp. And he would always be grateful to Waugh for the lodgings above his business. The best funeral furnishers in Liverpool, Waugh's advertisements boasted.

But time to make his move, now. He could collect his few belongings from Waugh's later

Sunday, and he'd done his duty. Up and dressed early, then over to the All Souls mortuary. Just to check, like. Make sure all the paperwork was in order before the grieving families began their five-mile journey out to Ford Cemetery for the interments. The mourners for all the departed who may have been lying in rest at All Souls since the previous collective procession out to the Catholic burial ground earlier in the week. Just three such processions each week, Waugh had explained, and Tom wondered whether this might be another source of grievance to those of that Catholic faith. Even in death, denied equal treatment, they'd say.

Not that he cared much, mind. Papists, see.

And at least he didn't have to make the walk himself. There'd been these other things to do today. Tram into town. To the Haymarket, he'd decided. Then walked back here to Hunter Street from there. Followed them to chapel. To watch. To wait. But not a bad day for April.

Easter coming up. His Lord Jesus lived within him, of course, guided his hand. But things always got so busy for Him around Easter. So, good to get things moving now. Family things. Ties of blood. A reunion, of sorts, he supposed. Other things to be buried. Or, at least, the start of some grave digging.

11.45am

Where might a good Christian fellow be supposed to worship in this cold Liverpool place? Amos Gartee had no idea. Sunday. Though at least they still had a roof over their heads. On strike, but so far nobody from the Elder Dempster company's bossmen had attempted to shift them from the hostel.

The truth? They might as well have been invisible. For the bossmen did not seem troubled by their strike. And nobody else, either. He had spoken at the offices of their Liverpool newspaper – about their plight. Though he feared they had not been understood. And then, just a week ago, a big meeting. Some great distance away. They had walked, in the icy cold and the rain. To that meeting. Dockers and white seamen. Some had even congratulated them, told them a bigger strike was coming soon. All seamen together. Hold out, they'd said. Until the big strike. Then, nothing!

Yet they had food in their bellies. This morning, Cookie had served them up some gruel. It looked like the yellow *garri* they'd eaten back in Nana Kru, but without the flavour.

'*É guéu,*' he shouted from his table. Bon appetit. His own *Bété* tongue. Then repeated in the *Bakwe* of his brothers from the Kru's more westerly lands. These weren't all Kru, naturally. Many of them Bassa, or Grebo, or Sapo. But all from the Kru towns and using the cousin tongues. Mende boys, as well, with their Loma, Bandi and Loko allies. And Jonah Samba, the Mende man, always biting at his heels. Challenging his leadership.

Difficult. They would be expecting him to say something. Words of inspiration. From his bible, perhaps. His bible in this English, of course. It was the way the missionaries had taught him to read some of the English words. Read them slowly. Enough for him to be useful on the ships. No bible in *Bété*, though, nor any of the other tongues they shared. No paper-writing *Bété* at all.

They said some of the missionary pastors had begun to study the sounds of their speech, invent symbols to mimic the sounds. To set those symbols down with ink. The same with the *Mende*, which so many spoke in Liberia.

Well, good luck with that little venture, he thought.

How many bibles, he wondered, to capture all the sounds, all the dialects, all the tongues, even just of the six hundred miles of coastline he'd worked since he was a boy, from Abidjan in the south to Banjul in the north.

And Amos had seen no sign of these symbols.

He set down his spoon, opened the bible to a page he'd chosen this morning. Some of his Christian brothers had asked him whether to strike was a good thing. A Christian thing. Would Nyesoa be with them in their fight? So, he should answer their concerns.

Jeremiah, Chapter twenty-two. Verse three.

Thus saith the LORD; Execute ye judgment and righteousness, and deliver the spoiled out of the hand of the oppressor: and do no wrong, do no violence to the stranger, the fatherless, nor the widow, neither shed innocent blood in this place.

He read it through. Slow, as usual. Painfully slow.

This was not the English he used daily. No, that was their Liberian *Kreyol* – the cousins' tongue they *did* share, all along that six-hundred-mile shoreline. Cousins? Yes family. More or less.

'A'right,' he began to translate. 'Be so! This how our Lord say.'

Family. They must stick together as family. Because they had few friends here. Almost none. Except, perhaps, the *poto* woman. If she came, of course.

11.55am

The Census. Breaking the law. Yes, thought Cari. But, for now, seemingly just another opportunity for her tada to get back on his soapbox.

'No privacy,' he shouted from the parlour. Late morning in the Maddox household. 'Always somebody prying into your business these days. Spying on a man, it is. That's all. And you think these Johnny foreigners will all be waiting around to get themselves listed? I don't think so. Can't move for them. Just walk outside, girl, see how long it is before you hear anybody speak the King's English.'

As it happened, Cari knew that their neighbourly Italians, the Morettas, round in the court, had been in Liverpool for a full generation longer than her own family. The Morettas shared their misnamed and permanently forbidding passageway with a German family, the reputable relatives of *Herr* Jurks, who could also trace his roots here far deeper than hers. But she knew she'd have been wasting her breath trying to point out the irony. Instead, she inclined her head towards the kitchen doorway, smiled to herself.

'And on the Lord's Day,' her father said. She imagined the shaking of his head in despair. 'What are we supposed to do? Miss chapel tonight?'

'You've already been to chapel,' she called back. 'We only just got home. Don't have to miss anything, like. Just fill in the forms.'

He ignored that, but came to stand in the doorway, a crumpled grey copy of the previous night's *Football Echo* dangling from one set of prematurely arthritic fingers, the smoking fragment of a Woodbine dangling from the other.

'Not that you'd be bothered about chapel, mind,' he said. Then he softened. 'Can I help you with that, *cariad*?'

'Women's work,' she snapped at him. 'Don't bother yourself.'

Daniel Owen! It was her favourite and mildest oath. Times, even for me, Cari thought, when this chief cook and bottle washer thing wears a bit thin. And no help from Nesta, as usual. Off on this latest of her crusades – in company with the old German's nephew, Ernst.

'No need for sarcasm, see,' said her tada. 'I've cooked for you enough times, girl.'

He had, she supposed. Sometimes, anyway. After their mam died. When he'd been sober. And only until she was old enough to take up the burden herself. Yet they'd never wanted for a square meal. And she'd never bettered his cawl stew. Just regretted the time she'd lost from school. All those occasions hidden from the school board's kid-catcher. Hardly ever got there, to tell the truth. Had to teach herself, in the end. The Library on William Brown Street, her discovery of iambic pentameter. Her yellowed notebooks.

*

Go down to wells of literary fame,
And drink our fill of university.

'What's happened to you, Ceridwen?' her tada was saying. 'Good girl, you were. Always. And now – what? Mixed up with all this other nonsense.'

'Twenty-two, Tada. Not a girl. Not anymore. And nonsense, is it? Seems to me we're doing the Lord's work. Fighting for the rights He intended us to have.'

Yes, she wanted to shout, Cari cares!

She wiped a sleeve across her forehead, checked to make sure there was enough custard powder left in the tin. Steam from the suet pudding simmering on the hot plate, the salt-sweet smoky scent of a cheap gammon joint roasting in the chimney oven, thankfully washing out the odours of paper, ink and cleaning fluid from the printshop below, which normally pervaded their daily lives.

'According to Holy Scripture, *cariad*, a woman's only duty is obedience. "*For the husband is the head of the wife, even as Christ is the head of the church.*" And how can it be the Lord's work you're about? When it breaks the law. I might not like the Census, Cari, but it is the law.'

He so rarely used her nickname it caught her by surprise, yet she still trotted out the slogan.

'If women don't count,' she said, 'we won't be counted. Better if me and Nesta make ourselves scarce. Unless you'd prefer us to stay. Spoil the Census Form, like. Lots of others doing it, Tada. *No vote, no census.* Or, *No other persons – only a couple of women.* I could write that kind of thing.'

Huw Maddox, her father, couldn't have looked more horrified if Satan himself had appeared before him. But the thought of Satan sent a shiver down her spine, as though somebody had walked over her grave. A premonition of doom. More memories of Pryce.

'*Duw*, you wouldn't do that, *cariad*,' he said. 'Get me arrested, like.'

'They'll not be arresting anybody, Tada.' She smiled at him. It was almost her natural expression, teeth just a touch excessively prominent for her lips. But there were those who liked this feature. Her accidental grin. So they said.

'Too many of us,' she went on. 'Revolution, that's what this is. Census Night Revolution. Not a town anywhere without a boycott going on. But you and Taffy can give them what they need.'

She wrapped the peelings in yesterday's paper, dumped them in the scullery, kicked a cockroach into oblivion – oh, how she hated them – and fetched the plates, set them on the scrubbed table.

'Dafydd?' he yelled. Cari's brother, Dafydd – though the rest of the world called him Taffy. 'You don't see him being here, do you? He's another one. Know what it's like? Having to make excuses? Pastor Jenkins. About why my boy has no time for chapel anymore. It's a girl Dafydd's got. That's what I'm guessing. A girl. And no more time for chapel.'

He was right, of course. Cari knew it. Taffy, just two years younger than her, was indeed courting. But if their tada had known the truth of it, he'd have had an apoplexy. Bad enough that Taffy wasn't yet back from the boozer. Simply being in such a place was now an offence against her father's sensibilities, despite his own earlier problems. Maybe because of them. But on the Sabbath?

'You'd better tell me where you want to go, anyway,' he said. 'You and Nesta. Before I give my permission.'

She couldn't tell him, naturally. Hard to say which of their assignations – Taffy's, or her own and Nesta's – would have shattered him most. He thought it was bad enough that the girls were so involved with the fight. Time to put her foot down. Militantly. Oh, how she envied those women who could undertake the work openly with pride, without having to defend it all the time.

'Nessie'll not miss her Sunday dinner, Tada. Then we'll work something out. And we're not doing anything that needs permission.'

No, Nesta wouldn't miss dinner. Hopefully, anyhow. But Cari couldn't help worrying that, even with Ernst Jurks for company, her sister's assignation today might not have been her brightest idea.

But tonight? And open houses? That's what some of the women had organised. Couple of them over in Seacombe and Birkenhead. Another in Waterloo. They could all gather. Not sleeping there, so no need to put their details on any form. Just be anonymous women. Because that's what they were. No votes. No rights. Anonymous.

'Or we might go up to the George's Hall,' she said. 'There's going to be a promenade around the Haymarket until after midnight.'

They were going to none of those, though. Not straight away, anyhow. Nesta once again had other plans. Dear Nesta. Bone idle when it came to chores, but too precious for Cari to ever be vexed by it. Her present passion – and one that needed to be kept quiet not only from their father, but from Taffy, as well. It had already caused enough trouble. More than enough. All the meetings they'd attended.

'Walking the streets at midnight?' her father said. 'I'm just thankful your mam can't hear all this. What would she have said, girl?'

Their mother had died giving birth to Pryce, of course. Five kids in five years. Seventeen years and more he'd been without her and, Cari thought, never a day without missing her, without talking about her. Cari's inheritance from her mam? Nimble fingers, thimble fingers, and a gift for millinery. Upstairs in her room, a half-finished *Sans Souci* for a friend of Mrs Kaplan. And the bonnets for Easter, just a couple of weeks away.

'Anyway, you'll be wasting your time,' he said. 'Like it or not, the bobbies have been told to count any wanderers. So they reckon. Well, at least Winifred will do her duty, I suppose.'

'Wyn's wedded to chapel,' she said, and meant it literally.

At nineteen, Winifred no longer lived with them. Married, to the Victoria Chapel's harmonium player. Though Cari had never taken to him. Rhys Fingers, they called him – because of the harmonium. And because – well, she wouldn't dwell on this, not on the Sabbath.

His real name was Rhys Morgan. Ten years older than Wyn. Already beginning to lose his hair. In patches. Strange man. Something not right. But a good job – dock gateman. And renting a house down on Idris Street. Cari had tried to convince Wyn to join the WSPU, with herself and Nesta. But Wyn was cut from some different cloth. Didn't believe in violence she said. Neither did Cari, truth be told. Well, maybe just a bit.

When Cari and Nesta decided to join the fight, they'd gone window-shopping. Easy enough. Plenty of meetings going on. So they could listen to speakers. Some good ones as well and, personally, they liked Mrs Rathbone. Made her mark, she had. First woman ever to sit on the City Council. Real firebrand. Against low pay and Liverpool's Dickens-like slum housing. But Mrs Rathbone was with the Liverpool Women's Suffrage Society and they'd been around a long time. Nearly twenty years. Got them nowhere. Or so the speakers from the Women's Social and Political Union had said.

They'd got nowhere, in Cari's opinion, for the whole *forty* years – never mind twenty – in which women had been stretching through the bars of their cage for the vote. All those monster petitions. Back then. In the sixties and seventies. Long before Cari's time. Three million signatures. MPs returned to Parliament on the promise they'd stand with the women. Nothing. *Rargian fawr!* she thought. Good heavens. Forty years. One trick after another to stop them getting the vote. She hated them. The whole rotten bunch. The powerful. The wealthy. Oh, Cari get off your knees!

Five years earlier, though, a scattering of women had decided they'd had enough. Direct action, bellicose protest, that's what was needed. The Women's Social and Political Union was formed. And that's what they'd joined. Cari and sweet Nessie. A couple of years back, just before Cari's first meeting with them, there in the city, WSPU members had been attacked by a vicious mob. No qualms about violence, that bunch. And did you not need to fight fire with fire?

They started going to the meetings regularly, selling the WSPU paper. But not Winifred. Winifred wouldn't be joining anything without her husband's say-so.

'So yes, Tada,' she said now, 'Wyn will be dutifully in her place and Rhys will list her as sleeping there, all prim and proper for the enumerator. I'm sure she will.'

And this was when their Sunday morning was disturbed by knocking below. The street door. Strange time for anybody to come calling.

Cari doubled and ducked down the tight stairway with its creaking, precipitous risers, to the dank passageway. It led, in one direction, past the splinter-sharp bench at which her tada would mend their shoes, to the printshop – itself actually in the cobbled confines of Dawson Place where they'd played so often as children. Beyond the printshop, to the yard and the privy. The other way, with its single grey window, a threadbare stretch of red runner reached to the building's front steps on Hunter Street. Nothing else on the ground floor since the remainder of the building's Hunter Street side belonged to the Weights and Measures office.

She squeezed past the hand-made baby carriage which had served them all but was presently just one more souvenir of baby Pryce they'd found impossible to discard. Well, everybody dies, she reminded herself. Another way of trying to dispel the guilt – though one always doomed to failure.

It was raining, carrying the Mersey's prevailing essence of brine and old oakum, the door already half-open, awaiting the return of Taffy and Nesta. But Cari found there a young man, frog-eyed and hauntingly pale.

Like – well, like a ghost himself.

12.15pm

How many times had he watched her come and go? Still, strange now to be standing there confronted by the reality of so many desires. So many dreams. Even taller, more slender, than she'd appeared from a distance. Hair neither straight nor curly. Features neither plain nor pretty. Eyes neither grey nor green. Just the over-enthusiastic buck-toothed grin.

'I was looking for Mister Maddox.' He knew he spoke in a slow monotone – that he gave the impression of being somewhat simple. No harm in it, he thought. Often made things easier for him. 'Huw Maddox.'

Her head was cocked to one side. Listening. For what? His accent familiar perhaps? Like her tada's?

'What business?' she replied.

Estella Havisham, he decided, and he almost laughed. It was the one thing everybody remembered about Huw Maddox. His passion for Dickens. And *Great Expectations* in particular. His favourite. In English, that is. In the *Cymraeg*, he probably preferred Daniel Owen. From his own observations, Huw Maddox seemed generally an avuncular man, often more Pickwick than Pip, though perhaps lately the better side of his nature seemed shrivelled by circumstance. Great expectations, meagre realities, which contrived to anchor Maddox and his family in hard times. He supposed the girl would have been raised on Dickens as well, and he was pleased to have made the connection so early. Yes, Estella Havisham.

'Printing business,' he said, and felt the muscles in his right cheek begin to spasm. 'No – what about this? Family business. Family, girl.'

'You're no family I've ever seen,' the girl said. 'How? Family, I mean.'

'*Duw Annwyl*, Beanpole,' he told her. Good God. 'You'll never know if I die here on the step. Uncle Huw in, is he? Or not?'

And Beanpole? He looked for reaction. Saw his barb hit home. It had stung her, he was sure. Had she perhaps been called the same before? She was staring at him again. Trying to work things out? Did she imagine they'd already met? Maybe running through the faces of boys she remembered from her earlier years. Attempting to place him. A boy with a cruel streak, she'd be thinking. A lad with lank hair, no colour to his flesh. Bulging frog eyes. Yes, he knew how he looked, wore his ugliness with pride. And while she pondered these things, he stepped past her, into the hallway, out of the drizzle, shook his upturned jacket collar.

'Who shall I say...?' the girl had begun. 'And Beanpole? Who d'you think...?' But by then he was gone again, already halfway up the stairs.

He found the parlour easily enough. Not much to see. A table and four mismatched chairs. Two more against the walls beneath a couple of framed photographs. Linoleum on the floor. A dresser. A Cast Iron Plant, which had seen better days. And a flower-patterned sofa with holes in the arms. On the sofa, Huw Maddox, looking up at him, questioning, as the girl had done, a copy of the *Football Echo* on his knee, a cigarette in his hand. Filthy habit, that was.

The old man had something of the family about him, mind. A drop of pit pony in the blood. Short and stocky, broad at the shoulder. And with that forelock of early grey falling down thinly across his brow.

'Too soon, isn't it?' Huw Maddox said to him. 'Enumerator, like? Supposed to collect the forms tomorrow, aren't you?'

There wasn't much time. He could hear the girl coming up the stairs behind him, rushed over to the sofa and settled himself there. Like he owned the place. He whispered urgently in Huw's ear, watched as the *Football Echo* slipped from the old man's hand, pooled around his ankles. Yet Huw Maddox seemed to shrink before his very eyes, his mouth working but no sound coming forth.

'Best tell them I'm a nephew,' Tom Priddy murmured.

'Your cousin,' Huw Maddox dutifully stammered, as the Beanpole finally caught up with him. 'Cousin Thomas.'

She'd know there were relatives, surely. Her father's brother and sister. Bangor. Or was it Beddgelert? But estranged. Some parting of the family's ways he likely never discussed. Though, a cousin? Well, that might come as a surprise.

'I'd thought it would have been bigger,' he said, gazing around the room. 'Funny. All those stories about the big city. Streets of gold, like. And Uncle Huw making his fortune here. Who'd have thought?'

He tried to read her thoughts. *And what's this to do with you?* she must have wanted to tell him. Yet she didn't. To tell the truth, he felt he might have frightened her. Good. But if her tada wanted her to treat this Cousin Thomas as family, he knew she'd have to make the effort. Family was family, after all. Nothing more important in Beanpole's life, he guessed.

'Tada keeps wanting us to move,' she said. 'But it's home, isn't it?'

'Must be like a barracks,' said Thomas. 'Uncle Huw and – how many of you? Six? In this little place. There's comfy for you.'

He began to knead his fists, each in turn, making the knuckles and the joints of his fingers crack and pop in a fashion he knew was sickening to behold.

'How did you…?' Huw Maddox swallowed.

Cousin Thomas glanced at the Beanpole, and he thought he saw fear there.

'Get me a glass of water, Ceridwen, would you?' said old Huw. The girl hesitated, then did as he asked. 'Not anymore,' Maddox muttered, while the girl was busy at the sink. 'Not six. Winifred's moved out. Married, see. And we lost Pryce when he was little. He'd have been seventeen now.'

So, this one, the Beanpole – Ceridwen, was it? *Blessed Song*, that's what it meant. One meaning, anyway. Poetry to his ears. But wasn't there also a myth? Ceridwen, keeper of the cauldron of rebirth. Something must die so something new and better might be born.

'Fever, was it?' Cousin Thomas asked, though he knew the answer.

'No,' said Huw Maddox, as he took the glass from his daughter. 'Not fever. Not exactly.'

This was all. So, did they never talk about it? And the Beanpole, her look of soul-splitting guilt. Could she not even bear to think about it.

'So, just me, Ceridwen, Dafydd and Nesta,' the old man explained. 'But what about you, boy?' It was stilted, formal. 'What brings you here?'

Cousin Thomas decided it was one of those questions folk sometimes ask when they really don't want an answer. Fear of ill-fate awaiting release from a verbal Pandora's Box. But it caused him to stop kneading his fist and fingers. He needed to decide how best to answer this one.

'Been in town a while,' he said. 'Working for Waugh's.' The funeral furnishers. It seemed apt, though he knew he'd picked up the stink of the place on his clothes. Could she smell it as well, the girl? Embalming fluid. 'But mostly dried up now.' Did he intend that to be humorous? He wasn't sure. 'Still at the Rotunda though.'

'An actor,' said the girl. Sarcasm dripped from her lips. 'I should have known.'

He fixed her with his most frigid stare, then nodded.

'Actor.' Tom Priddy smirked as he spoke the words. He slowed his drawl still more. 'When I'm able. But stagehand mainly. Pay's poor though. So, I thought to myself: what about Uncle Huw? He must need some help with the print works. Well, I see his name on just about every poster in town. Handbills at the theatre. Programmes at the match. Posters for the National. Everywhere, see? Printer's devil – it's what you need, *ewythr*,' he said.

Uncle. *Ewythr.* He knew how to get the old man's ear. Done his research.

And printer's devil – the trade's jargon for an apprentice. Exactly what the old man needed. Research, see? Nobody else to help him now, the old man's son being settled in his job at the docks. At least, whenever he'd manage to grease the ganger's hand enough to get a tap, Thomas supposed. Meanwhile, more and more print work coming in, or seemed to be. Yet the prices being forced down with every week that passed. So, a printer's devil.

He glanced at the Beanpole. She'd know the same things, of course. Her father might *want* a printer's devil but the last thing he could afford. So, how would the old man jump? The daughter expected old Huw to say no. Of course, she did.

'Champion,' Maddox murmured, without a great deal of conviction, the Beanpole's mouth falling open with astonishment. 'Aye, champion.'

'Maybe a bed for me, too,' said Thomas, 'given Cousin Winifred's moved out.'

He fixed Cari with his frog's eyes. Trying to see. Why *did* she look so guilty?

'Wyn only moved out of the girls' room,' she told him. 'What d'you think this is? The Adelphi?'

He had an image of swinging cats, saw how the Beanpole still stood there, waiting for her father to refuse this further impertinence. But again, she was wrong. The world had shifted somehow. Well, it had shifted for the old Adelphi, now he came to think of it – work already started on rebuilding the place, scaffolding everywhere.

'You can share with Dafydd,' Huw Maddox told him. 'The Good Lord knows, he's here little enough.'

Tom almost imagined the expression on this Dafydd's face when he heard the news. The disbelief. It thrilled him. Yes, the world had shifted.

12.35pm

Cari thought her brother might just explode.

'My room?' he spat. They were all crowded around the oilcloth-draped table and their jostling dinner plates. Tradition. Her tada insisted on this weekly tradition. The whole family together on the Sabbath. And the family now at once extended. Not just Cousin Thomas himself, but also the seaman, Ernst – that nephew of their German neighbour – recently paid off by the Red Star Line. At times he'd been a drinking companion for Dafydd – Taffy – in Mad John's. Though today Cari suspected he'd been doing his duty as Nesta's bodyguard.

She'd warned her tada, of course. About how Taffy would react to the idea of sharing his room. But something about the look on

Cousin Thomas's face. Cari had once seen a similar expression, cruel ecstasy, on the features of a local urchin torturing a dappled mongrel pup in Cartwright Place.

'You don't bother with the *Cymraeg* any more then, Uncle Huw?' Cousin Thomas drawled, garnishing the words with his finest sneer. 'At table, like.'

Cari was making her way around the table, the handle of her pan wrapped in a thick green cloth, as she ladled out their vegetables, shoving them alongside the meagre slices of pink gammon.

'Well…' her tada struggled to explain, and Ernst Jurks struggled to understand.

'*Cymraeg*, Ernst,' said Cari, slowly. 'It means Welsh. My family is from Wales, see. I could teach you.'

She touched his shoulder, knew she was flirting with him. Didn't care. She caught Nesta's knowing grin, as well. Nessie had seen it but said nothing, still flushed after her hasty return to the house. *Duw*, it must have been a flying visit.

'Ach, Wales,' said Ernst. 'I know Wales. It is in Scotland, I think. *Ja?*'

Her father shook his head, mumbled the word *tramorwyr*. Foreigners. It made Cousin Thomas smile, she noticed. Common ground between them, maybe. And she saw his smile grow even wider as he watched Taffy still waiting for his objection to be answered. Well, she guessed, poor Taffy would likely have to wait a while longer.

'And how did you get this?' Thomas waved at Taffy's hare lip, almost caught Cari with his fork as she leaned over his shoulder with the serving ladle. He laughed as she recoiled from the fork's prongs. 'Watch what you're doing, girl,' he told her.

It was only a modest retaliation, a momentary revenge, but it gave her some satisfaction to slam the pan down onto the table, splashing him with fragments of potato, onion and carrot, a fine shower of gravy. She expected him to react, but he simply grinned at her, dabbed at the stains as he turned back to Taffy.

'Not born with it, I don't think,' he said.

'His first day at the docks,' said Rhys Fingers, his pipe and tin of Whiskey Flake on the table before him. Wyn's husband seemed to be losing more of his hair each time she saw him. 'Smacked in the face by a rope block. He was lucky to ever get the tap again.' Rhys made it plain – his own word in the right ear, of course, to get Taffy his docker's ticket in the first place. A dock gateman could wield that sort of influence. 'But thank the Lord Jesus for good friends,' Rhys prattled on. 'For Christian words and deeds. Like hospitality, Taffy. Sharing space with those less fortunate than ourselves. You know? Right, Ernst? Your family, all Lutherans, I think.'

Taffy's face assumed a dark and sullen expression. He chewed on a response, simmering just like the suet pudding. But by the time he was ready to spit it out, all eyes had turned to the German.

'*Nein*,' said Ernst. 'We are all – how you say? *Calvinsten.*'

'Calvinists,' said Thomas, under his breath. 'As good as heretics.'

Nobody else appeared to have heard him, for Rhys Fingers nodded sagely, and Wyn patted her husband's arm, looked up to reveal her ravaged face. A rare occurrence for her to display them in public, those scars. She gave her husband an uncertain, deferential smile. But Taffy was cowed into temporary silence, as he always had been, by his outstanding debt to Rhys Gateman.

'There's a palliasse,' said Huw Maddox. 'Downstairs. The boy can bring it up here.'

Cari had taken her pan back to the black-leaded oven chimney stove, and was just squeezing into her own place. But she stopped, only half-seated, when she heard her father's suggestion. The idea filled her with horror. Taffy would never accept it – never.

'Pa…' Taffy began, and he bounced so hard on the ancient chair that they all heard it crack. It wobbled violently and Taffy had to shift his weight to keep it upright. There was a collective gasp, though their father held up an imperious hand, seemingly unconcerned for either the chair or Taffy's equilibrium.

'No, Dafydd,' said her tada. 'We'll hear no more, see. Sunday, it is. Sunday dinner.'

Those simple words could have been a sacred text. Then their tada began picking at his food. Not his usual self, perhaps. Just how much of a shock had it been? Cari wondered. Cousin Thomas turning up on the doorstep this way. Nesta had maybe noticed something amiss as well, kept making little gestures of the face and eyes at her. Those gestures by which we silently ask each other what's wrong.

'Well, all settled then,' Nesta said, once Cari had shrugged her own lack of an explanation. 'And welcome to the family, Cousin Thomas.'

There were similar muttered endorsements for this sentiment from the rest of them as each tucked into the slender feast. Except Cari herself. And Taffy, of course.

'So, what's your other name, then?' said Taffy, helping himself to one of his pa's Woodbines. 'Not Maddox, naturally. You'll be a Priddy, I suppose?'

They all knew tada had taken his stepfather's name, Maddox, when he was just a boy. Well, William Maddox was the only father he'd ever known, really. So, they were all Maddox too. But their tada had been born Huw Priddy, of course. They knew it, though the knowledge was buried somewhere. Stored away for posterity.

'It would be good to know, see,' Taffy spluttered through his spuds, his lips dripping pure bile. 'For when you become a famous actor. So we can tell people. We used to know him, we'll say. Before he became overly grand for us. Slept on a palliasse in my room. I can boast about that to the lads, eh?'

Sticks and stones, Cari decided, as her father dropped his knife on the floor, ducked beneath the table to retrieve it. He almost smacked heads with poor Ernst, who'd tried to rescue the implement on her tada's behalf.

'Oh, I'll never grow too grand for this family.' Cousin Thomas grinned at Taffy. Was it a pledge of loyalty, or an insult? She couldn't quite make up her mind. 'And my name? Yes, Priddy. Thomas Priddy, see? Proud of it, I am.'

'You must be our uncle's boy,' said Cari. 'Tada's brother. From Bangor. I can hear the accent.' It was a bit of nonsense, naturally. She spoke Welsh, this was true. But it was a child's Welsh, she knew. Gaps in her vocabulary big enough to drive a horse and cart through. Certainly not good enough to recognise one district's dialect or accent from another. She suspected Cousin Thomas knew it, as well.

'Beddgelert, as it happens,' he replied. 'You worked near there, Uncle Huw – Penrhyn Quarry?'

Now, this was certainly news. More than just news. Something of a riddle. Surprised faces, all around the table. Cari knew how he'd gone back to Bangor for a few years, before they were all born, of course. Then returned to Liverpool with their mam. Yes, that much they knew. But a quarryman? And the Penrhyn Quarries were something of a legend – the workers there on strike and then locked out for three whole years at the turn of the century. Long after their tada would have worked there, of course, but still, news.

'Not the Great Strike, like,' said Taffy, almost admiration in his voice. 'But the others, when they started the union – you was there?'

'After the '74 strike,' said his father. 'Short, like. Of men, they were.'

'The Quarrymen's Union,' said Rhys Fingers, almost mocking. 'Don't suppose you had much choice but to join. Not then.'

'Didn't mind, see. Done well, they had. Pay was better. Got rid of some of those managers. *Duw*, a bad lot. Profits were up. Before the rot set in, like. Those idiots at Dinorwig. Didn't know when they had a good thing going. Another lock-out. Lasted until Saint David's Day, that one. '86, see? Came back to Liverpool after that.'

'Your only reason, then?' Cousin Thomas almost growled at him. 'For coming back to Liverpool?'

But their tada never replied, outside a brief twitch of his head.

Then talk around the table turned, as it always did, to sport and politics, while Cari was left wondering whether there was yet another story here. She went to fetch the pan again, extra helpings, though there wasn't much left. Still, a skivvy's work was never done. Wasn't that what they said, these days?

Fly me on Angel wings to Saint Mark's Square,
At Caffè Florian to take my ease.

Pipe and cigarette smoke began to fill the room, Cousin Thomas with a theatrical coughing fit, making a great play of wafting away the offending fog.

Rhys Fingers, for whom boats of all shapes and sizes were a passion, waxing lyrical about Oxford's easy win by three lengths the day before. Ernst Jurks, laboriously amusing with a story about his favourite team, Rostocker FC. Tom Priddy joined in as though it were his place to do so. Everton's latest transfer, Tom Gracie from Greenock Morton. Taffy's taunt that Gracie'd not be there long, how the Reds would snap him up next season.

'You got this nonsense from your mates at the boozer, I suppose,' said their tada, rising from his silence to take Taffy's bait. In truth, Cari had already been convinced Taffy only supported the Reds to spite his father. Another rift between them.

'You're a drinker, Taffy?' Cousin Thomas Priddy sounded astonished, the first time Cari had heard any real feeling in his voice. A change from the usual drone. 'I'd have thought this would be a good temperance house. You're a temperance man, aren't you, Uncle Huw?'

'No swindler like a self-swindler,' said her tada. *Great Expectations* again. At least, his own paraphrase of the sentiment. 'No self-swindler like the man who seeks his solace in the demon drink. It's what the scriptures tell us. And I should know, see.'

'Isaiah five,' said Cousin Thomas.

'Verses eleven and twelve,' Rhys Gateman replied, extending to Cousin Thomas a look of sincere approval. Biblical fellowship, Cari supposed.

'Just a few jars with the lads, Tada,' said Taffy. 'Nothing wrong. Not against the law, is it?'

'More's the pity,' his father replied.

'Not like these two.' Taffy waggled his own knife between Cari and Nesta. 'Law breakers. What d'you think of your sisters, Wyn? Planning to dodge the Census. That's what they're up to.'

'Census?' said Ernst. The German was trying hard to follow the thread.

'Suffragette,' said Cousin Thomas. The muscles in his cheek began to work once more. 'You don't believe all this nonsense, do you, Beanpole? And what did I read the other week? The *Post and Mercury*. Some woman who had a go at Haldane when he arrived at Lime Street. Made a point of her being very tall, if I remember right. And a dark cloak. Do you have a dark cloak, Cari?'

She'd bristled again when he called her Beanpole, but she had to think twice about fighting on two fronts. Either defend herself, or defend her cause – that was the choice he'd forced upon her. And she felt the warm glow of revolution pulse through her veins.

'Suffragettes,' said Cari, now back at the table, eating again. 'Just a name the *Daily Mail* gave us.'

She saw how it made him smile. The defiance in her voice.

'But that's the difference, isn't it?' Cousin Thomas replied. 'Law-abiding suffragists. Criminal suffragettes. Which are you, Beanpole?'

She bristled once more, swallowed it.

'The *Mail* might have thought it was an insult, Cousin. But for those of us in the WSPU, a badge of honour, like.'

'Just imagine,' murmured Wyn, into her food. 'If it had been our Cari. Imagine. Do women have the vote in Germany, Ernst?'

Yes, just imagine, thought Cari.

'Not now,' said the German. 'I regret, no.' And Cari sensed the apology was aimed at her, personally. She was grateful, caught his eye, felt some spark pass between them.

'I keep telling them,' said their tada. 'It'll all end in tears. Come to no good.'

'Each to his or her own place,' said Cousin Thomas. 'The Lord's rule, isn't it? *Likewise, ye wives, be in subjection to your husbands.* Clear, I think. A woman's place in the world.'

'Well, I'm not a wife, as it happens,' Cari snapped. 'Nor a Beanpole, neither. And what does Holy Scripture tell us about voting rights, precisely? Nothing. Not a word. Not for men. Not for women. But I work as hard as any man. I pay my tax the same as any man. Yet I'm not allowed a say in electing my MP. Nothing to do with Holy Scripture, Cousin. Just men, being men.'

1.30pm

Almost blasphemy. Nerve of the girl. But the Lord would put Miss Cari Beanpole in her place soon enough. With Tom Priddy's help, of course.

'It's about how the world's run, girl,' said old Huw. 'Men who govern. Men who have the power. That's what Holy Scripture tells us. Women must obey their husbands. Their men.'

'Many in Germany are, who say same,' said Ernst. 'But wrong, I think.'

'Think you know better than Uncle Huw, Fritzie?' said Thomas. He congratulated himself when he saw the German grapple with a riposte. Then he turned to Cari, deliberately devoured her impiety with his eyes. 'Women must obey men. And you don't need a vote just to be obedient, Ceridwen.'

'Women too impulsive to have a vote, *cariad*.' Her tada had assumed a more soothing voice. 'Don't reason the same as men, see.'

'Well, it may be the Conservatives' argument, Pa,' said Dumpling Nesta, 'but it doesn't hold water. Half of the men in this country can't vote either. No property, no rent, then no vote. So, what about you, Thomas Priddy? Taffy's got an excuse. Not twenty-one yet. But you, Cousin – get a vote, do you? Not capable of reasoning the same as other men who pay rent?'

Rent? Tom had no intention of paying rent. He hadn't taken much notice of Nesta before. Yet now? Perhaps he needed to afford her more attention. Where Cari was long and thin, Nesta was short and stubby. The pit pony again. Frizzed hair. Tendency to play with the ends of her tresses. Twitching nostrils, like a suspicious rabbit.

'Got a sharp tongue, you have, for such a young girl, Nesta,' Thomas sneered at her. 'Mind it doesn't cut you now, see.'

'The problem with the world,' said Rhys Gateman, puffing on his pipe. 'Nobody knows their place anymore. Look at these palm boat boys down at the Harrington. Strike. Equal pay with decent white sailors. Who do they think they are?'

Tom Priddy watched Nesta put her head down, a spread of scarlet rising from her neck to her cheeks. Another guilty secret?

'Well, the seamen's union can't have it both ways,' The Beanpole jumped in as if to stop Nesta saying something she'd regret. Yet she seemed to know a thing or two, did Cari Maddox

'They try,' she lectured them, 'to campaign against the employment of blacks or Chinese on British ships. Why? Because they reckon it undercuts white sailors' pay. Then boycott them when they strike to get their wages up to a decent level. And not asking for equal pay, by the way. Just better than the pittance they get paid right now. What do you say, Ernst? You're a sailor.'

'Same work, same pay.' The German shrugged, as though her question was stupid. Yet his narrowed eyes never faltered from Tom's own gaze. Perhaps not a fellow to tangle with.

'Black workers get paid what they deserve,' Taffy barked. 'Everybody knows it. They're not worth the same as whites. How can they be?'

'Oh,' Nesta spat at him. 'There speaks the big union man. Hurrah for the Empire. King and Country.'

She waved her hands as though they were flags, while Taffy almost choked on a piece of gammon. Rhys Gateman had to thump his back until the offending lump of pink meat flew onto the blue-patterned plate.

'Men have the power,' her tada repeated. 'Only natural. White men, at that. Obvious, isn't it?'

'Only obvious,' said Cari, 'if you read the nonsense in the *Mail* and the *Express* every day. Supremacy of men. Supremacy of *white* men. Supremacy of *British* white men. Drip, drip, drip.' She aimed this part specifically at Cousin Thomas himself. It almost rocked him back in his seat. 'Every day,' she said, 'until even honest workers believe the lies. As though we didn't have enough problems without fighting among ourselves. Blaming each other.'

'You sound like some sort of communist,' said Thomas. 'Or anarchist, perhaps. You'd have us all buried in revolution.'

At his mention of the word communist, he saw the German's head lift. Proud of it, maybe. Interesting. And what did Thomas know of communism anyhow? Utopia. Workers of the World Unite! Karl Marx. The chaos in Saint Petersburg six years earlier.

'There's a difference, you know, Cousin,' Nesta told him. 'Between anarchists and communists. And what's wrong with them anyway? This world needs shaking up – breaking apart and then all the pieces put back together but better, see.'

'Cousin Thomas is right, Nesta,' said the Beanpole. Miss Defiance. 'I *would* bury us all in revolution. Telling Tada earlier, I was. A night for revolution. Census Night Revolution. And working people all over the place just now, fighting battles for their own causes.'

She was becoming dramatic, emotional, but it seemed she couldn't help it. 'Singer workers in Glasgow,' she raged. 'Eleven thousand, isn't it? All those miners in Clydach. Even more there.'

She was right. Troublemakers everywhere. Revolution. And Tom Priddy? Yes, a modest revolution of his own in prospect. Or was it retribution? A bit of both, maybe. But, one way or the other, there were spells to be woven here. Enigmas to be forged.

'Last year,' said Ernst. He wiped his hands on the brown Sunday suit trousers, mimed a hammering action. *'Peng, peng,'* he said. 'Sixty thousand – sixty thousand? *Ja*. All not can work. In – *werften*. Place make ship.'

'Shipyards?' offered Cari. She received a heart-melting smile in response. It made Thomas feel sick.

'Revolution, revolution,' laughed Thomas. 'Only in your dreams, Beanpole. All a fancy. Like this nonsense about war in Europe. Every time somebody coughs in Morocco or Serbia you're all there. Doom and gloom. As though the Lord Jesus would allow us to go to war over heathen places like that.'

No, he thought, I hope He would not. But Thomas would make sure to ask Him later, whenever He saw fit to reappear. There were days when he believed the world was becoming a little unhinged, some collective mud-stained madness growing within them. Something you could almost smell on the wind.

'I don't know about Serbia,' said old Huw, 'but those fools in the Rhondda will be getting short shrift. Lancashire Fusiliers sent off there yesterday to break them up.'

Tom Priddy had read this news also.

'They're working men, Pa,' Taffy protested, still coughing after the episode with the stuck gammon. 'And bloody Churchill's a bit quick to set the army on working men.'

Home Secretary Churchill had done the same in the previous November against strikers in Tonypandy. But no excuse for profanity, Tom decided. Not on the Lord's Day. Not really on any day.

'Mind your docker's tongue, now,' growled Huw Maddox. 'Sunday, see. You leave that sort of language where it belongs.'

Nesta shouted over her tada's words, not allowing an opportunity to pass.

'Working men,' she reminded them. The girl's mouth was full but she couldn't contain herself. 'That's right. Like the Krooboys at the Harrington,' she spat.

'Those are coloureds, Nessie,' said Taffy. 'For pity's sake. Can't compare our own working men and women with those buggers brought all the way here from Africa to cut white men's pay. Them and the Chinese.'

'He's right, Nesta,' the old man told her. 'No comparison, see.'

'Isn't there, Pa?' she said. 'What's worse then?' She glowered at Taffy. 'Blacks or Catholics?'

The Beanpole was just getting to her feet again, to collect the now emptied plates. Tom Priddy saw the moment freeze. Proffered plates and dirty cutlery suspended in mid-air. Glasses of water poised 'twixt plate and lip. But where lay the slip?

'No, Nesta,' she shouted. 'Don't...'

Mouths open. The cusp of a revelation? A Pandora's box about to be opened? Tom looked at Huw Maddox, but the old man seemed blissfully unaware. The atmosphere which, seconds before, could have been cut with a sharpened blade, remained unperturbed.

'Now,' said their father, lighting another Woodbine, 'there's silly for you. Just need to look at the law of the land. At what's good for the king. That's always my question. The king can marry anybody he likes. A Jew. Or a black'un. Anybody he chooses, see. But not a Catholic. Not allowed to marry Catholics, they're not. And why d'you think this would be, *cariad*, if there's nothing wrong with them? Catholics,' he snapped. 'Nothing worse than Catholics. And Irish Catholics? Worst of the lot.'

8.35pm

'A nest of nits,' Cari told her sister when they'd jumped on the tram, with its dog-damp smells, gentlemen passengers spitting on the floor slats and cigarette smoke drifting in from the outside benches. 'That's what you'll stir up. Need to curb your tongue, Nessie.'

'I don't know how he can live with himself – Taffy, I mean. Rattles on about dockers and how badly they're done to. Strike talk all the time. And those poor lads at the Harrington. On the cobbles for six weeks already and nobody gives a fig. Certainly not Taffy or his precious union. Hardly a mention in the papers either.'

True enough, but Cari already sensed the world was coming off its rails a bit, everybody bogged down in their own small corner. Every corner its own pit of despair. And those of them fighting for the vote almost as bad as the rest. So many suffrage societies in Liverpool now, she couldn't count them anymore. Forty different groups? Fifty? And most of them wouldn't have spat on the others if they'd seen them on fire.

Fine, perhaps she exaggerated – but only a little. Everybody else had got together for the big rally on St. George's Plateau last June, but the WSPU stayed away – held their own event a few weeks later. And the movement no nearer working together than it had ever been. Yet those of them in the Women's Social and Political Union reserved their greatest scorn for the snooty mares in the Women's Suffrage Society – regardless of everybody's admiration for Eleanor Rathbone.

'Well,' Cari said, 'Tada would soon put a stop to your little gallop if he knew. So, no point goading Taffy. No point at all. Anyway, Ernst seems to have the right politics. But did you see the way he bridled when Cousin Thomas mentioned the communists? Maybe some of it will rub off.'

Cousin Thomas. Tom Priddy. They'd talked about little else all the way to the tram stop. Cari swore she'd lamp him if he called her Beanpole just once more. Cari, get off your knees! Yet she found she also feared him. As though he could read her mind. See and understand her guilt. The wicked thought from all those years ago. Pryce and Winifred both so ill and her only preoccupation about how their passing might simply leave more room for the rest.

More space. More affection. She'd been no more than an infant herself, naturally, unable to understand even the concept of death. How could she? Not even old enough to understand her own mortality, let alone the impossible thought that another's life could simply disappear, never to return. Not for all eternity. Unless, as Tada insisted, they might meet again in the Kingdom of Heaven after they, themselves, had undertaken the same unfathomable journey.

'And you were flirting with him, Cari. Ernst Jurks. No, don't shake your head. Funny name, though.'

'I was not,' Cari protested. 'Flirting, indeed. And I should never have let you drag me into this.'

There they were, clattering along St. James Street on the Outer Circular. Sunday night, but through the windows there were lights in the darkness. Lights of the Wapping Goods Station. Lights from the steam bakery. Lights from the Brunswick Brewery. As much traffic as she'd have seen on any daytime of the week, though now all with lamps burning. A stink, as well. The sewers. She held a handkerchief to her nose – afraid, as usual, of catching something incurable.

They were heading for the part of Toxteth Park they all called Sailor Town. Dark Town. Tada'd skin them alive if he knew. Probably throw them out on the street, where they belonged. Because only a certain class of women went to this part of the city, and on the streets was precisely where those women plied their trade. But Cari was just glad to escape from the house. From the leering gaze of Cousin Thomas.

Yes, leering. He made her feel dirty. And then calling her Beanpole all the time. She could scream.

'We'll not stay long,' Nesta promised when Cari reminded her they really shouldn't be there. 'Then where? Posh Florrie's?'

'It's a bit of a haul, luvvy. All the way to Crosby. Better than going over the water though, I suppose.'

'I thought Tada was going to have a fit when the penny finally dropped and he realised we were really going to do it.'

He'd worked himself up into a fine temper, that was sure – certain he'd end up in the Cheapside Bridewell if his daughters weren't there to be counted.

'And Cousin Thomas didn't exactly help,' said Cari.

'Got his slimy feet under the table fast, that one. Seems a bit simple, at first. But he's not, is he? Pa's already promised him his own keys.'

'You should have seen him bolt up the stairs when I let him in. Making sure he got in a few words with tada before I caught up with him. Just wish I knew what he'd said. And slimy? Doesn't really do it justice. Bet he's got webbed feet.'

They giggled, drew stares from the other passengers as the tram rattled across into St. James Place and they stood up, went swaying downstairs for the next stop, carrying between them the Pegram's woven straw bag they'd smuggled from the house with their contraband.

'But Pa can't afford to give him a job, can he?' said Nesta.

'We've not got two ha'pennies to rub together. You're right. Must think he can make it work though, Ness. He's been looking after us a long while. All on his own. Without Mam.'

Their tada could be infuriating, and his outlook on life was often difficult for them to swallow. They'd seen him fight his way through the booze, then through hard times, with a big heart. Yet Cari knew his heart wouldn't stretch to this. To tolerating what they were about.

They'd dodged a couple of big carts – plodding in towards the docks from somewhere plainly paying no heed to either Sabbath or Census – then wove their way between heaps of steaming dung into Upper Stanhope Street. To Cari, it felt entirely foreign, despite the churches and chapels, stopped her in her tracks.

'Come on, Cari,' said her younger sister. 'Where's the girl who had a go at Haldane?'

'Haldane?' Cari smiled. 'Wasn't it you, Nessie, who sulked with me for a week because I'd done it on my own?'

It wasn't every day the Secretary of State for War dropped into Liverpool for a visit, and there'd not been time to get the other girls together. Just a mention in that morning's paper, and sometimes a body needed to seize the day. Other women in the WSPU had been doing this for the past couple of years, seizing the day. Attacks on politicians – it's what the papers called them. So why not Cari? She'd yelled at Haldane a bit in Welsh, unfolded one of their posters – *Votes for Women* – then got away sharpish in the crowd when the bobbies tried to grab her. It had made a few headlines. The whole point. And made Cari laugh like a loon afterwards.

'Oh, that was then,' Nesta grinned. 'This is now. And nothing to worry about here.'

Easy enough to say. Yet it was threatening. A thin sea mist from the river, punctuated by the sound of ships' horns. Depressing too. Seagulls screeched above a large redbrick building at this nearest corner and, squatting in the meagre shelter of its outside walls, a dozen sad castaways of Elder Dempster's African hands.

They frightened Cari as well, though in a different way from Cousin Thomas. Some library book residue of mud huts, she supposed. Of tribal savageries. Zulu massacres. Cannibalism. All the rest. Absurd. Most of the men looked too debilitated even to stand, let alone pose any threat.

'All these on strike?' she said.

'Don't know,' Nesta sniffed. 'Didn't have time to find out properly. Before, like.'

Cari imagined not. Nessie had escaped after chapel, of course.

With Ernst to keep her company. To see what was needed, she'd said. Though, between the tram journeys, there and back, she couldn't have been here long.

'But suppose so,' said Nesta. 'All of them, I reckon.' She was scanning their faces, plainly looking for somebody she knew. 'Most of them just get taken on for a single trip. One way. The company pays them off when they get here, charges them for the privilege of staying in this fleapit while the cargo's unloaded and a new one put on board. It can take weeks. Then, when their money's all gone to whatever crimps have cheated them for food and gewgaws, and they're still in debt to Elder Dempster for the lodging, the company takes them on again, if they're lucky, for the return trip.'

'And if not?' said Cari.

Nesta shrugged, while the men muttered among themselves, and Cari had the distinct feeling they'd angered them. If so, she couldn't blame them. They must have given the impression of intrusiveness, of treating the men like exotic specimens in a zoological garden. It was far from their intention. At least, Cari hoped so.

Yet they were an intriguing bunch. The jaundiced sky of her hometown reflected in their doleful eyes and a mismatch of vagrant clothing, supplemented by woollen caps, shawls of hessian sacking or the occasional army greatcoat. All this Cari tried to absorb as Nesta drew her past the corner, the hostel's entrance, where a further cluster of black seamen stood out quite distinctly from the others. They seemed, to her, more solid, less ethereal, not stocky but broad-chested, darker, somewhat aloof – happier, if it wasn't too foolish a word to use.

And, for her sister, smiles that cut through the late afternoon's gloom.

8.45pm

'*Duw*,' said Tom Priddy. 'What am I going to call you, now we're on our own, like?'

'What is it you want, boy?' old Huw replied.

'To be honest with you, *uncle*, I'm still trying to make up my mind.' It was true. He'd not yet decided. And so many possibilities. 'But what are you going to do with these?'

He fingered the Household Schedule and the detailed instructions, pushed them around the table. The enumerators would have delivered them a few weeks earlier. But Huw Maddox gathered them back into his hands, held them jealously. He was still wearing his Sunday suit. But he'd discarded his neckerchief.

'Fill them in, of course,' he said. 'Only problem is how to list *you*, see.'

Tom Priddy ignored him.

'And the girls?' said Tom Priddy. 'It would be a laugh, wouldn't it? Write their names anyway. Like they were sleeping here. One in the eye for them, that's what it would be.'

'But against the law, boy. Just as bad as them not being here.'

He reached for his ink pot and the eyedropper to fill his pen, while Thomas looked around the place again. It had been an interminable afternoon. Dinner and suet pudding out of the way and old Huw had insisted on bible readings. Then dominoes. A break in the weather gave Beanpole and Dumpling Nesta a chance to excuse themselves. A stroll around St. John's Garden. But they were back in time for more readings – Dickens this time. More readings, then upstairs to their room. To work on bonnets. For Easter, they said. Later, over bread and a cuppa, the girls repeatedly dreaming of the day they might be able to afford a gramophone for the house. Some hopes! And before too long, it would be Tom Priddy's tune to which they'd be dancing.

The big question? Where had they gone? This sad little protest they'd planned.

But more room at least, now Rhys Gateman and the scarred little shrew Winifred had gone home. Taffy and the German off to the boozer, he supposed. But Cari and Nesta? Something not quite right. A secret. He could smell secrets. Though his first concern had to be Taffy. Palliasse on the floor? Not for long, he determined.

'Tell me about Dafydd,' he said. 'Your Taffy. How come he's a communist?'

'Communist, you say?' Huw Maddox sat bolt upright in his chair, almost spilled the ink. 'Dafydd's no communist.'

'Liverpool then,' said Tom Priddy, and laughed to himself. 'Football. Liverpool supporter. And there's you, with the Toffees' programmes to print. The contract, like. Wouldn't look good, would it?'

He'd have to take himself to Goodison one of these days, he decided. Yes, he'd drop into Ma Bushell's famous toffee shop, see what all the fuss was about. Fond of a bit of toffee, now and again, was Tom Priddy.

'Don't expect they'd care,' said old Huw, and began to fill out the Schedule, tongue between his teeth as he added his own name. At least, his stepfather's name, Tom noted. 'So long as I keep giving them a good service. Right price, sort of thing. Not that it's any of your business, mind.'

Maybe not quite yet, Tom thought.

'Still, just a shame Dafydd's not more – well, grateful,' he said.

'The young? Never grateful. Too full of themselves. Pip, see? With Joe and Biddy. *"I was better after I cried."* You know the part? Dickens? *"More sorry, more aware of my own ingratitude."* But not mine, like. Mine just never seem grateful and don't give it a thought.'

The old man's eyes pierced Tom Priddy's soul. Was Huw Maddox including him in this general condemnation?

'Raised five of them,' he was saying. 'And here.'

He waved his hand around the room.

'Not exactly Lark Lane,' said Tom Priddy. 'Thought I'd find you in the leafy suburbs, I did. Not here. A bit – well, beyond the edge, isn't it? Wild, like.'

'Inherited the place. That's what happened.' From his stepfather. William Maddox. Tom knew this much. 'But, one day. I've told Ceridwen. One day we'll not need to live above the shop. Not anymore.'

'Yet here you are,' said Thomas. 'Only a stone's throw from Little Italy.' He sniffed, imagined he could smell them, the papists, even from here. 'But Hunter Street. Good honest traders like yourself, isn't it? All Protestants, I'm guessing. But over there...'

Tom Priddy jerked a thumb over his shoulder.

'Shoeless slummies,' said old Huw. 'That's what I call them. Catholics. Hordes of the devils.'

Huw Maddox banged his fist on the table, caused an ink blot to stain the corner of the Schedule.

Tom Priddy had spent many weeks familiarising himself with this world. Friendly Protestant territory beyond the heights to the east, with its dividing line along Netherfield Road. Inside the enclave bordered by Islington, Lime Street and Parliament Street. The centre of town also, naturally. And the South End, or the Welsh streets near the canal.

But the rest? Those wards edging the river – the river with which every single aspect of this city was so firmly anchored – would mostly be forbidden ground, so far as Huw Maddox was concerned. Catholic ground. Apart from the occasional beleaguered enclave here and there – isolated streets where nothing but Welsh was spoken, and where Methodism or Presbyterianism was the proper order of the day.

'Slummies with pull, though, I suppose. Papists, like. Italian. Or Irish. Doesn't make much difference. It's them always get to work the strings. And mind if I make a brew?'

'Help yourself,' said old Huw. 'I suppose you would, anyway. But you've got it right, you have. About Catholics. Influence is what they've got. But honest Welsh folk...

Tom Priddy turned back from the scullery door. He turned just in time to see the old man adding Thomas himself to the Schedule; crept silently over to see what he wrote. His name first. Then the final column. Language spoken. The explanatory note – if able to speak English and Welsh, write *Both*.

Thomas watched him write *Both*.

Birthplace Bangor. Assistant. Funeral furnisher. Worker. All fair enough.

Single. Age? Twenty-five.

So, he remembered that much, at least.

Finally, the relationships column. *Boarder*, he'd written. Boarder. Was that all? Then to hell with you, he thought. To hell and damnation. You and all in this house.

9.00pm

The white girl had brought another *poto* with her. This one tall and slender as a coconut palm, while the other, Nesta, was short and solid as the black afara growing along the banks of the Dugbe near his family's home at Nana Kru. Amos Gartee was pleased to see them both.

'Miss Nesta,' he cried, and saw the other girl take a step back, her eyes fixed on his face. Not on his eyes, though. Did she not know? Disrespectful, not to lock eyes with those who speak with you. But no, she would be thinking about the scar patterns, the raised arrowheads at the sides of his eyes, the line down the centre of his forehead. A savage, she might decide, for she could not read the story they told. Or maybe he was wrong. Perhaps she simply admired him, thought he was a handsome fellow. For there was, indeed, a hint of admiration in the cloudy eyes of Missee Coconut Palm.

'You good news?' he said and saw Nesta smile. She had told him she loved his voice. Sing-song, was the word she'd used. He liked that. So, he sang some more. '*Ay-yah!* And bring things.'

He pointed at the straw bag she held out towards him, almost snatched it from her hands, then pulled out each of the threadbare blankets, until he discovered the tin of tobacco hidden beneath. He read the words. Navy Cut. Cigarette rolling papers as well. And a box of matches. Swan Vestas, spoke the box.

'Only these, I'm afraid,' Nesta told him. 'All we could manage. And this is my sister, Cari. I told you about her earlier. Remember? Cari, this gentleman is Mister Gartee.'

Amos stretched out his hand to Missee Coconut Palm, shook it gently, then clicked his fingers. A gentle click, fit for a young woman of such stature.

'Amos, Miss Cari.' He regarded her with his head tilted to one side, wondering – and not for the first time – why these people could not find more beautiful names for their daughters. 'You is tall. Tall past sister.' It was a thing of wonder, truly. He smiled at her, yet duty to his brothers soon turned his attention back to Nesta. 'No news? No money?'

The tall one cast no shadow. Yet Amos could discern a shape. It followed her. Maybe, more correctly, a shade. The shade of a child? His mother always said he had the gift. Like the men from the Alligator Society.

'No money,' said Miss Nesta. 'But I've spoken with our own leader. We have a plan.' Well, this was interesting. The words were delivered with care. 'Yes,' she was saying to her sister. 'I spoke to Alice. A plan.' Then she turned back to Amos. 'And I rather hoped you'd have news of your own. No movement from the company?'

'*Aan*,' he said. Yes. 'Messenger now come. Tell us we sign with *Zaria*. We go, they give us early our pay. But not more than come here. You know what us pay, Miss Cari? Half. Half pay of white man. Same job, half pay. Not just pay. Half food too.'

Miss Nesta tried to tell him they'd been talking about it earlier. She should have known. It wasn't right to talk when another person was already speaking. These white *poto* people!

'So, I says no,' he said. 'I tell them we are Kru. Kru never be took as slave. Kruman starve himself until dead. Every time slaver take him. So why be slave for this Elder Dempster bossmen? An' they say: "Fine. Plenty white men for sign to ship." Them right. He shrugged, looked down towards the river. 'Stand at them shed and watch. Plenty white men. Bossmen pay them all money. But not Kru. Now *Zaria* him sailed, and Kru still here. Many.' He flicked out the fingers of both hands, again and again, to illustrate the point. 'Many. But not give in. No, not never.'

'They let you stay here, though?' said Missee Coconut Palm. 'Even though you're striking? Not work?'

For now, Amos explained. Only for now.

'They say we learn. Normal time, we get small money for be here. Small. Too small to live. But some. Now, no more.'

It was true. As soon as they'd collectively decided not to ship out again until the wages were improved, their meagre retaining allowance had been stopped. Now they had to find enough money to pay for all their rations. It wasn't the way Amos had imagined it. His father had led a strike back in Freetown, twenty years earlier – and won. But here, in this Liverpool place…

'Why doesn't the union fight for you all to get the same pay?' said the tall girl. 'I don't understand.'

'*Ay-yah*, Miss Cari,' he said. 'Is justice like this any place here?'

It felt biggity, arrogant. But Amos knew it for perfectly fair comment. His mother, her bones now in the ground, had played an important part in her women's society. But queen of all she surveyed. It was fitting. For there they were, as their missionary pastor kept reminding them. Already in the twentieth century. A century, they'd been told, promising science, logic and invention. Yet here were these white people, still arguing about whether their women should be entitled to a simple vote. For some gathering of old men. In some faraway London. A gathering which seemed to have no bearing on their lives. It was strange. By then the tall sister had touched her hand to his arm. Some gesture of solidarity?

'Cari!' Miss Nesta scolded her, lifted Missee Coconut Palm's hand away. 'I think we should each promise to speak with our brother again. See if the dockers may help, after all. And Mister Gartee,' she said, almost interposing herself between Amos and the tall sister, 'please do not worry. One way or the other, we'll get you some help – and some money too.'

This was even more interesting. Amos was pleased. Perhaps both sisters? Was it forbidden? To consider marriage, here, with two sisters at the same time?

Chapter Two

Monday 3rd April 1911

2.55am

'Police!' hissed Florrie Thompson-Frere as she pulled Cari Maddox towards the plush maroon bedroom curtains, held them slightly apart so she might see. 'My goodness, I wonder if there's ever been a police raid in Waterloo Park before,' she laughed. 'I suspect the rest of this tour may have to wait, Cari.'

Her house on Haigh Road was palatial, even boasted its own crenelated turret, for heaven's sake. A long, long way from Hunter Street, and Cari was curious to see how the other half lived. Florrie had made them welcome enough, but had coming here been a mistake?

Most of those middle-class women lived on a different planet entirely from Cari and Nesta. No wonder, in a country with more people employed as domestic servants than almost any other trade. And those curtains – they were probably worth as much as all the Hunter Street furnishings put together, even though there were few enough other worldly goods left in the place. She couldn't help but wonder how different life for her family might be, if only…

'There's nothing amusing about this, Florrie,' snapped one of Mrs Thompson-Frere's friends, a cheroot-smoking Little Crosby woman who seemed even more uncomfortable there than Cari did. 'If I'm arrested…'

'Oh, you'll get used to it,' said Florrie. 'Being arrested. They're usually quite sweet about it. But Cari,' she whispered in Cari's ear, 'be a darling and ask the girls to turn off the music. I shan't be able to hear myself think otherwise.'

Below, the bobbies were hammering at the front doors again, so they went down the wide staircase together – Florrie to the generous vestibule and Cari to the almost bare reception room their host had turned over to her WSPU friends for the purpose of this gathering, which Alice Davies, their paid organiser, had insisted on calling a "field night."

Alice hadn't long taken over as Organiser for the WSPU and seemed to have her hands full with the campaign. She came to mind now, did Alice, as Cari tried to take command. Nessie had encouraged her sister to apply for the position, but Cari had decided against even making the attempt. It was all she could do to hold down her job and look after the family.

'Please,' she yelled at the dozen women dancing some mockery of a Highland Fling on the Thompson-Freres' exposed floorboards to the scratchy strains of Harry Lauder. 'Please, ladies,' she tried again, 'the bobbies are here – I mean, the police.'

Nesta wasn't among them, though she soon emerged from the card school she'd arranged in the grandiose dining salon, wagering her own money, she'd announced, on the basis that any winnings would contribute to the Elder Dempster Strike Fund.

'Is this what you meant by a plan, Nessie?' Cari snapped. 'Gambling your money away, mind?'

The dancing women seemed either deaf to Cari's pleas or entirely unheeding, and a couple of them were more engrossed in each other's company than she thought natural. What would Pastor Jenkins say about all this? Cari wondered. But she clapped her hands as loudly as she could, while Nesta took the more direct action of lifting the gramophone needle.

'There's bobbies at the door,' Cari shouted, just too loudly, into the sudden and comparative quiet simultaneously being filled by the two policemen in question. Already in the room, helmets under their arms and grimacing at the scene they now confronted.

'Ladies,' said Florrie Thompson-Frere, 'please allow me to introduce Sergeant Miller and Constable McCann. I fear we have incurred the law's wrath, yet again.'

'It's no laughing matter, Mrs Thompson-Frere,' the sergeant said. 'Not an issue for levity, I don't believe. And good evening, ladies.' It was a strange greeting – for three o'clock in the morning. 'I'm sorry to have to inform you we've received a serious complaint.'

'This is still a free country, isn't it?' said one of the posher women, Victoria Something-or-Other. 'If we choose not to take part in this silly Census, there's very little you can do about it, Sergeant.'

'Well,' he replied. 'I see the enumerator has left the forms in the hall, miss.'

Victoria Something-or-Other must have been forty and flushed with pleasure at this flattering form of address.

'And I can only advise you,' said the sergeant, 'to complete them. But the complaint concerns another matter entirely. The noise, you see? Complaints from the neighbours. So, I'm going to ask you nicely, just this once. To keep it all down a bit. Can you do that? Or should you prefer if I speak with *Mister* Thompson-Frere? He is at home, I assume.'

'My husband's away on business,' Florrie told him with frigid composure. 'But I'm hardly likely to ignore your warning, Sergeant. On the last occasion, as I recall, it cost me my furniture.' She gestured around the echoing reception room from which all her possessions had been seized some weeks earlier.

'Just doing my duty, ma'am,' said Sergeant Miller. 'You're a clever lady. And my wife's a great admirer of your work. I'm not one for poetry myself, but my Martha seems to like them. You make money from them, though, and that means you have to pay income tax like anybody else. Refuse to cough up your taxes and you must accept the penalty.'

'I earn my own income from the produce of my brain, Sergeant,' Florrie laughed. 'Yet I'm considered insufficiently intelligent to understand the difference between one parliamentary candidate and another. So, in the words of our American cousins, no taxation without representation. Fair, isn't it?'

'Perfectly fair if you don't mind having your possessions seized and auctioned by the authorities to pay off your debts. But I suppose you'll have enough wealthy friends to bid for them and get them back again this way.'

'The auction's tomorrow, Sergeant. So, we shall see, I suppose.'

There. It's what Cari meant. As if any of *them*, the ordinary working girls, could afford to protest in such a way. A different planet, indeed. Bad enough that, even in their Sunday best – which Nessie and Cari had both been reluctant to wear, lest it made them seem over-dressed, primly formal – their blouses and skirts were so plainly Blackler's. Yet here they were, in a house attired entirely by George Henry Lee.

And yes, even in this leafy northern suburb they could still vaguely smell the wharf-weary drift of a thousand dockside cargoes, but they were among folk who could afford to have all their worldly goods taken by the bailiffs, simply to purchase them afresh at auction the next day through their equally wealthy friends. They stuck together – Cari had to give them that. But it seemed to her very far from revolution.

If you're going to break the law, she thought, it should have some impact. Real impact. The point of the WSPU, surely. If they simply wanted to campaign peacefully about voting rights in general, they'd line themselves up with the Adult Suffrage Society. If they wanted to campaign peacefully for women's votes in particular they'd join one of the Women's Suffrage Societies. If they simply wanted to break the law as a protest – refusing to pay their taxes, that sort of thing – but refused to go the extra mile of taking direct action, well, they should have gone off with the splitters who'd left to join the Women's Freedom League.

But peaceful protest wasn't going to win this fight. And nor would it get women the wider respect, their equal place in society. Cari didn't think so, anyway. Nor, in theory, did any of those other women gathered at Florrie's, posh or not.

The WSPU might not be perfect but Cari considered it their best chance. And she had this moment of madness. The fantasy that there were enough of them here to overpower Sergeant Miller and Constable McCann, imprison them, hold them hostage against some concession for the cause. Yet, by then, Florrie Thompson-Frere had escorted the bobbies out through the vestibule, and the ladies were all picking up their sashes, draping themselves in the purple, white and green. In the case of the two sisters, sporting the cream straw boaters – with the appropriately coloured flowers – which Cari herself had finished the week before.

They followed the policemen up the hallway, down the steps onto the gravel driveway, where they began to sing *The March of the Women* at the tops of their voices. For the benefit of the neighbours, naturally, and as yet another gesture to the authorities.

"Shout, shout, up with your song!
Cry with the wind, for the dawn is breaking."

It was a ragged performance, the lyrics too new for familiarity, yet apt for the hour, the harmony quickly falling apart so they faltered early in the second verse and the sergeant spared them not even a backward glance.

'Cheek of the man,' said Cari, as they processed indoors again, gathered in the hall. '"Your husband is at home, I assume."' It was a fair imitation.

'Only doing his job, I suppose,' Florrie replied. 'It could have been worse, don't you think? I've always suspected Sergeant Miller has some sympathy for our plight.'

'Sympathy?' said Cari. 'Is this our goal? Suppose I was hoping for something more, see. But I'm guessing sympathy's about all we'll get until we decide to shake things up a bit more, anyway. Right is on our side, isn't it? How can we fail?'

'That's my girl, Cari,' Nesta laughed. 'Beginning to see sense at last. We need to stop thinking about Pastor Jenkins and his Holy Scripture and start fighting for justice. Proper fighting.'

'I'm sure we can reconcile godliness with a little more direct action,' said Victoria Something-or-Other.

But Cari knew how her own resolve so often faltered. In her moments of outrage, she could see the path clearly. Breaking the law, breaking windows, it was all the same to her. Yet at other times she wondered at the wisdom of their actions. Too many years of dutiful adherence to chapel, she supposed.

'Yes,' said Nesta. 'Something to make them sit up. Really sit up – stop poking fun at us.'

They were all still stinging from the poem in Saturday's paper, a cruel satire.

'I don't think I want to hear this,' said the timid lady from Little Crosby. 'It all smacks too much of illegality. It would be so easy to endanger our cause as the result of some ill-conceived impatience. Some foolishness.'

Another one. Cari wanted to ask her why she didn't join one of the other groups, in that case. But she knew the answer. There were always a few who stayed with the WSPU for no better reason than pressure from their friends or because they thought it fashionable. Not many, perhaps. But enough to hold them back.

'Well, I'd be thinking twice about any foolish action, as well,' said Cari, then caught herself recalling the impetuous attack she'd made on Haldane. 'But impatience? How long are we supposed to wait?'

'We'll be like those poor Krooboys at the Harrington dock,' Nessie snapped. 'Waiting for an offer that's never going to come.'

'Oh, them!' said Mrs Little Crosby. 'I don't think they're interested in anything except getting themselves a British passport or a British wife. As though there aren't enough foreigners here already. Either that or – well, you've all heard the stories.'

'No,' said Nesta. 'I haven't, for one.'

'Come on, Miss Maddox,' said the woman. 'You must have done. All those stories about them being mixed up with White Slavers. Not a strike. They're simply here so they can ply their trade. You should be ashamed if you're mixed up with those rascals.'

It was rare to see Nessie stuck for words, but her mouth simply hung open, her nostrils twitching more violently than normal.

'Dear me, ladies.' Florrie Thompson-Frere threw up her hands, a silent plea for peace. She reached for the gorgeous little gold watch hanging from a chain around her neck, flicked it open and studied the time. 'Perhaps we should start to think about what we'd like for breakfast.'

6.45am

Tom Priddy couldn't recall when he'd spent a worse night. *Iesu*, the palliasse. And the idiot of a brother, snoring like a pig. *Mochyn budr*. Then kicked him when he was getting ready for work. On purpose? Yes, on purpose, he was certain.

Tidy though, like. Had to give him that much. Clean shirt from the chest by the bed. Rest of his work clothes didn't look too foul. Smell of the docks. Smell of this whole city, really. But still not enough to overpower the stink of beer on Taffy's breath.

He was damned if he was going to wash in the same bowl Taffy had left on the nightstand, either. He lit a candle, carried bowl and candle down to the kitchen, emptied the contents into the sink and filled it afresh.

'Got to go,' he muttered, as he turned towards the parlour door for the trip back up to the bedroom. 'Daft Taffy's simply got to go.'

He was thinking about the various ways Taffy might be exorcised from his life – almost jumped out of his skin when he saw the dark outline of Huw Maddox on the sofa once more. How had he not seen him on his way through? The lamp above the sofa itself was lit, but the old miser had turned down the gas so much it provided no more than a glimmer, outshone even by Tom's candle flame.

'Talking to yourself now, is it?' said old Huw. He was peering at a notebook, held only an inch from the end of his nose, and from the spectacles perched there. 'And going? So soon?'

Tom Priddy pulled himself together. He grinned.

'Just out to buy the paper,' he said. 'You'll not be seeing the back of me so easily, *ewythr*. Not for a while, like.'

'Still didn't tell me,' Huw grumbled. 'What it is you want.'

The old man was more composed this morning. Definitely. More composed.

'True, that is,' Tom replied. 'But more's the point, where are *you* going?'

Huw Maddox was wrapped in his outdoor sack coat. Long, and the colour unfathomable in this gloom. His cap was on his knee, cigarette in his hand.

'Parcels Office. Work I finished Saturday. Need delivering today, they do.'

'Just the job for your very own printer's devil, then. Old Haymarket?' Huw Maddox nodded by way of reply. '*Iawn*,' said Tom. Fine. 'Five minutes. I'll give you a hand, see.'

It took longer than five minutes, naturally. Tom Priddy's wash and shave. Mug of tea and a crust of bread with a meagre smear of dripping. Another candle. Downstairs to the passageway.

'Planning on more?' Tom Priddy laughed and pointed to the web-strewn baby carriage.

'Can't bring myself...' Huw began, then closed his lips tight once again.

Out into the yard. A visit to the privy. Raining a bit now. The first glimmers of morning light. To the printshop.

'Not the worst smell in the world,' said Tom, and breathed deeply of the heady aroma. Ink, paper and cleaning fluid. The candlelight flickered across the press, a guillotine, sorting table, typeface racks, stacks of printing paper and piles of wrapped packages. Brown paper packages, tied with string.

'These,' said Huw Maddox, and they each took an armful from the table.

Tom Priddy followed him out through the printshop's side gate into Dawson Place. Sounded grand, it did, but wasn't much more than a paved yard. Flaking whitewash patches to marginally brighten segments of the soot-stained brick walls. Along the cobbles, stepping stone progress over the puddles of filth, to reach Hunter Street itself.

'This is it, then?' he shouted over the rumble, clatter and snorts of laden carts, the screech and rattle of trams, as they turned the corner past the Byrom.

'Mad John's,' said old Huw. 'That's the place. Den of iniquity, like. Dafydd. Boozing his money away like every other dock walloper.'

'But this many?'

Tom glanced back along the road. Streetlamps still lit. A few shops, early openers, with their yellow lights already showing. And though it wasn't yet possible to see all the boozers, they both knew they were there. Just about every corner. Byrom Street, then all the length of Scotland Road. Further. Dozens upon dozens. For mile after mile. An infinite outpouring of the devil's brew. But here, next to Mad John's, praise the Lord, the Temperance Hotel and Popular Café. A beacon of hope in all this dark iniquity.

'And those girls,' Tom pressed the old man when they'd crossed Clayton Street, passed in front of the Technical School's grandeur and entrance steps. 'Even worse than Taffy and the booze. Out all night? Not right. Clip their wings – that's what you need to do. Put the fear of God into them.'

They waited while a tram sparked its way down William Brown Street, followed as it swung into the oval terminus at the Old Haymarket.

'Not easy,' said Huw Maddox. 'After their mam, an' all…'

They pushed their way through the comings and goings of

passengers to reach the green and cream wooden confines of the Parcels Office on the farther end of the terminus platform, where they were quickly surrounded by a dozen Parcel Boys. Urchins, all of them. Dark blue uniforms not quite fitting their undernourished frames. Treated old Huw Maddox like some sort of saint, though.

'Still,' said Tom, pushing open the Parcels Office door, 'Cari and Nesta. Maybe you need a devil on your side for more than the printing, *uncle*.'

7.05am

Amos Gartee was happier than he'd been for weeks. He'd been dreaming about the two heavenly women. Dreamed of them white, naturally. But white with the kaolin clay, breasts and belly painted with lines and spirals of green-black kola nut paste. Dreamed of them back home, in Nana Kru.

But now it was time to rise, to face the day. To see whether this happiness could last, burn away the challenges he must overcome. He climbed from his hammock, lit the candle, pulled aside the blanket separating him from his brothers still sleeping in the dormitory. Yes, separate. The privilege of his rank, his election as their *krogba*. He had, after all, been their headman on board the *Mendi*, which had brought them here. And now, as the voice of their fight for fair pay.

'Awake, awake!' he yelled, first in the *Bakwe* spoken by so many of them from the Kru western lands, then in his own *Bété*.

They shared some good-natured banter, as well as the pitcher and bowl of washing water, then processed down to the basement mess hall, carrying their eating bowls. The room was already full. The Mende boys. Ready for a fight, Amos could tell. The averted eyes. The tensed shoulders. The clenched fists. The petulant silence. The acrid stink of skittish sweat. Atmosphere tight as a drumskin.

'No word?' One of the Mende, the fellow he knew as Jonah Samba, stood from his table, stretched a jittery finger towards Amos, and spoke in his own *Krio*. It was, after all, the *lingua franca* of Sierra Leone. But Amos chose to reply in the *Kreyol* version of English with which they were also all familiar. They had to be. For the ships. For the bossmen.

'Word come, brother,' said Amos. 'Word come a'right. Word

come that Mende want end this strike. Correct, Jonah?'

'Strike isn't working. An' you know it, Kruman. We need go home. Get paid. Maybe in Freetown the Kru click them fingers and get what they want. But not this Liverpool place.'

Amos knew he was right. He was proud of it. Ship work along the coast from Freetown. The Kru and their allies were kings. And the Mende, others, despised them for it. Jealousy. But jealousy was a powerful thing.

'In this Liverpool place,' Jonah Samba went on, 'you ain't no better than rest of us. No better past shit. Time to go home, Kruman.'

'Then go home, Jonah. Tell women how you run from them bossmen.'

He turned his back on the Mende boys, led his own brothers to the tables where the hostel's cook and his *poto* wife had laid out baskets of *fufu* bread and congealed *geebee* soup. Yes, they were still fed. Like the lodging, the Company knew most of these men would have to give in and pay up sooner or later. The bigger the slate they built up now, the less they'd have to be paid when they eventually and inevitably were forced to sign on for a return passage to Freetown. Without the few shillings of their weekly waiting allowance, the slate simply grew bigger faster.

He supposed the Company could have starved them back to work. But this would have made martyrs of them, perhaps. And anyway, what use was a starved seaman. Aboard ship, they only received half the rations of a white man. Half the pay, half the food. But just sufficient to keep them strong enough to stoke the boilers or perform their other duties.

'This what you call food, Cookie?' said Amos. The cook came from some place, the name of which Amos couldn't even pronounce, the fellow's face painted all over in blue tattoo patterns.

'Eat, no eat,' the cook grinned at him through the gaps in his teeth. 'All same, dog-eater.'

It was a game they played, daily. The insults. The ripostes. But, by then, members of Amos Gartee's inner circle were already scooping the stew into their bowls. Barkuh Togba, a Kru prize-fighter from his own town of Nana Kru. George Janjay, a yellow-skinned Guere person, short-tempered, like all the Guere. And Samuel Nimene, almost as tall as Missee Coconut Palm, with his strange dreamlike gait. Amos would have filled his own bowl as well, but he felt somebody grip his arm, spin him around. Jonah Samba, of course, backed by those who ran at his tail.

'Not this time, Kruman,' he yelled into Amos's face. 'You think bossmen will settle just with us? Need us all. And if them did, then what? Some day you come home to Freetown too? Tell whole world we have no balls? Shame us?'

'An' you, Mende man,' Amos laughed at him, though he knew there was no laughter in his eyes – no, quite the opposite. 'What you do? Hold my hand?' He was fast when he wanted to be. Lightning fast. Jonah Samba didn't even see it. The way he snatched the Mende's wrist, shook it like a wet fish, made the fingers flap in empty air. 'Make me sign bossman's papers?'

He saw the anger in Jonah's own eyes turn to fear. Amos flung the man's wrist away from him, then stared down each of the Mende's followers.

'No,' he snarled. 'Today. Big meetin'. Today *will* be word.'

But how, he wondered, am I going to make that happen?

7.25am

'For pity's sake, what were you thinking, girl?' Cari demanded for the fourth time since they'd left the Five Lamps.

It was barely light and they had, indeed, been fed breakfast by Florrie Thompson-Frere before starting the journey home. Tram from Five Lamps to the Sands, then another one back to the Haymarket. Yet most of the way they'd been silent. A sulking silence. To tell the truth, Cari thought, it was pitiful. But she couldn't help herself.

'She'd never have missed it,' Nessie hissed at last.

'Her best cruet?' said Cari. 'No, of course not. And who, d'you think, she'd have blamed? Mrs Snooty from Little Crosby? I don't think so, Nesta.'

Cari thanked the Lord she'd seen her sister do it. Slipping the silver pot beneath the napkin and onto her lap, under the table. The trick had been to get the thing back before anybody else around the table decided they wanted pepper on their savoury scrambled eggs.

'Remember Mister Gartee,' said Nesta. 'I promised. Money,

Cari. Money. And it doesn't grow on trees.'

'Nor from gambling away your shillings at whist, you silly goose,' she said. 'But stealing – and from our friends.'

'Hardly friends. Didn't you see the way they looked down their noses? And there they'll be, later, throwing around their guineas like they're going out of fashion – plenty to spare for Florrie Thompson-Frere's leather chesterfields.' She wrinkled her nose and switched to a very passable English upper crust accent. 'And, oh my dear,' she mimicked. 'My beautiful Turkish divan. I brought it all the way from Istanbul, you know.'

Almost at their end of Scotland Road, a couple of early shops opening up, their gas lights flickering through the gloom.

'Don't think you can wriggle your way out of this, Nessie. How would we ever face them again? At the meetings.'

'Oh, Mrs Bloody Thompson-Frere.' Nesta shook her head. 'The likes of her, she's never going to help us change anything.'

Cari was on the verge of leaping to Florrie's defence, then recalled her strange comment about getting used to being arrested – how sweet the bobbies might be. Well, it didn't chime with the stories they'd heard from many others who'd suffered the same experience. Nor the reason they'd all demonstrated for so long last January outside Walton Gaol against the forced feeding of women imprisoned there. At least, the forced feeding – oral violation, as many of them saw it – of the Gaol's working class women. Maybe this was the difference. Wealthy women like Florrie Thompson-Frere were spared such indignities.

'It's a broad church we've got – you know that,' said Cari, but she laughed. A sarcastic laugh. 'We need the Florrie Thompson-Freres,' she insisted. 'And you'll not help Amos if you end up in the Bridewell. Or worse.'

'Oh, it's Amos now? I saw the way you touched his arm, Cari. And the way he looked at you. Well, if you care anything for him – for the other Krooboys, as well – it will take a little more than fluttering your eyelashes at him. Anyhow, you've already got the German hanging on your every word.'

Cari felt herself flush.

'What total nonsense,' she snapped. 'How dare you, Nessie?'

In truth, though, she'd struck a nerve. Ernst Jurks and Amos

Gartee had been somewhat equally on Cari's mind several times through the night. They each intrigued her. Perhaps a little more than that, a thrill of excitement, if she was honest. Several thoughts she knew would never have met with their good pastor's approval. A couplet, which wouldn't quite leave her.

From Africa he blows a dream to me,
To fill my days with visions of the East.

But then there'd been those comments about White Slavers. About the African sailors only seeking wives or British citizenship.

'And are you so sure,' she said, 'Amos Gartee's not playing you for a fool?'

'They're on strike, Cari. Starving. You wouldn't have asked that question if they were white. You wouldn't. You know it's true. And Taffy wouldn't have turned his back on them either.'

The heat crept up Cari's neck again. Anger and embarrassment, both. An overwhelming sense of sadness. She knew her sister was right, and she had no answer for her. Not then.

In any case, they were already turning into the Old Haymarket. And there was their father, at the Parcels Office. They both saw him and neither of them remarked on the fact, for they'd fallen into another huff as they joined the press of passengers leaving the vehicle at one end while the conductor tried in vain to hold back those pushing to alight at the other.

The pre-dawn press and bustle. In the middle of it, their tada, surrounded by his admiring supporters among the Parcel Boys. Paper package, bundles of flyers for businesses all across the city and its suburbs. His regular routine.

She saw him place a paternal hand on the shoulder of a child at his side. Fourteen years old like all the Parcel Boys. They were a favourite and deserving cause of her father's. Sixteen-hour days and paid a pittance, their miseries only exceeded by those of the marginally older Points Boys – out in all weathers, working the control box levers at each junction of the network, and trams coming at them every couple of minutes out of the dark, the rain, the driving snow, the fog, or a rare blinding sun. And Tada was right, of course. These lads could hardly have been treated worse if folk had still been shoving them up chimneys.

Cari had hoped they might sneak past, but Nessie's tongue had engaged before her brain, once more.

'I'd have thought that was a job for a printer's devil, Pa,' she shouted. 'If he was any use, like.'

She failed, of course, to notice Cousin Tom Priddy emerge from the Parcels Office immediately behind her.

7.45am

'Funny, that is,' said Tom, and delighted in the way both girls started, spun around to face him. Those stupid, shocked faces. 'I was just saying, like. How much your tada needs me for more than just the printing.'

'Oh, you're back, are you?' Huw Maddox turned on them as soon as he saw his daughters, gave them a look of such disgust, after their night away from home. 'Back from the House of Rahab. It's these lads who deserve your pity,' he shouted. 'Not those – those harpies you're mixing with.'

Tom Priddy saw the shock the Beanpole's face, while the other one, Dumpling Nesta, simply giggled.

'Is that the way of it, Tada?' the Beanpole answered him. Insolent. But she was in full flow. 'What you think of us? House of Rahab. No better than street women? And doesn't Holy Scripture tell us to stand against all evils – not just those we personally dislike? Not a competition, see. Enough evil in this world to go around us all.'

Pretty speech. But evil? She didn't know the half of it.

'*In the little world of children,*' Huw Maddox began to quote, though his face immediately creased with pain, '*there is nothing so finely perceived and so finely felt as injustice.* Dickens, see. Injustice to children is the worst injustice.'

What hurt him so? The hands. Of course, the hands.

'Maybe, Pa,' said Dumpling Nesta. 'But look at you, out here with no gloves on.' Old Huw was fishing in his pockets, searching for coins with which he might reward the lads but barely able to handle the coppers with those ugly twisted fingers. Tom Priddy wondered how on earth he managed the typesetting. 'This how they got in such a state?' Nesta asked. 'Your hands. The quarry, like Cousin Thomas said?'

She almost spat his name. He was about to slap her down but Huw Maddox got there first.

'Enough, now,' old Huw snapped. 'The boy's your own flesh and blood. And a man has to find work where he can. You know it, both of you.'

It wasn't much of an explanation but it was all he was going to give them.

'Oh, we know more than that,' said the Beanpole. 'All of us working now, Tada. Not just the men. Pull our weight, we do. Though we get little enough credit for it.'

Same old story, Tom thought. He yawned and was rewarded with a frown of exasperation from the girl.

'Not from the powers-that-be,' she snapped, and deliberately turned from him, back to her father. 'No fairness. And these boys? It's a good thing, you taking them under your wing and all, Tada. But how much d'you give them each week? More than you can afford, that's what. More than *we* can afford, now we've got Cousin Thomas to feed. How long can we go on like this?'

Huw Maddox handed out the last of his addressed packages, paper and string, red sealing wax. He distributed his final few coppers. And he seemed to revel in the occasional ironic salute or grin of false gratitude from the blue-uniformed boys. Old fool.

'*Duw*,' said Huw, at last, 'you might be right, girl. I suppose there's nothing else for it – one of you will just have to rob a bank.'

Tom Priddy explored his face, trying to fathom whether this terse comment was intended as humour, though he thought not. Sarcasm seasoned his words.

'Me and Nessie,' said the Beanpole, 'we've both got work in an hour. So maybe the bank robbery later. Will you walk us home?'

'Now you want to look respectable, is it?' Huw Maddox sneered. 'No, I think I'll pick up the *Post and Mercury* first.'

And off he went towards the kiosk.

'Don't worry, Beanpole, he'll get over it.'

Tom Priddy surprised them both by sliding between them, seizing an elbow of each girl. Before they knew it, he'd crossed them over the bottom of William Brown Street.

'Don't you think?' he said, but he knew she wasn't really listening.

'What?' she said, returning from whichever reverie into which she'd sunk.

Tom had the feeling she was still thinking about what her father had said. About the bank. That comment about robbing a bank.

8.05am

Amos had no meeting planned, though he couldn't admit as much. There was no word coming. Yet, as was their routine, he organised as many of the men as he could muster, led them to the gateway for the Harrington Dock, spread them beneath the shelter provided by the overhead wonder of the raised electric railway, scattered them so far as the railway's Toxteth Dock Station.

Placards, which the *poto* girl, Miss Nesta, had helped them put together.

Black or White, Equal Pay

A dozen other slogans. And a galvanised bucket. A few of the carters, at least, stopped to give them pennies, to wish them well. Good union men, those horse drivers. Many of the dockers, as well. But the rest? Passed them without a second glance. At best a second glance. At worst…

Pickets. This was the word he had learned. Though for what purpose? The *Zaria* had sailed and there were presently no more of the Elder Dempster bossman's ships in the berths. Yet Amos had convinced the men they must continue their protest, draw attention to their plight. And once they were set to their duties he needed to make himself scarce, to give the appearance of making good his boast about the meeting.

As he'd done several times before, he cut back up through the streets of terraced houses and warehouses, to the place they called St. James' Mount, where the great House of God was slowly climbing from the ground. Magical, bound on one side by a valley of the dead. On the mount itself, mighty blocks of carved and fluted sandstone piled one upon the other. Archways under construction. All set against a spider's web of metal threads, criss-crossed between legs of sturdy black iron. Clouds of white or amber dust. The beat of a hundred masons' hammers. The grind and screech of steam cranes.

A House of God.

Could God already live in a house not yet built? Amos had no idea, yet he pulled the bible from his pocket, clutching it in his hands. He prayed anyway. In *Bété*.

Rather, he argued. It was his nature.

'How can this be, Lord? The Kru, we are a Christian people. If Thee saw fit to put us on this earth in one place, and these white folk in another, was this not Thy will? And did Thee not make us equal in Thine eyes? If so, how have You allowed them to treat us like dogs?'

He knew the answer. Of course, he did. The fault of song-sayers. Tellers of tales. A myth invented. These people, or those, they would say, have some special power. An unnatural power. A power they used for evil. They ate babies. They placed curses upon their neighbours. They brought diseases or foul weather. They ruined crops. They stole livelihoods, caused poverty and starvation. Whatever it was, this special power always for the same purpose – so they could control the whole world. The myth within the myth. And the myth was repeated, generation after generation, until it was bred in the bones of the weak-minded.

From the weak-minded came the hatred, the persecutions.

'But why, Lord,' he said, 'do Thee allow it?'

Here, in this Liverpool place, Cookie had directed him to those who might help their cause. To the Seamen's Friend Society, who had offered them books and blankets, coats and clothing. To the Seamen's Mission, which had given them both blessings and boxes of food. From both, advice to speak with the Sailors' and Firemen's Union. He'd made the journey down to Canning Place, the union's offices just across from the Sailors' Home. And there he'd sat for half the day, speaking to one white man after another, each of them so short-tempered he'd come to believe they must all be related to the Guere. For the Guere were indeed a short-tempered people.

The strikers needed help yet could not be helped because they were not members of the union. They were happy to join, Amos had confirmed, but had never been allowed membership. And now, they were told, they could not be taken into membership because they were undercutting the pay of existing members. But wasn't it the point? Amos argued. A fight to increase their own pay so they should not be cheap labour for the bossmen.

It had all fallen upon ears that were deaf. At that meeting, more than a week ago, they'd been congratulated on their strike, told to "hold on" for the bigger strike to come. But how long must they wait?

So, no. Word not coming. No further meetings. And here he was, on strange ground. Sailor Town – or Dark Town as he'd heard some call it – was a true melting pot. Malays and Chinamen. Arabs and Greeks. Lascars and Africans like himself. Followers of Jesus. Followers of Islam. Followers of a dozen other faiths. Yes, on the streets and in the lodging houses, there were insults. Beatings. Sometimes worse. But in the hostel at least they were together, among their own. Though the section of this Liverpool place through which he now walked was a different world. Very different.

Yet there was an omen, surely. He trudged along the road behind the valley of the dead. A terrace of houses like a palace. Hope Street. Hope. Yes, he must continue to hope.

A left turn. Past a great school, down the hill towards the edge of Liverpool's Chinatown. He kept walking, desperate to find an answer to his problem. And behold, another omen. Bold Street. Bold, of course. He must be bold.

Amos ventured down this thoroughfare of banks and elaborate boutiques. He thought of the *poto* girls. Their promise of money. That would help, but it would not be enough. The people here were dressed well. Elegant dresses and hats for the women. Suits and coats for the men which reeked of wealth. A sea of white faces among which he felt entirely and unutterably alone. Afraid. He realised he was afraid. And Amos saw their questioning glances, knew they were fearful also, crossed the street to avoid passing him. As though he possessed the evil eye.

The street drew him onwards. Down. Down into territory more alien to him than any other place he'd ever been. A long way down. To the bottom, a junction of roads with trams thundering around the corner – a corner with another stone-built palace, gentlemen in tall hats coming and going. There was a smell here. A smell of eggs gone bad. Another station for their railways. Billowing smoke.

He knew he was lost now, ran between trams and carts, turned past one of their beer houses – no, a whole row of them – and found himself in a square with hotels on each of its four sides. More shops. Floor upon floor of shops.

Why have Thee brought me here? his brain whispered to the Lord. But he should have known. For good omens always ran in threes. Hope. Boldness. And there, not twenty paces away from him, was the answer. As sure as day, there she was Missee Coconut Palm.

12.15pm

'Back promptly, please, Miss Maddox.' Mister Kaplan made a point of poking his lugubrious head around the typing room door as Cari shrugged into her coat and tried to hurry out for lunch.

'Yes, Mister Kaplan,' she shouted back and made an effort to flash him her most reassuring smile.

But she'd been on the verge of tears all morning. Lack of sleep. Time of the month also. The curse. And she knew she was on borrowed time. More late returns from meetings at the WSPU office, and then her feigned illness last November when she'd been moved to join the march on Parliament. Borrowed time. A good job at Kaplan's she could ill afford to lose.

Yet Wyn had asked to meet her and she knew her little sister had been troubled lately. It was her mixed blessing. Being the eldest. Bestowed on her as long ago as she could remember. Surrogate mother for each of them, though all their woes to shoulder, as well. The truth was that Wyn was too young to be saddled with a man like Rhys Fingers – but not much to be done about it just then. She needed to leave, yet felt her face crumple, her eyes fill for no good reason, while Kaplan shook his old head in exasperation. 'Yes,' Cari repeated. 'Back prompt, like.'

Then, as she ran around the corner from Seel Street into Hanover Street, where the hurdy-gurdy man churned out his tunes, the newspaper kiosk's billboard screamed at her.

Prime Minister Condemns Census Dodgers.

Asquith! Well, what else could you expect from that dishonest creature? Asquith the great Liberal.

He'd promised a debate on a private members' Conciliation Bill all through the previous year – a modest proposal simply to give voting rights just to a million women. Cari had never believed it would happen anyway, even this much of a sop, though it was enough for most of their women to agree a temporary cessation of activities. A truce, they called it. No more than a truce. But in November he'd made it clear there was no time for such a debate. Yet another General Election to be called.

Outrage. The march on Parliament, which Cari wouldn't have missed for all the tea in China. Nor the bit of window-smashing later. And yes, she'd expected the bobbies to be rough. But the violence. The animal fury of those men. Black Friday. Poor Mary Clarke, Emmeline Pankhurst's sister. Holloway and forced feeding. Then died, just before Christmas. Brain haemorrhage, they said, but Cari reckoned it was the beatings she'd taken.

So, Asquith. Snap election in December, and there he was, back in power. More Liberal promises. Of course, a fresh Conciliation Bill to be considered. Cari argued like the very devil. They shouldn't fall for it again. But they did. So here they were. Another truce. Another break in the campaign. Not that it meant much to them locally, mind. Liverpool, after all. So, Cari was tempted to call at the office, pick up some more leaflets – the leaflets her tada had refused to print for them – though, in the end, she decided to go straight to Clayton Square.

She'd laughed when Nessie tried to persuade her to stand for the paid organiser's post but now Cari found herself on every visit wondering how she would have handled each crisis landing on Alice's desk. Today she convinced herself the priority must be to find out what was wrong with Wyn.

Cari wasn't certain it was the best place to meet. They used it, normally, because Nessie worked there. And because it was only five minutes' walk from Kaplan's. The Japanese Café, an exotic name which was more than it deserved, perched above the Clayton Brothers' oriental emporium and up flights of rickety stairs. But Nesta hovering about was unlikely to be helpful if Wyn did, indeed, have anything confidential to impart.

She was intrigued. But as she reached the emporium, Cari heard a voice.

'Missee Cari! Missee Cari!'

She turned to see a crowd of shoppers part as though a leper had appeared in their midst. Amos Gartee. Surely, it must be. Though she'd only met him last night. Yet this man knew her name. And the scars across his ebony face and forehead. Were they the same?

'Mister Gartee?' she said. He smiled, the relief upon his face palpable. 'What are you doing here?'

'Should I not be? Here?'

'No,' she said, then realised the blunder she'd made. 'I mean, yes, of course you should. Be here, see. I meant – oh, never mind. You have business here, in town, like?'

Cari saw the way they were regarded by the passers-by. Frowns. Sneers. Whispers behind hands.

'I think God send me to find you, Miss Cari.'

'Really?' She glanced up at the windows of the Japanese Café, two floors above. Confused. Those thoughts she'd entertained about Mister Gartee. Pleased to see him, though somewhat embarrassed as well. Did she give a fig for what these folk around her might be thinking? No, indeed not. Well, perhaps just a little. It was more – the timing of the thing. Yes, that was it. No time. Wyn waiting for her. And the pressure to get back to work.

'I'm afraid the Almighty may have chosen a poor hour to send you, Mister Gartee. My sister, see. I have to meet her. Up there. Think she needs my help with something.'

His gaze followed the direction of her pointing finger.

'Must call me Amos, Miss Cari,' he told her. 'Need help too. Us.'

'We have some ideas. Nesta and me. For raising money…'

'Not money. More than money. We need union. For fight.'

There was a desperation in his voice. And she knew, deep inside. Amos Gartee was not a man who would normally plead for anything.

'Then we'll see what we can do, yes? My brother is on the committee of his own union. Perhaps…' Yet she knew Taffy would be no help at all. Still, she needed to get upstairs. 'Look,' she said, 'I promise. I'll speak with Nesta. Somehow we'll work something out.'

She touched his arm, smiled at him, looked up at the window again. 'But now…'

Cari was on the second flight of stairs, his face still haunting her. That expression. His disappointment at her condescension mingled with a sense of abject abandonment. And she realised she had no idea whether he might even know how to get back from Clayton Square to Dark Town. What did the verse of Exodus say? *A stranger in a strange land.*

12.25pm

Tom Priddy was happy in his work. For the most part, anyway. Waugh paid him decently enough for his occasional duties in the yard, helping the stable boys, or the fellows who kept the hearses in such exquisite condition. Polishing. Always polishing. But pleasurable equine memories of his youth, of Beddgelert.

Yet it was the assistance he gave to Mister Clamp the mortician which most delighted him. Cleaning the equipment. And, on joyful occasions, the chance to use them. The mouth clamps and syringes. Arterial and drainage tubes. Trocars, or the metal and rubber vacuum hand-pumps. The fluids. The formaldehyde. The razors and whetstones. The curling irons for styling the hair of their gentlemen customers, as Clamp called them.

And therein lay the problem. Clamp was content enough to accept his help with the deceased gentlemen. But never the women. Tom was never allowed near the women. It vexed him.

'Working tonight, Thomas?'

Clamp wiped some wax from his fingers onto the apron he wore to protect that expensive suit.

'They don't need me, see. Just the variety tonight.'

The Rotunda Theatre, right next to the funeral parlour. Handy enough. John Waugh & Sons, at 407 Scotland Road. An arched gateway behind the theatre, the yard. And behind the yard, the funeral furnisher itself.

Well, plenty to keep you busy here, young man,' Clamp smiled at him. 'Soon have him looking the part again, yes?'

'An artist, you are, Mister Clamp. Artist, like.'

After the scalpels, the bistuaries, the aneurism hooks, had come the fine-toothed saw for the skull, then the plaster and, finally, moulding the wax. Whole side of the head. So much damage. Oh, the indignity of death.

'Simple reconstruction, Thomas. We've seen far worse on this cooling table.

He watched Mister Clamp at his creative best, while Tom gripped the small pump between his fingers. He worked the plunger with his thumb, slowly sucked more of the foetid gases from the man's stomach cavity. Gentle farting noises as the pump and the rubber exhaust tube did their work.

'You enjoy your work here,' Clamp observed, standing back to check his handicraft. 'Time for a little colour, I believe.'

Tom dutifully passed him the leather case of powders, brushes, creams and paints.

'Gives me time to think,' he replied. 'Peaceful, like.'

Peaceful as… And there was plenty to think about. The brother, Dafydd, for one. Taffy. How many times had he heard the word Taffy flung about as an insult since he arrived there? An idiot with an idiot's nickname. Needed some way to bait him. Not just the football thing. But he'd have to go. So, what was it little Dumpling Nesta had been on the verge of spitting out? Blacks or Catholics, she'd said. Which was worse? Yes, that was right. What had she meant? And then there was the booze.

'Drunk, did you say?'

Tom Priddy almost leapt out of his skin, thought for a stupid moment Clamp had read his mind, realised he meant the source of his latest creation.

'Oh, as a lord,' said Tom. 'Rude, he was. Real rude, like.'

More than just rude. Tom had been working the theatre's cloakroom. A simple mistake, he'd made. Anybody could have done it. But *this* fellow…

'No need to speak to me that way,' he murmured. 'We all have rights, Mister Clamp, isn't it?'

Rights. Yes, proper rights. Not all this nonsense the girls whined about. He'd have to put Cari Beanpole in her place, as well. Teach her something about rights. Teach her the Good Lord had placed men above women, and that's the way it would stay. He knew her weakness, of course. Family. All the stuff about blood thicker than water.

But beyond the literal, what was the reality? Families as likely to stab you in the back as look at you. *Iesu*, you could trust total strangers more. Yet there *was* the dead child to think of. Baby Pryce? He could read her guilt about Baby Pryce. A lever. Just needed to know how to exploit it. Yes, a lever.

'Rights?' said Clamp. 'Even this poor wretch, drunkard or not. What d'you think, Thomas? More rose?'

He'd already added too much in Tom's opinion. Looked like the deceased was blushing. Well, maybe not a bad thing, going to meet his Maker with embarrassment painted on his features. It made him think of Nesta the Dumpling. Her own flushed face and neck when the palm boat boys were mentioned. Interesting. Then old Huw's jest about robbing a bank. What *was* it he'd seen written behind her eyes?

'Perhaps just a little more,' he said. 'Just this side?'

The side crushed by the steam wagon, he thought. Accident, they'd decided. Unfortunate accident. No witnesses, of course. Sad, it was. The theatre closed and there he'd been, all alone crossing Scotland Road. Came out of the fog, the driver had said. Out of nowhere. Almost running, he'd reckoned. Strange, see.

'No,' said Clamp. 'I think not. On this occasion, I must disagree, Thomas. Enough, as they say, is enough.'

Clamp moved his head from side to side, took a step back. A masterpiece. It was the thing Tom Priddy needed, as well. A masterpiece. For Huw Maddox. He'd put the fear of God into him, of course. Those few words he'd managed to spit in the old man's ear when he'd arrived. But what *did* he want from him? In the end, like. The business? The Hunter Street house? He'd imagined something better. Yes, he needed to work on his plan. His own private revolution.

'Always room for improvement, though. That's what I say, Mister Clamp. Reach for the future, see. Even at the Rotunda. Talk of a bioscope next year. Moving pictures, like.'

Clamp laughed.

'Moving pictures?' he said. 'Only be a passing fancy, I expect.'

Perhaps he was right. But imagine, Tom thought, to be able to catch a person's essence. To capture their living selves forever. Important. Because he wondered whether this dead fellow's family would even recognise him now. Hard to tell, though. For Tom Priddy's recollection of him was from those final seconds – the scream as he'd fallen forward under the wheels of the steam truck.

12.30pm

The place was quiet and Nesta wasn't waiting on tables but seemingly confined to the kitchen today. But as she entered the Japanese Café, Cari was still brooding about Amos. Guilty, guilty, guilty.

'Has Nessie spotted you?' she said, sitting at Wyn's window table. The place was ripe with the smells of freshly ground coffee and baked sponge cakes, overlaid with the scented teas in which they specialised. The same scents, she imagined, which must pervade a cottage garden.

'You seem distracted,' Wyn said to her, but Cari simply shook her head, turned her thoughts from Mister Gartee. For now, at least.

Wyn was pushing a piece of confection around a willow-pattern plate with a fork she must surely have brought with her. An obsession, using her own cutlery, almost regardless of where she went. If she was honest, Cari was astonished her sister had even deigned to use the café's crockery.

'Boiled or poached, Wyn?' she said, and nodded towards the slice of ginger cake. Cari thought it was funny.

'It's neither, of course. But I felt obliged to order something. Would you like it?'

She slid the plate in Cari's direction.

'I'm sure there can't be anything wrong with it,' Cari told her. 'It's been baked, after all.'

Her sister merely smiled apologetically, as though Cari was simple. Unless food was boiled or poached, Wyn normally wouldn't touch it. They'd had the conversation countless times, though Wyn was far beyond reason on the matter. Since Pryce. The smallpox which had taken the poor mite and almost claimed Winifred as well, left her with this tragic face so pitted and scarred, this soul so similarly flawed, and this obsession with fastidious cleanliness.

'It isn't my favourite place,' she whispered, and glanced at the neighbouring table where some braggart was boring his wife or lady friend with repeated outrage about the Norwegians – Amundsen's temerity at stealing a march on Captain Scott's *Terra Nova* expedition. 'Too many people,' said Wyn. 'And none too clean.' She drew a fingertip along the table's edge, showed the result for emphasis, though Cari could see no sign of grease or dirt.

'Well, it will have to do,' said Cari, as the pallid waitress – Nesta, she thought, had said the girl's name was Annie – took her order for tea and a cheese sandwich. 'And we've not got long, Wyn. Old Kaplan's watching the clock again. So, what is it? Something wrong?'

'How can you, Cari? Work for a Jew, I mean. And wrong? Why should you think something's wrong?'

'You wanted to meet up.'

Cari chose to ignore her comment about Kaplan entirely, and also resisted the temptation to say they only met when Winifred needed something. They were hardly close, yet Cari felt a special responsibility for her sister. Even more than the others. Yes, Cari cares. The guilt again, from those days when the pestilence had gripped both Wyn and Pryce. Cari's childish musings about how life might be better without them. Then Pryce's death as though in answer. Cari's rapid back-pedalling. Fevered prayers to the Lord Jesus that Wyn, at least, should be spared. The offer of a deal. He should take Cari instead. Or, as an alternative, pledges about her future godliness. She had no doubt from whence the guilt arose. She was a girl, after all. A female. And did the whole world not talk about feminine wiles? Her female guilt.

She understood Wyn's obsessions, therefore, but they annoyed her, and especially the obsession with chapel. They'd all been raised the right way and Cari was – the result of her pledges – as true a believer as everybody else in the family. But, for her, Holy Scripture gave them all a moral framework, their traveller's guide through life's more troublesome pathways while, for Wyn, it had become a justification for so many stumbling prejudices and the worst sort of crutch. Without it she was incapable of walking independently. Scripture, Cari always thought, should teach them to resist tyranny, not impose its own tyranny upon them.

'It's nothing, really. Just – well, you know so much, Cari.'

'Do I?' In truth, Cari believed she did not know herself at all. 'And it's you that's the married woman now, Wyn. Look how you've grown up.'

'There's the trouble, see.' She almost raised her head, but only enough so she could look Cari in the eye. 'Thought I knew how girls were supposed to behave. Read all the books, I did. How to make yourself attractive to men. Where you fall down, Cari. You know so much, but…'

But? Cari wondered. She might be unfashionably tall, yet she wasn't entirely lacking in the graces, was she? And there was interest in her, she was certain. Ernst Jurks. Perhaps Amos Gartee also. That trembling excitement again.

'Make myself attractive – for what, exactly?'

'So men will want to marry you, silly. Have their children.'

'Not high on my list right now, Wyn. But you? Why so quick to marry Rhys Fingers? Scared of being left on the shelf?'

If she was honest, they'd all secretly suspected they may have been entirely wrong about Miss Prim-and-Proper. An obvious reason why she would be in such a hurry to wed him. Almost disappointed when, all this time later, there was still no babe.

'He's not just anybody, Cari. My husband's a man of substance.'

'Well, it's not for me. Not yet. Having some man's children. Then having to do whatever might please him.' She shivered at the thought. But the words had spilled forth just too loudly, causing the fellow at the next table to choke on his sandwich as Cari's own arrived and the tray was set down before her.

Wyn lapsed easily into the *Cymraeg*.

'*Paid â bod mor ffiaidd*,' she hissed. Don't be so disgusting. 'And anyway, it's not like you think. Always choices. Far easier to just close your eyes to all that side. Let him take his pleasures elsewhere. Natural, it is – in a man, I mean.'

Cari stared at her for a long time, the cheese sandwich poised halfway to her open mouth.

'Is that…?' she whispered. 'Does he…?' There was no reply, and Cari was almost speechless, as well. 'You must be – well, angry.'

'Why would it make me angry, Cari? My husband's a good man. The best. He's just the way Our Lord Jesus made him, isn't he? Shaped from the same clay as Adam. A woman's only duty is obedience. *For the husband is the head of the wife, even as Christ is the head of the church.* All there is to it.'

The same nonsense her tada had quoted yesterday, though Winifred's situation seemed to take Holy Scripture to a whole different level. Cari was used to it, of course. A man's role in life was defined as closely as a woman's. They were the roles society set for everybody. Society. And chapel. Yet this confession, the trembling of her hand – Cari could hardly believe what she was hearing. So, she lifted the napkin to her lips, murmured into its folds, even though they were still speaking in Welsh.

'Do you mean he has another woman, Wyn? Or does he do it with —?'

'There are things. Things he likes. Things that make me ashamed. Of myself, mind. Only ashamed of myself. Not him. Never him. It's just the way Our Lord Jesus made him, see.'

'Winifred, you bring Rhys to dinner every Sunday. How do you expect me to sit across the table from him and not – why, in the name of heaven, did you want to tell me all this? Do you want my help in some way? Poor girl, I don't know what else to say.'

'I certainly don't want your pity, Ceridwen,' she snapped. 'Why should I? I just wanted you to tell me it's the right thing. For him to take those things elsewhere. I've been looking. All through the scriptures. But it's confusing. The main thing is believing in the Lord Jesus, of course. Like in Matthew. *The tax collectors and the prostitutes are entering the Kingdom of God ahead of you.* That's because John the Baptist came to them, showed them the way of righteousness, and they believed him. Forgiveness, Cari. For all those who believe. And my Rhys, he's the godliest man I know, see. But I thought…'

'You thought you'd get a second opinion from your big sister.' Then Cari experienced an epiphany. 'No, wait – maybe you're worried I'd hear it from somebody else?'

'Men gossip so much,' said Wyn. 'You know what it's like, Cari. On the docks there's always tittle-tattle going round.' She used the phrase *clebran-tattle*, of course, and Cari saw the man at the next table slam down his teacup. He'd been muttering about "the bloody Welsh" since Wyn slipped into the *Cymraeg*, and they'd obviously now replaced the Norwegians on his list of hated nations. He clicked his fingers for Annie to fetch his bill and "make it snappy." But Winifred didn't seem to have noticed. She was in full flow. 'I was just worried,' she said. 'If Taffy heard anything…'

'He'd come to me, you mean? Champion. That's all I need. But perhaps you're right.'

Taffy. Awkward. She needed to speak with Taffy about Amos, of course. It wouldn't do any good, but she'd promised, after all. But somehow this all conspired – Taffy and Amos Gartee, Wyn and Nesta, Cousin Thomas – to create a sense of doom within her. Premonition. Some bombshell waiting for them all. Or perhaps a whole shower of bombshells.

3.20pm

The beating Amos had taken left him barely able to walk, trousers ripped to shreds. He'd lost count of the hours spent on his agonising return to the hostel. And if he had not found a friend, the Wolof who called himself Charles Tuohey, he doubted he would have survived.

'Who these men?' Cookie winced as he opened the torn and tattered shirt, Amos himself writhing in the hammock. Sheer agony. He managed to get his head over the canvas edge, retched once more, though there was nothing left in his stomach but bile.

'Hair like straw,' he replied. It was all he could remember. There had been words. Words filled with hatred. But he'd not understood even one of them. 'Big past others.'

'Norway men?'

Amos had no idea. He'd sailed with Norway men before. But how could you tell? Faces all the same. Them, and the Dootshies. And what was the difference between Dootshies and Doitshies anyway? He'd never been sure.

He looked around at the anxious faces of his brothers gathered in his space at the end of the dormitory, the curtain held aside.

'Everything a'right,' he said, and tried to force a smile, though his face ached. He'd been kicked, was certain it had loosened some of his teeth.

'Union men do this?' said Janjay the Guere.

'You a foo', George,' Amos whispered. 'Union men good friends.'

At least, he thought, they are the enemies of our enemy. 'No, this was bossman's doin'. To be sure.'

In truth? His own doing. He knew it was. He'd been angry with Missee Coconut Palm. Angry and lost. Well – angry, lost *and* afraid. Tried to find his way back to more familiar territory. He'd wound his way through an alleyway, stumbled across another palace, this one with a courtyard and iron railings. Another omen. Liberty Buildings, he read. Yes, liberty.

After all, were his people not from the lands known to the world as Liberia? Was Liberia not created as a home for freed slaves? Or Freetown in neighbouring Sierra Leone, where his Kru people also plied so much of their trade – did the name not ring out as the very symbol of liberty? Wasn't Liberia unique in keeping its independence – in all Africa the only lands to have avoided the grasping hands of the Doitshies, the French and the English?

And yes, yes, yes, Amos Gartee knew how his own Kru and Grebo people – all the others who had been here long before those freed slaves had arrived from America – had been forced to fight for their own rights as citizens of this Liberia. Had some of those freed slaves not sometimes made slaves of the Grebo, the Mande and others? Though, never the Kru, of course. The Kru were slaves to no man. And had Amos's own father not been part of the fight for their rights, a fight they had only won just before Amos himself reached manhood? Certainly, he had, and the flame of liberty still burned brightly within this son of Nana Kru.

'Ribs here,' said Cookie, and poked them for emphasis, caused Amos to scream. 'Some broke.'

He screamed even more as his so-called brothers helped to sit him upright, while Cookie brought bandages, wrapped them so tightly around his chest that Amos could hardly breathe. And before this cruelty was done, here came more trouble. The Mende boys with Jonah Samba, pushing their way into the room, through the half-circle of his own fellows.

'So,' Jonah shouted, 'this the big word for which we wait?'

Amos allowed his eyes to roll back in his head, summoned through his hurt a mystical murmur, like a man possessed.

"*Neither by blood of goat or calf,*" he began to intone, repeating the scripture as best he was able, *"but by his own blood, he enter a'right some holy place and have obtain there redemption for we all."*

'Praise the Lord,' shouted George Janjay in his own Guere tongue.

'So now,' said Jonah Samba, 'you think you're the Lord Jesus?'

But the assembled seamen largely ignored the Mende.

'Where this place you been, brother?' said Samuel Nimende.

Where, indeed? Amos wondered. Streets without end, past mighty warehouses, or dwellings packed so tightly together they must surely allow neither light nor air to enter. A factory where the smell of liquor was so strong it almost made him drunk on the fumes alone. Until he found himself in a street so long and straight, he could see no end. Yet it had climbed uphill, and he'd been certain that, near its upper reaches, he would find St. James' Mount again and the great House of God.

'This place I been called Liberty,' Amos whispered. 'An' I see a vision there. Union men. All them streets full o' union men. Thick like the monkey-fruit trees of Gamu and Ghanpa.'

A vision, he thought. None of us can resist a vision.

'Then how this happen?' said Jonah Samba, waving his hand dismissively towards the hammock. 'They beat you in this vision too?'

It earned the Mende snarls of disapproval, even from his own followers. Wrong to mock a man's visions. And Amos managed to shake his head.

'No,' he said. 'Later. But the Lord's light still in my eye. Like a foo' I not see them. Men with straw hair. Walk into them. An' then...'

It was almost true. He'd been weary, slogging his way up that endless slope. All manner of stores. More depositories. Alehouses everywhere. And hostels. Seamen's hostels, one with words he couldn't read. He'd still been trying to fathom the language, hadn't noticed the straw-haired men playing some game on the steps, stumbled over their feet. Or perhaps they'd tripped him deliberately. It made no difference. They'd beaten and kicked him anyway. Kicked him into the roadway as though he had no more substance than the *akua'ba* doll his married sister had carried on her back to help her fertility. Kicked him until he was senseless.

They may have kicked him until he was dead. But then a saviour had appeared. A big fellow. An African face in this ocean of white faces. Charles, he'd said. What sort of name was Charles? He had half-carried Amos into yet another world. Streets where the faces carried all the colours of the Lord's rainbow. And through those streets, home to the hostel.

5.50pm

'What was so secret, then?' Dumpling Nesta demanded as she shared out the chips and a pie from Gianelli's. That was her job also, Tom Priddy had gathered. A short detour on the way home from her work. Mondays and Fridays, to the corner of Islington Place. Yes, an Italian chippy. Italian Catholics, no doubt. Just one of those things Huw Maddox, it seemed, was able to ignore if it suited him.

'Secret?' said Tom. 'I like secrets. How many have *you* got, Beanpole?'

He wiped his hands on his trousers, bothered he'd not had a chance to wash, his fingers still stinking of formaldehyde.

'What's this?' said old Huw, his mouth stuffed with chips and a smear of grease on his chin. 'We don't have secrets. Not in this house.'

'Just Cari meeting Wyn at my place,' said Nesta. 'But not a word to me, mind. I had to find out from cock-eyed Annie. My own sisters. And there they were, whispering in the corner.'

'Wyn in the family way, after all?' Taffy growled, a cigarette dangling from the corner of his damaged mouth.

He'd already complained about only being given a half-day's work. But the rest of it must have been spent in Mad John's. Tom could smell the ale on Taffy's breath from his own side of the table, and his damaged lip was having even more trouble than usual spitting out his words.

'Women's problems,' said Cari, which caused Tom to laugh, a high-pitched braying sound he knew would annoy them all.

'*Na fo*,' he said. That's right. 'World's full of women's problems, it is. Bet you had a fine time last night. No end of fun, discussing them all.'

He gazed at the chip between his fingers, wondered what the Beanpole's fancy friends were eating tonight. Not chips, he reckoned. Nothing wrong with chips, mind. But yes, a world apart from Hunter Street, he was sure.

'Not that sort of problem,' Cari sneered. 'You want me to go into detail, Cousin?'

Rather stopped him in his tracks. Disgusting, like.

'Think we've got mice again.' Old Huw sniffed the air. 'Anybody else smell it?'

'Been like that for days,' Taffy told him. Tom might not have been there long, but it was plain the place was usually riddled with them.

'Well, it looked like more than a natter about the old curse,' said Dumpling Nesta, as stomach-churning as her sister.

'*Duw*, that's enough,' their tada snarled.

'And you could at least have said hello,' Nesta grumbled to her sister.

She'd been sharp with just about everybody since she got home, though Tom couldn't tell whether this was normal or not. Bad day at work, she said. Bad enough without getting ignored by her sisters on top of everything. So, they were all forced to sit through Cari's laborious explanation about how she'd been in a rush, slapped it on thick, about her boss keeping his eye on her. *Iesu*, did the girl never know when to close her mouth?

'Was it here before the German came to visit?' Tom peered at a newspaper headline among the chip wrappings, hoping to shut her up. 'The smell, I mean. Only, I thought – well, it was interesting what he said. About German women not having the vote either. They wouldn't, would they? More manly than us, the Germans. I'd not be surprised if this was a German plot, see. Paying your lot to do all this, Beanpole. You and these Pankhurst people. Votes for women. Weaken our men. Smelled a rat, I did.'

Clever, see? Rat? Smell of mice, like? But even old Huw looked askance. Did none of them get it? They certainly all ignored his witticism.

'He's not a bad bloke,' Taffy stammered. 'For a Fritzie.'

Pathetic, Tom thought.

'And I've never heard such nonsense,' said Cari. 'Are you another one, Cousin – German spies around every corner?'

'Good union man, at least. Ernst Jurks,' said her brother. 'Knows what it's all about, he does. Workers of the world…'

'Just not those poor Krooboys at the Harrington,' Dumpling Nesta replied.

'Oh, not again,' Taffy told her. 'Change the music, will you, Nessie? It's this bloody Cousin Thomas I'm talking about. Mad as hops, he is.'

Me? Tom Priddy laughed inwardly. One more insult to be added to the tally.

'And you, Cousin,' said Tom, 'so drunk you couldn't see a hole in the ladder.'

'That's right now, is it?' Taffy snarled, began to get up from the table.

'Personally,' said Cari, 'I was still thinking about the Pankhursts. How fine it must be. At the centre of things. The chance to make things happen. And if Taffy was drunk,' she went on, 'he'd have given you a bunch of fives by now, Thomas. But what it is, Taffy – well, you should sit down, mind.'

'Been drinking the devil's brew again?' said their father. 'I'll not have it, Dafydd. Not in your mother's house. Where's your respect, boy?'

'If you spent a bit less time at Mad John's,' said Nesta, wrapping up the last of her chip scraps and thumping the balled paper for emphasis, 'and a bit more with your mates at the union office, perhaps you'd be able to muster some help for the Krooboys.'

'Who – Sexton, you mean?' Taffy sat again. 'You'll wait a long time for him to get off his lazy backside.'

Sexton, Tom knew, was the leader of the dockers' union in Liverpool. Couldn't miss him, really. Not a day went by without his stupid face in the local newspapers.

'I thought you'd been working,' Huw Maddox said to him. 'But you've been wasting your time in the boozer.'

'Not wasting my time, Pa. I was with some of the Committee men.'

'And what did they say about the Krooboys?' Cari asked.

'Oh, forget about those black buggers, Cari, won't you?' Taffy shouted. 'We've got bigger things to think about. They had their chance. Came to the meeting at Paddy's Market, didn't they? All drippin' wet, like. Couldn't understand a word they said.'

Interesting, Tom decided. Things would be easier than he'd imagined. This bunch already falling apart, without any help from their Cousin Thomas.

'More important,' said Dumpling Nesta, 'than a whole bunch of seamen who've now been on strike for weeks and not a scrap of support?'

'If Havelock Wilson has his way,' Taffy replied, 'we'll soon have every seaman in Britain on strike. And us dockers along with them. He'll show the bosses then, Nesta. But only when we're ready.'

And Wilson? Tom had followed the news. President of the National Sailors' and Firemen's Union he'd helped to create.

'So meanwhile,' Cari snapped, 'they just starve.'

'Yes,' said Nessie. 'While Taffy drinks our money away or goes necking with his Catholic girlfriend.'

There was a silence so profound that Tom could feel and hear his own pulse quicken, his heart tremble and race – a silence running straight into his sense of premonition, this strange thing, which we sometimes experience, of having lived through a moment of time before. There was a French name for it, he recalled. But before he could remember it, old Huw had broken the spell.

'Catholic,' he said. Just that.

'Taffy – ' the Beanpole began.

Tom guessed Cari was trying to fathom how the clock might be reversed. Not for long, mind. A few seconds, he supposed. It should have been possible, shouldn't it? Yet he saw no more than an instant of doubt, of conciliation, on Taffy's face. The merest chance Taffy would deny it, give Nesta a chance to take it back, turn it into some stupid joke.

But I hope not, thought Tom. This is just too precious.

He wasn't disappointed. An instant. Before Taffy's features hardened. Stubborn lad.

'That's right, Pa,' he murmured. 'Catholic. And what's wrong with it?'

'You're courting a papist?' Tom pretended incredulity.

'Worth ten of you, she is,' Taffy sneered at him. 'And why's this your business anyway. Turn up yesterday. Think you own the place. This is our house, see?'

'Not anymore,' shouted his father. Another silence – from which, Tom supposed, they each tried to determine what he meant. Then he repeated himself. 'Not anymore. I've warned all of you. Often enough, mind. We'll have nothing to do with Catholics. So, you can pack your bags, Dafydd. Pack them now,' he yelled, slammed the table. 'Either that or finish with her.'

'Tada,' said the Beanpole, 'you don't mean it.'

'Yes, he does.' Taffy's chair fell backwards as he jumped to his feet. 'Bloody old bugger.'

'Taffy, I'm sorry.' Dumpling Nesta had begun to sob. 'I didn't mean – '

'No, you never do, Nessie,' said her brother. 'Well, good riddance, that's what I say. And you!' He turned to Tom. 'No need for you to spend another night on the palliasse. Should please you. But think on this, Pa – he's not worth a blow on the rag man's trumpet, this one. You're welcome to him. And I'll not finish with her, not ever.'

No more nights on the palliasse? Tom considered this unexpected bonus. Priceless. Worth a dozen indignities. And old Huw's face was set like stone as Taffy stormed out of the room and up the second staircase to the top floor.

'Stop him, Tada,' said Cari. 'Can't let him go like this. The family, Tada.'

Tom grinned at her. He could feel the eyes almost popping from his own head. Her family was finished.

'You're right, Beanpole,' he said. 'Tragedy, that's what this is. When families fall apart. Why don't you go and talk some sense into him. He'll listen to you, I reckon.'

She ignored him. Or tried to do so.

'Tada –'

But her father simply struck out with his hand, swiped the remains of his chips from the table, all over the old, red-patterned rug, reached for his Woodbines and matches. And then Nesta had also pushed herself from the table, eyes brimming with tears as she ran for the scullery. He watched the Beanpole, panic on her face, looking first to the stairs, then to the kitchen.

She doesn't know which way to turn first, he thought. Her dear Nesta, who seemed so lost just then. Or her brother, about to burn his bridges. He imagined her turmoil. Nesta first, she'd be thinking. She'd talk to Nesta first, then Dafydd. That would be her choice, he was sure. And it pleased him greatly when Cari followed her sister into the kitchen.

Some instinct caused him to follow the girls. But cautiously. He'd rolled up the chip wrappings, made a theatrical show of spilling them again at the kitchen doorway, dropped to his hands and knees to clean the mess. From there he could surreptitiously watch them both. He saw Nesta had something in her hand. A slender roll of banknotes. Ten bob notes, so far as he could tell. And a small purse.

'Cari,' he heard Dumpling Nesta whisper, 'what a mess. I didn't mean it, honest. Talk to Taffy. And better take this.' She thrust the money into Cari's hands. The purse also. 'It's what I've been putting aside. For Amos Gartee and the boys.'

The Beanpole turned to make sure they weren't observed, and Tom just had time to pull his head back, out of sight.

'Where did you get all this, Nessie?' Cari murmured. 'There must be – what? Nine or ten quid?'

Tom peered around the doorway, saw her hefting the purse in her hand, holding up the ten bob notes.

'Nine pounds, sixteen and sixpence,' hissed Nesta.

'But how…?'

'It doesn't matter, Cari. Just look after it for me. I'll explain later. After I've been to the privy.'

Tom was back on his feet, making great play of having come straight from the table. Nesta pushed past him, headed for the landing as well, and he heard her clattering downstairs. From the corner of his eye, he saw Cari stuffing the banknotes into the purse, the purse into her skirt pocket.

He went quickly back to the table, where Huw still sat like a statue.

'*Duw*, that boy of yours,' Tom dripped a few more drops of poison into the old man's ear.

'Making more trouble?' Cari asked him. 'Think we've not got enough?'

'This is no trouble, Beanpole,' Tom smirked. She looked confused, trying to calculate whether she should have asked what he meant, exactly. But she didn't.

'Tada, please,' she begged, instead. But there was no response, so she also made for the landing, maybe intending to follow Taffy, make some futile attempt to patch things up. Yet she'd only put her foot on the stairs when there was a hammering below, at the front door. She turned, waited to see if anybody else could be bothered to answer.

'As usual,' she shouted, 'left to me again.' More hammering. Impatient. And the Beanpole bellowed down the stairwell like a fish-wife. 'I'll be there now, in a minute.'

6.45pm

Duw Annwyl, thought Cari, as she opened to them. More police. More premonition of doom. The hint of a storm coming in from the Mersey Bar. Stink of rotten fish.

'Nesta Maddox?' said the sergeant. He seemed reasonably sober, a rare thing for their local bobbies.

'Her sister, Ceridwen,' Cari told him.

'Is Nesta Maddox at home, Miss?'

Cari probably took too long to answer, but she needed to think a moment, sensed it was important to buy some time.

'No,' she lied, at last. 'Not back from work yet. Can we help you?'

'I'd like to come in, if you don't mind.'

'No problem, Sergeant. Just up the stairs, there.' She let him pass, him and a constable who looked twice his age. Cari glanced along at the privy, then shouted up the stairs. Top of her voice. 'Tada! It's the police. Looking for our Nesta, they are.'

The sergeant glanced back down at her.

'I hope you're telling the truth, Miss. About your sister not being here.'

She smiled sweetly at him but said nothing.

Back in the kitchen he introduced himself and his companion. Sergeant Ladysmith. Constable Cooper. 'C' Division. That would be the Bridewell on Argyle Street, then. Not their local bobbies from Cheapside at all. Across town, these boys. Was this why they were sober, though? Cari didn't suppose so.

'And what is it you'd be wanting with young Nesta, Sergeant?' said her tada. All sweetness and light again on the outside, but inwardly still seething, she could see. The twitch in the muscle at his jaw.

86

Taffy had also appeared in the doorway behind the policemen, a stuffed kit bag on the floor beside him. Cari hated her brother's prejudices as much as her tada's. But she knew that if you could just get Taffy on your side...

She squeezed her way through, saw the chair still lying on the floor, hurried over to stand it upright once more.

'Knocked it over,' she muttered. 'All that banging...'

'I'm afraid we have some questions to ask her, Mister Maddox,' said the sergeant, though he was staring at the chips scattered across the rug. 'I've got it right, I take it? You're Mister Maddox?'

'Oh yes,' said Cousin Thomas in his tiresome monotone. 'He's Huw Maddox. Definitely.'

'You're his son, Sir?'

'Well – nephew, really, I suppose. Yes, nephew, like.'

He had that smirk on his pasty face.

'I'm his son,' said Taffy. 'Though you'd not know it.'

'I see I've interrupted something,' said Sergeant Ladysmith, then turned to Cari. 'And you, Miss. Sister, you say?'

'You want proof, Sergeant?'

'Won't be necessary, Miss. If you can just tell me where she is?'

'Like I said, not back from work. That's right, Tada, isn't it?'

The moment of truth. But her father simply stared up at the sergeant, his mouth open to speak but no words coming forth. Cari wondered whether he was thinking about Dickens, another favourite saying. *"Ask no questions and you'll be told no lies."*

'It's right,' said Taffy, from the doorway. 'Not back from work. Didn't you see her there a while ago, Thomas?'

Cari was astonished. Was he an idiot? Trying to enlist Tom Priddy to support Nesta.

'*Duw*,' said Thomas. 'Yes. Saw her myself. An hour past, I suppose. Said she'd be working late.'

To be fair, this shocked Cari even more. Perhaps he was really family after all. Yet he lied so smoothly.

'I see,' said the sergeant. 'Well, that's a little strange, if you don't mind me saying. Because we've just come from her place of work. The Oriental Emporium. The café. They told us she'd finished at five o'clock. So – what? Two hours?'

'The Oriental?' said Cari. 'What were you doing there, Sergeant? Has there been an accident of some sort?'

'Accident? No, Miss. The small matter of theft. Mister Clayton's had his suspicions for a while, it seems. Been making a point of counting his takings as they come in. Then, this afternoon, there was a discrepancy. And only your sister with access to the tin. We need to ask her a few questions, as you might say. Now, shall we start again?'

Her tada had buried his face in his hands. Taffy snorted with disbelief. And Cousin Thomas was shaking his head, tutting loudly, muttering something from scripture about letting him that stole steal no more but rather let her labour.

'I'm not sure I've anything to add,' said Cari. 'But would you mind if I go to the privy first?'

'Downstairs, Miss?' Yes, she told him. 'Then you'll not mind if Constable Cooper escorts you there?' he insisted.

She protested, naturally, but there was nothing she could do about it. So, off they went, Cari and Constable Cooper. Downstairs. The gloomy passageway. Then past the workbench, through the printshop and the Dawson Place gate, out into the yard.

'I think that's far enough, Constable,' she said. 'You can see the privy from here.' She pointed, wondering what on earth she'd do once inside. Though she should have realised. For, as she tentatively tried the latch, found it unlocked, and opened the door on the dark, brick-built toilet, Cari found herself quite alone.

Nessie, of course, had gone.

Chapter Three

Friday 19th May 1911

6.05am

Eviction, this was the word they'd used. The Company's bossmen and the police who'd been there to help them. Another of Elder Dempster's vessels arrived in port, space needed for her crew. The Company's patience exhausted, and its strategy of leaving them to come to their senses, like errant children, plainly in tatters. But that had been weeks earlier. Since then, they'd tried three times to speak with the men now living in the hostel. Men from Banjul. Mandinka men. Muslim men. Slave men. Men now protected by the bossmen's guards.

'And this place?' Nesta said to him. 'How is it?'

Amos held his still troublesome ribs, turned to look up at the grey, soot-soaked exterior. Parliament Street. He'd tried to seek the omen in the name but, so far, he'd not succeeded. Except, somehow, the eviction had brought them more together, more determined. Apart from Jonah Samba, of course. Though even the Mende and his boys were still there. Housed further up the road, but still there, where his rescuer, Charles, had helped find them lodging.

'Friend Society, them send us,' he replied. 'But friends, so far, we not found. Except one.'

Charles. Charles Tuohey, who said he had stowed away as a boy from Serrekunda. Then, here in Liverpool, homeless, a white family had found him. A family of Irish people. Irish, a white people, but also from across the seas. But this Charles had kept his own name, Abdul Niasse. And kept his faith also. A follower of Islam. The Muslim Wolof with an Irish name. It amused Amos Gartee greatly.

'And me, Amos,' said Nesta. 'Am I not a friend also?'

He examined her face. How fine she was. But a friend? It was a pleasant idea, but he had been thinking more along the lines of a wife. Perhaps both things might be possible. He'd never really considered such a thing, never really got past the thorny problem of the bride wealth. Perhaps best to avoid the subject in its entirety.

'You, Miss Nesta? Not safe, come here. Them po-leese still lookin' for you?'

'Yes, still looking. Safe to come when it's early, though. Like this, Amos.'

Early, indeed. The sun only just come up. And, as she'd done many times since the eviction, she'd arrived to join Amos and his brothers on the front steps of their new lodging. Always bringing food, or money. Always in company.

She'd explained to him, carefully, what had happened. Accused of stealing money, though innocent, she'd said. And why should he not believe her?

In the early days, she'd had that big fellow with her. German, she'd said. A Doitshie. She'd been staying with a whole family of Doitshies. He couldn't remember how many, but a lot of Doitshies in a very small place. A court, Nesta had called it, though it sounded far from the grandeur its name implied. Crowded. But danger there because, if he had the story correct, the Doitshies didn't trust their neighbours. Hatred stoked up against them, a few years back, when everybody thought these English would go to war with them. Over Morocco, of all places.

'An' your new house?' he enquired.

'Good. With the Sanguinettis. But this is Luigi Moretta.' She pointed to the lamp post against which a slight youth was leaning, smoking a cigarette, a large flat cap pulled down onto his ears. The youth came forward to offer Amos a cigarette, and he accepted the gift with a generous click of his fingers.

'Lots of people say bad things about the Morettas,' Miss Nesta went on in a whisper. 'Probably all nonsense. Though there's certainly no love lost between them and the police. And – well, there's a part of the city we call Little Italy. Easy to vanish there. The Morettas know it like the back of their hand.'

Amos was struggling to understand all this, but he'd grown too fond of Missee Nesta's voice to stop her in full flow. And he hoped the slight youth might not also be contemplating the question of bride wealth.

'Anyway,' she went on, 'we had no money to give them, but what they had, they shared with me, kept me fed and warm. Like the Muscatellis, over in Bennett Street. I knew most of them already and they all seemed to take a shine to me. But now, yes, with the Morettas.'

Take a shine. Nice phrase. He'd have to remember.

Somebody tapped him on the shoulder. Barkuh Togba.

'Ask her,' said Barkuh in his own tongue, 'about the letters.'

The sisters had arranged collections of money for them. From the women who wanted to vote. Amos thought he understood the issue better now. But Missee Coconut Palm had been writing, as well. To the leader of the seamen's union. This Havelock Wilson.

'Why for?' said Amos. 'The Wilson man, he never write back.'

'Wait,' Miss Nesta put a hand on his arm, 'is he asking about the letters? If so, there's a glimmer of hope. Cardiff, see? Cari found out there's this other organiser for the sailors down there. He's called Tupper. *Captain* Tupper. Our brother knew all about him, like. Had no time for him, really. Seems this Captain Tupper's been trying to get other African sailors into the union. Of course, Taffy'd have no time for that. But Captain Tupper thinks the same as you, Amos. Everybody organised, they can't use you for cheap labour anymore. Right, it is. So, she's written to him, our Cari has – though nothing back just yet.'

Amos explained as much of this as he'd been able to follow – explained it to Barkuh Togba and the others.

'Writing to another white man?' laughed the Guere, George Janjay. 'Why would she bother?'

'We must not judge them all the same, George,' Amos scolded him. 'Remember the one who saved your life?'

They'd been moored at Dakar, picking up more freight, and George had fallen overboard during the night. A boat was eventually launched but, meanwhile, the ship's Second Engineer, Mister Willie, had jumped into the sea and kept the Guere afloat until the boat reached him. Pitch black. Sharks. But Mister Willie hadn't thought twice. Yes, a brave man.

'Got a medal for it, didn't he?' George Sanjay growled.

Oh, those Guere, thought Amos. No gratitude. Short-tempered hardly did it justice.

'Well,' he said, 'I know this much. Without them white man's union, we can't never win. How long we been fightin' already?'

'Yet there is a glimmer,' Miss Nesta smiled at him. 'Just a glimmer.'

7.20am

Tom Priddy held up his copy of the *Post and Mercury*. No work for Waugh's but he was needed for this evening's performance at the Rotunda. He'd hoped for a restful morning, but Beanpole Cari was especially strident today.

'I don't care, Tada,' she shouted, 'we have to bring her home.'

She pinched her cheeks to put some colour in them, ready for work. At least she was no painted harlot, he'd decided. They said there were "cosmetics" shops all over London now where you could quite easily buy powders and rouge, and nobody thought any the worse for using them. But at least here in Liverpool the Woolworths toiletries counter had caused almost as much scandal as their sale of sixpenny hunting knives.

The Lord Jesus who lived within Tom's heart spoke to him.

'There shall be no whore of the daughters of Israel.'

Plain enough, like, Tom decided.

'It's been well over a month already,' said the Beanpole.

Hard to believe. All those weeks without. Peaceful, like. But without any money coming in from Nesta or Taffy, they'd been living mainly on boiled cabbage and slops. He'd been paying his way, after a fashion. Not entirely honest about the income from his two jobs. The Beanpole paid a pittance, of course. And old Huw's business seemingly with more outgoings than profit. It had felt like a lifetime. Not what he'd expected.

Dumpling Nesta had escaped through the print shop, of course, and had the fortune to run straight into Ernst Jurks and his German uncle, making their way through Cartwright Place. All a terrible mistake, she'd told them. A great story. Another girl, cock-eyed Annie, she'd claimed, who'd had her fingers in the cash box. But how long would she have to spend in the Bridewell before anybody believed her? If ever. What if she was sent down? So, the Germans had taken her in. Hidden her, even when the local beat bobbies went door to door looking for her. Believe anything, he'd thought, those Germans.

'They're still watching the house,' said old Huw. 'That sergeant. Ladysmith. I saw him yesterday in the street. Dangerous, it is.'

He was only too quick to believe the Dumpling, naturally. One of Huw Maddox's girls, a thief? *"Rules are rules,"* he would sometimes say. *"A turnip is a turnip."* The detail about poor Magwitch stealing the turnip to stop himself from starving to death would have been quite lost on him.

Tom had to hand it to her, for she'd almost convinced him, as well. Insisted to their faces she'd been saving hard, scraping together every penny for the Krooboys. Such innocence on her face, nobody could bring themselves to call her a liar. That was families, he supposed.

'The bobbies haven't actually barged in for a while though,' said Cari. 'Not for a fortnight or more. If we do it when it's dark…'

They had forced their way into the house frequently enough at the start, usually far from sober and turned the place upside down.

'You want my opinion?' said Tom from behind the paper. 'I think she's right, Uncle Huw. Poor girl must be sick of it by now. Shoved from pillar to post every few days.'

He wasn't convinced about Nessie's innocence. Far from it. But he was, he supposed, trapped in it like the rest of them. An accomplice, at best. For he'd never really fathomed why he'd chosen the cock-and-bull story about seeing Nesta at the café. Except – well, he was always so much more comfortable with a lie on his lips.

'Who's she with now?' old Huw asked. 'More of the pope's lot?'

'I think all our Italian friends are Catholics, Tada,' the Beanpole told him, finally slipping into her coat. 'At least they've looked after her. So, you see? Not so bad.'

'I don't want to hear it, Ceridwen. Not one more word. That fool's no son of mine. Not anymore. Looking after Nessie's one thing. But courting a Catholic? *Duw, Duw*. Sinful's what it is. Unforgiveable. Now, leave well alone, girl.'

It must have broken her heart afresh every day. Both Nesta and Taffy gone from the house. Yet she kept trying. With her tada. Though this was the least of her problems. Because even if her tada could be persuaded to relent, Taffy was too stubborn for reconciliation. But Tom knew she'd see him later, anyhow. Try to talk with him again. Stubborn's what she was.

'And I've been looking at the shop,' said Tom. 'The loft. The one we use for the paper store. I can clear most of it. Make it snug, like. The old palliasse. Some other things. Home from home, like.'

Old Huw looked far from certain, but Tom meant it. His mood had been exceptionally good lately. Ever since his visit to Walton Gaol with everybody else, the morning they hanged Seymour the wife-murderer. Exhilarating, that's what it was.

They owed him, as well. Satisfying. He wasted no opportunity to remind them how, bad as things might be, he'd kept the business afloat, brought in some new orders from the Rotunda Theatre when the Everton contract dried up, as it did every year at the end of the season. But how they'd cope with Nesta to feed again, he had no idea.

'In that case,' said Cari, 'I'll sneak around now, make sure she gets things ready for tonight.'

Then she was off, down the stairs before Huw Maddox could argue with her. But she didn't get far.

'Ceridwen!' he bellowed.

'Yes, Tada?' Tom heard her groan.

'Friday, it is, *cariad*. You think we might run to some chips, now?'

The Beanpole promised she'd try – though she must have had no idea where the money would come from – and slammed the front door behind her.

7.45am

Cari hadn't much time, but at least Nesta shouldn't be far away. That was, if she was back from her sojourns at first light with the Krooboys. A bit further up the hill, with the Sanguinettis, opposite the Friends Meeting House.

Just as well, for there was a dusty drizzle falling and she had no rain napper. But it varnished the cobbles and paving slabs prettily enough, turned the dray horses silky-brown, deadened the hammer blows of plodding hooves and the more occasional throb of a lorry engine, or the hiss and pop of a steam wagon. It diluted the inebriating wickedness of the brewing processes across the street. And it distracted her, so that, as she crossed Dawson Place, she almost leapt from her skin when a hand grasped her left arm.

'You'd be telling me you're off to work, Miss,' said Sergeant Ladysmith, snug in his rain cape, 'except Seel Street's the other way, of course.'

'The same direction as the Argyle Street Bridewell, Sergeant.' Cari tried to be jaunty, though knowing her voice must betray her apprehension. 'It seems we may both be a little lost.'

'Speaking personally, Miss Maddox, I always know exactly where I am.'

'An essential quality in a policeman, I'm sure. That and an accurate knowledge of the time. But can I help you with something in particular?'

'Very amusing. Just a warning, though, I suppose. Hindering our investigations is one thing. Harbouring a wanted criminal – well, crosses a line, if you get my drift.'

Cari thanked him for the advice, made some fragile protest about her sister not being a criminal. The anticipated riposte about why he had no bigger fish to fry. Better, she told him, if he'd devote his time to tracking down the actual thief. This seemed to make him smile, but then she felt obliged to walk all the way up to Christian Street without once looking back.

At the corner, she waited and watched until she was satisfied he was gone before cautiously creeping down the hill again, stopping often, checking for the slightest sign of him hiding somewhere. There were plenty of places where he might have done so, but it troubled Cari more that he'd been there at all. Was it truly safe to bring Nessie home? And where did this leave her?

It wasn't as though she'd not herself broken the law previously – well, it was windows she'd broken. In the name of justice, of course. Justice for women. Her Christian duty, she'd told herself. But this? Sergeant Ladysmith was right. A line had been crossed. And she'd be crossing another if she was late at Kaplan's. Yet she daren't now approach the Sanguinetti house directly, not if there was any chance of the sergeant still hanging around.

As it turned out, it was Mamma Sanguinetti herself who helped resolve the dilemma. Or so Cari thought. For she was still edging nervously past the Meeting House when the old lady emerged like a bent crow from the grimy terrace across the street and hobbled arthritically down the front steps to the pavement. Her head and shoulders were entirely shrouded, as they always were, by a moth-eaten grey shawl from which she peered, waiting for a gap in the traffic. Yet her steps across the cobbles seemed just a touch too sprightly as she picked her way between some prominent heaps of horse dung. And she was distinctly more solid than Cari remembered.

'Help an old lady, *cara mia*?'

As Italian accents went, it was a poor show.

'Nessie,' said Cari. 'Ladysmith was here again. Just a few minutes ago. You shouldn't be doing this.'

Nesta straightened her bowed back, grimaced at the effort.

'Mercy, that's better,' she laughed. 'Saw you going up the hill, though. Just guessed you needed to speak.'

'You're good at guessing, Nessie. Like the day you ran. You knew, didn't you? Knew the bobbies would be coming.'

'Still bothering you, Cari? All this time? I told you. Just coincidence. Give it a rest, won't you?'

The story remained fresh in Cari's memory. Nesta insisting she'd genuinely needed the privy, then heard the knocking on the door and Cari shouting up the stairs. How it hadn't taken a genius to work out that if the bobbies were looking for her, it couldn't be good news. And how she knew about Annie McGuire's sticky fingers. Everybody knew, she'd claimed. Just put two and two together.

'Well,' said Cari, 'we can't stand here arguing the toss. And I've not got long. Look, we've a plan. Bring you home, like. Why don't you carry on being Mamma Sanguinetti? We'll head up to dairy and back.'

Nesta fell back into character, Cari taking her arm and helping this "old lady" with the climb towards Christian Street. Wilding's, the cow keeper.

'Still don't believe me, though, do you, Cari?'

'Just a lot to take in,' Cari replied and told her about the plan to bring her home.

'Cousin Thomas is making a little nest of your own,' she smirked. 'In the paper loft.'

'It stinks in there.' She looked up at Cari, wrinkled her rabbit's nose. 'But listen, I saw Amos again this morning. I was telling him...'

'You know the thing that bothers me, Nesta?' She had to shout to make herself heard above the clamour of a steam wagon as they passed the church. 'If everybody knew about cock-eyed Annie, surely...'

'Don't listen, Cari, do you? Thick with old man Clayton, she is. The others wouldn't say anything. It's not the money. We think she and him – well, you know. To be honest, I don't care whether you believe me or not. And I just need you to do something. Not for me, mind. For Amos. Ernst, he came to let me know there's going to be a meeting. Another seamen's meeting. So, do the Krooboys a favour? Pop round to the dockers' office. See if you can speak to them – about getting the Elder Dempster lads along there again, too.'

Cari's heart sank. They'd talked about her going to see Jimmy Sexton almost every day for the past six weeks. She knew she'd been making excuses, insisted it wasn't really an issue for the dockers. Or no time. Anyway, she'd been raising money, hadn't she? At the meetings. Collections and so on.

'Why not get Taffy to do it?' she said.

'What? Ask Taffy to do a favour for the Krooboys? And from Sexton? Taffy would have a screaming fit. How is he, anyway?'

'Still with the MacKennys,' said Cari. She knew Nesta had side-tracked her, thrown her off those questions she still had – about the money. But she was running out of time. 'You think Mamma Sanguinetti will let you borrow the disguise again?'

She was sure there'd be no problem, said she'd wait until it was fully dark and then make her way to the print works door.

Cari, for her part, and more to get away than through any enthusiasm for the task, promised to get herself around to the union office. In addition, she'd wait for Nesta that night in Cartwright Place. Nine o'clock.

Well, it's what families were for, Cari told herself. To close ranks around each other – no matter what may come of it.

8.50am

Raining again. Amos wondered how any place could be blessed with this much rain yet remain so grey, so lacking in greenery. But so many horses. He idly wondered whether there was a connection. Rain and horses.

This morning they were out in force. The carters, their wagons and their big horses. A queue, stretching from the Harrington Dock gates, all the way back along this Sefton Street, past the goods yards.

The *Burutu* was in port and, from where he stood, Amos could see the yellow of her funnel. He was keen to also see the colour of her crew, but there'd been no sign of them yet. And who would replace them? The Mandinka men from the hostel, of course, probably being paid even less than his own fellows.

Her passengers would already have come ashore – back at the Princes Landing Stage – and the cargoes, palm oil and the rest, were ready for carriage to whichever warehouses might await them. This whole city, Amos knew, was built upon its trade across the endless oceans – and the trade itself owed its existence to these horses. Countless horses.

He'd admired them, decked in their flowers and finery, just two weeks earlier in a great parade. The thing they called May Day. A celebration of workers. White workers, anyway.

'How long now, lad?' called the nearest of the carters, while Amos waved his placard in the air. 'On the cobbles – how long?' the fellow repeated.

Amos looked down at the cobbles themselves, at the train tracks buried within the stones. On the cobbles – what did it mean, exactly? He held the carter's gaze, as good manners required, but decided to interpret the question as he chose.

'Here all the day, uncle,' he said. 'All days.'

The horse driver laughed, fumbled in his coat pocket.

'Aye, well, maybe this'll help.'

He flicked a silver coin towards Amos, who caught it deftly with one hand, dropped it into the bucket at his feet. And the brothers, scattered in their line under the shelter of the Overhead Railway, set up a cheer, drummed a salute on the boards of their own placards.

The carter whistled to his beasts, a gentle touch of the reins as the queue moved forwards. The smell of wood, leather and animal dung. Rumble and clatter of iron on cobblestones, wheel rim and horseshoe. The painted signs of a hundred carting companies. Horses in all shades from palest pearl to darkest umber, dapples of every tone between, steam rising from their damp coats.

A gap in the traffic and, with the gap, a procession of men marching towards them from inside the dock gates. They carried wooden clubs. Silent. Menacing.

'Here, my brothers,' Amos shouted to his pickets. 'To me, brothers.'

Safety in numbers? He doubted it. He knew they'd give a good account of themselves. But placards and fists against billy clubs and hobnailed boots? Maybe worse? It wouldn't be good. And, as the ruffians drew closer, he recognised a few of them. From their clothes more than anything. The same men who'd helped evict them from the hostel? Who'd stopped them speaking with the Mandinka men? He thought so. And here was Jonah Samba at his side.

'So, Mende man,' said Amos, 'you wanted fight. Fight find us now.'

'But you, Amos Gartee? Another beating?'

It was a good point. He wasn't sure his ribs would survive any more punishment.

Yet, as the bossman's gang reached the tracks, another wagon broke from the waiting line behind them, the brace of huge horses coming at a bouncing run, flying manes and feathering around their hooves.

'Woah, woah,' the horse driver yelled as he swung his rig to a halt between pickets and bruisers.

'Now, boys,' he called down to the nearest of the bossman's boys. 'Bother, like?'

Beneath the carter's cap, the face was thin and hard, a long, drooping moustache. His heavy brown coat was tied about his waist with rope. Along the side of his wagon, the white lettering spelled Hatton & Cookson, African Merchants.

'No bother, lad,' replied the leader of the hyenas. 'Not so long as you shift yer arse, any'ow. Need to get these monkeys out o' the way, is all.'

Monkeys? Well, Amos had heard worse since he arrived in this Liverpool place but, ribs or no ribs, he'd make sure that, if he managed nothing else, this villain would be the first to feel his fury. Yet the carter was laughing in the hyena's face.

'You'll have a lot of explaining to do then,' he said. 'To whoever's paying you scabs.'

'Scabs, eh, King Billy…'

The rest of it was lost on Amos. But he got the gist of it. Threats back and forth. And then the carter making it painfully plain that if the ruffians didn't "bugger off" there'd be none of the wagons picking up cargo. Not this day. Not any day if these Krooboys told him they'd been back.

This was a man of substance, then, this King Billy. For the hyenas, after the requisite show of defiance, din and bravado, eventually returned to the dock gates and disappeared. The strikers crowded around the cart and Amos reached up to shake the driver's hand, then snapped his fingers at him in salute, as explosively as he was able. A snap fit for a hero.

'King Billy,' he said, 'we thank you.'

'No,' the carter laughed. 'Just Billy. He had that bit right. But must have known I'm with the Lodge.'

'Lodge, uncle?'

'Never mind. Just listen, I'm on the committee. Understand – committee? For the Carters.' Amos told him yes, of course he understood. Their *krogba*, the headman for these horse drivers. 'Well, there's a meeting. The seamen. Next Monday. St. Martin's Hall.'

Behind them, the horses and carts moved steadily onwards, more drivers shouting encouragement to the Krooboys, more cash thrown into buckets, banter exchanged with King Billy until the whole junction was almost jammed with traffic.

'We know meeting,' said Amos. 'Miss Nesta tell us. Tall sister speak to them docker man.'

Billy shook his head, and Amos saw he'd not been understood. He'd have to start again, explain more slowly. But the carter was still in full flow, repeating yet again. Next Monday. St. Martin's Hall. Amos realised they had a problem. One he'd not considered earlier. Two problems, in truth. Though something else was happening. His brothers shouting, pointing back across the street, to where the queue of wagons had started to move again, yet one in particular coming faster than the rest, some of the carters yelling.

Over their heads, a train rumbled along the tracks, made it

impossible to hear King Billy's words, but Amos was certain he'd heard him say "scabs" yet again. And the cart coming towards them had policemen in rain capes trotting in a line on each side, the wagon itself one of those for carrying people. Windows in its sides and an upper deck, with seats. Large white lettering. Bryant & May. The passengers? The Mandinka men from the hostel. The change of crew.

Yet they couldn't get through, the carters blocking their way.

'Well, here's your chance, lad,' said King Billy. 'You picketing, or what?'

Amos didn't need telling twice, ran across to the people wagon with its police cordon.

'Hey, Mandinka men,' he yelled, thanking the Lord Jesus that, like his own kin, the Mandinka would know the English. Know it very well. 'Why you steal the brothers' work? Bossman use you. Pay dogshite.' He'd added considerably to his vocabulary since he'd been there. 'Half white pay.'

The Mandinka men on the upper deck were standing, whispering, one with the other, those on the lower deck with their heads poking from the window openings.

Amos felt the grip of strong fingers on his arm. A policeman.

'Now, banana boy,' the fellow laughed. 'Enough. Move on, like.'

He pushed Amos, hard enough to make him trip on one of the raised cobblestones, fall on his backside.

Amos Gartee shouted a protest, found King Billy at his side, helping him to his feet, the carter scolding the policeman. But Amos was otherwise engaged, distracted, the rest of the police cordon in confusion as the passengers filed from the vehicle, every one of them. They began to mingle with the strikers, sharing their placards. Joined the fight.

'There,' King Billy said to him. 'Looks liked you've scored, lad.'

Amos experienced a surge of pride. Some small victory. But he was still troubled, unsure how to explain his problems. Even should Missee Coconut Palm succeed, as Miss Nesta had promised, where *was* the meeting hall of which they spoke?

'If them docker man,' he began, 'not say we go to meeting…'

'Listen,' the carter laughed, 'whether "the docker man" says yay or nay, we'll get you into the meeting. Or my name's not Bill Jones. And before you ask, we'll get you there in style too!'

12.20pm

The building at forty-six Hanover Street, just across from the tea warehouse, was nothing special. Red brick, with the ground floor entrance to Tyrer's Wine Merchant angled across the corner of the block while, just further along, a separate door gave access to the businesses above. No lift, just stone stairs, green and cream tiled walls, climbing up past the floor occupied by the administrative offices of Barclay Perkins, to the second-storey headquarters for the National Union of Dock Labourers. The place smelled of tobacco smoke. And leather – for the top floor was taken by a small workshop, hand-stitched travelling bags and portmanteau cases.

'You get used to it,' said the young woman serving, it seemed, as the NUDL's receptionist and sole secretary. Pretty, beige two-piece walking suit, a gold-trimmed badge gleamed at her breast. 'Except sometimes when they get the hides straight from the tannery. It gets a bit ripe then. Know what I mean, luvvie?'

Cari did, indeed.

'Is Brother Sexton in the office?' It felt like the correct form of address, though she'd never met a paid union official before.

'He's busy just now. Can it wait? Or Georgie Milligan's about. Maybe he could help?'

Cari explained her predicament. Only Brother Sexton. And short dinner break. Get the sack if she was late again.

'You need the union,' the woman beamed.

'Not a docker,' Cari replied, and instantly fell for a lecture about the National Federation of Women Workers. The receptionist was herself a member, tapped her thumb against the shield-shaped green badge. And she had some flyers. Cari dutifully took one, feeling guilty she'd not already joined. Guilty that, as a woman, trade unions were somehow seen as not for her sex. So yes, she took the flyer and gave her name.

A couplet sprang, fully formed, into her brain.

Where mountains quake when women shake their chains,
To stir the entire globe for justice gained.

'You Taffy Maddox's sister, by any chance?' And Cari sensed her friendliness leaking away when she said yes. Taffy was on some Area Committee or other, and never seemed to have a good word for the paid officials. Not this bunch anyway, he used to say. And not for Sexton, their General Secretary. And when Cari was finally ushered into Sexton's office, the greeting was far from friendly. It would have been the waterworks again. She knew it. The trembling inside. If she'd been there on her own account, she thought she would have fallen apart. But Nessie and the Krooboys were relying on her.

'Miss Maddox,' he said, as though Cari had invented the name to make life difficult for him. Mid-fifties, three-piece suit, moustache and thinning hair. Smelled of pipe tobacco. But the right side of his face had been smashed. An accident on the docks when he was still a lad. That much was legend. And the badly healed damage left him with this impediment, which turned much of his speech into a sibilant hiss.

Cari sat, as primly as she was able.

'Brother Sexton, I'm here – well, on behalf of some colleagues in the WSPU.'

'One of that lot, are you?' His accent was very Lancashire. St. Helens maybe. 'Should have known. Political matter, then?'

He began fishing in one of his desk drawers, removed some leather-bound books and then, incongruously, an ivory-handled revolver, before finally finding his tobacco pouch and pipe, curved, with a briar bowl.

'I suppose so,' she said. 'In the sense that every matter in our lives is political in some way or other. Wouldn't you agree?'

'No, I bloody-well wouldn't, as it 'appens. But perhaps we could save the philosophical chit-chat for another time, eh? I'm a busy man. Things to do.'

For emphasis, he took a small folding knife from his pocket and began to scrape the briar bowl, knocked the pipe's dottle into a dirty brass ashtray shaped like a seashell.

'We seem to have got off on the wrong foot,' said Cari. 'My fault. But let me get to the point. It's the Kru seamen at the Harrington. You know about them, I'm sure.'

'The Krooboys?' He paused in the process of filling his pipe. 'Aye, I know about them. But what's this to do with the WSPU?'

'They're in trouble and nobody seems to care.'

'Half this city's in trouble, lass. Or hadn't you noticed? World trade slumps, and who's supposed to pay the price? We are, of course. Working men.'

'And women?' she said. 'You're right, of course. But sometimes my belly feels like my throat's been cut too. We all suffer, Brother Sexton.'

The receptionist popped her head around the door.

'Tea, luvvie?' she said, and Cari accepted with gratitude. Why in heaven's name had she mentioned her belly? She could have happily eaten a horse. But she saw Sexton bite back on his impatience. Not a man to suffer contradiction lightly. And certainly not from some slip of a girl. But she thought she'd at least piqued his curiosity.

'Aye, well – working men and their families then. And nobody hit worse than workers in a city that only exists for this same world trade. For pity's sake, is there anything, anything at all, in this town *not* about the sea? About shipping? So, you think I don't care – about your Krooboys?'

He blew a cloud of white smoke from the damaged corner of his mouth. It made her think of Taffy.

'I didn't say so. In fact, you've a reputation for siding with the underdog.'

'Not according to your brother and his pals. And you've still not told me where the WSPU fits into this.'

'Officially? We don't. My sister, Nessie – she was handing out leaflets a couple of months ago. On the dock road. Near the Harrington. The Krooboys had just gone on strike. They were trying to talk with some of the men finishing their shifts and – well, it turned a bit ugly. She stepped in. That's Nesta for you. Been a bit of a crusade for her ever since. We've raised some money for them now and then. But not enough.'

No, not enough. Yet look at the mess in which Nesta had landed them.

'Rock and a hard place, then,' said Sexton. 'You know what Havelock Wilson says about them? Blackies and Chinese under-cutting the pay of his lads?'

Not just Havelock Wilson, she knew. Jim Sexton's views as well, she was sure from his tone.

'They were lucky to get invited to the meeting back in March,' he told her.

'Fat lot of good that did them. A pat on the back. Well done, boys! All you've got to do is hold out until the rest of us decide to hit the cobbles too. And isn't this why they're on strike? To close the gap? It does them no favours to be on low pay. Just plays into the hands of Elder Dempster and the other shipping lines.'

He stared at her for a long while, though she had no idea what might be going on inside his head.

'Aye, 'appen it does,' he said, at last. 'But that's the business of Joe's Sailors and Firemen, not my Dock Labourers.'

Joe? Havelock Wilson, Cari guessed.

Another billow of smoke.

'But it will be, won't it? Your business, I mean. Somebody told me there's another big meeting this coming Monday. Seamen's meeting at St. Martin's Hall. More word going around about a national seamen's strike.'

'No secret. It was in all the papers last Monday. And?'

'If it happens, they'll be looking for your help, won't they?'

'Whether they get it all depends on what they're after. If it's going to be pay and conditions, that's one thing. But I'll not 'ave this union used as a political soccer ball. Not by nobody. And we've our own battles to fight. Against clock time. Faster work, longer hours, less wages. Gettin' the shipping lines to recognise our right to bargain for the lads. So I don't see how or why I should help these darkies of yours.'

'You'll be at the meeting? On Monday?'

'Been asked, aye. But what are you expecting me to do, Miss Maddox?'

He'd taken the trouble to whistle his way through Cari's name again, and she took it as a sign they'd broken the ice between them. She wondered how long he'd been in hospital after the accident, how long for the shattered cheek and skull bones to settle into their present soup bowl shapes. But then the receptionist was back with the tray of tea and Sexton was rummaging in his desk drawers again. He'd set the pipe down in the brass ashtray and now unwrapped a waxed paper package of sandwiches. Doorstoppers.

'Want one?' he said. Cari wasn't certain whether she might be expected to politely decline. If so, Sexton would be disappointed. She accepted her cup of tea at the same time.

'Might you just get them invited back to the meeting?' she said and bit into the crust. Tongue and mustard. 'I'm sure things will just develop a life of their own once they're inside,' she spluttered.

'You've more faith in human nature than me then, lass. But I may be able to swing it – if you can give me a reason why I should bother, that is.'

He took a bite of his own butty.

'Just one reason? I can think of three, at the very least.' Cari counted them off on her fingers. 'One. Think of the pleasure you'd get imagining the look on our Taffy's face when I tell him Jimmy Sexton's helping me and Nessie get the Krooboys sorted.'

'I'm not sure this is goin' to do me much good,' he muttered, and wiped some crumbs from his waistcoat. 'But go on.'

'Two. You stood for Toxteth in the General Election, didn't you?'

'Not this last one. Five years ago. I lost.'

'But you'll run again?'

'Somewhere maybe. One day. If the Party wants me. What of it?'

'Just imagine if you had the WSPU backing you.'

'The way things are going, 'appen that'd be the kiss of death too. So, this third one, it'd better be good.'

To tell the truth, Cari thought it was the weakest card in her hand, but she waved the remains of the sandwich at him anyway, wiped a smear of mustard from her lip.

'Three?' she said. 'Well – because it's the right thing to do.'

He gazed at her again, fixed her with those eyes, which seemed as badly put together as his face until he set down his butty, put away his books. And the revolver. She was desperate to ask him about that, though she knew it would break the spell. Yet it naturally seemed odd for a man who, besides his work for the union, was also a city councillor – Labour's one and only representative on the Council, as it happened.

'You've got some brick, lass,' he said. 'I'll give you that. But if I do this, I'll expect the debt to be repaid. You know?' She nodded, and he stood up, shook her hand. 'Now, is there anything else?'

There are times when a person simply needs to seize the moment, are there not? *Carpe Diem*, she thought might be the phrase.

'Well, Brother Sexton,' she said. 'If you could see your way clear to lending me the price for a bag of chips.'

6.05pm

Tom Priddy had finished at the Rotunda Theatre earlier than he'd expected. Scenery shifted and costumes railed for the evening performance. *A Runaway Girl*. Powders and paints readied in the dressing rooms. Not so fine a collection as Mister Clamp's. Still, it had all helped to inspire in him a possible plan of action, and he'd managed to sneak out through the stage door with some of the things he might need.

He turned over the details as Cari the Beanpole opened up the chips for them to share.

'Thought you'd be working,' she snapped at him. 'Only had enough for one bag.'

'Somebody rubbed you up the wrong way, girl?' he replied.

'Busy day, like. None of your business, mind.' She turned to her father. 'Met Jimmy Sexton, Tada,' she said. 'About the Krooboys.'

'A mystery would have been nice,' said old Huw. He entirely ignored her mention of the Krooboys, his voice still modulated to be heard above the squabbling chatter which had once filled the room when Dumpling Nesta and Daft Taffy had been there.

'I barely had enough for the chips, Tada, let alone a sausage. And how was I supposed to know Cousin Thomas would be here?'

'Already eaten though, eh, Beanpole?' Tom tapped his own chin, saw Cari blush, hastily wipe the grease from her lips.

'Mister Gianelli was kind enough to let me have some of the scratchings from his early fry-up. Tide me over on the way home, like.'

Interesting. Tide her over? How much time *had* she been spending with those monkey boat boys?

'And you going to keep the Aged Parent company tonight?' Huw Maddox asked his daughter.

Just nod away at him, Mister Pip, Tom thought, remembering his Dickens.

'Sorry, Tada,' she said. 'Have to go out again, see? Soon, too.'

There it was – the colour riding up her neck. Tom had seen it often enough by now, though her tada seemed oblivious. A lie beginning to form.

'Meeting, I suppose,' said old Huw. 'Those harpies again?'

'Yes,' she told him. 'My harpies.'

Tom heard her relief. There, the lie created for her. So where *was* she going? Taffy, surely. It *must* be Taffy. In which case, his scheme...

'But I'll be back by nine,' she said. 'Meet Nesta, get her safely back inside. And settled, like.'

'Thanks to me, Beanpole,' said Tom. 'You forgot to say it's all thanks to me, girl. Where's your gratitude?'

She ignored him. And that was fine. Plenty of time to collect on this particular debt in due course.

'Won't it be champion, Tada?' said the Beanpole. 'Nessie home with us.'

Yes, champion, thought Tom. But, meanwhile, he'd have himself a bit of fun.

6.35pm

Cari's brother had settled into the MacKennys' place on Gerard Street, though when she arrived there, a little after half-past six, there was nobody home but Mrs MacKenny herself and two of her middle girls. She thought she'd recognised more of the brood out on the street, but it must have been a precious commodity, Mrs MacKenny having time on her own. How many did she have? Fourteen, she thought Taffy had said. So, woman to woman, she felt guilty disturbing this rare moment of tranquillity – though, of course, it was no such thing. Mrs MacKenny was working in the back room, wrapped in the strange miasma of fish, coal smoke, brasso and damp wool.

'Can I help?' said Cari.

'Mary, Mother of God,' Ma MacKenny laughed, heaving a pan carefully over the gleaming fireguard with its drying clothes, and setting it onto the hotplate. 'That'd be a fine thing, Queen. Don't you think, girls?'

They could have been twins, slim and sickly-looking, but hair the colour of flames.

'The little ones already eaten?' Cari asked them, though she got no answer, just shy glances as they looked up from the galvanised tub where they were swilling an assortment of pots and dishes in water that looked like tomorrow's stew. She couldn't help thinking of Florrie Thompson-Frere's place. Two homes, a few miles apart. Different planets, as she'd once before decided.

'Finny 'Addy,' said Mrs MacKenny. Friday, of course. What else? 'And the next bunch'll be here before we know it. Greedy little sods, the lot of them.'

Cari had grown fond of Ma MacKenny since Taffy moved in. Though how the family managed to make space for him, she had no idea. Compared to this place, even Hunter Street was a palace. And, to her tada, of course, this was the home of heathens. Antichrist papists. Those things rubbed off, too. Hard not to share at least a sliver of his fears as Cari avoided looking at the crucifix, or their brash print of the Virgin Mary.

'You're a saint, Mrs MacKenny,' Cari told her, running a finger along the books on a precarious shelf beneath the picture: Kipling; Mary Johnston; *The Wonderful Wizard of Oz*; Helen Keller. And, on the corner of the shelf, a single shilling, like an offering to the Holy Mother.

'Saint? Nah. Patience of one, maybe. Just play my part, girl. Like you play yours.'

The pallid redheaded girls passed Cari some of the assorted crockery, dried with a gingham cloth, handed them to her in turn for setting the table afresh.

'I don't know what my part is. Not really. Sometimes – well, sometimes when I'm at work, I get this feeling. Like, a door's just about to open and I'll be able to see outside. But it never quite does. Open, I mean.'

'But you're not saddled with a man,' said Ma MacKenny. 'Not yet. And take my advice. Stay that way.'

Cari had always assumed Mrs MacKenny was happy in her role, a larger-than-life woman who seemed to revel in her kids. Not the life for Cari, she was sure. But, in a way, she envied her. It seemed as though her family defined her. And if Cari could revel so in her own family, how much more bounty must there be in one so large?

'Don't give me that,' Cari laughed – and tried to decide whether there was some hierarchy about where specific plates should be placed. 'You love it,' she said. 'I can tell.'

'Love it? Just goes to show. We could all be on the stage. All of us. My fella goes out in the morning. Crack of dawn. If he's lucky, he gets a shift. The docks. Any monkey could do it. But it makes him feel like a man. An' when he gets home, I fetch and carry for him like I'm his personal slave. Makes him feel big. They've got to feel big, eh? Then he's off to the boozer, comes back pissed, knocks me about. Makes him feel big again.'

She dried her hands on the cloth, snapped at the girls.

'You two,' she growled. 'What are you gawping at? Empty the bleedin' tub.'

Ma MacKenny turned back to Cari.

'But you know what?' she went on. 'The truth is he couldn't look after himself to save his life. Can't cook. Wouldn't know one end of a washhouse from the other. Has no idea how to run a home. Bring up the kids. Not a bloody thing. Useless bugger. Hands over whatever's left of his wages, then leaves me to worry about how we'll stretch it through the week. So, no matter what he thinks, I know who runs this bloody house. And that's enough. Has to be, Cari, girl. Because I know it's all I'm ever going to get. But love it? Don't make me laugh.'

She tossed the cloth onto one of the chairs.

'There should be a hundred ways to argue with you, Mrs MacKenny,' Cari said.

'Only you're clever enough not to bother, Cari Maddox. Because you know none of them hold water. No way to escape once you're in the trap. And winning me the vote? Help me swap one MP for another – when we both know it's not them as runs the country. Just a clever way to make us *think* we've got a say when, really, it's all them faceless moneybags in control – who make the little boxes for us to fit in. Well, this is my little box. I can live with it. Just about.'

It plunged Cari into a fit of despair.

7.10pm

At the Upper Stanhope Street hostel, it was time for celebration. The guards were gone – at least, for now. And the Mandinka men were keen to make merry.

Cookie had conjured up plenty of *kala* dumplings, a smoked fish *palava* stew and an enormous pot of *jollof* rice. From somewhere, flagons of palm wine.

Amos Gartee squatted against the hostel wall, his belly full for once, his head dizzy from the wine, but basking in the noise and general merriment. It had always surprised him – both in Freetown and in this Liverpool place – how white seamen, regardless of where they came from, were two creatures. At sea, great sailors, perhaps as good as the Kru themselves. On land, hapless infants, a disgrace, with no ambition apart from swallowing as much strong liquor as they could consume and creating havoc wherever they went. It was beyond understanding. Like the walking of those strange small dogs along the streets, a thing which he had seen so many times here.

Yet this night was no occasion for sobriety, even for Amos. It troubled him hardly at all when Jonah Samba staggered towards him. Indeed, he was pleased to see the Mende. Were they not allies now? Yes, he was pleased.

At the corner, one of the Mandinka men drummed a ferocious rhythm for three dancers, and Jonah's unsteady gait seemed synchronised with the beat.

'So, brother.' Jonah gazed down at him, offered a crooked smile. 'Here you are. The big man.'

The smile remained. Yet, through his palm wine haze, Amos sensed this more resembled the ragged-toothed grin of a shark.

'Aye-yah,' Amos laughed. 'Do we not win? Friend women promise them speak with union man. For sailor meeting. Horse drivers too. Now Mandinka men, they join with us.'

Around the drummer, those three Mandinkas gyrated and pranced upon the pavement. Their white robes were the billowing clouds along the coast of his homeland, and their matching white caps bobbed and swayed, became the waves upon its shores. Clever of them, Amos thought, to stow such fine attire among their dunnage.

'But see, Amos Gartee,' Jonah was saying. 'If now they help, past so long time, how this your thing? Perhaps *poto* womans. And union man. Or horse driver, this King Billy. Or Wolof man. *Them* should be *krogba*, we thinkin'. Headman.'

It was a challenge to him. Plain as day. Amos was disappointed, angry his leadership was in question yet again.

At the corner, a small crowd had gathered around the dancers. Mostly the strikers. But a few white folks passing by, as well. Seamen, Amos guessed, with painted women on their arms, and beginning to stamp out their own drunken, stupid imitation of the Mandinkas.

But here, where Amos levered himself upright, a different audience came together. Amos Gartee's brothers on the one hand, Jonah Samba's scavengers on the other. Those who could smell trouble on the air as surely as they tasted the sulphurous grit of chimney smoke from the surrounding houses.

'Maybe we join dance,' said Amos, shaking his head to clear the fog. 'Let all choose. You or me. Best dance. Mende, Loko and Bandi. Kru, Guere and Grebo. Mandinka, Soninke and Dyula. Choose *krogba* this way. You or me, Jonah Samba. Yes?'

It spoke a great deal about the inebriation of both men that Jonah Samba agreed. Thus, they danced. And neither they, nor the men who watched and understood the purpose of the dance, not one person queried whether there might not perhaps be some better way to judge the qualities of a strike leader.

7.25pm

Tom Priddy understood this one inalienable truth. In life, you don't need to be clever in all things. Just one skill will suffice. And, for Tom, this was the art of deception.

While Cari had readied herself to leave the house, he'd been downstairs in the print shop, making his own preparations. A quick application of the theatrical make-up and his borrowed costume, a check in the mirror just in time to follow her.

A short step. The back way. Cartwright Place and round the rear of St. Stephen's, finally cutting through onto Gerard Street. A few hundred yards, but *Duw Annwyl*, another world. In the space occupied by just a single house on Hunter Street, small as *they* might be, here there were two. Narrow, pressed together, one upon another. Clean enough, for the most part. Two or three steps up to every front door all scrubbed, but the district dirt poor. Two storeys or three, often shared by a family on each floor. The long monotony of grimed brickwork broken only by an occasional shop window, or by the washing hung across the street below, or by the archways leading to the dark courts and foreboding alleyways beyond – jiggers, he'd heard the locals call them.

The heart of Little Italy and Liverpool's community of papists. All scrubbed, but the district dirt poor.

Tom had ventured here twice before, always on Fridays, as it happened. He knew the routine. Seen the parish priest on his rounds. Like clockwork. He'd wondered what it was all about at first. The old fellow in and out of every house, but only seconds spent inside each of them. What unholy ritual was performed there? And he'd laughed when old Clamp at Waugh's had revealed the mystery to him.

But this evening, would anybody here notice? He was half an hour ahead of the priest's schedule, and his disguise far from perfect. Yet there was a passing resemblance, the black beret pulled down almost to his eyes, the shoulders of his charcoal suit hunched up, and the crucifix around his neck, below the borrowed clerical collar. Yes, he looked the part.

Cari had been ahead of him, making for the MacKennys' house which, he knew, was almost at the top of the street. But as he'd passed the lower reaches, women and the babies, it seemed to him, on every doorstep, the street itself full of urchins playing their games, he'd been gratified by the greetings he'd received.

'Hello, Father.' Or, 'Ciao, Padre.' Or, 'Father, early tonight, no?'

It had made him so bold that, halfway to his destination, he'd ventured into his first house. In and out. In and out. Not a single family paid him any heed. And so great was his exaltation, he almost bumped straight into Daft Taffy himself, surrounded by infants and laughing like a loon.

7.35pm

The shouts and howls of laughter out on the street cut across any further discussion of Mrs MacKenny's world – though it was familiar enough anyhow. And she was right. About why Cari hadn't bothered with any trite comments or solutions to her situation. She tended towards optimism in life, though she wasn't stupid enough not to understand there were times when it was misplaced.

But Taffy burst through the front door just then, cigarette in his mouth, one of the smaller MacKenny boys under his arm, tickling him so much Cari thought the kid must wet himself. And Taffy's girl, Theresa, a thin linen frock, pale blue, giggling along behind. But she couldn't shake off the gloom, seeing in this ostensibly happy scene merely a perpetuation of the snare.

How long before Theresa would, herself, be burdened with a dozen children and Taffy drowning in the same cycle of self-delusion, falsely weighing his own worth in a world which valued him not the slightest. How long before Theresa became her mother, never to become a Florrie Thompson-Frere.

'Cari,' he cried, setting the boy down, 'how are the lost causes today?'

'Funny,' she said and looked up from the table. 'Mrs MacKenny and me, we were just talking about the same thing.'

'You'll have some with us, Queen?' Mrs MacKenny heaved the pan back over the fireguard and set it on the corner of their parsimonious table. 'It's good Finny 'Addy, even if I say so myself.'

The room became a dust-devil of scraping chairs and rowdy, jostling bodies, plates and spoons.

'I had some chips before,' said Cari, but this didn't prevent a muggen bowl being pushed into her hands, a portion of the milk-poached haddock and onion slopped into the deep-brown depths.

'So, which one was it?' Taffy cried, over the general clamour. 'The lost cause. Krooboys? Or your precious vote?'

Not enough chairs to go round, so he shared one with Theresa.

'No, neither,' Cari told him. 'It was men in general. About them being too big for their boots.'

'Krooboys?' said Mrs MacKenny, dishing out more portions. And Cari saw how she crossed herself. 'You're not mixed up with them godless blackies, Cari?'

'They're workers,' she said, breaking up the fish with her spoon. 'Good Christians, all of them.' At least, Cari thought so. 'And they're on strike. But I think the union's going to step in at last.'

'What are you going to do, Cari?' said her brother. 'Break Elder Dempster's windows?'

'Hasn't there been enough of that just lately?' said Mrs MacKenny. 'Window-breaking.' She was right. It had become the favourite pastime of local gangs again. Catholics and Protestants. Attacks on each other's churches and all beginning to turn very ugly. 'And Theresa,' she said, 'go and get the other little buggers in here, right now.'

Theresa made some feeble protest but she did as she was told.

'Not the WSPU, Taffy,' Cari smiled, wiping a dribble of fish milk from her chin. 'Your lot. I met Jimmy Whistle at dinnertime.'

It was cruel – repeating Sexton's nickname. Taffy was about the only union man she knew who didn't use it. His own harelip, she supposed. But she wanted to sting him. Just a bit.

'Sexton. You went to Sexton without speaking to me?'

He'd balled his fists, his face livid white.

'And what would you have done, Taffy? Nothing, that's what. Don't know whether he can help but he's going to try getting them into the seamen's meeting on Monday. At least it'll be something. Anyhow, you might be out on the cobbles soon yourselves. And who knows? Maybe it'll be you dockers looking for *their* help.'

'What d'you mean?' said Mrs MacKenny. 'Strike?' She set down her spoon with such force that it splashed Finny 'Addy juices all over the table. 'My fella's not said anything about a strike. Mother of God, how does he think we're going to feed this lot if he's on strike?'

Taffy on the defensive now, fighting on two fronts.

'Take no notice, Ma,' he said. 'Not much chance. And if it does happen, Cari, we'll certainly not be needing help from no blackies.'

So, Cari thought, it's Ma now, is it? Cousin Thomas wasn't the only one with his feet under another's table. But he'd done it on purpose, of course, knowing how much she'd hate him calling anybody else Ma, other than their own mother.

'It was good, Mrs MacKenny,' she said. 'Thanks.' And one of the twin-like girls jumped up to take her bowl, while Theresa returned with four more noisy urchins in tow.

'Anyway,' Taffy sneered at her, 'that all you come for? Rub my nose in the Sexton thing?'

Had she? Maybe. But she was also trying to make the family whole again.

'We're bringing Nesta home later,' said Cari. 'Thought you'd want to know.'

'And what? Give me the lecture about making peace with Pa?'

'You should, son,' said Mrs MacKenny. 'Life's too short.'

She surrendered her place at the table to the extra mouths Theresa had fetched. More bowls and plates, the kids crowding each other, pushing and shoving around the table's corner. Cari could barely hear herself think for the noise.

'He knows where I am,' shouted Taffy. 'Wouldn't do any good anyway, Ma. He'd never accept our Theresa.' He put his arm around the girl, gave her a squeeze. 'So, to hell with him.'

8.00pm

'Teach white children swim?' Amos Gartee's voice echoed in a strange way around this shimmering cavern of water, empty now of swimmers. The smell of the place stung his nostrils.

Charles Tuohey smiled at him, leaned on the carved walking stick which seemed to be his constant companion. Many years older than Amos, they shared the same build, stocky, solid, but Tuohey's features distinctly Senegalese.

'It seems I had a natural gift,' the Wolof replied. 'Began in the bath house. Cleaning, of course. My adopted father knew the Superintendent here. One day, old man Tuohey persuaded me into the pool. And I floated. Like a cork. After that, learning was easy. So yes, now I am a teacher of swimming.'

His English was strange, as well. Like birdsong. Charles had explained how the lilt was Irish. It was the way those Irish folk, from across the seas, spoke the English tongue. Irish folk who had taken him in.

'This way, brother,' said Tuohey, and led him back along the corridor separating the warm bathtub closets from the cold plunges, to the building's entrance, then past the office and through the wash houses. Out in the yard, at the side of the engine room, a spiral iron staircase led to the upper floor. 'It won't do,' Tuohey went on. 'You need to defend yourself. Good footwork, but not enough. Not by itself.'

He'd appeared while Amos Gartee and Jonah Samba still danced. At the end, straws had been counted, Amos maintaining his leadership by a comfortable majority. But Tuohey had been unimpressed, insisted there was much more for Amos to learn if he wanted to survive and prosper in this alien land. And when Amos had told him he had no intention of staying beyond winning the strike, the Wolof had laughed in his face.

Now, on the landing at the top of the stairs, Tuohey produced keys from his jacket pocket and unlocked the door. It was still not dark, but once inside Amos took a moment to adjust his eyes to the gloom, while Charles turned the gas on a wall light and set a match to the mantle.

A gymnasium. There'd been such a room in the vessel on which he'd sailed here. For the passengers. Smaller, of course. And, as well as the parallel bars, the vaulting horses, the exercise ladders and climbing ropes, this one boasted a boxing ring.

They were soon stripped to the waist, Amos equipped with a pair of cumbersome gloves and the Wolof similarly attired, holding up his own mitts, encouraging his new disciple to hit them.

'Jab!' Tuohey yelled, circling around.

Amos followed, obeyed the instructions, fell easily into the routine.

'You need to understand this place,' said Tuohey. 'Double jab!'

Ay-yah, the Wolof wasn't even breathing heavily, while Amos was already gasping. He was fit enough. All that work as a stoker. But this…

'This place is built upon the blood of our people, Amos Gartee. Jab to the body! The blood of slaves.'

Amos jabbed. But he'd already had the lecture. The day Charles Tuohey had helped him back to the hostel, after his beating. Amos had only heard and understood snatches of the story, yet he remembered it well enough. Lifetimes ago, and there had been slaves in Merica. A time when the people of that place had been fighting to free themselves from the English king. Many slaves had escaped from the Merica people and fought on the English king's side. But when the English king had lost his war, some of those slave soldiers had been brought for safety to this Liverpool place. Settled here. Well, that was what Tuohey thought had happened, anyhow. More soldiers and sailors of the English kings had followed. Generation after generation.

'Jab to the head,' cried the Wolof.

'But not understand,' Amos gasped. 'You told me slaves here as free men.'

'Those from America, yes. Jab! Double jab! But there were others, brought here as slaves themselves to serve the town's rich and powerful. Jab!'

Rich and powerful, he explained. Amos became more and more exhausted, as Tuohey detailed the trade in which the slavers had engaged. Liverpool to West Africa. The death ships from West Africa to the American colonies. Much of the story, Amos already knew. You couldn't know Freetown, or any of Sierra Leone, or his own home in Liberia, or the Gold Coast, without knowing the story of slavery.

'Not my people,' said Amos. 'Not the Kru.'

'No, not the Kru. The Kru are a bold people.'

'Bold, yes. I was on street called Bold.'

Tuohey laughed.

'You see? Bold Street. I regret to tell you, Amos Gartee, but Bold Street has its name thanks to Jonas Bold. Jab! Jonas Bold the slave trader.'

It shattered Amos Gartee's illusions, sapped his will, and he felt his punches weaken. There was a litany. Streets and buildings he did not know, though each carrying the name of yet another merchant of death. Even their town hall, it seemed, had been built with the proceeds of slavery. As the litany came to an end, Amos saw the Wolof lower his fists.

'Finish?' Amos hoped so. He'd had enough, drenched in sweat, feeling as though he would vomit.

'You are weak, brother,' said Tuohey. 'Now the bag.'

He led Amos across to the opposite side of the gymnasium, where a long, filled bag hung from a chain. More instructions. His feet thus. His fists like this. Sequences to be followed. Jab. Right cross. Left hook. Right cross. Amos slogged away, wishing he'd turned down the Wolof's invitation.

'Look up,' Tuohey told him. 'Look at your target. And when you walk the streets of this city, Amos Gartee, look up also. Open your ears. For, though we are many thousands here, have been here two hundred years, there is no other city in all England which equals Liverpool for insults to black people. The reason you stand alone against Elder Dempster. Yes, look up. See how they celebrate the enslaved. Carvings of crocodiles and elephants. Carvings of slaves themselves.'

Crocodiles and elephants, thought Amos. How he wished he were home in Nana Kru, rather than this place where a Wolof from Serrekunda – now bearing an Irish name as well as his own – was teaching him this boxing foolishness.

'Rest now,' he said, and flopped onto the floor, arms and legs all a-tremble, sweat running in rivers across his torso. 'And you, brother. You Islam. How?'

'This city has good people as well,' said Tuohey. 'People who knew the evil of slavery when it was happening. Quakers and others. You know Quakers?' Yes, Amos knew Quakers. 'And here,' the Wolof continued, 'we had a mosque. An Englishman, Quilliam, who'd converted to follow the word of the Prophet, blessings be upon him.'

Amos watched him touch a hand to the small leather pouch tied around his bare neck.

'But the mosque is closed now,' the Wolof told him. 'Sold. And each must observe the teachings of the sacred scriptures in his or her own way. Though it's your own teaching to which we need to attend this day. If you're going into the seamen's meeting, come Monday, you'd better be able to fight your way out again.'

Perhaps it might be good advice, after all, though there was no fight left in Amos Gartee just now. But he nodded.

'You fight here?' he said.

'Like the swimming,' said the Wolof. 'I learned to fight early. This way.'

His fists moved so fast Amos could barely follow the movements. Punching the air, though Amos wouldn't have wanted to be on the receiving end of those fearsome blows.

'A strange thing,' Tuohey went on. 'Once you know how, there's really no need to fight anymore. That's what I've found, anyhow.'

'Then why keep white man's name?' said Amos. 'You. Abdul Niasse. From Serrekunda.'

The Wolof laughed again.

'Why? A reminder, brother. My Irish family were good people as well. But there was another. Another Tuohey. No relation, I don't think. A man called David Tuohey. From Tralee. County Kerry.

A place in Ireland. But he came here to Liverpool. A slaver. I have no idea how many hundreds, thousands, he sent into slavery, but I keep the name. To remind me. So my ears and eyes are always open here. So we don't forget.'

8.05pm

This must be the girl, surely, Tom Priddy decided. Taffy's girlfriend. Small and thin, freckled. Pretty enough – for a papist. Blue summer frock that had seen better days.

She'd gone into the house five minutes earlier and come back out again almost immediately afterwards, screamed like a fishwife at those of her siblings still kicking a ball around the street, eventually gathered them together and dragged them up the front steps. Like herding cats, he decided.

He followed them. Up the steps, at least. Stopped at the front door, which stood ajar.

Inside, he could hear Daft Taffy.

'Last time I saw Rhys,' he was saying, 'he was talking about Nesta. And this Thomas Priddy character. Wanted to know all about the bobbies coming to look for her.'

Tom's interest was naturally piqued. Though he was thinking about the old saying. About eavesdroppers never hearing good of themselves. Well, he'd have been disappointed if it had been any different, and he peered through the gap, saw Taffy turn to an older woman, heavy-set, presumably the mother of this heathen tribe.

'Great Finny 'Addy, Ma,' said Daft Taffy. 'The best. And did I tell you this? The bobbies. They want to know where she is. Our Nessie. Well, she's down in the privy. But I tell them she's not back from work yet. And then I do a stupid thing, see. Pass the ball to Cousin Thomas, who's sitting there, smug as you like. "Didn't you see her there a while back, Thomas?" I says. Why did I do it? No idea. And my heart's in my mouth. Then he just chimes up about how he's seen her there 'imself. An hour past. Working late, he tells them. They catch him out, of course. But he doesn't care. Just stares them down. Still haven't fathomed that one.'

Funny, Tom smiled to himself. Not fathomed it, like. But it had helped put him further into old Huw's good books.

'And what did Rhys Fingers have to say about it?' Cari asked him.

'Oh, Rhys thinks a good chapel-going lad like Cousin Thomas,' said Taffy, 'must have cause to try and cover for her. Says if Nesta swears she did nothing wrong, that should be good enough. But me? I wouldn't trust Thomas Priddy as far as I can spit.'

Cause? Tom thought. Sometimes it's good to merely follow one's whim. And Daft Taffy not trusting him? Sensible lad. But he needed to catch a better look at the girl, Theresa. He couldn't see her from the step. Though he saw the Beanpole get up from the table, surrender her chair to a pair of the urchins and go to help at the washing tub.

'Tada's talking about making him a partner,' Cari told her brother. A cry of protest from Daft Taffy.

'What?' she said. You've no interest in the business, Taff. Nor in Tada.'

Quite right, Tom thought. But he couldn't stand on the step all evening and he was beginning to attract attention from some of the street's busybodies. He pushed the door open, stepped inside, saw Daft Taffy with his head buried in his hands.

'Hello, Father,' said Mrs MacKenny, though she barely spared him a glance and Tom certainly didn't trouble himself to reply. Instead, he kept his back to the family, surveyed the room quickly, spotted the shelves, saw the votive shilling, gleaming, ready for collection. He began to edge his way around the table.

'We know nothing about him, Cari,' Taffy was saying. 'No more now than when he showed up. Aren't you curious? Just a bit? About how and why he dropped like a stone into our lives. You think Pa would have turfed me out like that? Printer's devil. Oh yes, he's a devil all right. And the business – well...'

Interesting. And gratifying if it were true. Would old Huw have kicked Taffy onto the street, with or without Tom being there? Of course, he would – once Dumpling Nesta had let the cat out of the bag about Theresa. He ranted for days afterwards about it. Catholics. Catholics. Catholics.

'Tada shouldn't have said what he said,' Cari told her brother. 'You're right. But you didn't waste any time leaving either, did you? And the business? You just thought it would sit there. Like money in the bank. Until Tada's not with us anymore. Waiting for you to get your share.'

'Cari Maddox!' cried Mrs MacKenny. 'That's a wicked thing to say.'

Tom reached the shelves, picked up the silver shilling, kept moving, completing his circuit of the table, squeezed carefully past the Beanpole, who'd fetched the end of a loaf from the scullery and sliced a few cobs for the MacKennys' brood to mop up their slops.

'No, Ma,' said Taffy, and took one of the crusts. 'She's got a point. In a way. But it's not just me, Cari. It's all of us, see. Look where we all are, for pity's sake. Any of us so well-heeled we can let Thomas Priddy get his hands on the only bit of family silver we're ever likely to have?'

He was right, of course. Tom knew it. The house on Hunter Street was no palace. But without old Huw's inheritance from his stepfather, where would they be? Still in one of Bangor's back streets. Or crowded like sardines in one of the courts. In a place like this. It was a family thing, Tom decided. Yes, family silver. Might not be much, but *Iesu*, it would be his. He glanced at the girl, Theresa, saw she was otherwise occupied helping feed the little ones. He studied her, made sure he'd fixed her image in his head.

'What are you saying, Taffy?' the Beanpole demanded. 'Planning to spy on him, is it?'

Tom reached the door again.

'Goodnight, Father,' shouted Mrs MacKenny.

Tom kept his face averted, waved his hand at her, something resembling the sign of the cross, and he slipped out onto the doorsteps, paused long enough to hear Taffy's reply.

'I didn't say spying,' Taffy told the Beanpole, as the front door closed again. 'But isn't there somebody in the family you could write to? You'd know what to say, Cari. And me? Maybe check him out at the Rotunda, like.'

Oh, you will? Tom Priddy smiled to himself. Well, we shall see.

Chapter Four

5.00pm

At the meeting room, which Alice Davies had hired on Ranelagh Street, it sounded like war had already broken out by the time Cari arrived.

'You simply cannot trust the Germans,' Florrie Thompson-Frere was saying, as Cari took her seat just behind the Crosby contingent, all expensive afternoon dresses, summer coats and dusters, wide-brimmed hats or flowered jaunties. This was a world away from Ma MacKenny and Gerard Street.

A few curt nods of greeting from some of the two dozen women gathered there – as well as the two gentlemen, both regular representatives from the Men's League. But Cari was usually met with more warmth. Or was it just her imagination? Word has spread, she thought. About Nessie and the police. 'Give the Germans an inch,' Florrie continued, without sparing her even a glance of recognition, 'the slightest hint that we'll turn a blind eye to their shenanigans in Morocco, and…'

Poor Germans, thought Cari. On the receiving end of Florrie's tongue again. She didn't understand the fuss. All the Germans she knew were perfectly decent people. Just look at Ernst Jurks, for example. Yes, just look, she smiled to herself. She felt a pleasurable shiver run down her spine.

'Who says?' shouted Patricia Woodlock – not much older than Cari, but a very formidable young woman, she'd decided. There'd been some controversy at the previous meeting when Woodlock had announced how, apart from her membership of the WSPU, she'd also joined the newly-formed Catholic Women's Suffrage Society – in an effort to counter the bile being heaped on them by so many church leaders and the *Catholic Herald* in particular.

'Who says we can't trust the Germans?' said Woodlock. 'The *Daily Mail*?' The *Mail* was obsessed, as it always was, with any perceived threat to British superiority. And their headlines had been dominated recently by war-mongering attacks on Germany's territorial ambitions.

'Ladies,' said Alice Davies. 'Ladies, please. It was helpful to have the report but it's time we moved on to the business at hand.' The report in question, Cari guessed, must have come from the Peace and Propaganda meeting held a couple of evenings earlier at Byrom Hall. She'd not been there, but the outcome had been predictable.

'It's a dreadful mistake, that's all.' Florrie Thompson-Frere sat down again, reluctantly. 'As if anybody's going to take us seriously,' she murmured in a loud stage whisper to the woman next to her, 'if we keep supporting silly resolutions against re-armament and war when everybody knows war is exactly where we're heading.'

'And is this the best we can do for a room, Miss Davies?' It was the elderly Mrs Avery, Birkenhead's *Votes for Women* secretary. 'At least when we had the shop...'

Oh, for pity's sake, Cari thought. Really? She was already anxious, and this nonsense – besides now apparently being ostracised – just made it all worse. Worrying about Nesta, finally installed in the paper loft back home, but taking far too many risks with her visits to Amos Gartee's strikers. Worse that Nessie, who should have been happy to be back in the bosom of the family – well, with Cari and Tada, at least – now seemed to possess a permanently haunted look about her eyes, had become somewhat distant and could not, or would not, give any reason for this change in her normally exuberant manner.

Worrying also, though hardly as important, about the strange incident on the previous Friday evening during her visit to the MacKennys – the hullabaloo when the real Father Doolan had come protesting about imposters and sacrilege.

Finally, worrying about this meeting of the sailors' union on the opposite side of town. Sexton had sent the briefest of notes. *Get them there.* That was all. Three words. Nesta had been foolish enough to insist on delivering the message to the Krooboys, returned with a mysterious response from Amos Gartee. King Billy, he'd seemingly insisted, was helping them as well. So yes, they would be there. But who, in heaven's name, was King Billy? And worse, Nessie was insisting she would go to the meeting with them.

5.05pm

King Billy had been true to his word, arrived at the hostel to collect Amos and his chosen men. To transport them safely to this meeting of seamen. Not like last time, when they'd had to slog from one side of the city to the other in the cold and rain. He must indeed be a person of standing, the horse driver, for their working day could hardly have been finished and there he'd been, with the wagon belonging to his masters, the carter proudly displaying a button on his jacket which, he said, marked him as a union man. Oh, for such power, such freedom, thought Amos.

He rolled himself a thin cigarette, asked the carter for a light.

'We thank, King Billy,' he'd said. 'But friend Tuohey,' he pronounced the name as he'd learned from Charles himself, *Too-ee,* 'say must walk.'

'Walk?' said the carter. 'Not ride?'

'Tuohey say walk. Walk, look up. See, hear this Liverpool place. See bad story. See good too. Respect.'

'Fair enough,' said King Billy. 'We'll make it a procession then, eh, lads?' He made a clicking noise with his tongue, gave the horses just the merest tickle of the reins. 'Walk on, Jackie. Walk on, Prince.'

They plodded away, all gleaming brasses and shining black leather. Amos Gartee followed with his placard, the other strikers in a straggling line behind. They turned the corner towards that great House of God they were building on St. James' Mount and there, waiting for them, was a woman. An old woman, Amos thought, wrapped in a shawl. A woman who hobbled towards them, fell in alongside.

'Miss Nesta,' Amos laughed when he saw through the disguise. 'Think witch come. But good medicine. No bad.'

'Police,' she said. This was a more serious Miss Nesta, the normal dancing light in her eyes extinguished today. 'Still looking for me. But I couldn't miss this. Not for all the world.'

She looked fine, even with the disguise, even without her usual spark. He wanted to sweet-mouth her, tell her she was beautiful. He'd wanted to tell her the day before, when she'd arrived at daybreak with a message. The other union man wanted them at the meeting also. She'd been confused when he'd tried to tell her about King Billy. So, when he'd wanted to sweet-mouth her, he feared the words would not sound right. Not in his apparently faulty English. It had always seemed so perfect, back home, or on the ships. But here? The English of the *poto* girls, of King Billy, of the Wolof Charles Tuohey, it seemed like a different tongue entirely. One he could understand from the mouths of others, though one in which he could often not, himself, be understood. Another strange thing in this strangest of lands. Yet, now, he lost himself in the music of Miss Nesta's voice, the serious running commentary she kept up as they passed from one place to another, and King Billy sang his song.

'*Tramp! Tramp! Tramp! The boys are marching…*'

Upper Duke Street, she explained. And Berry Street. She certainly seemed to know a great deal about her city. Though perhaps not *so* much. For, just then, she pointed down Bold Street, spoke of its virtues.

'Bold?' Amos snarled. 'Look up. See names. Jonas Bold. Evil man.'

He remembered the Wolof's lecture very well, remembered Tuohey's warning also – that despair was not the correct response to a history stamped into every wall of this Liverpool place. Not despair. It was the wrong strategy for one's life.

'Really?' said Miss Nesta. 'I never knew.'

She pulled the shawl closer around her face, and he realised she did so because they were beginning to attract attention. King Billy's song. This tail of black faces venturing down streets where, he guessed, such a thing would rarely, if ever, have been seen. Passers-by. And a pair of laughing policemen, one of them making monkey noises.

The road was long and wide. Beer halls and tall buildings creating a valley through which trams and carts competed for space. And where the valley opened out – its lower reaches – another great station for their railways. Not the one he'd seen on the day he'd been lost. Yet the smell the same, those rotten eggs. The noise also, so deafening it had eclipsed King Billy's singing.

'I was enjoying that,' said Nesta as they swung left down the slope alongside an enormous, pillared temple, dark-walled gardens at its rear.

'Me sing, Missie Nesta?' he asked. He hoped it might cheer her, restore her customary smile. And he was at once excited, certain he might explain his feelings better in his own tongue. The words may be unfamiliar to her, but the sentiments must shine through, would they not?

'*O gio te bo*,' he began. She has come for it again.

The Mandinka man had brought his drum. And the Guere, George Janjay, kept up the accompaniment with a pair of ebony rhythm sticks.

'You have a beautiful voice, Amos,' she told him, and he raised his voice to the grey skies, so the Lord Jesus Nyesoa Himself might hear. He sang loud enough to drown even the sparks, rattle and rumble of trams circling about an oval island of paving, beyond which they marched out onto another busy thoroughfare.

'There!' Miss Nesta tugged at his sleeve. 'My house.'

She pointed to the corner of a street climbing up and away from them, but Amos was unable to properly distinguish any single dwelling from the monotonous rest. It seemed to him the *poto* girl's home should stand out. And she had spoken her words without joy. Indeed, he could see something in her eyes akin to fear. Fear of her own dwelling? How could that be? The police, perhaps?

'You feared, Miss Nesta?' he said, as his song came to a close.

She looked him in the eye, squeezed his arm, shook her head, wiped away a tear.

'Nearly there,' she told him. 'Look, tobacco factory.'

It was meant to distract him, he knew it. He could smell it, caught glimpses of its bulk rising behind a side street to their right. More onlookers here and, off on the opposite side of the road, quite a gathering. A building with a wide and ornate façade, women of all ages, vendors, clustered around the outside with their wares. Clay pipes and pinafores. Chequered mauds and stained skirts. A market. Unmistakeable. The traders' cries. The aroma of fish and meat, fruit and vegetable. Stacks of clothing, rags and shoes spread out against the walls of adjacent streets. Subtle differences from the markets of Nana

Kru, maybe. But a market. Lord Jesus be praised. A market. Familiar. So familiar. And yes, the same place to which they'd walked two months earlier, freezing and soaked to the skin.

The gathering here today? Dozens of men. Sailors again, he thought. They must be sailors. Some of them anyway. Those, from their dancing gait, not long ashore. The coal heavers' smocks. Top-buttoned jackets and tanned faces of deckhands. Something about their demeanour as they crossed from the beer houses all along the road, pushing and jostling their way into the market building.

'Here we are, brothers,' shouted King Billy and brought his horses to a halt. 'Over to you, Tom.'

The fellow must have been waiting for them. Whiskers and thinning hair. Sad eyes, resting on sacks of weary old age.

'And what's going on?' Amos heard King Billy ask. At the same time, Miss Nesta slid behind him.

'How did they know?' she murmured, though Amos didn't entirely understand her meaning.

'The bobbies?' said Tom the Elder, for an elder of King Billy's tribe he must surely be. 'Looking for somebody – that's my guess.'

Amos gazed around, seeking enlightenment, saw the number of policemen wading through the crowd. Looking for somebody. Looking for...

'For me,' Nesta hissed. 'They're looking for me.'

5.30pm

The clock above the Rotunda Theatre's main entrance told him it was half past five and Tom glanced back along Scotland Road. Somewhere there, past Saint Anthony's, their towering temple of papist iniquity, on the opposite side, beyond his vision, stood the market. St. Martin's Market. Paddy's Market, for reasons he'd never quite fathomed – unless, of course, it was the number of Irish tinkers who plied their trade there. Above the market hall, a meeting room. And there, he assumed, Dumpling Nesta would by now have been arrested. Something else he no longer needed to worry about. And he hoped she'd rot, in whichever pit Sergeant Ladysmith might throw her.

He stepped inside once more, tipped his cap to the passing ghost of that wretch he'd pushed under the steam wagon. It was a frequent manifestation. Something, he'd decided, to do with their later relationship, some form of bonding arising from the cosmetic work on the fellow's broken corpse at Waugh's.

'Priddy!' The manager, Mister Mantlemere, yelling at him from the ground floor bar and café, the far end of the plush red carpet and the gilded mirrors. 'The scenery, if you please. Are you not supposed to be manipulating the scenery?'

'On my way, Sir,' Tom replied with his most supercilious smile. 'This moment, see.'

Opening night for the new production. *Another Man's Wife*. Farcical comedy, they called it. But he could find little in Fenton MacKay's script to amuse him. Four acts. Too many scenery changes. Some of the props to be wrestled from the storage room at the rear of the billiards hall, the rest down in the basement beyond the bowling alleys.

Duw, bowling alleys. Who'd have believed it? Americans. Today, everything was American. Disgrace, that's what it was.

And, after all the scene shifting, he'd be on his knees, pooped as a pit pony. Yet he'd have his moment. The final act and his chance to perform. The footlights beckoned. No lines, like. Was it worth it? The money he'd spent on the strychnia solution and the phosphoric acid – just enough to inflict a serious bellyache on the troupe's regular walk-on. No lines, but a start. The play's old family retainer. Talcum powder to whiten his hair. Pale greasepaint.

Yes, his moment. He'd make a name for himself, he was certain. And by the time Dumpling Nesta had served her time – well, maybe she'd have learned her lesson, learned to respect him better.

He unlocked the double doors beyond the smoke-shrouded billiard tables, dragged forth the sofas for Act One. Tom Priddy ignored the complaints from the gentlemen whose game, they muttered, he'd disturbed, though in practice their carping rekindled the flame of his anger.

It had been good, at first, to have the girl back at the house. The paper loft. He'd prepared the place carefully – well, to perfection. The palliasse and bedding. Wash bowl and jug. Rail and chest for her clothes. Home from home, it was.

And the spy hole.

He smiled, should have seen it coming. How one thing would lead to another. Too much for a man's flesh to endure, see. A Jezebel. He'd been certain she must have known. Flaunting herself. Wasn't that what she'd been doing? Intolerable temptations. The allure of her soft warmth to shatter the fast of his celibacy. The enchantment of a leap from the heights of his faith into the dark depths of her mocking eyes. The enticement of the pleasurable vinegar essence upon her skin promising to quench his own thirst. The snare of gentle rustling from the seductive cotton of her undergarments, inviting him to worship her in return for all the immoral pleasures of the flesh. But when he could contain himself no more, when he'd burst into the room – well...

There was indeed only so much a man could stand. All the pretence. Her lying protests. The stupid tears. *Iesu*.

'You're no cousin,' she'd screamed when he'd first caressed her. Well, she was right about that, of course.

So, a lesson to be learned. And the sergeant, Ladysmith, still sniffing around. But Tom Priddy couldn't have his prying eyes on Hunter Street. Not with everything else going on there.

But when she'd stormed off to this meeting, it had all been easy. Anonymous message for Ladysmith. A lie about how the policeman's quarry remained at large in Little Italy but today could be found at the seamen's meeting, above Paddy's Market.

5.50pm

'What I want to know,' called out Bessie Butler, another girl Cari knew from along Great Homer Street – though she only ever seemed to take an active part in their various social gatherings, 'is what's our position going to be on these strikes when they happen?'

Bessie was another union member. Worked at one of the factories. Normally demanded to know why the WSPU – and the NUWSS also, for that matter – weren't even more involved in campaigning for government legislation on decent working conditions for factory women. Fair question, Cari thought, though Bessie tended to dominate the meetings a bit. And it rather ignored the stand taken on behalf of factory women by some of the WSPU's leaders.

'I'm sure the Trades Council will keep us informed,' Alice Davies told her. 'And we'll play our part so long as we have shared objectives. But I think you're forgetting how much support we already give to the issue of women's sweated labour. To the iniquities of sweated labour as one of the very reasons ladies like you should have the vote! Though I have to tell you this, Bessie. Some of the union leaders – well, they leave a lot to be desired when it comes to supporting our own cause.'

Cari felt herself blush, knowing Jimmy Sexton to be just such a case in point. But needs must when the devil drives. Still, it turned her thoughts briefly, once more, to the Krooboys and Nesta. How was the meeting going? She hoped Amos Gartee had been given the chance to speak.

By then, however, Alice had brought the meeting back to some semblance of order. Yes, their own cause. The relative euphoria within some of the ranks when, earlier in the month, a revised Conciliation Bill had passed its second reading. Another "foot in the door", they'd been told. Good news. And, this time, a promise of a full week's debate in Parliament with a view to bringing the principle into law.

'And now the bad news?' shouted Doctor Ker. She couldn't be far off retirement, Cari guessed, but famous locally for her work at the Wirral Hospital for Sick Children.

'It's very disappointing,' Alice Davies told them all. 'Bitterly so, in fact. But, from our meeting yesterday, Adela tells us they have it on very good authority that Lloyd George will make an announcement about there being no further time for the Bill during this session.'

Cari was on her feet before she knew it.

'Well, there's a surprise, isn't it? It'll get pushed back to the autumn, I suppose. And then fall through the cracks again. How many times? How many? They must think we're idiots. And they're right. We are!'

'But what does Mrs Pankhurst say?' asked another of the women. 'And why wasn't she at the meeting, instead of Adela?'

There were many there among them who didn't entirely trust Emmeline Pankhurst's younger daughter – Cari included – though Adela had a certain following within the moderates. She worked hard, though, by all accounts. You had to say that for her. And a real pacifist. But it seemed to Cari her stance against war had now extended to a hatred of confrontation in all its forms, even here, where they were defending their rights as women.

'What's she proposing?' said Cari. 'We write some more strong letters? A few more petitions?'

'As it happens, Cari, no. There's to be a major demonstration on the Saturday before the Coronation.'

'London?' Cari was on her feet yet again. 'Always London. And the Coronation's still a month away. Presumably, this major demonstration will take place after the horse has bolted. After Lloyd George has made his announcement? We need action here, Miss Davies. In Liverpool. Here and now.'

'I made the point myself,' said Alice. 'But you have to accept, this is something special. We expect to put forty thousand on the streets. Fifty thousand, perhaps. One of the biggest demonstrations we've ever organised.'

'To celebrate the Coronation,' said Florrie Thompson-Frere. 'To remind His Majesty that we, also, are his loyal subjects. We deserve his intervention.'

Somebody sniggered. And Cari gritted her teeth. She supposed His Majesty might indeed intervene on behalf of the Mrs Thompson-Freres of the world – but the Mrs MacKennys?

'I think the point,' said Alice, 'is to attract the attention of the press. To show the level of our support. But we'll need to spread the word. There'll be plenty of materials. So, newspaper secretaries, all hands to the pumps, as they say. Just the problem of Liverpool North to settle.'

Each of the districts had its own secretary to distribute and sell *Votes for Women*. But the secretaries also acted as general communication agents as well – circulating information and notes about meetings to local members. But their Liverpool North secretary, Eileen O'Donnell, had died during the winter – pleurisy – and Alice Davies had been covering ever since. Yet it wasn't working very well.

'If it's London,' said Cari, 'I doubt there'll be too many able to go from our end.'

An understatement. The cost, apart from anything else. And oh, how Alice loved these London events.

'We have enough in the funds to subsidise a few train fares,' said Alice. 'But if you'd deliver some leaflets, Cari? Try to drum up support? I'm sure you could do it. A Liverpool North contingent. What do you say? Perhaps you might even think of taking over as secretary?'

There were a few discreet coughs. An uncomfortable silence. Acting as the *Votes for Women* secretary involved collecting the penny price for each copy sold and keeping the local accounts. In truth, it was the last thing in the world Cari wanted to do. Enough on her plate already. Yet she knew she could not admire, or even envy, those women who were making a mark – Mrs Pankhurst within the WSPU, and even more formidable heroines, like Besant and Macarthur – without herself once setting a foot upon the ladder. In addition, there were those discreet coughs. Less than discreet. *Trust a Maddox with the money?* Cari imagined them thinking.

'If my sister, Nesta, was here,' she began, 'I'm sure she would be more than honoured to take up this responsibility, Miss Davies. And to fulfil her duties as scrupulously as our friends here. Or as Eileen did before she was so unjustly taken from us. But Nessie cannot be here through injustice also.'

And what *is* the matter with Nesta? Cari wondered. So subdued. Changed.

'A different form of injustice,' she pressed on, 'but injustice all the same. So yes, I shall take up the duty on her behalf. On a temporary basis, at least. Though I give the branch fair warning. We cannot simply go on this way. All these promises. *"Jam tomorrow, but never jam today."* Know what I mean?'

Cari almost called her Alice. It would have been appropriate in more ways than one. For there was something about their approach to this fight – indeed, about Cari's whole life – which often reminded her of *Through the Looking Glass and What Alice Found There*.

But the thought now immediately conjured an image of rabbit holes, a premonition of falling. Falling a long, long way.

5.55pm

He had hoped Missee Nesta might have joined him once more. But no. She'd vanished as surely as a sea mist is wont to do. Yet she had escaped the clutches of the police, that was the main thing. And while Tom the Elder had indeed succeeded in getting Amos inside the gathering hall, it had not been without considerable dispute, and then only on the condition it would be Amos and no more of his fellows, the chosen men forced to wait outside.

'It's a joke, right?' Tom the Elder had yelled once they were past the doors. 'I bet half these buggers aren't even members.'

The room was full. A table at one end, long, bow-legged polished pine. Some chairs in the centre of the hall. But most of the men standing. And here at the entrance, a brace of doorkeepers who might have been twins, each of them short, though wiry as cheetahs. Hard faces. Cold eyes. Drooping moustaches.

'But they *will* be, Tom,' said one of them. 'They'll be queueing up to join after today. Not 'im, though, eh?'

He nodded in Amos Gartee's direction, a sneer on his lips.

'This lad's got more right to be here than most,' Tom the Elder told him. 'Anyway, he's with me.'

'Aren't you on the top table?' said the man.

'Not today, son. Not today.'

He led Amos to the side of the hall, received warm handshakes from a cluster of obvious admirers, all sporting the same button badge as King Billy. More horse drivers, Amos assumed, as his own hand was pumped in welcome. They laughed, friendly enough, at the clicking of his fingers and within moments they were all doing it. Cigarettes shared. Strange, but it warmed his heart, this fellowship. Yet they hushed when the speakers' table began to fill.

'Union bossmen,' Amos muttered, almost to himself.

'*Two* unions,' said Tom the Elder. 'Well, three, I suppose. Dockers, as well. But mainly the seamen and firemen – the deckhands and stokers, like. Yes?'

'Know that place,' Amos grimaced.

Indeed, he did. If there was truly a hell, it had to be the bowels of a ship, where they toiled for endless hours at the furnaces, drowning in their own sweat, sometimes drowning in reality – for he had seen men driven mad by this labour and hurling themselves overboard to meet their death in the merciful ocean.

'And Joe Cotter's boys,' Tom the Elder went on. 'Stewards, cooks, bakers and the like. Hate each other, for the most part. Remains to be seen whether they'll join any strike.'

Small world, thought Amos. For he had known a man named Jocota in Nana Kru, also. Yet this hatred? So many tribes among the white men. He'd spoken with the Wolof, Charles Tuohey – Abdul Niasse – about this. With their own peoples, he could understand. Or those they called Lascars, those from different places. A question of tongues. Customs. But it was known that the bossmen would also avoid like a pestilence the mixing of crews from one part of this England with those from another.

Amos had decided the bossmen must like it this way. More divisions, though the white men did not seem able to see them. It was difficult enough already, the Wolof had insisted. The seamen all employed by the different shipping companies, dozens of them, and then usually only for one voyage at a time. The dockers also, turning up each day to see whether one shipping company or another would want them, to load or unload a particular vessel. A slavery of their own.

Tom the Elder whispered names to him. The men themselves and the bodies they represented. Amos would never remember, saw only images, registered them as caricatures through the haze of tobacco smoke and the familiar stink of rope and sweat and diesel oil.

From the seamen's and firemen's union, a fellow with the square bulk of a rhinoceros, another with the proud moustache of the guenon monkey, and a third man, a proud silver fox. The stewards' and cooks' union was represented by one with the piercing eyes, the ebony thatch and facial hair of a mountain greyback – this Jocota. And though he'd never seen a walrus, Amos knew them from pictures, saw one now sitting alongside the stewards' headman. Finally, the dockworkers. A giant, a hippo. And, at the table's end, a man whose face was horribly shattered. This one Amos *did* remember by name, for both Miss Nesta and Missee Coconut Palm had spoken of him. Sexton.

Silver Fox spoke first. Between fits of coughing. The man, thought Amos, cannot be long for this world. And though he did not follow it word for word, Amos understood the drift of things. Praise for those who were there. Those from ships berthed in the port and those presently ashore, here in this Liverpool place where they lived. Those in the union and those who were not – though the Silver Fox railed at them. They must soon join. For this fight they must now all make. A fight for better pay, yes, but a fight also for the right to have their union heard. To be seen by the bossmen. Demands to be made. If the demands not met, then yes, a strike. Across all the land and sea.

There was heckling, of course. Shouting. This seamen's union was too small, too weak, to battle the shipowners, some said. Others, who had been in Chicago or New York, the places of the Merica people, and who wanted the fight to be led by Wobblies.

'Wobblies?' Amos murmured.

'International… Workers… of the World,' Tom the Elder whispered to him. 'One big union, that sort of thing. Anarchists, like.'

It sounded to Amos like a good thing. But the heckling went on. What about Hull? What about Southampton? And the Silver Fox told them there was no need for these Wobblies since, here it seemed, they had something called a Federation – this Federation having planned for a great gathering, in this very Liverpool place, the following week.

Yet this brought more opposition. Men who did not trust this Federation. Or, indeed, did not seem to trust those who led the unions themselves. And were the shipowners not already prepared for this strike? Was this not the shipowners' chance to crush their unions almost at birth? They'd had enough notice, after all, for there'd been the promise of a seamen's strike for two months and more.

The big docker man, the hippo, tried to keep order, thumped upon the table, though it had little effect. The protests went on.

'A ten bob rise won't do us much good,' yelled one of the men, standing on a chair, 'if our pay's still undercut by bloody blackies.'

He turned to point a finger in Amos Gartee's direction.

'These lads have already been on the cobbles,' Tom the Elder shouted back, 'nearly two months.' His voice carried across the hall, loud and clear. 'Stupid bugger. Their fight's the same as yours, lad.'

The heckler was pulled down from his chair and the Silver Fox now pointed at Amos also. An injury to one, he was saying…

'What is this tenbob?' Amos asked.

'Ten shillings,' said Tom the Elder. 'That's the demand. Recognition for the unions and ten shillings all round on their monthly pay.'

Amos made the calculations. He was good at numbering. If the seamen, the stokers, won this increase, as things stood, his own brothers would receive only half. If they were lucky. A white seaman with five pounds each month presently earned two pounds and ten shillings more than a black seaman. If they won this fight, the white seaman would now have five pounds and ten shillings. The Kru and others like them? Two pounds and fifteen shillings. The difference? Two pounds and fifteen shillings also. The gap would widen! His brothers worth even less compared to these white sailors than before. It would not do.

'A tenbob for all!' he found himself crying out.

'Ten bob for all!' one of the white seamen shouted back, and the war cry was taken up by others. 'That's right. An' we'll not be waiting for Havelock bloody Wilson to fire the starting pistol!'

Chapter Five

Saturday 17th June 1911

8.15am

The sun might be piercing the clouds this fine morning but, on the Mersey, a chill wind blew, and Huw Maddox rubbed at his painfully deformed fingers.

'Even in summer, like?' said Tom Priddy.

A long blast from the yellow funnel of the *Winifredian* drew his gaze in the liner's direction as she began her long crawl between the lines of anchored vessels waiting for a berth, out towards the Bar and, beyond, all the way to Boston. The ferry danced across her wake, swung across the brown swell, the engines throbbing for their own destination at Woodside. More ships anchored along the river even than usual, with few empty quaysides available inside the docks, now the strike had caused so many to be laid up – though the *Winifredian's* crew must plainly have refused to answer the call. Good to see they weren't all sheep, like.

'The river, see,' said old Huw. 'Always the same. Always a wind.'

Tom gripped the stanchion rail. He wasn't enjoying this. No pleasure in boats. Not safe. And how long before these ferrymen joined the strike as well? For now, the noise, those screeching seagulls. The stink of engine oil. But needs must, he supposed. His associates happy to play their part, to get the ball rolling. Not in Liverpool, though, they'd said. Too many who already knew them. So no, it was Birkenhead Park.

Yet it had fallen into place well enough, old Huw keen to see the grudge match there against Bootle, especially with Arthur Berry, Everton's outside right, spending his summer at the crease for Birkenhead.

'Well, who knows?' said Tom. 'Play our cards right and we might be able to put a word in the right ear, as well. Fixture list and programme contract for the Park?'

He knew it was nonsense. Business might be bad, but Birkenhead Park Cricket Club wasn't the answer. Not for Tom Priddy, anyway. They had their own printer over the water, of course. And yes, no problem in itself. A modest amount of arson could open up the market overnight. But Tom had other plans than simply acquiring new business.

8.30am

The station was ablaze, even so early in the morning, burning with the white light of their dresses and summer linen, the glow of banners, the heat of chatter and song, drifting through the steam and coal smoke – a number such that Alice Davies, in conjunction with the other organisations, had needed to book a special train. So, while Cari may have had her doubts about yet another London event, about whether they could whip up sufficient local support, as it turned out she could not have been more pleased to see those doubts so roundly swept aside.

'You look like a mother hen,' said Taffy. She'd bumped into him on Lime Street itself. He was on his way to a meeting, placard tucked under his arm. *War Declared: We Strike For Liberty*, read the poster glued onto the board.

And this was accurate enough, for the seamen had been out since Tuesday. Five hundred of them, according to the papers, and the dispute spreading every day. Tom Mann now also in the city, brought in to lead the strike. A real legend – at least within the unions – and, to Taffy, only one step removed from the Lord Jesus himself. Outside the unions? Professional troublemaker, her tada said, both at home and abroad.

'Lost your new chicks?' Taffy laughed.

'It's the first time for most of them,' Cari told him.

She was pleased with herself. She'd spoken at a gathering of the Women Clerks' Association, a couple of Wednesdays earlier, at Hardman Hall – not on her Liverpool North patch, of course, but Alice hadn't been available. Cari had been sick with fear. Naturally.

Literally. But she'd tried to sound enthusiastic about today's Women's Coronation Procession and nobody more surprised than Cari herself when thirty of the girls – yes, thirty – had signed up there and then both for the WSPU and the Procession as well.

A few more and they would have doubled Liverpool's WSPU membership – well, almost. It also created a problem, of course. No chance for any of them to purchase their regulation white frocks from the fancy haberdashers and dressmakers advertising in the pages of *Votes for Women*, nor from the relevant departments of Lewis's, Bunneys or George Henry Lee. So, they'd all pitched in together: material from Blacklers; and each to her turn at cutting and sewing.

Cari's task? Hats, naturally. For herself, a pretty misses' boater. The makings all bought cheap at the market. White Java straw. A trail of flowers around the brim. Purple, white and green flowers, of course. From material scraps.

'They probably won't show up,' said Taffy, 'now they've had time to think about it.'

'No? Wasn't it you who told me the whole train would be empty, Taffy? Nessie'll find them.'

But where was Nesta? She'd moved out of the paper loft weeks before, the night of the seamen's meeting above Paddy's Market. No explanation. And barely willing to even tell Cari where she was going. With the Gianellis, it had eventually transpired.

'They're probably just late,' Cari went on. 'Or lost in the crowd. Plenty of time still. Until nine. So don't you worry, *cariad*. We'll go to London and win ourselves the vote. Then, when we've done that, all you men who can't vote either – well, maybe you'll get the urge to fight for some proper liberty.'

She rapped her knuckles against his placard.

'In your dreams, Cari girl. We've got our fight here. Better pay. Stop them treatin' us like donkeys. Force the bosses to bargain with us. Your precious Parliament's never going to do it, no matter how many of us get the vote.'

'The Gospel according to Saint Tom Mann, I suppose, is it?'

She couldn't be bothered to argue really. Too busy trying to spot her little army in the middle of all those crowds. There was a brass band playing as well now. *Goodbye, Dolly Gray*, for some reason.

'If you like,' said Taffy. 'But found out anything interesting about our favourite cousin?'

It had been a busy few weeks. The weather had turned glorious and Cari had tried to take advantage by working on her new duties as one of the *Votes for Women* secretaries, albeit a temporary one. Great title for a glorified paper seller. But she'd got better at it – worked out the best places to make her pitch. Byrom Street, the Temperance Hotel and Cocoa Rooms. She'd stopped apologising each time she offered a copy for sale, switched to pressing one on every single person who passed. No longer worried whether they bought from her or not but made a point of getting them to speak, at least. Used this to gather a few together, block the doorway, get noticed. Eventually she'd be moved on as well, and start over again outside Dickson's Teashop.

Besides these things, there'd been the many meetings to get this Coronation Procession sorted, despite her reservations. Then, of course, there was Nesta. Settling her in the new hideaway with the Gianellis. Trying to find out what had driven her from the paper loft. A few scares when the bobbies had come sniffing around. Tricks to be employed so she could get out and about without being seen – with the regular assistance of Ernst Jurks, Cari was pleased to say. And a few more visits to Toxteth and Amos Gartee.

'Too busy,' she told Taffy. 'The Krooboys. All that.'

'Still?' he said. 'You never satisfied? Sexton got them into the meeting, like you wanted, didn't he?'

'Fat lot of good it did, as well. Round of applause. Plenty of promises, like. But not much support. And then what happens? Big surprise. Your national seamen's strike starts. And all those who've been taken on by Elder Dempster to scab on the 'blackies', as you call them, find themselves on strike too. And the company now threatening to bring in depot ships with gangs of non-union labour to replace all of *them*. Justice, I call it, Taffy. It'll be interesting to see whether Amos Gartee's boys stand up and fight alongside the scabs who took their jobs, won't it?'

But she already knew they would. Cari and Nesta had met them just last night and, today, they were planning to march down to the Harrington, make common cause with those who, at best, had ignored them for the past three months and, at worst, had previously helped keep them on the cobbles.

'Life's not so simple, Cari. You know bloody-well it isn't. Those blackies and coolies were undercutting pay. At least Elder Dempster had to pay full whack to the lads who replaced them. We all knew this was coming. The national strike. If your Krooboys had any sense, they'd have kept their powder dry for a while. Look where we are. The seamen only out for a few days and the big shipping lines already making noises about offers to settle. It won't be long before Elder Dempster toes the line, as well.'

'Champion,' said Cari. 'And, of course, the sailors' union will stay out until they're all on the same better pay, blacks, Chinese and whites alike. Right, Taffy?'

'Either that or agreement they'll stop using foreigners in the first place.'

Cari threw up her hands in exasperation.

'Are you serious?' she said. 'Then what happens to them? They just get stranded here.'

'Not my problem. There's enough to do, looking after our own.'

'You sound like Tada.' Cari knew he'd hate the comparison. '*Duw*, I sometimes wonder. How we could all have been brought up under the same roof, share the same blood, and all turned out so different.'

'Still believe all this nonsense about blood thicker than water, Cari? And what? Think you're better than me now? You and Nessie? We're not so very different, girl. There you both are, looking down your noses at Theresa and the MacKennys. Maybe not as bad as Pa, but not so much better, either. Not in the end.'

'Look down our noses? How…?'

'Well, at least she's not black. Or German.' He was ranting now.

'German,' she repeated. 'You mean Ernst?'

'Oh, don't give me that. Pretending you don't know. About Jurks and our Nessie.'

What was he talking about? Ernst had been a great help. Without him, Nesta might have been trapped in her hideout far more. And, this aside – well, there'd been no specific words between herself and Ernst Jurks but he must know she was fond of him. Surely.

142

'You're talking nonsense,' said Cari. 'They're just friends. And I thought he was a friend of yours, too.'

But then she saw her. Nesta. She was waving with a rolled parasol, some of Cari's women clerks bustling in her wake. A glance at the station clock. Twenty-five to nine. 'And anyway, Taffy…' Cari had the speech all worked out in her head. About how, regardless of skin colour, creed or nationality. But then she noticed something else. That damned police sergeant. Ladysmith. Three or four other policemen spreading out through the crowd. And Nesta blissfully unaware of their presence. 'Look.' Cari gripped Taffy's arm. 'Bobbies.'

'Oh, yeah.' He gave them barely a glance. Then he laughed.

'Think of something,' she said. 'Quick.'

'Don't think so, Cari. I've got my meeting. And besides, one good turn deserves another, eh?'

He strolled off, left Cari there. And the awful sick feeling deep in her stomach. Ladysmith being there, it was just chance, surely. Or maybe some calculation on the sergeant's part. Where else would Nesta be this morning except here, on her way to London with the rest of them? But if it was that straightforward, what had Taffy meant?

One good turn deserves another?

8.40am

He was warm. The first time since he'd arrived in this Liverpool place. Yes, a freshening breeze running the length of the river and mewling around the iron supports of their overhead railway. But here, out of the wind, close to the dock wall, the sun on his face, he was warm.

Inwardly? The same.

The internal glow had begun to consume him during the week after the meeting – the gathering itself having been such a chilly disappointment. If Amos had expected some sudden acceptance, a conversion of the unions to his cause – a moment like that of St. Paul upon the road to Damascus – his hopes had all been dashed. The longer the meeting had run, the more venomous it had become. One speaker after another demanding to know what the union bossmen were going to do about the monkey boat boys, Lascars and Coolies. Even Missee Coconut Palm's union man, Sexton, had spoken the same.

Yet now, just a week later, and this massively greater gathering the meeting had promised. A monstrous procession with bands and embroidered banners came snaking its way from the city's settlements just to the south. A living and breathing creature. The *Ninki Nanka* dragon of legend. More legs than a millipede.

Amos and his brothers had joined, in as much finery as they could muster, finding a place for themselves behind the standard borne aloft on one side by King Billy. And when they finally reached the open space before that temple of giants they called the Hall of St. George, near their other cavernous rail station, a second column had joined them from the north. More men than Amos had ever seen in one place. Carts set here and there among the crowd, so the speeches of their big union men might be relayed to those too distant from the orators themselves.

Demands. This tenbob. The bossmen, the ship owners, to be pressed for *recognition*. This was the word. A desire for the unions to be seen, heeded as a voice for their people. If not, a strike. And promises. Yes, the sailors and stokers would strike. There'd even been a mention for Amos and his men – though it was hard to know whether this mention meant anything in practice.

Patience. They would need more patience. Well, that was fine. For Miss Nesta – the admirable Miss Nesta who, this very day, would travel the length of this country, to their London – and King Billy as well, were now bringing regular donations of food and money. Then, more sunlight. Three days earlier. Charles Tuohey, the Wolof, had carried the news.

'It begins, my friend,' he'd said. 'You have heard?'

Amos had not.

'North End docks,' Tuohey had told him, and Amos now knew what this meant. For he had made the journey one day with King Billy himself. The length of this Liverpool's dockyards. Mile upon mile upon mile. A wonder. 'Five hundred,' the Wolof had continued. 'Sailors and firemen. Refused to sign on for the *Empress of Ireland*. Then for the *Teutonic*. Oh, and the *Baltic*.'

Those names meant less. But important vessels, surely. And a messiah arrived to lead the strike. Like the Lord Jesus Nyesoa himself. Carrying the name Tom Mann.

Today? More news. Some of the ship owners had already agreed to meet the seamen's demands. But this wouldn't end the strike. Of course. Not until the other bossmen agreed as well. More seamen joining the strike with each passing day. More and more ships laid up. Only a very few able to find a crew. Scabs, Tuohey had called them. Like scarring on a weeping wound. Or blacklegs. Like – well, he wasn't certain. No matter. For the first time, white seamen came to stand with them at the Harrington gates.

Yes, today Amos was warm.

8.40am

Tom Priddy was glad to set his feet again upon solid ground. Or, at least, upon the relative safety of the landing stage's more gentle undulations. He was pleased to leave it all behind as they climbed the incline of the covered gangway, separated from the outbound ferry passengers by a waist-high bottle green barrier.

'*Duw*,' muttered old Huw. 'More of them.'

A gaggle of women coming down the other side of the ramp, all decked out in ribbons and silk sashes, straw boaters, waving their placards and yelling slogans, laughing like loons at the echoes they created.

'You shouldn't have allowed it, see,' Tom told him. 'London? Never know what might happen.'

He had a good idea, though. At least so far as Dumpling Nesta was concerned. It had been a difficult few weeks. Disappeared back into the depths of Little Italy, she had. And the Beanpole unwilling to say precisely where she might be hiding. But today? If Cari was going off on this stupid procession in London, he could be reasonably certain the Dumpling would be there as well. At the station, like.

'Ceridwen's under the spell of those harpies,' said Huw, as they reached the top of the ramp, came out at Woodside's tram terminus.

'And Nesta?'

'How would I know?'

How, indeed! It was all something of a mystery. Dumpling Nesta flown the nest but seemingly said nothing to her older sister about the reason. Otherwise – well, in practice, the Beanpole had been exceptionally pleasant to him. Relatively speaking, anyway. But spying, of course. That was the reason. All those questions. Those supposedly innocent questions.

'Your mam?' she'd said.

His mother lay abandoned in Beddgelert's burial ground and all about her were the faded heads of frigid lilies, the desiccated emblems of eternity.

'Now with the Lord Jesus,' he'd told Cari.

The pretence of commiseration.

'And your tada?'

He'd almost been tempted to tell her.

'Wasn't around either, see?' he said, instead. 'Raised by mam's brother.'

Owen Hughes, who ran the carriage service for the Llewellyn, ferrying tourists back and forth between the hotel and the train station at South Snowdon. Taken them in when his mam was dying, though he'd been too small to remember. Not much more than a babe. By the time he was ten, Tom Priddy had learned the trade. Learned much more besides. How to take a daily whipping from Uncle Owen. How to take everything else Uncle Owen chose to inflict upon him. Filthy things, best not to dwell upon. Best not to dwell, either, on the fate of Uncle Owen Hughes. Would anybody, he wondered, ever discover the body?

Yet Cari the Beanpole's prying had eventually dried up. Foolish probing. She'd have done better to worry about the here and now, rather than the past.

'They'll be there, will they?' said Huw Maddox. 'Those friends of yours?'

Tom peered from the open deck of the tram, onto the greenery, the leafy trees, the memorial, the statuary, of Hamilton Square, with its fine town houses. Elegant, it was. More elegant than parts of Liverpool, though both cities a wonder. A true wonder.

'*Duw Annwyl*,' he said. Good Lord. ''Keen, they are. Proper keen. Big chance, this is. For the Society, like.'

It amused Tom Priddy. A credit to his powers of invention. Orphans. Yes, the irony. The hypocrisy. How this old fool should care so much for other orphans when…

'Sometimes…' Huw began.

'Wish you could talk it through with Taffy, I suppose?'

'It *will* all be his, one day. The business, like.'

'Not much interest though, has he? In the business.'

'Come around, he will,' murmured Huw Maddox. 'Once he's settled. Seen the error of his ways with that papist of his.'

'Perhaps,' said Tom Priddy. And in his mind he shuffled the playing pieces once more. They swung briefly right onto Conway Street, swayed immediately left again towards the tram's destination at Claughton and the south side of Birkenhead's impressive park. He caught a glimpse of the white clock tower above the Electric Light Works. Dumpling Nesta – surely in the Bridewell by now. Then Taffy's comeuppance – the plan, he decided, finally formed, simply waiting the proper opportunity. And old Huw himself, of course. Afterwards, he thought, as the tram turned along Park Road South, just Cari the Beanpole to think about.

8.40am

Cari couldn't shake Taffy's words from her head. Some stupid revenge for Nessie spilling the beans to Tada about Theresa MacKenny? But by then she was running for the brass band. The Liverpool Clarion Brass Band, she could now see. Playing the *Marseillaise* at that precise moment.

'Stop!' she yelled. 'Stop!' And she gripped the sleeve of the conductor's blouse, pulled down the baton, causing the music to fall away also. 'Play *The March of the Women* instead. Play it now.'

'Now?' the woman said and shook Cari's hand from her arm. 'And a polite request would have sufficed.' But she turned to her band in any case. 'Now, ladies. *The March of the Women.*'

The lead trumpet offered Cari a smile, put the mouthpiece to her lips and blew the dozen familiar notes of the introduction. It acted like a magnet. Always did. She'd seen it so many times.

> *"Shout, shout, up with your song!*
> *Cry with the wind, for the dawn is breaking."*

The song not only served to lift a body spiritually but, at the same time, inevitably and unfailingly, brought them to also seek physical contact in their sisterhood, one with the other.

> *"March, march, swing you along,*
> *Wide blows our banner, and hope is waking."*

To any eye unfamiliar with the phenomenon, it would have seemed those several hundred women were, at once, sucked towards the centre of some maelstrom created by the bandswomen. And they were less than polite in their coming together, the words rising from their lungs as they pushed aside other passengers, bystanders, station porters and policemen alike.

> *"Song with its story, dreams with their glory*
> *Lo! they call, and glad is their word!"*

Yet now Cari could see neither the sergeant nor their Nessie, simply a gathering surf, indistinguishable whiteness, above which there was the occasional mast or sail of banner pole and placard, the singing like whitecaps breaking around Formby Point.

> *"Loud and louder it swells,*
> *Thunder of freedom, the voice of the Lord!"*

Where was she? Cari found herself shaking all over, afraid her ploy was too little, too late. Visions of Nesta already being hauled into a Black Maria, a hurry-up wagon. But no. There. Laughing like a loon as she pushed her way towards her sister.

'Cari,' she cried. 'You goose. This your idea? To get us all on the train?'

> *"Long, long — we in the past*
> *Cowered in dread from the light of heaven."*

Cari lunged for her, yelled into her ear.

'Bobbies,' she said. 'Right behind you.'

Nesta spun around but, a head shorter than her sister, she stood no chance at all of being able to see them. Not see them. But hear them?

Oh, yes. Even over all those voices. The stentorian tones of Sergeant Ladysmith. Close, as well.

'Make way there, ladies. Make way. Police business.'

He should, in truth, have known better. A dog catcher could have expected more by way of cooperation from the strays whose litters of pups he was threatening. These were women with their blood already risen today against the forces of law and order which, in their eyes, were responsible for keeping them in a state of subservience. Worse, these were Liverpool women. Divided, perhaps by individual affiliations but stitched together, at least, by several strong threads – just one of which was a collective antipathy to the police.

"Strong, strong — stand we at last,
Fearless in faith and with sight new given."

Cari watched, therefore, as so many of their number turned, voices lifting ever louder, and it seemed some pushing and shoving had begun. There was a police whistle. Ladysmith shouting again.

'Come on, ladies. You don't want any arrests. Not today.'

Cari grabbed Nesta's wrist.

'Let's get out of here,' she said. And then they were hurrying through, aiming for the Lord Nelson Street exit.

'What about your new recruits, Cari? You can't just abandon them.'

'They'll be fine, Nessie. Just run.'

"Strength with its beauty, Life with its duty,
(Hear the voice, oh hear and obey!)"

She'd stopped, dragged Cari to a halt. They both looked back, hard to make out exactly what was happening, but it felt ugly, the general air of celebration turning sour, as the stations sometimes stink of rotten eggs.

'No, they won't,' said Nessie. 'Besides, you need to be in London. And me? I'm sick of hiding, Cari.' She pulled herself free. 'Really, I mean it. Take them to the Big Smoke. And when you get back – well, you know where I'll be.'

"These, these — beckon us on!
Open your eyes to the blaze of day."

Before Cari could stop her, Nesta had headed back towards Sergeant Ladysmith and his men. And Cari herself? All she could think was that she'd not asked her about Ernst Jurks.

10.05am

Huw Maddox jerked forward, as best he was able, in the Birkenhead Park Cricket Club's green canvas deck chair.

'*Diawl gwyrion!*' he yelled. Silly devil. Berry — his hero — had missed an easy catch from Bootle's star player, Ben Johnson.

'You don't mind meeting here, Mister Maddox?' said one of Tom Priddy's associates. Rees, this one. From Flint. It seemed appropriate somehow. Grey men, both of them, hard as Welsh granite on the inside, he was sure, despite the affable exterior.

'Good as any for me, like,' said Huw. 'Long way from home for you boys though, isn't it?'

'Get lots of support here, we do.' The other fellow, the one who called himself Lewis. 'For the Society.'

But what had they said to set old Huw on his guard like this? Tom could read the suspicion on his face.

'And what say I get us a tray of tea?' Rees beamed. He glanced back at the pavilion behind them, dappled grey by its surrounding trees.

'Think they'll have *bara brith*?' said Tom Priddy. 'Good, that would be, Uncle Huw.'

A ripple of applause from the crowd as Ben Johnson batted the ball to the boundary through deep square leg. Tom clapped his hands, appreciative of the shot and ignoring old Huw's support for the other team. He'd played a bit himself. Blaenau. After he'd freed himself from Owen Hughes. When he'd found his voice. More ways than one. The Blaenau choir, as well. In his mind a smile formed, though as usual it failed to find an escape route to his lips.

'Tea?' said old Huw, and it seemed he may have dropped his guard. 'Nice.'

Rees picked his cap from the grass, pushed himself up out of his chair, headed through the gate to the pavilion.

'So, what d'you think, Uncle Huw. The lottery, like?'

'What's it going to cost me? That's what I need to know.'

The satisfying smack of leather on willow, the Bootle batsmen making two more runs.

'Why, bless you, Mister Maddox' said Lewis, 'nothing at all. Some modest outlay at the beginning, of course. We need a small fund, see? Prizes for the first winners. But after this – well, from our experience elsewhere, this one will fly.'

'Done fine everywhere, they say. More than just fine. Welsh Orphans Society. Can't fail, see. Not in Liverpool.'

'Both seem to have done nicely for yourselves, too,' Huw Maddox snapped at Mister Lewis, surveyed the man, from the top of his straw boater, past the well-cut blue blazer and flannels, to the toe tips of those two-tone casual shoes.

Duw Annwyl, Tom thought. Not going well, this isn't. He stared out past the white glare of the scoreboard, towards the bandstand beyond the pitch.

'Mister Maddox,' said Lewis with a distinct note of reproof, 'here are the costs. All the costs. Income from sale of the tickets. Amount yet unknown. The most modest of payments to the vendors. The commercial rate paid to yourselves for the printing work undertaken. A mere five percent administration fee for myself, and for Mister Rees, including all administrative disbursements. The rest, every penny, to those poor unfortunates. Think of them, Mister Maddox. Poor wee orphans.'

Old Huw Maddox threw a glance in Tom Priddy's direction. Was that a trace of guilt, perhaps?

Rees returned with a tray of tea and cakes while, out at the crease, some altercation, a dispute with the umpire.

'Sorry,' said Rees. 'No *bara brith*, I'm afraid.'

'And all proper?' Huw Maddox asked. 'Legal, like?'

'Good gracious, sir. How *can* you put such a question?'

10.15am

The creature clawed at Cari's stomach, tore at her flesh and roared in her ears, its breath rancid in her face – a beast sprung straight from Pastor Jenkins's hell. Guilt. It pursued and tortured her all the way to Crewe, where they picked up another considerable contingent of women. To Crewe and far beyond, as she swayed along the train's corridors, unable to settle in one compartment or another, and wondering where Nessie would be at this precise moment. They'd have hauled her off to the Bridewell, of course. Charged her. With what? Embezzlement. Simple larceny. Bare whitewashed walls. A single suspended plank to serve as both seat and bed, bone-bruisingly uncomfortable for either purpose. And there she would stay until Monday, when she'd be taken before the Beak. Magistrate's Court.

'Won't you come and sit with us, Cari?'

Alice Davies. And Cari had been caught unawares.

'Did you see them?' she said. 'The arrest, I mean.'

'It was all a bit confused,' Alice replied. 'Has she nobody to speak for her? Some mitigation perhaps?'

Cari had heard them, Alice and her middle-class women. No smoke without fire, they'd said. And worse.

'I sometimes think it's what we're all about,' Cari told her. 'Mitigation. Pleading for some crumb of comfort. A few votes here. A lessening of sentence there. But what about justice, Miss Davies? What if my sister's simply innocent? What if we're not happy to settle for the same mockery of democracy afforded to our menfolk?'

'I understand you being upset, my dear. It's natural. But you should be prepared. They're likely to come down heavily on her. A fugitive all this time. And being one of our members, a thorn in the authorities' side already. She will need her family around her.'

Cari hadn't yet calculated how Tada would respond to all this. Her natural inclination had been to abandon this excursion, tell him the bad news, but she'd been swayed by Nesta's own insistence she should proceed. Nesta was right. Nothing to be done. So, she'd scribbled him a note, caught one of the Parcel Boys and tipped him thruppence to deliver it. But beyond this? Family? Cari convinced now that Taffy had been complicit in her arrest.

'They cannot give her more than a month, surely,' she said.

'You have to be looking at six,' Alice replied. 'And hard labour. Not unusual in petty larceny cases.'

Six months? How was it possible? A slummy neighbour of Wyn's, old man O'Dare, had been given only two for beating his wife half to death, no more than a few weeks before. It was all too much, and Cari wept, choking on her tears.

'There could have been a riot,' she sobbed. 'If she hadn't given herself up.'

'A riot you would have instigated, don't you think? I rather wish you'd not taken that upon yourself. The band, I mean.'

'Ideas above my station, I suppose.' Cari had intended no pun. But at least it made her smile, lifted her spirits somewhat.

'I shouldn't say so. Though some of the other ladies have certainly expressed concern. Discipline, you know? It's very important to our movement. And when there's such a large and sudden influx of new members – well, it's bound to excite some attention. Questions about whether all those women you've brought us are truly committed.'

Did she see Cari as a threat to her authority? Cari and her little troop of women clerks. Had she not been so distressed, she should probably have laughed. It was nonsense, of course. Or so she thought at the time. Yet we are shaped by our memories, she knew, and wondered whether it might be these events, or those still in her future, which would bring her destiny.

Memories are not fixed, however. This she also knew. Often dishonest, fluid as water. Capable of interpretation to suit changing needs, the passing of years, the diversity of circumstance. And sometimes folk were proficient at warping even recent memories. An example had been that stupid image of the Krooboys' homeland – mud huts and cannibals. Yet, even just a few months later, she already saw it as something she may have heard from a third party. Her own guilt as an ignorant girl assuaged. Somebody else's actions, or a denial of her own.

Like her confrontation with Haldane. Like her first involvement with window breaking. Like her volunteering as a paper seller. Like her recruitment of those women. Activism thrust upon her, she liked to think, knowing it for a lie. An understanding that, not born to it either, it was activism she sought to acquire. So, she wondered. Whether Alice Davies was correct to sense some seed of insurrection in Cari, even then.

1.25pm

Amos Gartee sipped at his drink. Pleasant. Refreshing. Fruits and herbs. A Vim Tonic, the Wolof had told him. A colourful red and blue tin plate promoting the beverage was screwed to the front of the counter, just below the two collecting jars, one "For the Striking Seamen", the other for the "Elder Dempster Strikers". It was something, he supposed.

'This new king,' said Amos. The Vim Tonic was better than beer, Tuohey had remarked, though Amos would have preferred a palm wine. 'Him already king?'

Charles Tuohey set down his own glass.

'Came to the throne a year ago. But their coronation next week. These things take time – to arrange properly.'

Amos had spent all morning at the Harrington gates with his brothers and a few of the white seamen – though those had mostly stood apart. But by midday there'd been little activity and he had been pleased when the Wolof suggested they might combine some business with a little pleasure. So, this temperance bar, near Tuohey's home, near the swimming cavern, the wash houses and gymnasium where he worked. No work today, however. Some mechanical fault, the swimming cavern closed while their Corporation made repairs. Yes, a magnificent thing also. The great Corporation of this Liverpool place, an enterprise so vast that it controlled everything, it seemed. The spider's web of tramways, the electric lights, the very water with which their Vim Tonic was mixed – well, everything. Another wonder.

'Women think this king, he give them votes?'

'I believe that's their general idea. A show of loyalty to the Crown. A show of their strength, their numbers, at the same time. The hope King George and Queen Mary may somehow tip the thing in their favour.'

'King George,' Amos laughed. Since they'd learned about the coronation, the brothers had begun to bestow this title upon the Guere, George Sanjay. It was a fine joke. Now they had their own King George, as well as their own King Billy.

'The fifth monarch of that name,' Charles Tuohey told him. 'I imagine the square was named for one of the others.'

Just a few paces along the street. The Wolof had taken him there. Leafy trees surrounding a garden with pathways, the whole thing surrounded by elegant houses – though many of them, it seemed to Amos, now fallen to neglect. But, among them, the boys' home, which had once housed Tuohey himself until the Irish family had taken him under their wing.

'Will king do so? Tip this thing?' Amos chose the words with care, in imitation of the phrase the Wolof had used. In a place like this temperance bar, where he and Tuohey were the only black faces, he was even more acutely aware of the way his tongue must betray him. Less here, in this quarter so filled with Chinese and others. But still…

'Of course not,' Tuohey laughed. 'But the women will have a fine time in London, I suppose.'

A fine time? Amos hoped not too fine. He felt a pang of jealousy. Miss Nesta there with Missee Coconut Palm. He had become more attached to the younger sister than he could have imagined, wanted to ask the Wolof how *this* thing might function here. The whole question of bride wealth. For true, his heart was pure in his feelings for her. Yet what might be her price?

3.35pm

If Alice Davies doubted Cari in any way, it did not prevent her being selected as one of the procession's *Votes for Women* vendors, and thus setting her upon yet another fateful course.

From Euston, some of them had caught the tram, already bedecked in its coronation finery, to the Thames Embankment from where the march was due to commence at five-thirty that evening. Yet even two hours before the allotted start time, chaos already reigned. In the way of such events, perhaps, with white-dressed women milling around, seeking direction but receiving little from the WSPU stewards except exhortations to be patient.

Cari supposed they could blame Mister Gladstone. He had, after all, before she was even born, set down a taunt. If women truly wanted the vote, they would have to take to the streets in great numbers. Demonstrate their ardour. A challenge he plainly believed they would never meet. Yet he'd been wrong. And there had been large demonstrations ever since. But surely never such as this.

It was daunting simply to be there. A part of it all. Overwhelming. So Cari was relieved when Alice approached her about selling papers along the route, sent her off to the van where she collected a knapsack full of yesterday's edition, and where she was given instructions. Follow the river only so far as Waterloo Bridge, then north along Lancaster Place to reach the Strand, where she turned left until she arrived in Trafalgar Square.

Her relief was short-lived, however, for the solitary walk across London, though efficacious in itself, served only to fuel her fears for Nesta's fate. Yet little time for introspection once, as instructed, she took up her stand outside Morley's Hotel.

She'd determined to follow her usual strategy, to engage folk in conversation rather than worry too much about sales. But she had barely taken the first copy from the canvas satchel when a woman snatched it from her fingers, pressed a penny into her palm and beamed at her with a pearly smile.

'Well done, my dear,' the woman cried. 'Oh, well done. And look.' She waved the front page in Cari's face. 'How clever. Who'd have thought? Such a gathering.' There was a picture of Old Father Thames, rising from the river and watching their great procession, marching along the Embankment. 'How remarkably accurate,' said the woman. 'Such prediction.'

Even so, Cari was shocked. More so when the experience was repeated only moments later. Then again and again over the intervening hour or more when, with her bag almost empty and over five pounds in her pocket – from both sales and small donations of half-crowns, shillings and even a ten bob note, gifted to her by some foreign lady – the heightened excitement upon the air and the sound of martial music announced that the procession was finally approaching.

Cari thought her heart should break for the sight of it, since the apparent chaos she'd left at Blackfriars was now turned to a thing of orderly elegance and staggering beauty.

There were crowds by now. Well-wishers in numbers she could not recall having seen at any of their previous activities. Crowds, cheering as the head of the column came into sight. Their "General", of course: Flora Drummond, mounted, in military tunic and officer's peaked cap. A little overweight, Cari thought, but smiling happily as she had every right to be, for she had organised most of this day, along with the redoubtable Mrs Downing.

Next, another of their number Cari recognised from pictures in *Votes for Women*: Charlotte Marsh, given the honour today of bearing the WSPU colours, for she had been the first of their martyrs, the first to suffer the outrage of forced feeding. Behind Charlotte, one of the principal pageant figures – a woman on a white horse, helmet, white surcoat, lance and banner. The programme said that Joan of Arc represented the militant women's ideal, though Cari wondered what her tada would have said about them venerating such a symbol of Catholic France. There was even talk about the Vatican considering making her a saint – Joan of Arc, naturally, not this woman, whoever she might be.

Behind her, their New Crusaders, all glorious in purple, green and white, as a fitting escort to the true leadership of this Holy War. Mrs Tuke, Mrs Pethick-Lawrence, Christabel Pankhurst and her mother, Mrs Pankhurst herself – proud as a lioness, the very image of implacable determination.

Yet it was those who followed in Pankhurst's wake for whom the crowd raised the roof. The Prisoners' Pageant. Seven hundred-strong, gathered from every one of the participating organisations. Seven hundred who had already seen the inside of a prison cell or worse. For the cause. Seven hundred in virginal white, each carrying a lance of silver with the pennon of liberty. Seven hundred, preceded by a simple banner. *From Prison to Citizenship.*

Cari was not the only one there, at the corner of Morley's Hotel, with eyes clouded by tears – though, for Cari, there was the added poignancy of concern for Nesta. Those women had served their time but were now free once more. Whereas Nessie – albeit an innocent victim of a different sort…

4.35pm

Tom Priddy was pleased with his day's work, so far.

'Going to help with the rest?' Huw Maddox asked him, as the tram from the Pier Head trundled up Dale Street. Tom knew the old man had left a big print job for the Co-op on City Road, half-finished this morning. But now he'd just have to manage on his own.

Tom had bigger fish to fry. And he wanted to let old Huw wallow a while longer in his despair at Birkenhead Park's performance, beaten so easily by the Bootle team, his Evertonian hero Arthur Berry's dismal performance and even Marshall – who'd scored a century just the previous week against Formby – unable to turn the tide.

'The Dearly Departed beckon, see,' Tom smirked. 'Grieving mam and dad. Waugh's at half-past five, sharp. After that – well, tonight's big show.'

'An' this lottery business. You're sure, like?'

'Safe as houses, *uncle*.' Tom patted him on the shoulder as old Huw got to his feet for the Byrom Street stop. 'Firm as family.'

Tom thought about it some more, alone on the seat now, and heading for the Rotunda. He still wasn't entirely sure where the venture might lead him. No intention, certainly, of inheriting some down-at-heel printing business. This much, at least, was plain. Yet the scheme had merits.

First item of business, he mused to himself. He thumped his hand against the wooden slats of the bench, demanding order from the audience populating the meeting room of his mind. His Lord Jesus among them. The business must yield me a tidy profit in as short a time as may be possible. The lottery will fulfil this end. Agreed? The audience was unanimous. Aye, agreed.

Second item. For the sake of efficiency, the lottery scheme should also serve to hasten old Huw's downfall. Agreed? Again, not a single nay-sayer. No abstentions either.

Third agenda item. I propose, Tom Priddy argued, that the business, even following such setbacks as the lottery might inflict upon its owner, shall still be sufficiently viable for sale to a new proprietor. All in favour?

For the first time, he heard the sounds of dissent. Doubts.

In any case, they were passing St. Anthony's and approaching the Rotunda.

Item deferred, he decided, and promptly closed the meeting.

5.55pm

After the heads of the procession had passed, much of what followed was a blur of brass bands, the ranks of their marching multitude, five abreast and so finely in step, wheeling in such precision from Northumberland Avenue, past the Charing Cross and into Pall Mall, they might have been the Brigade of Guards. Pageant groups or floats, as well. Groups from all across the world. More famous women from history. Druidic and Roman priestesses, Victorian crinolines, Florence Nightingale, and Grace Darling.

A couple of women stepped from the pavement, asked for the paper, and thus left Cari's knapsack entirely empty, a further guinea added to the amount already collected, and it occurred to her, despite the modest size of the WSPU's membership, that most of those sections she'd already seen had either originated from, or been arranged by their own women, while the far more numerous ranks of the NUWSS, with their red, white and green, were still to come. She knew it from the programme. And not simply the NUWSS but all the other organisations. Dozens more. It could be an hour at least before the tail of the column came along.

With no papers left to sell, it seemed only proper she should make haste, put a spring in her step and catch up perhaps with Mrs Mansell Moulin's Welsh contingent. Yet she stopped just long enough to purchase some sustenance – bitter Bramley apples from the barrow of a fruit and vegetable vendor. Cooking apples, but the only ones he had left. She'd eaten worse and, while she dropped her rations into the knapsack, the barrow man took the trouble to complain about the rubbish left behind by the event. Discarded placards and the like.

But she had no time to argue with him and had not long left Trafalgar Square, running along Pall Mall, when she almost literally collided with the only sign of opposition she'd seen all day. Hired sandwichmen, with boards on their backs and chests, bearing the legend, *Women Do NOT Want the Vote!*

'Shame on you,' Cari shouted into their faces.

'Shame, lady?' a fellow laughed at her. 'A man has to earn his living, don't he? Nothing wrong with an honest day's pay.'

'And who is it – pays your wages?'

'Why, it's Lord Curzon his-self, dearie,' cried another. 'Can't say no fairer than that.'

She had no real idea who Lord Curzon might be and did not greatly care. The men seemed to have recently emerged from an elegant portico on her left – the Reform Club announced an ironic polished plaque. And, as Cari glanced up, she noticed women leaning from a first-floor balcony, heard snatches of their deliberately loud conversation.

'Look at this venomous snake,' shouted a horse-faced harridan. 'Just look.' And she stabbed her fat finger towards the procession.

'A slithering serpent of discontent,' called another, a woman in her thirties, with an American accent, who theatrically waved a champagne bottle in one hand and sipped from an overflowing glass in the other.

Somebody from a passing contingent – the Catholic Women's Suffrage Society – noticed the Antis, or perhaps heard the comment. In either case, Pall Mall was filled with the singing voices of this multitude, while placards, banners and pennants were waved in defiance towards the open windows.

'Don't take it personal, missie,' said one of the sandwichmen.

But by then she was moved to personal rage, admiring the measured composure of the marchers, yet entirely unable to share it. Fatigue, perhaps. Or this sense of being a stranger in a strange place.

She remembered the fruit vendor, the small pile of broken placard staves, and ran back there, pulled a stout length of wood from the heap, hefted the thing in her hand. It seemed perfect and, as Cari reversed her steps, approached the sandwichmen again, she reached into the knapsack and took out the firmest of her apples, calculated the distance, then – using the formidable skills learned while playing rounders with neighbourhood children in Cartwright Place – she tossed the Bramley into the air. As it rose, Cari gripped the stave firmly with both hands, brought it down and behind, then swung with all her might, smiling in anticipation of the retribution it might wreak, fearful that, when it struck, the apple might simply shatter.

But it did not. It was firm, crisp and lacked all sweetness, flew straight and true, caught horse-face with a sickening crack to the side of her face so that she fell, crashed into the woman with the champagne. The bottle dropped from her fingers, plummeted into the crowd below, spraying them with froth and barely missing an infant in a baby carriage. It splashed down, banged and bounced instead upon the head of a sandwichmen, floored him, senseless, while the bottle itself exploded on the paving in a final eruption of shattered green glass and spume.

Screams. Cries of outrage from the crowd. From the open windows of the Reform Club, as well. People stared at her, at the makeshift bat still in her guilty hands. Behind her, the fruit vendor yelling at the top of his voice. Then a police whistle. So Cari dropped the stave, clutched the knapsack close to her side, and she ran, pausing only long enough to see the sandwichman was conscious, rubbing at his head and therefore, she felt certain, not mortally wounded. But this was little consolation. Her child-like, tangy relish at the prospect of the deed had turned to bitter cider in her mouth. How close she had come to injuring the babe. And how swiftly had the joy at Alice's faith in her crumbled to dust.

5.55pm

At Waugh's Funeral Furnishers, the bereaved parents, supportive aunts and uncles, all draped in black, sought advice – through their racking tears – about the service. Advice about appropriate hymns. For they were incapable of recalling whether their poor daughter might have had one or two favourites. Something apposite. And Waugh himself, Tom noted, seemed incapable of helping them, touched as he was by his own familiarity with the family, sharing the devastation of their loss.

Into this uncomfortable silence, Tom Priddy raised his counter-tenor's reedy yet astonishingly soothing voice to the parlour's ceiling.

> *'I hear Thy welcome voice,*
> *That calls me, Lord, to Thee.'*

An American hymn, of course. But popular enough here now, as well. He'd have preferred to sing them the Welsh version, *Gwahoddiad*. Oh, how the Blaenau choir loved it!

> *Mi glywaf dyner lais,*
> *Yn galw arnaf fi.*

It was not what they'd expected, but after they recovered from the initial shock, yes, they said, *I hear Thy welcome voice*, a perfect choice. And might he sing it for them during the funeral?

'Don't really sing in public,' he told them. 'Too nervous, like.'

But he allowed himself to be persuaded, of course. He kept a close eye on Mister Waugh, as well, spotted the moment when the fellow realised he might have an additional asset here.

For his own part, Tom would have preferred to sing the lullaby, *Suo Gân*. Appropriate, in one way, he thought. The Welsh so very beautiful. And what would be wrong in putting the fun into funerals?

> *Huna blentyn ar fy mynwes,*
> *Clyd a chynnes ydyw hon.*

But the English so woefully lacking. And not a hymn, of course.

> *Sleep my darling, on my bosom,*
> *Harm will never come to you.*

He'd sung it to himself – well, to the girl, really – all the time he'd worked on her with Mister Clamp the mortician. How old? Fourteen? Fifteen? Not for the first time, he'd found himself distracted, pitifully distracted, by the naked flesh now brought back to some semblance of life.

Something in the girl's reconstructed features, as well. Reminded him of Cari the Beanpole. And somehow, in this moment of strange ecstasy, his distraction had metamorphosed towards Cari herself. In his head, while Waugh resolved some further details with the family, he heard that song again. *Ceridwen.*

6.45pm

She ran until she lost both her pursuers and herself in the gathering dusk of late evening. But she eventually and cautiously found her way back onto the route. By then the last of the procession had passed and the great tide of London's traffic and population had closed again over the streets so recently filled with the shifting sandbanks of women's suffrage. So long after, in fact, that by the time Cari arrived outside the Albert Hall, having asked on several occasions for directions, it was impossible to gain admission. First, it was apparently packed to the rafters for the main rally gathering. And, second, there was a cordon of bobbies outside, which she did not dare try to approach. So, she rather miserably continued along Kensington High Street to the Empress Rooms.

The rallies had been staggered to some extent, to allow those here in this overflow meeting to still enjoy several of the speakers. And, by the time she'd pressed herself into the back of the throng – still expecting to be arrested at any moment and sharing Nesta's fate – Mrs Besant was already on the platform, delivering her speech for the second time that night. And such a clear delivery. She was, by then, in her mid-sixties, Cari thought. But what did she know about her? Some notoriety recently in the pages of the *Post and Mercury* for her part in bringing the young Indian boy, Krishnamurti, to England, claiming he was a reincarnation of our Lord Jesus Christ.

The movement she'd established to replace Christianity entirely – The Star in the East, she called it. Her advocacy on behalf of the Theosophical Society – all of which Tada condemned so violently as "atheist dabbling with the occult." But, personally, Cari had been schooled by others in the WSPU about Mrs Besant's part in the Great London Dock Strike and the famous Matchgirls' Strike, both over twenty years earlier. Mrs Besant couldn't have succeeded without the strike committees of workers who must actually have made these disputes effective, but this was a woman of substance, and Cari admired her. Exotic, here on one of her rare return visits from India.

'The question you are here to support,' Mrs Besant was saying, 'is not a woman's question, but a human question, as important for men as it is for women. For men and women cannot be separated into two separate halves. They are one humanity, halves of a single whole, and all humanity is the poorer, all humanity is wronged, when in any question it divides one sex from the other and tries to range them in opposite camps.'

Try telling this to Tada, Cari thought. Or strange Cousin Thomas who seemed, with each week that passed, to have an even tighter hold over her father. Or Taffy, so contemptuous of their cause and yet such an advocate of solidarity in most other circumstances. Taffy the police informer? Taffy who had betrayed the sanctity of family loyalties?

'What will you do with the vote when you have it?' Annie Besant was demanding. 'It is the practical question of tomorrow, because the vote is nearly won.'

'Hear, hear!' screamed a woman just off to Cari's right. The woman was jumping up and down to see the platform better – a problem which, thankfully, Cari didn't share. She saw that it was Bessie Butler, one of the newer members and, Cari was fairly certain, a worker at Bibby's oilcake mill. She had the yellow jaundiced appearance, which seemed so typical of those employed at the factory. Cari edged closer to her, needing some companionship, while Mrs Besant continued with her oration.

'And it is on your use of it,' she said, 'that the value of the vote will be judged by history. For men have had the vote by thousands, and hundreds of thousands.'

'Oh, Sweet Jesus,' said Bessie, as Cari touched her shoulder, 'I'd have thought you'd be off at the Albert Hall with all the big knobs, Cari.'

'Couldn't get in,' said Cari.

'The whole of the last century,' the distant but clear voice of Mrs Besant reminded them, 'was a continual repetition of widening out the suffrage. And yet, in spite of this, you see misery today, drunkenness today, ignorance today, wretchedness today.'

'You can say that again,' Bessie shouted, and drew reproachful glances from those standing around them. 'Bloody men! Better off without the buggers.'

'But why should you say so?' Cari asked her. 'I mean, about me being at the Albert Hall. With the big knobs.'

'Oh, come off it, girl,' she laughed. 'You're one of them, eh? Posh, like.'

Posh? Cari wondered what she meant. They were certainly better-off than many. She knew it. But posh? Surely this wasn't how Bessie saw her? Or how others might see her? Yet Mrs Besant demanded their attention.

'Oh,' she cried, 'if women cannot use their vote any better than men have done, I fear we shall hardly repay the expenditure.'

'She's got that right, too,' said Bessie, and incurred yet more wrath from their neighbours, straining to hear the words of wisdom. 'Got to grab it,' Bessie hissed in Cari's ear. 'Like Jeannie Mole says. No bloody politician's ever going to give us anything unless we fight for it. Not to the working class. The real working class.' She gave Cari that look again. 'Have to use our industrial muscle. Take it for ourselves, girl.'

It was precisely the line Taffy would normally take – for men, at least. Syndicalism, was what he called it. And Cari had never heard Jeannie Mole speak. She was old now. But another Liverpool legend. Well, a legend among the women, she should say. Organising women workers into their own unions. The Women's Industrial Council. All those campaigns against sweated labour.

'But if you bring it,' said Mrs Besant, 'to your women's hearts and women's brains; if you remember how the nation is only the family, and cannot do without the mother any more than it can do without the father; if you realise that, when men and women join hands in legislation, as in other things, you are not simply doubling a vote, you are multiplying a nation.'

Is it like this? Cari wondered. The nation as a family? Most of the time it didn't feel much like one – unless she meant one of those families divided against itself. And Cari thought about her own. About the bitter rift between Tada and Taffy.

'For the women will bring new elements into legislation,' Mrs Besant inspired them. 'The women will bring a new type of thought, a new power of application and administration.'

And I must do the same, Cari calculated. This should be my goal. To bring a new power of application, which might heal the rift, regardless of what Taffy may have done.

Mrs Besant concluded her speech with an exhortation that they should now go forth, grown into the noblest sort of women, fighting for their cause with all the strength given them by the power which is neither male nor female, but expresses itself equally in both.

Cari had no idea what she meant. Was this a Theosophical reference? Perhaps. Yet she was more concerned with Bessie's surprising view. That Bessie did not consider her working class.

Not working class? It had stung her, and Cari determined she should speak with her further on the subject. But, for now, she was keen to get back to Euston, catch the overnight train home again.

She left the hall early, remaining only long enough to hear the joyous announcement that Prime Minister Asquith had, this very day, promised the next session of Parliament would afford a full week's debate to the Conciliation Bill. Surely, this time, there could be no going back. Victory was in sight. A limited victory, of course, but a step along the way – this seemed to be the general mood.

'Well, we've heard it all before,' Bessie sneered.

Something else Cari determined she should discuss with her. That cynicism.

6.55pm

Yes, not a bad day's work, Tom Priddy concluded yet again. Bootle's victory, of course, and old Huw's hopes so badly dashed. The ease with which Tom's associates had baited the lottery trap. The praise heaped upon him by Mister Waugh for his performance. And later, when he'd bought the evening paper, more cricketing good news, an easy win for Lancashire on this third day of their match against Gloucestershire. Yes, his time in Liverpool had turned him into an avid Lancastrian.

Then, there was Dumpling Nesta. Arrested, surely. Hopefully now in a cell and beginning to learn some lessons. Of course, she wouldn't know he was responsible for her incarceration, but that would come soon enough. Reject him, would she?

Yet the icing on his cake? Tonight's performance at the Rotunda.

He recalled how somebody had once described *Gipsy Jack* as a *"splendid farrago of meretricious buffoonery"*. A play about rogues and brigands. It was supposed to be a satire about Bonaparte. It said so on the billboards. *Gipsy Jack, or the Napoleon of Human Life*. Well, he didn't know about Bonaparte, but there were threads of Gipsy Jack's character with which Tom closely associated himself. The iniquities of his birth. The mother who'd died and dumped him into the proverbial ditch of his childhood. The battles he'd been forced to fight. His escapes. His lust for revenge.

'Well?' the theatre manager had asked him. 'The Harman part, can you do it?'

The member of the troupe who should have played beggarman Harman had simply failed to turn up at rehearsals, and still hadn't put in an appearance even now, half an hour before curtain-up. A speaking part. Only a few words, but a speaking part, all the same. Even a single snatch of song.

'*Duw Annwyl*, Mister Mantlemere,' said Tom Priddy, conjuring the image of a future career, the footlights of London's West End theatres, imagining his glittering prospects, 'lucky you've got me, like.'

7.35pm

Amos Gartee had developed an irrational contempt for Germans. In part, it was the fault of the Wolof, Charles Tuohey. A lecture after they'd earlier passed the German church on Renshaw Street.

'Them Germany men,' Amos had remarked. 'See? Even own church here. We let them, take all world. *Ene?*'

'Been reading the *Daily Mail*, brother?'

Amos did not like the tone of reproof in the Wolof's voice. He'd been doing his best, after all. King Billy had brought them newspapers and Amos had been using them to improve his English. Rather than simply skim through them, he was attempting a deeper understanding. And *Daily Mail*? He had no idea, but he had rather revelled in the pages he'd read.

'Newspaper, them not say it true?'

The rebellion in Morocco against their Sultan. The French sending soldiers to quash the revolt and Spain seizing a chunk of Morocco for itself. To protect all those white folks who, it seemed, were settled in those lands. Colonists, the newspaper called them.

'Sometimes not the whole truth,' Tuohey had said. 'Did you never look at a map of Africa, brother?'

Of course, he had. The colours. A patchwork blanket like those his mother had once stitched together. One colour each for France, Belgium, Italy, Britain, Portugal, Spain – and Germany. Hardly an inch of the entire continent free of these colours.

'Don't you know what's been happening there, my friend? The great nations of Europe carving up our lands? Fifty years. Grab, grab, grab. Any excuse. They might call them Protectorates, but what they practiced was invasion. Invasion after invasion. Were you never told, in Nana Kru, that you'd been invaded?'

There were troublemakers, agitators, who said as much. Yet it had never mattered greatly to Amos. The *poto* Englishmen were simply there. Like the trees were there. Part of the landscape. A name written across the skies, on almost every factory and warehouse. Mister Alfred Jones. Ivory, tin, timber, cotton, gum, cocoa, maize, palm oil, rubber – and, of course, shipping. The owner of Elder Dempster itself. A great gnashing of teeth when he had died two years earlier.

But Amos's own life, his family's life, went on regardless. Ignoring them. Mostly. Until he had shipped out with the Company. And now, Amos was here, in this Liverpool place. Becoming part of *their* landscape. True, largely ignored as well. In the months since his arrival, he had sometimes been defamed and suffered insults frequently enough. But mostly he had simply felt invisible.

'But them Germany men, send boat with gun. War come.'

It's what the newspaper had said. He thought so, anyway. The French had told them to stay away. And if the Germany men stayed away, the French would reward them somewhere else. All they had to do was stay away. Yet the newspaper did not believe they would do so, believed the Germans would send their gunboats to Morocco. And, when they did, yes, there would be war.

But Amos Gartee's prejudice against the entire German nation arose far more from his recent encounters with the man called Ernst Jurks. Hard enough to even work his tongue around the fellow's name. He wasn't entirely worried about the Germans taking over the whole world, so long as they kept their hands off Miss Nesta.

She had brought the German to the Harrington gates several nights earlier.

'We make collection,' Jurks had told him, a beaming smile plastered onto his ugly square face. 'From market. There now a few days I work.'

Amos had made an effort to express gratitude as he took possession of the can filled with coin and a few banknotes. But now, here they were again, visiting the pickets. Laughing together. Laughing just a little too much for Amos's liking. A shared jest which Amos struggled to properly understand. If his own English was limited by the *Kreyol* of Liberia and everywhere else along the coast, he still considered it superior to the harsh and almost incomprehensible efforts of this Germany man.

And the laughter? He was reminded of the cavorting he'd seen within the first stages of courtships between men and women at

Nana Kru. The seemingly forced merriment by which they sought to persuade each other that here was a potential mate with whom an entire lifetime of amusement might be enjoyed.

'Nesta,' said the German, 'now safe she is. With *mein Papa* and me again she lives.'

Living with the German? He turned towards Miss Nesta, hurt and confused. He had thought...

'Yes,' she smiled at him. 'Good heavens, what was I thinking? Such a narrow escape.'

Chapter Six

Tuesday 18th July 1911

10.25am

'I have to know, Cari,' Alice Davies insisted. 'About this allegation. A woman claiming she was assaulted during the Procession. I'm required to make a report. To Emmeline.'

Oh, Cari thought, it's Emmeline now. Pure pretension, of course, for Alice would never dare address Mrs Pankhurst this way face to face. Yet Cari knew she herself had also been slightly inebriated by her own experience of rubbing shoulders with the great and the good. Was it enough, though, to warrant Bessie Butler's assumption that Cari was part of the "posh" elite? Of course not. She was working class to her very roots, and could never have seen herself addressing Mrs Mansell Moullin, for example, as *Edith*. Not under any circumstance. But had her adventures in London somehow fed an ambition to become more active in the fight? To play some loftier part? Oh, yes. Most definitely. So, she gazed around the whitewashed WSPU office, with its posters and leaflets, its unsold curling copies of last week's *Votes for Women*.

'I could have taken those off your hands,' said Cari, hoping to remind Alice of her worth, ahead of whatever interrogation might follow. 'I ran out completely.'

She reached into her shoulder bag, took out the pocket ledger detailing the allocation of papers for the previous week, the consequent amount needing to be remitted at a penny per copy, and a separate column for additional donations received. She handed the accounts book to Alice, along with the small yet bulging brown banking envelope with its assortment of coins.

'One of the girls fell sick,' said Alice, peering appreciatively into the envelope. She signed the docket and tore it out for her own records, leaving Cari with the carbon copied page still in place. 'It was too late to redistribute them.'

'So why exactly am I in the spotlight?' Cari asked. It had been weeks since the procession but, for some reason, the papers only seemed to have caught up with the story this past few days.

'I think you know very well. A lady of note, who wishes to remain nameless, seriously injured by a rock, she says. And a man knocked senseless.' Cari tried hard not to smile. 'Somebody wearing our colours, according to witnesses. A tall woman. Very tall. And just the excuse the newspapers needed to paint the procession in a negative light.'

'Only the *Daily Mail*,' said Cari. 'What else would you expect? If it hadn't been this, they would have found something else.'

'You admit it?' Alice stammered. 'And never bothered to speak with me.'

'Alice, it was an apple. I hit the woman – one of the Antis – with an apple. And I thought we believed in breaking the law.'

'Good gracious, Cari. Not personal violence. It's barbaric. But an apple – did you say an apple?'

'I did. And besides, I had other things on my mind when I got back from London.'

'Oh,' said Alice. 'Your sister. You must have been surprised.'

Something about the way she spoke the word *sister* annoyed Cari again. Disparaging. Disappointed, perhaps, at how matters had transpired. It occurred to her that Alice Davies probably dismissed them both for precisely the opposite reason to Bessie. Too middle class for the latter, too working class for Alice. Yet "surprised" hardly did justice to the thing. Nessie had indeed been apprehended, taken to the Bridewell.

But during a moment of professional negligence, or perhaps underestimation of a woman's wiles, Sergeant Ladysmith and his bobbies left her unattended and without restraints. Nesta apparently then decided that being sick of hiding was still preferable to a period of hard labour in Walton and had simply walked casually from the police station before hiding within the crowds.

'It's been a month of surprises,' said Cari. 'Some more pleasant than others.'

Tada, at least, had received her note about the arrest at precisely the moment when Nesta had let herself in through the Dawson Place door. She had, it seemed, made him laugh like a drain with the story of how Cari had brought their cohorts into action, the diversionary singing. Of course, when Nesta repeated the way she had cheered him, the yarn lacked some of its lustre simply by virtue of it being overshadowed.

Two things. First, Cari's recollection of Taffy's damning assertion that one good turn deserved another. Had he truly turned informer against Nessie? Snitched to Sergeant Ladysmith about where to find her? And, second, his insistence there was something between Nesta and Ernst Jurks. It had eaten away at her ever since. It was made worse by *Herr* Jurks, Ernst's uncle, so readily taking Nesta under his wing and providing sanctuary to her once more. However, life – or rather death – had already intervened, and Nesta's cheerful account of Tada's amusement might, perhaps, be one of the final moments of humour and good times any of them would enjoy for some while.

'Yes,' said Alice, and Cari saw her anger dissipate. 'I'm sorry to drag you in here, today of all days.'

'Don't distress yourself. The funeral's not until later this afternoon.'

'Tragic accident. I read about it in the papers. It was Mary Robson who told me. I hadn't realised the connection with your family.'

'Why should you? She was my brother's girl.'

Theresa MacKenny had fallen victim to a terrible fate, almost two weeks earlier. She had died in hospital a couple of days later and there had, naturally, been an inquest.

10.45am

Tom Priddy wasn't entirely unfamiliar with the procedures of the Coroner's Court. But he'd been keen to see how those procedures might differ here in Liverpool from those he'd seen in operation at Bangor.

Naturally, evidence had been called from representatives of the Corporation Tramways Company. From other passengers, as well.

As Tom had expected, the statements were somewhat confused.

An inspector and the tram's conductor had been on the vehicle's platform but provided conflicting details, the former claiming he had seen Miss MacKenny making her way through the standing but orderly passengers – he assumed for the purpose of alighting at the next stop – and then simply stumbling from the platform and onto the street as the tram jolted and turned through the St. Anne Street and Islington intersection, after which he gave the signal for the tram to stop.

The conductor, however, had an entirely different tale to tell. Concerns about the number and behaviour of some of the passengers. He claimed to have observed excessive jostling among them just before Miss MacKenny made her way onto the platform. He had not observed her final moments, however, and simply heard a scream.

There were no other witnesses who either supported this version or came forward, however.

The surgeon-superintendent from the hospital then detailed the time at which Theresa had been admitted and the nature of her injuries – extensive fracture of the skull with significant blood clots on both sides of the brain. The other organs were normal, however, he had confirmed, as though this should be a consolation. The deceased never recovered consciousness and cause of death had been recorded as fracture of the skull and haemorrhage of the brain.

A verdict was returned. *Death due to a fractured skull, caused by accidentally falling from a moving tram.* The Coroner added that no one was to blame for the accident, and an order for burial was given to the family of the deceased.

Tom, of course, had not been identified as a witness, and nor had he come forward voluntarily, though he'd almost wished he had done so during the portion of the inquest when the inspector had presented his statement.

'Oh, yes,' he would have said. 'A simple stumble from the platform.'

But, of course, he could not have given evidence without…

10.45am

'They were engaged to be married?' said Alice.

'Not officially, I don't think,' Cari replied. 'There were difficulties. Theresa's family, all staunch Catholics. And my father – well, he's not spoken a word to my brother since he found out they were courting.'

'But the rift now healed, I assume.'

'If anything, it seems worse. As though Dafydd believes the whole sequence of events might have been different if only Tada'd not taken against them.'

'How can we ever know these things, Cari? You make one tiny change, a seemingly insignificant change, and the whole of history is affected. Except you can't, can you? Change the past, I mean.'

Of course, she was right, though Cari still wished the possibility had existed. Even at the most basic level, if she could have turned back time, she would have left Taffy to reconcile himself with his grief a little longer following the inquest, rather than rushing to the MacKennys' to pay her respects.

Mrs MacKenny herself had appreciated the gesture, but the encounter with Taffy had been unpleasant. And Cari had forgotten the custom of Catholic families in bringing home the deceased until the funeral – the vigil, she thought they called it, with friends, neighbours, sometimes almost total strangers, squashed into the house to keep watch with the family. Or perhaps to simply excite their curiosity, their passion for the macabre, the grotesque, rather than to find collective strength in the presence of our Lord Jesus.

So, there she'd been: the open coffin in the already cramped living room; the waxen, doll-like features of the corpse which Cari couldn't reconcile with the Theresa she'd known in life; and the unnatural lassitude of her brothers and sisters. As though the loss of Theresa's life had sapped the vibrancy from their own.

11.30am

The scene at Waugh's had been unpleasant, but he wouldn't have missed it for the world.

'What's he doing here?' Taffy had yelled when he'd seen Tom in the reception parlour. 'I don't want him anywhere near my girl, see.'

So, not much chance they're going to ask me to recommend a hymn or two, Tom had smiled to himself. After that first time, word had spread. It was now almost a standard practice. Waugh would have him at most meetings, impressed by Tom's ability to perfectly match hymns to the mood and background of the bereaved. And, just a week before, he'd had his first challenge.

'This him, then?' one of the mourners had asked. 'The bloke

who knows all the tunes? Bet he doesn't know *Ah! Lovely Appearance of Death.'*

Well, of course he'd known it. Wesley. An easy one.

Yet there'd been nothing easy about their meeting with the MacKennys.

'Mister Priddy is a valued member of staff, sir,' Waugh had told Taffy, as deferentially as possible.'

'But look at him,' Taffy had growled. 'Looks like a corpse himself.' He'd turned to the girl's mother. 'Ma, tell them…'

'Just bloody get on with it,' the father had said. 'This is costing me.'

Tom could see he was the worse for drink, turned up in his work clothes, while the mother was shrunken within her mourning weeds, surrounded by those same children he'd seen when he visited the house in the priest's disguise.

'I just don't want him anywhere near my Theresa, is all.'

Taffy had begun to weep. Pitiful, really, thought Tom. And, of course, he didn't object when Waugh diplomatically suggested Mister Priddy might perhaps return to his other duties. He'd backed out of the room, bent over his pale, clasped hands, in a gesture of humility which would have made Uriah Heap proud.

'Just nowhere near my Theresa,' Taffy said again.

Far too late to be worrying about that, my friend, Tom would have liked to tell him, and had recalled with pleasure the time he'd spent with Mister Clamp on the girl's preparation.

11.30am

It should have been the happiest week of Taffy's life. Yet they found themselves, Cari and Nesta, shivering in the shadows of Gerard Street, despite this otherwise being a day so hot, the sun had sucked sand from the paving stones, sprinkled it across the slabs to grate and scratch beneath the soles of their shoes on the way round, once more, to the MacKennys' house.

'Mrs MacKenny reckons Theresa agreed to marry him,' Nesta whispered to her, as the bell at St. Anthony's began to toll in the distance, and the bier was loaded at the front door with its sad coffin. 'Only the day before the accident.'

'I had no idea,' said Cari. 'Alice was asking me earlier – whether they were engaged.'

'Did she give you a hard time, Cari? About the apple?' Nesta tried to suppress her giggles, failed somewhat, and attracted glowering anger from others in the black-clad clusters, gathered along the cobbles and watching while the coffin was lifted into the back of the hearse.

'Even Alice couldn't help but be moved by Taffy's tragedy,' Cari murmured. And nor could any of them. It was cruel. Desperately cruel.

Besides, the revolution for which their brother had waited so long seemed, at last, to have come to Liverpool.

11.30am

It was the fellow Amos had seen at the meeting. And then at each of the great gatherings in that open space before the Hall of St. George, the place they called the Plateau. Two more such gatherings, and this fellow had spoken at each of them. The one they had called Jocota. The man leading the union of ships' cooks, stewards and others – many of them now also on strike. And here he was, come to speak with his members at the Harrington gate.

'Jocota,' Amos had accosted the fellow when the meeting was over. 'You talk Kru men now?'

Jocota fixed him with those piercing eyes, held his gaze. It was good. But he was not happy. The black moustache, downturned, gave him a permanent scowl. A serious man. And yes, with the proud and menacing stance of the mountain silverback.

'Listen,' he said, 'I've got nothin' against you lads. An' they reckon down in Cardiff there's blacks out with the rest. Tupper and the NSFU. Know what I mean?'

Amos didn't have a clue, turned to the rest of his brothers now crowding around them. Jonah Samba and the Mende boys at his shoulder. The Mandinkas. And his own Kru fellows.

'But 'ere,' Jocota was saying, 'well, the members won't 'ave it.'

Amos knew it. The largest shipping firms had surrendered to their striking seamen, and thus expected them to return to their duties, though there was no progress with Elder Dempster for Amos Gartee's Krooboys. And, at this very moment, the dockers had presented their own demands – that their union should be granted an agreement by which they could negotiate improvements in pay and conditions for the members.

Thus, the seamen refused to go back to their ships until those demands were met also, and those dockers who had previously seen no value in joining the union were now flocking to sign up in droves. And while the African seamen might at last be a regular feature in the mass meetings, their own strike fund, there was still no widespread support for their cause.

'You a big rusty man, Jocota,' said Amos. 'Talk much, do nothin'. A'right?'

Jocota's already piercing eyes were no longer friendly. They had become as black and incandescent as the coal Amos once shovelled into the bossman's boilers. The man took a step towards him, and Amos fell back by the same distance. His brothers followed suit, though George Janjay, the yellow-skinned Guere, had to be restrained from taking any of the violent actions twhreatened by his shouting. Did Jocota not understand these things? How, in a discussion between two people, an arm's length must always be maintained. Simple good manners.

'We've done good, lad. Don't you forget it. Two weeks since the first of the companies caved in. Just some of the big boys still to be brought into line. Know what I mean?'

'Yet this Elder Dempster, Jocota?'

'You don't get it. Bigger than this, see? Not a day going by without news of other comrades taking up the cudgels. Steelworkers at Hawarden Bridge. Tugboatmen, cotton porters, labourers from the tobacco and wool warehouses. Miners out in Skelmersdale. Thousands more just waiting for the word. Railwaymen and tram worker. Sugar refiners, and flour millers. The papers are calling it a transport strike. But they've got it wrong, lad. Much, much more than that. Yeah?'

'But we are here. This Liverpool place. Where is our tenbob?'

'All I can tell you, lad, is we 'eard this mornin'. The big boys, Elder Dempster among them, have agreed to meet us. Next week. If all you're after is your ten bob – well, I'll promise to see what we can do.'

Amos supposed it would have to suffice. For now, anyway. And there were other things to worry about today. Missee Nesta among other things. A funeral, wasn't it?

11.45am

It would indeed otherwise have been Taffy's proudest hour had he not, at this moment, been emerging from the house and taking his place among the leading mourners for the maudlin march around to the church. He was unsteady on his feet, though Cari couldn't tell whether it was through grief, or ale, or a combination of the two. Yet, as the sable horses set off down the street, the sisters fell in further back, towards the rear of the procession, not wishing to impinge upon his distress.

'Must have cost a pretty penny,' said Nesta.

As it happened, Cari knew precisely. Mrs MacKenny had told her. Two pounds, one shilling and ninepence. From their weekly payments to the funeral club. A penny per week for each of the kids. Tuppence for Mrs MacKenny. And a regular thru'penny bit to cover Pa MacKenny's eventual demise.

'Not a family to allow themselves the shame of a pauper's funeral,' Cari agreed.

'And Kaplan? He didn't mind giving you the time off?'

'He wasn't very happy. The old miser has strict rules. Bereavement absence. A half-day, no more. And only for immediate family members. But I must have caught him on one of his better days.'

They were turning into Byrom Street, towards Scotland Road, back in the blazing sun, and Cari saw Nesta stoop a little, shrinking herself to hide among those walking nearest to them, then peering back and forth, scanning the thoroughfare on which all traffic had momentarily stopped in respect.

'Relax,' Cari told her. 'I doubt even Sergeant Ladysmith would try to pick you up during a funeral.'

'You've too much faith in human nature, Cari.'

'Have I? Yes, perhaps. But there's a great deal of good in the world. You just have to look for it. And you've been blessed with your fair share as well. Look at how Old Man Jurks has taken care of you. Ernst as well.'

The words almost stuck in Cari's throat, but Nesta didn't seem to notice. It was hot, especially in their funeral weeds, and Cari envied those sheltering in the cool shade of shop awnings along the route, up the hill and past the innumerable street corner pubs, each disgorging its customers in turn, leaving a silent wake astern of the cortège as they passed.

'He insists I call him Ernie now,' Nesta said at last, sweetly, and Cari found it hard to reply, suppressing the jealousy seething within her. 'They've taken him on permanent, by the way,' she went on. 'Did he say? At the fruit and veg market. Only a porter, and some of the men have taken against him, but…'

'Because he's German?'

'The papers seem to be stirring up such hatred against them.'

'He's not going back to sea, then? You must be pleased.'

'Oh, I'm sure he will. If this German nonsense gets any worse. Or once the strikes are all settled. Until then? Well, yes, it's good to have him watching out for me. Guardian angel. That sort of thing.'

Guardian angel? Cari thought. Lucky you, Nesta. But by then they'd reached St. Anthony's, its bell still tolling. The pall bearers had lifted Theresa's coffin from the glass body of the hearse and carried it through the wall of wailing grief gathered around the church entrance.

'Now what?' said Cari. 'Do we go inside?'

It was a momentous decision. Neither of them had ever set foot within a Catholic temple and Cari had to confess she'd no idea what to expect – let alone how their father would react if he discovered they'd even contemplated such a thing.

'You're thinking about Tada,' said Nesta. 'He won't be watching us, Cari.'

'No need. He'll know though, see. Smell it on us. The incense or something. It just feels wrong.'

'It's absurd. But my heart's beating so fast. Feels like my chest will explode.'

So Cari took her sister's hand.

'Perhaps if we just stand at the back,' Cari told her, though they had little choice in any case about whether or not they entered, because those behind were now pushing them forward. 'At least it's only St. Anthony's,' she said. And there was, in truth, some consolation in this because the building had been a neighbour all their lives. Yet

179

they remained at the rear anyway, even though they were frequently offered places along the pews.

1.00pm

Tom Priddy knew one special thing about funerals – that nobody ever looked the featherman in the face. *Anlwcus.* Unlucky. Superstition, of course. Same here as home in Wales. So, he had no fears he'd be recognised by any of the mourners. Even the Beanpole and Dumpling Nesta had given Waugh's featherman a wide berth. Taffy the same.

It had been interesting to observe their various behaviours. And now, the chance to experience this heresy. The service. Something of a mystery to him. All the gilded idolatry of the interior, naturally, but the liturgy in Latin served to remind him this was a faith entirely foreign to these lands. Foreign in every sense of the word. Old Huw Maddox spoke of them as papists, but the language of their worship he called Romish – as if, somehow, those who practiced Catholicism were a last remnant of history's invading legions.

But at least today they were spared the burial itself for, at the conclusion of the service, the coffin was loaded again into its hearse and, with Tom Priddy the featherman at its head in his long black coat and tall top hat, they processed back towards town, turned left into Collingwood and crossed Cazneau Street to reach the All Souls mortuary chapel where Theresa MacKenny's remains would spend the night.

Then, on the following day, the closest members of the family would make the five-mile journey out to the Catholic burial ground at the back of Ford Cemetery. And yes, with the other mourners who'd been waiting to bury their papist dead since the last procession on Sunday.

The sisters, Cari and Nesta, however, seemed destined for another unpleasant encounter with their brother Taffy.

Tom watched them from the corner of his eye, careful to keep his face averted. They were apparently trying to sneak away from the chapel with no fuss. Yet the Beanpole must have had second thoughts, turned and loitered on the sunbaked pavement, shielding her eyes against the glare, and raising a hand in tentative greeting when Taffy briefly gazed in her direction.

1.00pm

She simply could not resist trying to catch his attention, let him know she and Nesta, at least, had attended. A gesture of solidarity, she hoped, which might help to salve wounds – this goal again, to heal her family's rifts. Yet she should have known better.

His face, she saw, was streaked with tears, stricken by grief, though it hardened in an instant, features turned to gravestone granite as he pushed folk aside, roiled towards his sisters like a summer thunderstorm.

'That's right,' he shouted, turning heads all around him. 'You can bugger off again. Consciences clean again now, is it? Done your duty.'

'Dafydd,' Cari tried to sound soothing, placatory. 'It was just to pay our respects. Your sisters. Love you, see?'

'We both liked Theresa, an' all,' said Nesta.

'Nah,' he spat. 'Just came to see how the other half lives.' He stopped abruptly, realised the absurdity of what he was saying, or maybe just deepened his own grief.

'Why not come home?' Cari asked. 'Tada misses you. I know he does.'

'Where is he, then? Today, I mean. Oh, I bloody forgot. Catholic service, isn't it? He'll not give this a second thought. Or maybe he will, an' all. Glad there's one less papist in the world. That'll be our Pa.'

'Tada's a good Christian...' Cari began to protest.

'Christian, Cari?' he cried. 'What's that to do with anything? You're going to spout religion at me as well now? I had enough at St. Anthony's. But at least I couldn't understand all their bloody nonsense. All the mumbo-jumbo. You think if there was really a god, that this...'

He turned back towards the chapel with a look of such despair and hopelessness, Cari thought her heart would explode for him, while Nesta grabbed his sleeve with both hands and buried her face in the woollen fabric, crying pitifully.

'I don't understand,' she sobbed. 'None of us do.'

'But we all feel the pain of it,' said Cari. 'Tada too. Even Cousin Thomas.'

Taffy spun back to face her, gave Cari such a look of disbelief she might as well have told him Britain had become a republic or given up its claim to Empire. 'It's true,' she insisted. 'They were talking about the accident…'

'Accident?' he said. 'Accident. There's a polite word for you.'

'Yet accident it was, Taffy. Cruel. Tragic. Terrible. Impossible to fathom. But an accident.'

'I bet they think I deserved this,' Taffy sneered. 'Didn't they? Some nonsense about God paying me back for something or other.' He looked Cari in the eyes, recognised guilt there. 'See? I knew it. What was it? Some prodigal son thing? God moving in mysterious ways?'

He may, of course, have simply seen the pattern of Cari's own thoughts. Her own philosophy. Each bad deed begets another. And she had fought this internal struggle since the day they received the news, trying to suppress the nagging thought. Here might be divine retribution for Taffy's betrayal of Nesta to Sergeant Ladysmith, that day at Lime Street – a battle Cari couldn't quite win, like trying to force the family's winter blankets back into the summer storage Lipton's tea chest which was simply too small for them all.

'They said nothing of the kind,' Nessie protested, and diverted Taffy's searching scrutiny from Cari's own. 'Heard them talking, I did. Respectful, they were. Both of them. Just – well, talking about what happened.'

Her voice trailed away towards the end.

'Just talking?' he said. 'Something else to blather about over Friday's fish and chips. Like – what else? Next week's print orders. Or the footie results.'

'Not like that,' she said. 'I can't stand the man, but Cousin Thomas was at least on the scene soon after – after it happened. He was there when they took your Theresa away.'

This was news to Taffy – and to Cari, as well.

'You never said, Nessie. When was this?' Cari asked, but she saw also how Taffy's whole demeanour had changed, softened.

'What?' he murmured. 'What did Tom Priddy see?'

1.15pm

He'd managed to hear most of the argument. *Iesu*, most of Liverpool must have heard them. And Dumpling Nesta, Tom Priddy the featherman decided, must have nine lives. Each of his attempts to make sure she was arrested had failed dismally. So, perhaps, not what the Lord Jesus intended. In any case, he'd been there, the night she'd turned up to tell old Huw about the papist girl's tragic end.

Iesu, the performance of his life, that night.

She'd looked upon him with open disdain. No, not simply disdain. Open hatred. Yet he'd found himself enraptured by her afresh. Confusing, he'd thought. The memory of her softness, perhaps.

'Tada,' she'd said. 'I have some terrible news.'

She'd told the story, becoming increasingly disturbed by her father's seemingly total absence of compassion. Tom Priddy had been proud of him, had waited for just the right moment.

'This afternoon?' he'd said. 'St. Anne Street? *Duw Annwyl*, it was the girl? Your Taffy's girl?'

'You saw it?' She'd had to force herself to address him.

'On my way home, see. Commotion. Putting her on the stretcher, they were. Didn't know who she was, like. Curious though, I was. Spoke to some of the passengers. Who'd have thought? Shocked, I am.'

'Coming back from work,' had said Nesta to her father.

'Should have realised,' said Tom. 'And she was still alive then. On the stretcher, like. But still alive.'

Now, outside the All Souls mortuary chapel, before he followed the coffin inside, he risked a last glance at the sisters, at their stupid brother Taffy, tried to read their lips, imagined Dumpling Nesta breaking the news to him. Yes, still alive, he smiled to himself.

3.30pm

'She was still alive?' said Taffy. 'Then? They said she was unconscious. But maybe she spoke. Did he hear her speak, Nessie? For God's sake, did he?'

'I don't think so. No, he can't have done. Why would he? He didn't know who she was. Not then.'

Taffy fell silent, looked confused, his fingers lifted to his hare lip, dragging at it.

'He wasn't on the tram itself, then?'

'Dafydd,' said Cari. 'If he'd been on the tram and seen anything, he'd have been called as a witness. Or made a statement. I can't begin to understand, but...'

Though, of course, she *could* understand perfectly. Her mother and her brother Pryce, both lost to them. The pain, which never disappears yet merely subsides to a permanent ache in the chest. Or the soul. The guilt, the recrimination, the confusion.

'I should just get over it. Trot back to Hunter Street and pick up where we all left off. Right, Cari?'

'But you can't stay with the MacKennys,' said Nesta, gently.

'No – right again,' he replied. 'I can't, neither. So maybe there's room for me with that Fritz boyfriend of yours.'

'Not my boyfriend!' Nesta protested, and with such passion Cari felt her stomach lurch. A vehement denial, and a seemingly heartfelt one. But could she dare believe it? 'And you were Ernie's pal.'

'Ernie?' He guffawed. 'Ernie.' Then he shook his head. 'I had a couple of pints with him, Nesta. Doesn't mean I liked the bugger. Bloody Fritzes. Not much better than your darkies, girl.'

'Well there,' Cari snapped at him. 'You've got this much in common with Tada and Cousin Thomas, at least.' But she knew it was the wrong thing, went straight on without drawing breath, without giving him a chance to reply. 'I'm sorry, Taffy. It's not the right day for this. Look, the MacKennys are waiting for you. Maybe just think about it? For me – and for Nesta?'

He said nothing. Just nodded, once, then turned and walked back towards the chapel.

5.00pm

Strike-breakers. But unlike the Mandinka men, Amos had no way of converting these to his cause.

The *Nigeria* had docked during the afternoon, sailed here from some Plymouth place after her voyage which, according to the newspaper, had begun in Forcados, with stops at Accra, Winneba, Abidjan, Freetown and Dakar.

These seafarers had been placed beyond Amos Gartee's reach by Elder Dempster, the company having converted part of a warehouse within the gates, a barracks to house the Yoruba and Igbo men pending the return voyage. And the same fellows had been used, it seemed, to offload the *Nigeria*'s limited cargo – limited since she had principally carried passengers and mail.

'You think we can win this fight, brother?' said Barkuh Togba. A relief to speak in their own *Bété* tongue, to set aside, even if only for a while, the *Kreyol* they all shared each day.

They had wandered across to the corner of St. James' Mount, to watch the work upon the great House of God. Late in the day, yet still the masons' hammers chipping away at the sandstone, the steam cranes bellowing under the strain of heaving a finely fluted block into place, high above them. A warm afternoon, though not warm enough for the two men to shed their overcoats. In the pocket of his coat, the bible, for additional comfort.

'Truly?' said Amos. He gazed down the slope of Upper Parliament Street, out across the river, handing over the cigarette he'd just finished rolling. 'How can we ever know these things? All I know is that those who do not fight can never win.'

There were still ships. They said there was a great canal, stretching all the way to another of their cities, one far from the coast, and perhaps those vessels were heading to this place. Pursuing the screeching gulls. Another wonder.

'But after,' said Barkuh, 'you will go home? To Nana Kru?'

'Who can say? This Liverpool – it is a place of miracle and wonder.'

'Beautiful women,' Barkuh laughed.

It seemed he had read Amos Gartee's thoughts.

'You remember the story, brother? The Beautiful Bride?'

'I think you see yourself as Goat,' said Barkuh.

'Certainly, I have a rival. Perhaps more than one.' Amos pictured an image of the German, square and strong like a bull buffalo, hair the colour of dung. The story was strong within him. How Goat had determined to win Leopard's daughter for his bride. But to do so Goat needed to defeat his rivals in a contest set by Leopard. Goat was the suitor least likely to succeed. Simply Goat, after all. So, he would need all his wiles to succeed.

'But I have a plan,' said Amos.

5.45pm

It ate away at her, of course, for the rest of the afternoon as Cari picked up a few spuds and carrots, some scrag-ends of mutton and a cheap slab of bacon for the night's cawl. Her father insisted she used her mam's special recipe so there'd also been lentils soaking overnight. And they were just sitting at the kitchen table, with her questions for Cousin Tom Priddy as carefully prepared as the lobscouse, when Wyn and Rhys Fingers turned up out of the blue to join them.

'That's if you don't mind, see,' said Rhys – though, by then, he'd already settled himself in Cari's chair, and scratching at a rash around his mouth. 'But what's this, Cari? Cawl with lentils? Not the way we used to make it at home.'

'Beggars and choosers, isn't it, Rhys?' Cari told him, then put her arm around Wyn's bone-thin shoulders. 'And before you ask, Wyn, it's been steaming away on the hot plate for an hour and more.'

She'd brought her own knife, fork and spoon, of course, but insisted on going to the sink and washing her bowl again before she'd allow Cari to ladle out her food. Still, it gave Cari a chance to drag out the spare chair.

'Nesta not here?' Wyn asked, and Cari didn't bother to reply. Evidently not, though she'd set a place for her. It felt as though Wyn had turned a knife in Cari's old wound. *"Not my boyfriend!"* Nesta had said. Yet if she wasn't here, with them, it was highly likely she'd be with Ernst and his family. And Cari might feel responsibility for Wyn, yet it seemed like she'd delivered a deliberate jibe.

'So, how's it going down there, Rhys?' Tada asked, setting down his copy of the *Post and Mercury*. 'They've not dragged your boys into this stupid strike too, I hope?'

The gatemen, of course, had always considered themselves as several cuts above all other grades of ordinary dock worker – their own Mutual Society, and their comfortable granite cottages for those on duty overnight – and Rhys therefore launched into his now familiar tirade, about the city's total dependency on the river and its traffic, and how these misguided revolutionaries like Taffy would kill the goose that laid the golden egg.

'There's pretty, Wyn,' Cari said to her, though mainly because she couldn't be bothered listening to Rhys. Wyn wasn't one for frills and finery as a rule, but this evening she was wearing a very fine scarf around her neck, embroidered with minute dark blue flowers, which seemed somehow to reflect the shadowy scars upon her face. Yet Cari forced her thoughts back to the material itself. Silk, she was certain, then caught the faint scent of liniment. 'Sore neck, *cariad*?'

Wyn had been fingering the fabric since she came in. A bit self-consciously, truth be told. And Cari just wondered, stupidly, if this was one of Wyn's ways to make herself more attractive to her husband. Wayward husband, she thought to herself, and looked over at him, caught him staring back. It made Cari feel – well, dirty was the only way she could think to describe it. Dirty and hotter than even their airless kitchen could justify.

'Think I must have been sitting in a draught,' said Wyn.

'Since Sunday? You'd have been lucky to find any draught at all these past two days. Like an oven, it is.'

'Anyway,' Rhys was saying, 'that was about the size of it. They needed us while they were bringing in the depot ships and the strike-breakers. But now there's not much moving one way or the other. Stupid, see, and – well…'

He thrust his emptied plate towards her, as though she were some serving wench. And she could have bitten his head off, though she chose a different path, angrily spooning out more of the lobscouse, the medley of pea green, sliced carrot, orange lentil and glistening ochre. She slammed the plate down before him, so it splashed upon his necktie. He glowered at her but said nothing.

'Locked-out, is it?' Cari tried not to smile. Another irony of the strike. The seamen who'd not been troubled by watching Amos Gartee's Krooboys fight the good fight alone all those months and then been forced to swallow it whole as other white seamen had scabbed on them in turn. And, here, the dock gatemen, these fellows of substance, now dumped by the Docks and Harbour Board once they'd outlived their usefulness.

'It's only for a while,' Rhys snapped, dabbing at the fresh stains on his tie. 'You don't understand these things, Cari. None of this will last long and the Board always rewards loyalty. It's where you women go wrong, see? Need to understand what makes the world tick.' He'd picked up her tada's paper, tried to change the subject. 'At last!' he said loudly, and showed the picture from the front page. 'Official opening.'

Cari had learned the lesson early – that folk were, within, rarely as their outward behaviour might suggest. Those who made the most show and noise, she had found, were usually those suffering from the deepest self-doubt, while the most retiring and quiet often those most confident and contented within their own skin. Those who watched and listened patiently, making the least comment, were always those who possessed the deepest pools of data, while those with the most outspoken views about their own intelligence were, for the most part, the same people who in practice knew the least. It was not the ignorance of folk such as Rhys which made them dangerous but, rather, their unwavering illusion of being knowledgeable.

'Official opening,' smirked Cousin Thomas. 'But I'm guessing it'll be a while before we get to hear how *that* place ticks.'

6.00pm

It seemed to Tom Priddy that here was the wart on Liverpool's many wonders. There they were, about to be blessed with the fine new skyscraper headquarters for the Royal Liver Assurance Company and they'd still not managed to get the clocks working. So, the jest pleased him.

'Ticks,' he said again. Not even a smile, not from any of them.

Apart from the clocks, no sign either of the enormous sea birds which were supposed to grace its waterfront towers. And then there'd been all the furore a while back when the local union troublemakers, the Trades Council, had exposed the company for using casual labour at poverty wages to do all the skilled work on the building. Well, wasn't this the way of the world? Hardly short of cash, of course. But they'd had to fork out tens of thousands to sort out the pay issue and get the work finished.

'The girls went to the funeral,' old Huw was saying. 'Ceridwen and Nesta. It was today.'

Tom knew it was the nearest he would come to saying that Rhys Morgan – Rhys Gateman – shouldn't be too hard on Huw's wayward son. Not today, at least. And not that Tom cared very much.

'Papist funeral?' said Rhys. 'Not one of Waugh's then, Cousin Thomas?'

'I believe Waugh's did make the arrangements,' said Tom Priddy. 'Though I wasn't there, of course.'

He found it hard to hide the smirk behind his spoon, thought the Beanpole had perhaps detected it. Tom couldn't help himself, coughed, spat out a gobbet of pinkish mutton. It landed on the tablecloth and he brushed it quickly onto the floor.

'Taffy,' said the Beanpole. 'He was hurting very badly, Tada. Angry with all of us. But strange, too. About you, Cousin Thomas.'

He felt his eyes bulge even more than usual, allowed his deathly features to settle into a quizzical expression, as though Cari had amused him.

'Nesta told him,' she went on. 'About you being there. When it happened. Well, he seemed to take some comfort from it anyway.'

She smiled at him, serene like, though it seemed to him her brain might be working around other questions she wanted to ask.

'On her way back from work was she?' said Rhys. 'The papist girl?'

'Theresa,' Cari reminded him. Making a point, she was. It made Tom smile. 'Her name was Theresa MacKenny.'

'Worked at Penny's,' said Huw Maddox, and caught his daughter by surprise.

Tom could read her thoughts. Penny's was well-enough known among the city's pubs. Rathbone Street. But it would never have occurred to her that old Huw might take sufficient interest in Theresa to find out where she worked.

'A right dive,' Rhys sneered. 'I suppose it's all you'd expect. Edge of Darkie Town. Stone's throw from Flukey Alley. Our own Sodom and Gomorrah. *"And the cities about them in like manner, giving themselves over to fornication, and going after strange flesh, are set forth for an example, suffering the vengeance of eternal fire."* Jude One, Verse seven.'

6.45pm

Cari tried to remember. What was it Wyn had said about her hypocrite husband? Let him take his pleasures elsewhere? He seemed to know enough about the fleshpots of the south end. But there were places just as close to home. Hard to avoid, either with your own eyes or through popular gossip. You could find worn-out street-girls hanging around just about every court in the town. Outside Paddy's Market any time of the day, then Lime Street during the evening. Or – so they said – the boozer and bordello in the basement of the Hotel St. George, Grossi's Trocadero. A dozen other places besides. And she glanced at Wyn, saw her fiddle with the scarf's edge as she took another spoon of stew.

'Now, what's going through that pretty head of yours, Beanpole?' said Tom Priddy. 'I can almost hear the cogs going round.' He stared hard into her eyes. Menacing. Daring her to ask.

'I had no idea tada knew so much about Taffy's girl.'

'Tom found out,' said old Huw. 'After the inquest, like.'

'Was this the best he could do for himself?' Wyn looked up. 'A pot girl at some bawdy drinking den?'

Rhys pulled the pipe from his suit pocket and gripped it between his teeth, reached for his tobacco pouch. Cari thought he didn't look quite well. Feverish.

'Oh, that's how you met their mam,' said Tom Priddy, with a saintly grin. 'Wasn't it, Uncle Huw?'

Huw Maddox visibly slumped in his chair a moment, took a few uncomfortable seconds to compose himself again. He lit a Woodbine. His loss, still missing her, of course. But when he raised his head again, it was Cari's old familiar tada, the avuncular smile.

'God could not be everywhere,' he said, 'and therefore he created mothers.'

'It's an extraordinary thing, Tada,' Cari reminded him. 'From all those *Seisnig* writers, and apart from Dickens, you have such a fondness for the only two who shout so loudly against votes for women. Kipling and Conan Doyle. What a pair they are!'

'I think you'll find Holy Scripture said the same thing long before Kipling,' said Rhys Fingers, setting a match to his pipe and wiping sweat from his brow. 'And are you denying God's purpose for women is in the home and with their families? Some of your friends preach abomination, Ceridwen. Those among them who – how should I put this?' He spared a look in his wife's direction, though Wyn seemed to be occupied once more with other matters than her husband's prattle, drawn back within herself again. 'Let me see! Women who practise unnatural acts.'

A cloud of smoke filled the room. But where had he picked up such nonsense? Cari could barely imagine.

'We could hardly accuse you of being one of that sort, Beanpole.' Tom Priddy to her rescue. 'You're just a bit misled. But good point, what Rhys says. If women got the vote, no doubt about it, they'll lose their motherliness, their womanly ways. And then – if they forget the fairness of their sex, who knows what might follow! Interesting, Rhys.'

'Interesting, Cousin?' said Cari. 'You should have been at last month's procession in London. Seven hundred women in the prisoners' parade. Most of them had been through the torture of forced feeding. Barbaric. Brutal. And yet all still women to the core. All their maternal instincts intact, so far as I could tell.'

'Propaganda,' Rhys sneered. 'Forced feeding. Torture, indeed! Harmless. Been proven, see. Nothing more than a simple medical procedure. Always proper doctors who do it. Or nurses, like. Necessary as well, maybe. To save the lives of your foolish demonstrators, see. Though I wonder why we should waste public money on them. On any of you, Cari.'

Cari, however, took no notice. More interested in Cousin Tom Priddy. Something nagging at her brain.

7.00pm

Amos felt more secure now in wandering the streets alone – at least, so long as he remained within those boundaries of the city set for him by the Wolof, Charles Tuohey. And when he did so, as Tuohey had advised him, he always tried to look up, above the shop and office fronts, to see the reminders of how this Liverpool had grown so fat. But, *eh bye!* He could still not fully understand how those shops and stores could have so much. Surely, there could be no King Hunger here, as so often reigned over them back home. No, this would be a good place to take a bride. If only he could afford the bride price. And therein lay his plan, to prove he had sufficient wealth of his own, and the Germany man did not.

He tried to look up. Yet always his attention was drawn to the alehouses, the tea shops, the temperance bars and cafés – so many of them, even here within these outer fringes of the city's heart. He stopped many times, peered through their windows, amazed at the numbers within, at the richness and variety of the foods and drinks on offer. But he moved on at great speed each time he found himself observed in his turn. He knew how strange he must appear, nose pressed against the glass, with his army overcoat, his woollen cap, the scars upon his face. And with the bundle of clothes upon his shoulder, on the way to the wash house and another of Tuohey's lessons in pugilism, as he called his art.

Now, however, the lesson was finished, his few spare items of clothing, at the cost of a penny's worth of soda and soap, all boiled, scrubbed upon the washboards, rinsed, mangled and strung, still steaming, along the drying racks below. Cleaner? His mother might not have thought so, he decided, as he sat against the ropes of the boxing ring, sweat soaking his vest and sipping at a brown earthenware jug of water.

'In Nana Kru,' he told the Wolof, who was unlacing his own gloves, 'all...'

Amos paused, searching for the word. He made a smoothing gesture with his hands.

'Level?' said Tuohey. 'Flat?'

'No, same. All days. Sun. Work. People.'

In his own tongue? Uniform, he decided. Consistent. Yes, there was a uniformity about Nana Kru.

'But in England, so many variables,' said Tuohey. 'No two days the same?'

He was correct. Here, the unpredictable weather. The many grey shades of light and sky. The gluttony of building styles. The skin colours of its citizens. The many languages which filled his ears. It bewitched him and terrified him at the same time. An incomer. But could this Liverpool place ever be his home.

'*Ay-yah!*' he said. 'Fight too. In Nana Kru, fight be easy. Here, no.'

He'd thought about this, long and hard. At home, the stronger creatures ate the weak. Unless, of course, the weak possessed enough guile, or speed, or numbers, to escape those who would feast upon them. Yet, in general, an order to things. A natural cycle. A law of the wild, perhaps, but a law, all the same. Here? It seemed to matter very little that the weak possessed guile, or speed, or numbers. No, here it seemed there was no way to escape the bossman hyenas.

*

7.15pm

Tom Priddy wasn't exactly comfortable with the direction in which the conversation was heading.

'Funny thing,' the Beanpole said to him. 'Nessie was telling me about Theresa. About how she broke the news to you both. The accident. She says it shook you up, Cousin Thomas. Almost been there when it happened. And then something about how you should have realised. Poor girl on her way home from work. That kind of thing.'

'Shook me up?' said Tom. 'It did, too. Somebody on the tram must have known her though,' he lied. 'Some mention, I reckon. Maybe they even told us the name of the boozer. D'you remember, Uncle Huw?'

He watched Huw Maddox shrug, take another drag on that filthy cigarette, waited while he considered how to proceed.

'But no,' he said, at last. 'It was only after the inquest, see. About Penny's. Yes, that would be it! The inquest. Or maybe something your Nesta said. Made me put two and two together. Why so curious though, Beanpole? Ah, I know. Like me, you'll be hoping the girl dying – well, you wouldn't wish this on anybody but it's an ill wind, isn't it? And who knows, maybe it'll bring your tada and Taffy back together in the end. Great minds think alike, eh?'

Precisely the opposite of his plan, naturally, but no need to share it with the Beanpole.

'Just a price too high to pay though,' she told him. 'But interesting. That you wouldn't think so, like. And you're sure you didn't know already? Where Theresa worked, I mean.'

'We all know now,' said Tom. 'Worked in one of Rathbone Street's sawdust joints. Beer hall. Devil's brew, *cariad*. And everybody else here also knows, like your tada, I'm a temperance man. So how else, exactly, d'you imagine I'd know where she'd worked? And why would it matter if I did?'

The Beanpole had begun to clear the plates, almost dropped them when he stood from his chair to help her. He could see there was something in her head. Half-formed, perhaps. But maybe refusing to quite fulfil itself. Something to do with performance, she'd be thinking. Her Cousin Thomas still holding down his part-time job at the theatre. Was she wondering how much of the thespian's art had rubbed off on him?

It distracted him. Made him think of the Rotunda. No performance tonight. Cancelled, it was. Some problem with the touring troupe. Shame, really.

'Just curious,' Cari was saying. She'd collected herself, continued to collect the dishes as well. 'And you must admit, Cousin, it was quite a coincidence – you being in just the right place, just the right time. I think Taffy was hoping you might have heard something. Theresa's last words. Did she ask for him? At the end. That kind of thing, see.'

Huw Maddox wiped a dried dribble of the cawl's juices from his chin with the ball of his palm.

'*Duw*, Ceridwen,' he said. 'You sound like some barrack-room barrister. What's eating you, girl?'

There, his opening. Time to distract the Beanpole now, in her turn. Twist this conversation in a more helpful way.

'Coincidence, Beanpole? It was, an' all. If Uncle Huw hadn't asked me to run up to London Road...'

'No need to go into that now, lad,' old Huw cut across him. He was flustered, though Tom Priddy wasn't about to pay him any heed. This was perfect.

'What's this now?' said Cari. 'More secrets?'

'No secret, *cariad*,' said Huw Maddox. 'Just business. Or it may be. Not final yet, though. Don't want to count our chickens.'

Tom Priddy made a pretence of looking innocent, made sure he appeared to be failing badly.

'No harm in telling them, Uncle Huw,' he said in a stage whisper, then brightened, a more optimistic note. 'This could be the making of your tada, Beanpole. We're going into the lottery business.'

'Is it legal?' Rhys Fingers asked his father-in-law.

'*Duw Annwyl*,' said Huw Maddox. 'How could it not be? And it's a bit more than just a lottery. Tom's idea, see? We sell the tickets but, after the prizes have been paid out, most of the rest goes to help the Liverpool Welsh Orphans Society. Good cause, it is. Some initial outlay but, after that...'

'Initial outlay?' said the Beanpole, almost gagging on her amazement. She'd be thinking there were barely two ha'pennies to rub together. But typical of her father, perhaps thinking the same, maybe – to get himself, the rest of them, into debt to help others out of their own. 'How much outlay?' she said.

'Don't fret, *cariad*,' Huw Maddox gave his widest smile. 'Just a few bob. That's what Tom was helping me with. The bank. London Road. Small loan, is all. Get us started.'

'On my way back across Islington and spotted all the fuss,' Tom Priddy insisted, the lie tripping from his lips.

'How much, Tada?' said Cari. 'How much debt has this landed us in?'

'Go and see, if you like. Letter from the City and Midland. In my box.' Then he seemed to think better of his suggestion, some doubt crossing his mind. 'And take your sister with you, isn't it,' he suggested, as though this somehow solved whatever conundrum was troubling him. 'Yes, that's it. You should both have a look.'

There, thought Tom. Perfect!

7.30pm

Cari's sister Wyn appeared keen on the idea, enthusiastically agreed. Even took her arm as they stumbled up the stairs to their father's room. Books everywhere. The smell of camphor and hair oil.

The old mahogany box was something of a legend within the family. An ancient, large tea caddy which, her father claimed, was an heirloom almost two centuries old – a solid, ornate yet redundant lock from the days when tea had, literally, been worth more than its weight in gold. The key was long lost, but not the two tin containers in which the caddy must once have held different blends. Yet it was a convenient receptacle for their father's most valuable correspondence.

'Here it is,' Wyn said. And she lifted out the brown envelope with Huw Maddox's name written upon it in very fine copperplate. But as she opened the loan agreement it contained, Cari noticed the silk scarf had slipped and there, upon Wyn's neck, clear as day, was some ugly bruising at her throat. She caught Cari staring, of course, and quickly pulled the silk higher up her neck.

'I feel foolish now,' Cari smiled. 'As if this proves anything one way or the other.'

Yet Wyn wasn't interested in the family's finances.

'Not what you think,' she sneered. 'He's a good man, my Rhys.'

'But you might as well let me have a look, now we're here. At the evidence.' Cari meant the agreement, naturally, and held out her hand to receive it. Or, at least... 'Two hundred pounds! What's got into him? And the house and shop for collateral.'

'Did you find out from Taffy though? About whether there's been any tittle-tattle. On the docks, like.'

'They're in the middle of a strike, Wyn. And then all this with Theresa. I don't think he'd care too much what his mates were saying about – about your husband.'

'What were you going to say, Cari? Go on. What?' Honestly, Cari had simply lost her thread. She was still staring at the agreement but, at the same time, she was drawn to the other contents of her father's mahogany box, idly flicking aside a couple of bills and her attention taken by a neatly typed envelope, which screamed the word "solicitor" at her. But Wyn's strident protest dragged her back. 'That's what you were thinking. My Rhys, a dock-walloper. Weren't you?'

'I was not,' Cari replied, though she was finding it hard to concentrate. Collateral? What did this mean? 'Unless, of course, the cap fits, Wyn. Or have you got a better story about the bruises?'

'Who are you to judge me, Cari Maddox? At least I've got a man. A proper man. Not some German. Or some darkie. Or those disgusting women you keep company with.'

'You forgot to mention the Jews, Wyn. Old Kaplan and his family. For somebody who loves our Lord Jesus, you've got a lot of hate in your heart, my girl.'

Wyn gave Cari a look of withering venom and tossed the loan agreement's envelope on Huw Maddox's bed before storming off downstairs. Cari picked it up, replaced the invoice itself and dropped it back in the box. Below, Wyn was being hysterical, though she could neither hear nor imagine precisely what she was saying about their conversation. Not the truth, that was certain. She'd closed the lid and was halfway to the door, intending to find out what she was supposed to have done, and resigned to playing along with whatever nonsense Wyn had told them, but then found she couldn't resist, turned back and quickly lifted out the other letter. From a solicitor indeed. Mister

Watkin-Evans. Carnarvon. Just a few lines. Lines giving Cari a deep sense of foreboding.

And her father was already at the foot of the stairs.

'Ceridwen! What are you doing up there all this time? And what have you said to your sister?'

He sounded concerned, and Cari could hear his steps on the creaking treads.

'Ceridwen!'

So, she read it fast. Very fast.

Dear Mr. Maddox

I act on behalf of Mister Thomas Priddy, recently domiciled at 12 Smith Street, Beddgelert, in connection with matters concerning his late mother, Mis. Myfanwy Priddy, late of that parish. As a result, I write to seek confirmation that you are the same Mr. Huw Maddox, previously and legally known as Mr. Huw Priddy, and once domiciled at 31 Tan-y-Graig, Glan Adda, Bangor. I should be obliged if you could provide such confirmation within fourteen days from postmark or, in the contrary, evidence that you are not, in fact, said person.

But, by the time she'd reached the end, Huw Maddox was on the landing.

Chapter Seven

Sunday 13th August 1911

10.45am

This Liverpool place had been invaded. Soldiers, *poto* soldiers. Guns. So many guns. Soldiers on horses, as well. White horses. Some war had been declared, which Amos did not fully understand.

Still, now he marched. To war, also? He did not know war, though he imagined it must feel something like this, and he rubbed at the brass buttons upon his old greatcoat. A great procession of men – some women as well. A procession greater than all the others. But banners, flags, musicians, the singing of battle cries. A host of thousands. And their own horses. Horses – and carts.

'We push soldier men in river, *eh bye?*' he shouted up to King Billy.

'Not today,' the carter laughed. 'Just a show of strength. Tom Mann calls for the biggest protest and demonstration Liverpool's ever seen, and here we are.'

King Billy clicked his tongue at the horses, glanced back over his shoulder at this army Amos had joined several miles to the south. In truth, only part of their army, this southern column, many more joining from the north and elsewhere. From across the river. And King Billy sang.

> '*Tom Mann commands and we obey,*
> *Over the hills and far away.*'

Amos had studied the newspapers, often with the Wolof's help. So there was another image in his head. The entire world on strike. Seven hundred hewers of coal had won a victory at some place with

198

the strange name, Skelmersdale. It had become his favourite word, rolled it now around his tongue.

'Skelmersdale,' he murmured.

'Eh?' said King Billy, though Amos simply shook his head, reflected on the other news.

A thousand tram workers now with their own union. Brewery workers, as well.

The dockworkers gaining ground in their talks with the ship owner bossmen, an agreement signed a week earlier.

Strikes in other places all across their country.

It seemed to him that no problem, no complaint, no grievance, could now be without resolution. Except two. Their own demand. And then the sadness which he still saw in the eyes of Missee Nesta, the women's fight for justice. Perhaps when they reached their destination. The place they called the Plateau. Though, when he sniffed at the air, he sensed something was amiss – a feeling which had troubled him most of the day.

10.45am

Tom Priddy had mixed views about whether the city had been invaded. It was certainly true that the people of this divided Liverpool were all affected differently.

'Better than mob rule,' he said, giving his widest smile to the truckload of Tommies grinding and billowing past on Crosshall Street.

Old Huw waved at them as well and received a cigarette stump flicked in his direction by way of appreciation. They might have been friendly protectors and liberators to those who shared Tom's views but he suspected that, to the Tommies themselves, these onlookers were clearly nothing more than the potentially dangerous savages of an occupied dominion.

'It's martial law, Tada,' Cari told her father. 'Not far from it anyway.'

'There'd have been blood on the streets by now if they'd not sent for them, Beanpole,' Tom Priddy replied on her father's behalf. He managed to do this a great deal lately.

The Victoria Chapel was a stark place, well-suited to the Calvinists and strict Welsh Presbyterians who'd funded it, and who came there from far and wide to share their equally austere worship. Tom and the others were sheltering in the shadows of its arched portico, waiting for the rest of the family and nodding greetings to those entering ahead of them.

'*Croeso.*'

'*Shwmae.*'

'*Sut ydych chi?*'

'*Da iawn, diolch.*'

'Not to mention the extra guineas you've been able to make, Cousin,' said Cari.

Tom Priddy shrugged, feigning embarrassment when all he felt was self-righteous pomposity. The Police Watch Committee and the Lord Mayor's Office had gone to great lengths, explaining their decisions in posters and flyers – demand for which had necessitated additional copies being urgently printed. It was a contract the Maddox Printing Company Limited had been more than willing to fulfil.

'Puts food on your table too, see,' Cousin Tom sneered. 'Haven't heard you complain, girl. Not once.'

'Makes me feel sick, all the same.'

Tom was certain she must be telling the truth. In just a couple of days they seemed to have consumed the streets. Companies of khaki-clad soldiers, rifles and bayonets, with old Huw quoting chunks of Kipling every time their boot studs could be heard crunching along the cobbles. Or the power of their passage felt through the pavements, through their very limbs, with each column of grey-mounted cavalry. Or the catcalls which could be heard, catcalls especially reserved for the men of the Royal Irish Constabulary – here for a week already and drafted in to supplement the extra police from Birmingham, Leeds and goodness knew where else besides.

'And don't forget, Ceridwen, you need to apologise to Winifred,' Huw Maddox told her.

Tom watched the Beanpole bite her tongue. Her sister Winifred had spun this story that Cari had made some reference to Rhys Gateman being a scab. The evening, a few weeks earlier, when he'd manipulated the girls in the direction of the letter. It had been Winifred's excuse for running, weeping, back down the stairs and, in turn, sending her father up to his room. How he had failed to catch his daughter red-handed – reading the demand for confirmation of old Huw's identity from Mister Watkin-Evans – was something of a mystery.

But no matter. She must surely have read it, for it was plainly eating away at her, hardly a day going by without the Beanpole picking away at the blister.

'You know,' she said, as if to prove his point, 'I don't remember you ever mentioning your wedding day, Tada. Was it a very grand affair? Cousin Tom's family there?'

Tom Priddy snorted. Derision.

'Go on, Uncle Huw,' he said. 'What was it like? And when would that have been again? Let me think. Beanpole's how old?'

'Twenty-two,' she reminded him, though he could see the doubt on her face. Yes, she knew this was all playacting.

'*Duw*,' said her father. 'With all you kids to raise, and your mam gone, there wasn't really time to fuss about remembering wedding day. Only posh folk have the luxury, isn't it?'

'And it must have been painful,' Tom interrupted him. Deliberate sarcasm? 'Remembering, like. Never talk about it, you don't, Uncle.'

'When you get to my age, it feels like you've already talked about everything there is to say.'

'You're fifty-six, Tada,' said Cari. 'And yes, there's a bit of grey hair. Your poor fingers too…'

Huw Maddox examined the deformities around the knuckles of each hand.

'Quarry,' he said, as if his daughter didn't know.

'But apart from those,' she said. 'Well…'

'*If she favours you, love her,*' Huw Maddox quoted. '*If she wounds you, love her. Love her, love her, love her!*'

What was the old fool rambling about? Remembering something? But how could anybody know? These random quotations. *Great Expectations* and the rest.

'You've still not told us, Tada. What time of year it was, when you got married.'

'September. Thirtieth of September, see.'

Tom Priddy caught old Huw's eye, smiled at him, saw him flinch.

'But what year?' said Cari, while her father shook his head in exasperation.

'You can work it out for yourself, *cariad*.'

He was saved from further interrogation by the first strains of a band, following the same route earlier taken by the soldiers' trucks. Not a military band, though. This was the Rimrose Road Shamrock Band, according to the writing on the big bass drum, and marching at the head of a dockers' contingent, thousands of them, ranked behind a large linen banner. The dockworkers' North Liverpool No. 12 Branch. All in their Sunday best.

Papists, of course, Tom decided. All these damned dockers seemed to be papists. So, a pox on their strike. And this view, at least, he shared with Huw Maddox.

'Let's hope the Almighty's going to pour down his wrath upon them,' said old Huw, and mopped his brow with a handkerchief. It was hot. Sultry. A tropical heat. But thunder clouds gathering in the distance, a storm in the making

'See,' said Tom Priddy. 'Your Taffy.'

There he was, in the thick of them, and Theresa MacKenny's father, as well. Tom recognised him from the funeral, though he wasn't about to admit it. They were out on this nearer flank, working the guide ropes helping take some of the pressure from the pole-bearers, though there was little or no breeze to trouble them that day. The air still, heavy with suspense.

'Fools,' said Tom Priddy. 'Risen to the bait. Should never rise to another's bait, see.'

11.00am

Cari supposed she must share some of his concern. It felt like war had been declared.

Yet how was it possible Tom Priddy was still there? How had he inveigled his way so firmly into their lives. She was reminded of a performance she'd seen at the Adelphi Theatre on Christian Street the previous year. *Trilby*, and one of its main characters the mesmerist Svengali, who exerts such hypnotic control over others. More recently, a picture in the newspapers. From Russia. It was almost all she knew about the Russian court – how the Czar Nicholas, and his empress, were susceptible to an entire entourage of such charlatans. John of Cronstadt. The Virgin Triapkina. Father Vostorgoff. Olga the Tartar. But this latest grainy image had shown the Czarina and others of her high society, taking tea with an exotically bearded monk, one Grigori Rasputin, she recalled. And apart from the long beard, the rest could have been an image of Cousin Thomas. The lank hair, the ghostly features, the bulging wild eyes.

She shook her head, tried to expel the picture from her mind. For now, at least.

'Shall I see if Taffy'll come to chapel with us?' She wrapped her fingers around her father's arm.

'You must do what you think fit, girl. Doesn't trouble me.'

How long had it been now? Far too long. Each of them as stubborn as the other. But she'd not quite given up hope. So, she ran after the marching dockers until she caught up with her brother.

'Taffy,' she shouted, and skipped alongside him. 'Didn't you see us? Me and Tada.'

'I saw him.'

'You learned nothing, lad?' Mister MacKenny scolded him. He still wore a black armband, and she could smell the ale on his breath. 'Life's too short to bear grudges. And she's a good girl, this sister of yours.'

Cari smiled at him, mouthed a thank you, but saw also the way he'd aged over those few weeks. She'd only seen Taffy once, as well, and plainly even more bitter than the day of Theresa's funeral service.

'Too short for some,' said Taffy. 'For our Theresa, like. The rest of us? Well, life's long enough not to have to put up with other people's shit. Family or no family.'

'Hey,' Mister MacKenny snapped. 'No need for that, lad. Your sister…'

'Just wondered,' Cari murmured. 'We could all go to chapel, see? Together.'

'We've got the meeting,' Taffy replied, but at least his tone was less harsh.

'Doesn't start 'til three, Taffy,' said MacKenny. 'Plenty of time to see the family first. Heading up to Scottie Road,' he told her. 'Meet up with the Carters and maybe – well, you know the way it is, girl.

A man needs to wet his whistle on a day like this.'

'How many?' she asked. 'How many will be there?'

'Another procession coming in from the south-end. A third from over the water. Sixty thousand, maybe? More?'

'Hey, who's this then, Taff?' laughed one of the pole-bearers. 'Can't be one of your lot, lad. Too good-looking.' And there followed a torrent of amiable jibes, aimed her brother's way and, Cari suspected, for her benefit far more polite than they'd have been on the quayside. But the dockers, she'd found, were like this. Hard men, hard workers, hard drinkers for the most part, maybe hard on their wives. But outside those attributes, more gentlemanly manners than your average toff.

'Better behave yourselves,' MacKenny shouted back into the crowd. 'This one's high up in the glass-smashers. She'll 'ave a brick through your windows, soon as look at you.'

And she played along, laughed with them, glad to be distracted from Taffy's sour face.

'Or worse!' she threatened. 'So be warned.'

Somebody yelled.

'Hey, you know what we call your Taffy? At work?'

Cari had no idea.

'Give it a rest, Kipper,' Taffy yelled. 'For Christ's sake, give it a rest.'

'There was a time,' she scolded her brother, 'you would have laughed at that, Taffy.' She twined her arm in his. 'Come on, just say hello to Tada.'

But he wouldn't, and after a few minutes she gave up, promised to find him later at the rally, with Nesta, and walked back along the dockers' ranks towards the chapel, with Kipper's harsh voice ringing in her ears.

'Dai Surgeon, we call him. He's Welsh. Has us all in stitches – an' I don't think! Miserable bugger, 'e is.'

Yes, miserable. So long since she'd seen him smile, and she was still saddened by it all when she got back to the chapel. Rhys and Winifred had arrived, though he'd already gone inside. Nesta, as well. She could hear the harmonium being played, a few practice scales and chords. And the notes to one hymn in particular.

He who would valiant be, 'gainst all disaster.

Disaster? She found the soldiers had left an alien smell in her nostrils. She had no idea quite what the stink of cordite might resemble, though she imagined it must be something like this. Yet Cari shook the thought from her mind.

'Is he on good form this week, your Rhys?' she said, and kissed her sister's cheek.

Wyn looked at her suspiciously, perhaps wondering if she was being cryptic.

'I told you, Cari. He's always good. A good man.'

'I know. And I'm sorry. If I caused any offence, Wyn.' The words stuck in Cari's throat, but they seemed necessary. And she was, at first, touched when her sister reached up to return the kiss. But that was also short-lived.

'There is no hatred in my heart, Cari,' Wyn hissed, 'except for the godless heathen.'

11.00am

Amos Gartee considered himself a good Christian. But he also had a leaning towards the various deities and spirits celebrated across the coastal lowlands and mangrove swamps, the upland forests and the northern mountains of his homeland. It always seemed to him there was space within this multiplicity of beliefs, each leading its adherents towards some form of eternal salvation, for folk to worship as they wished. Yet he knew, with some shame, that it was a Christian thing for every one of its many branches to require adherence to only their own narrow interpretation of God's word – and at times to hang, burn or crucify those whose interpretations might be marginally different.

Yet here, on their procession towards justice, there was a priest outside one of the city's many, many churches, blessing them as they marched past. In the priest's honour, Amos chanted the opening line of a song, taking the part of the Strong Man, Nyanwule the *Krogba*.

'*Who shall help me heave these nets?*' he sang in their own Kru tongue.

'*Tobogee-o, Nyanwule,*' came the harmonised response. We will do this thing, Nyanwule.

It was, Amos considered, appropriate – for was their Lord Jesus not a fisher of men? Yet he saw the priest flinch when he heard the song, regard them with horror and make the sign of the cross not towards the marchers but for his own benefit, as though to ward off the evil eye.

Amos also watched King Billy's response, the carter shaking his head, then turning towards their contingent.

'Good banner, by the way,' he shouted, and lifted a thumb in salute.

A length of old cloth, nailed at each end around a pole. White cloth, with words painted in black along its length. Above, *Black Sailors Equal Pay*. And below, *God Bless Tom Mann*.

Miss Nesta, of course, had brought it for them. Miss Nesta and the Germany man.

'How much further?' Samuel Nimene complained in their own tongue. Samuel was carrying one of the poles, the other borne aloft by the Mende Jonah Samba.

'Not far,' Amos replied. 'See? Remember this place?'

They'd passed it on their walk southwards to join the starting point of the march. It was one of the local alehouses, at the junction of two roads so that the building had been squeezed into the shape of an arrowhead. Iron-grey. Not far from the Elder Dempster hostel, presently occupied by the Company's bossmen yet again, while the Mandinkas who had joined the strike now thrown onto the streets. At the mercy of the David Lewis hostel and other benefactors.

Benefactors. The word caused him to think of Miss Nesta again. Her visit with the German buffalo and his dung-coloured hair.

'Sunday, you will walk?' the Germany man had said when they'd arrived at the lodging houses on Parliament Street.

'March, Ernst,' Miss Nesta had corrected him. 'Amos and his men will march. We say march for demonstrations. And Sunday shall be huge. So, we have brought you this gift, Amos.'

She'd unwrapped the banner, presented it with great reverence, and he had told her how fine it was, though he was thinking all the time about how she had scolded the Germany man for his faulty English. And Miss Nesta, for her part, had been distracted by the Kru brothers. She was expected, of course – had said she would visit. So they, in turn, had prepared a modest spectacle. To make a point on their *krogba*'s behalf.

'Yes, march,' Amos had said. 'To win.'

Samuel Nimene and the others had been hard at work. Masks. One for each of the beasts in the story. Made from anything they'd been able to scavenge. Easy enough in a city where every street and alleyway now had its own midden, heaps of garbage left where they lay.

'But first,' Amos had told the German, 'tonight, we dance.'

He'd done his best to explain – to Miss Nesta, at least. Leopard King's challenge. His daughter's hand to the creature which could best show its skill as a provider, which could catch and consume the most food in the shortest time.

For a gathering crowd of appreciative onlookers, Samuel's mane of Lion had swirled and rustled as he stalked his imaginary gazelle, pounced and gnawed – but then had laid himself down to sleep.

George Janjay's trunk of Elephant swayed from side to side, gathered roots and grasses, fruit and bark – though had to cover great distances for his foraging.

'This one?' Miss Nesta had asked, when Barkuh Togba lumbered forward, horned with dung-brown hair.

'Buffalo,' Amos had told her, hoping she might not spot the similarity between Barkuh's mask and the Germany man's features.

Buffalo, of course, has quite an appetite, yet spends so much time chewing the cud that he must surely fail the test. And the winner? Miss Nesta had seemed genuinely entranced when Amos had donned his own mask, Goat's horns and wispy beard. For Goat, it became clear, eats anything and everything, a veritable and insatiable eating machine. None may beat Goat for the extent of its eating.

At the performance end, there had been applause, backs slapped, Miss Nesta making the rounds to congratulate each of the performers.

'Goat winning, he did,' the German told Amos.

'Goat have bride price,' Amos had replied with his broadest smile. 'You have, Germany man?'

Now, marching with the procession, the recollection caused him to smile. But as they tramped towards their destination, towards the Hall of St. George, he happened to glance up one of the streets running upwards to their right. And there, though some distance away, he observed another column, seemingly moving parallel to their own. A column of uniforms.

Yes, thought Tom. Godless heathens. Papists. Darkies. It was all the same.

'That's my girls!' Huw Maddox beamed, deaf to Wyn's whispered venom. 'You see, Tom?'

He led them all inside without even a question to the Beanpole about his son. But Ceridwen and her brother were on Tom's mind through most of the service.

The sermon from Pastor Jenkins was all fire and brimstone, as usual, and not for the first time, took a moralising stance on the conduct of the Strike Committee – called on the Lord to look into the hearts of the ship owners and the other involved employers, to turn them from the paths of avarice, but also to search the souls of the union leaders and to lead them from the damnation of dishonesty.

Quite right too, thought Tom Priddy.

'And I don't blame Mister Mann,' Pastor Jenkins thundered. 'Nor their new Transport Workers Federation. No, not at all. For when they are sent to negotiate on behalf of the seamen, and they do so in an organised way, settling firm by firm – well, that is honourable. Honest men return to work as a result, yet only to be met with representatives of the dockers' committees, who say: "Hold fast. What about us? Where is our own portion?" Dishonesty.'

Yes, thought Tom Priddy. You can never trust a papist.

'The negotiators,' the pastor raged, 'are forced to begin afresh, the men to remain on strike, now with both the seamen and the dockers in dispute. Until new agreements are reached. Honourable agreements. And honest men returned to work once more. Yet now to be met with representatives of the railwaymen, who say: "Hold. What about us? Where is *our* portion?" Dishonesty once more.'

Tom wasn't sure about the railwaymen. He'd never taken railwaymen for papists, but…

'So, it all begins again, while the food our Lord provides is left to rot in warehouses. The stench of pestilence upon our streets.'

Yes, stench, Tom Priddy thought. And I should do something about it. Time to take sides, like. See my plans through. Not a problem. But take sides in this, as well. Show my worth, see.

'It is a great deception,' cried Pastor Jenkins. 'And those involved should heed the words of Holy Scripture. *The bread of deceit is sweet to a man; but afterwards his mouth shall be filled with gravel.* Thus sayeth the Lord. And when the newspapers call this Red Sunday, we should heed them. For this stench of pestilence is the deception of revolution. Of communism. Of the godless hordes.'

Red Sunday? Tom considered the words. Godless hordes. Communists. Yes, take sides against all this filth. Nothing wrong with a bit of rebellion, mind. Weren't his own modest schemes a form of rebellion? Whereas this…

'At least he's leaving *us* alone this week,' he heard Dumpling Nesta murmur to the Beanpole from behind the Welsh prayer book, which she couldn't read.

It was true. And amusing. Barely a week had gone by without Pastor Jenkins finding something in the women's demand for the vote to displease both him personally and, apparently, the Lord Himself. Well, Tom could cope with this. He was right about the stink on the streets as well. They were hardly scavenged anymore and there were heaps of decaying garbage on almost every corner. On the other hand, he also found the growing support for this swelling of labour unrest especially putrid.

12.55pm

Cari wasn't alone in the view that the WSPU should have been more directly supportive of the strikers.

Many of the local meetings had ended badly when they'd tried to push the matter further up the agenda. Alice now had Cari marked, she believed, as something of a rabble-rouser and while there'd been promises to forward each of the several articles Cari had written for the editorial team of *Votes for Women* – about the strikes and about the possibility of enhancing involvement in them – none of them had ever appeared, and she had begun to doubt Alice had ever sent them. Cari had even attempted to send one of the articles herself, direct to Clement's Inn.

No response. Instead, the pages were still filled with all the regular news and opinion. Yet it had become clear to Cari from the various disputes elsewhere – like the pit-brow women on the Lancashire coalfields – that women were no longer simply campaigning for the right to vote but, rather, often for the right to live and work. And to be paid proper wages. For while many of the strikes had involved women from the sweated trades, they were generally fighting for pennies extra each week, while the men, more often, might reasonably expect to gain shillings.

Well, there would be a contingent of their women during today's rally, and her women clerks would certainly be there. Along with some recently joined shop assistants who had promised to attend and protest most strongly about how they'd been forced, because of the strikes, to take a week's so-called "holiday" – basically, locked-out when their employers had decided to board up their properties in case of possible rioting.

Though how silly the prospect seemed, as Cari's family left the Victoria Chapel on this fine mid-August morning, and she became aware of a small man, bustling among them, while her eyes adjusted to the pavement's brightness.

'Ah, Mister Maddox,' the man beamed. 'And Mister Priddy. *Sut wyt ti ddau?*' How are you both? 'Hopefully, we'll see some dividend soon from our little venture.'

'*Bore da*, Mister Hughes,' her father told the man. Good morning. He went on to thank him for asking and yes, fine dividends in due course. Then Tada assured the tousle-haired and rotund old fellow that they were all fine, before introducing Cari, Nesta, Wyn and Rhys Fingers. He already knew Rhys, of course, though he still expressed delight – perhaps it was something he'd chosen not to take for granted – when he discovered the harmonium player's good lady wife to be equally fluent in the language. But it was left to Cari, with her usual curiosity, to ask him how he came to be acquainted with her father and cousin.

'Business partners, we are,' he told her. 'Now, that is.'

Though he was surprised her tada hadn't mentioned him. Mister Hughes, he explained. Mister Maldwyn Hughes. Superintendent of the Liverpool Welsh Orphans Society. And such generosity. For her father to have arranged this fund-raising venture on behalf of those poor children. A saint. Truly. And if Cari should like to see more of their work – her tada and Cousin Thomas already being regular visitors to their offices, it seemed – then she would be most welcome.

'I should like it very much, Mister Hughes,' she told him in her best Welsh. 'And where would that be?'

'Best to come to the offices first, see,' he replied. 'Can't miss us. Halfway along Rathbone Street, we are.'

2.30pm

'You've 'eard the good news, lad?' said Jocota.

The man had disentangled himself from the morass of men, women and children – though mainly men – now filling the area between the station and the Hall of St. George. A morass so dense that the spider's web of tram lines had entirely disappeared from view.

'You have seen soldiers, Jocota?' Amos replied. 'Po-leese might be.'

'No police or soldiers today, my friend. Tom Mann's done a deal. Understand – deal? And yes, looks like we've also got a deal with Elder Dempster.'

Amos had stopped just around from the great oval entrance and roadway into the station itself, stopped to peer in the window of the oyster bar adjoining the Royal Hotel. He loved the smell. Salty. Fishy. Reminders of home to eradicate the Liverpool aromas of tobacco, hemp, sweat, sewerage and discarded refuse. Stopped, also, because he admired the view from here. This Liverpool place, running down towards the river so that, from the station, the city presented the illusion of being somewhat below him. Spires, towers, clocks. A gilded dome shone in the afternoon sun and, in its honour, Amos unbuttoned his overcoat.

'Deal?' he said. 'Same pay – or tenbob?'

'Think it's as good as it's goin' to get, mate. Know what I mean? Ten bob, yeah, we got it. So not on half the rate anymore. Not quite. And you'll get more again when you're shipping out from 'ere. And both ways, you'll be getting more than the lads they hire in Lagos. Make sense?'

Amos wasn't certain. He asked Jocota to explain it again until, finally, he was sure he had the thing in order. With the tenbob increase, white seamen would now be paid five pounds and ten shillings per month; Kru seamen hired in Liverpool for the passage back to Freetown, three pounds; Kru seamen hired in Freetown itself, two pounds and fifteen shillings; and for other Africans – like those who arrived on the

Nigeria, from Lagos or Forcados, or other places – no more than two pounds and ten shillings. A victory, yes, though it felt like a small one, given the time he and his brothers had been fighting. Still…

'Yes, make sense, Jocota.'

He glanced across at the crowd, growing ever larger by the minute. He had never seen so many people in one place at one time, could not have imagined there might even be so many people in Liverpool. Yet all of them fighting. Scratching for their tenbob. Here, surrounded by these palaces and temples, by this wealth. And he remembered the wise words of the Wolof, Charles Tuohey. How the English, the French, the Germans, the Belgians used the argument that they had brought civilisation to Africa. To India, also.

'But do we truly believe,' Tuohey had said, 'the English brought their railways to India for the benefit of the Indians?'

A good question. And Amos was proud of his people's culture. They already had a civilisation of their own, one which had not been improved by the arrival of the English. And how, thought Amos, can they have claimed to bring civilisation anywhere when, from his own observations, they had plainly never troubled to bring civilisation to the poor of their own cities?

3.05pm

It was impossible to count them, and Cari had certainly never seen such a multitude in all her born days. Tom Mann had opened his address by claiming they were a hundred thousand in number, and she saw no reason to disbelieve him.

Those who knew the city would be familiar with the setting. The huge, level space bordered, back along its eastern edge, by Commutation Row, the Empire Theatre, the row of shops with Silverman's at its end, the palatial North Western Hotel and the broad façade of Lime Street Station.

A recollection here always made her smile. She'd been going to work, a carthorse dead in the road outside Commutation Row's piano shop, a bobby trying to write down the details in his pocketbook, glancing frequently up at the street sign. Scribbling. Crossing out. Scribbling. Crossing out. Until he finally yelled to a bunch of lads crowding in the doorway of the pub next door.

'Oy,' he'd shouted, 'get yerselves over 'ere an' help me drag this bugger across to Lime Street.'

She'd never told Taffy the story, thought of doing so now, yet he seemed intent on the opposite, western rim of this space. The looming bulk of Liverpool's own Parthenon, their gargantuan temple to Victorian enterprise, St. George's Hall. The hall's steps ran down and down in lines a hundred yards long onto the cobbled plateau between, a space that could have accommodated, they said, six or seven soccer pitches.

'Can you smell it, Cari?' Taffy asked her and filled his lungs. 'Freedom,' he said. 'Today we all breathe free. Look at them all.'

Such a crowd. A crowd undivided by sectarianism for once perhaps, she thought. No Catholic nor Protestant. No Jew nor Presbyterian. Not this day. And she had sold her satchel of last Friday's *Votes for Women* in the first half-hour. Could have sold a hundred more besides, and that despite the competition. For the Strike Committee members were out in force selling the first edition of their own new journal, the *Transport Worker*, or supplying placards from the back of an enormous wagon. She wasn't the only one of their WSPU women, either, with sashes worn as proudly as the men's union buttons. Cari, Mary Robson, Eileen O'Donnell, Patricia Woodlock, and young Bessie Butler. And Cari's little army from the Women Clerks' Association. No sign of Alice Davies though, but the NUWSS out in force and a decent contingent from the Catholic Women's Suffrage Society.

A crowd of a hundred thousand? Oh yes, so very easily. And Tom Mann had been careful to remind them, in his broad Black Country accent, how the authorities had agreed to allow the Strike Committee to police the event themselves, with only a minimum presence from the occupying forces. Allowed? That was the word they'd used, after all.

'How does it feel?' she said to Taffy. 'Being responsible for all this? Not a bobby in sight.'

"All this" was an eddying swell of varying sepia hues, which seemed to Cari a reflection of the brown Mersey itself. A tide of cloth caps and bowlers. Sunday waistcoats and straw boaters. Women's broad-brimmed bonnets and corduroy caps. Waving banners of the unions and, in one place, a fluttering standard of the National Federation of Women Workers. Almost the smell of the river as well, salty, something of sewage, mingled with the heady waft of tobacco smoke and horse manure. And the cry of gulls overhead to punctuate the powerful noisy flood of it all.

'Don't kid yourself, Cari. Thousands of them hidden away all over the show. You just can't see them. Well – don't make it obvious but have a glance along the roof. Behind you.'

She looked casually over her shoulder, to the parapet running above the columns of St. George's Hall. And there, sure enough were the flat caps of British Tommies. Not many, but enough.

'Anything goes wrong,' Taffy murmured, 'and they'll be all over us like a rash. Freedom or no freedom.'

This was pretty much what Tom Mann had said, but she still wasn't convinced.

They'd met near Taffy's branch banner, just across from Lord Nelson Street – itself packed with overspill from the crowd – close to a flat-bed wagon from which leaders of their North Liverpool Committee were taking turns to relay the speeches being delivered from the main platform, by the steps.

She could see four such wagons set up across the plateau, all the way from Wellington's Column and the fountain, past the great black lions and the huge plinths from which rose the equestrian and heroic statues to Liverpool's many glories – those plinths now dripping with spectators trying to gain a better view. And from each wagon, the Joint Strike Committee's stewards and officials coordinated the reading of the addresses in perfect simultaneous harmony, their voices carrying, clear and loud for the most part, to the several thousand clustered around their particular position, so that the applause and cheers, when they came – and they came frequently enough – were also simultaneous, great roaring waves of fervour which raked the crowd with quickening hearts and invincibility.

'And do you think he was right?' she said. 'This will turn into a general strike, if we don't get a settlement soon from the bosses? Some movement tomorrow?'

Tom Mann was due to put a resolution to that effect to the crowd and Cari expected it would be approved with deafening cheers, over and over again, at each of the other platforms.

'Might as well be a general strike already,' Rhys Fingers grumbled. 'Hardly any of us left in work anyhow. There may be a hundred thousand strikers, Taffy, and all of them here. But there's seven times that many in the city, lad. Suffering from this the more it drags on.'

'If we'd had solid support in the first place…' Taffy began.

'You'd never have been working on the docks, *in the first place*,' Wyn snapped at him, sarcastically, 'if it weren't for my Rhys.'

Taffy knew she was right and swallowed whatever he'd been going to say. 'If it weren't for my Rhys and the blessings of our Lord Jesus,' Wyn went on. 'Ashamed, you should be. Not even in chapel for months now. Shame on you, Dafydd. Shame!'

Nineteen, Cari thought, and always so distraught. There lay the shame. But Wyn hadn't finished. Not yet.

'You don't know how it hurts me. The idea that, on the day the Lord calls us to Heaven, the rest of us will dwell in His house forever – but not those who haven't fully taken Jesus into their lives.'

'This what you think, Wyn?' Cari said. 'The Lord would be cruel enough to divide us like that? Our beautiful family. For eternity?'

'Nah, never mind,' said Taffy. 'I'll make my peace with God in my own way, Wyn, when the time comes. And the day might come sooner than you'd think. If Tom Mann's right and they plan to send gunboats to sort us out.'

'I don't believe it for one minute,' Rhys sneered. 'About the gunboats. Fantasy, that's what it is.'

'You can scoff all you like, Rhys,' said Taffy, his hare-lip slurring some of the words in his excitement. 'But Mann's nobody's fool. He's right. Even without the gunboats, all these troops and extra police – why all this unless they mean to take us on? Challenge us, like he said. All of us. Challenge our rights. Our – our identity, like. As workers.'

Identity? Cari thought. There's a word, now. And it brought back to her the solicitor's letter, as it came to her every day. A dozen times a day. Only now, as she looked at Taffy's earnest face, etched with belief in his own cause and helping him overcome his grief, there was this second riddle. Mister Maldwyn Hughes and his Liverpool Welsh Orphans Society. Her tada's loan which the family could so ill-afford for this lottery venture. And his apparently frequent visits – or, rather, the visits of Cousin Tom Priddy – to the Society's offices. In Rathbone Street – where Theresa MacKenny had worked at Penny's public house.

3.20pm

The afternoon wore on, and it seemed to Amos that the crowd's appetite for more and more speeches must be insatiable. Among most of the remaining older spectators, at least. The children, for their part, had taken to playing football, or their crickety game, near the enormous column on the farther side of the Plateau, around the fountain of cool water, which spouted there for all to enjoy. Others were simply running around making a nuisance of themselves.

The crickety game. A reminder of home. The *poto* Englishmen, sweating in their equally white shirts and trousers. Their overfed *poto* wives and other spectators in their funereal white dresses and hats, their sun helmets. The boredom of the match.

There was something of the same boredom here, as well. The voices of the speakers now settled almost to an insect drone, broken only occasionally by a burst of applause echoing against the austere face and columns of the hall.

Boredom, Amos knew, was dangerous. For in the sleepy moments when boredom has you within its grip, this is when the predator strikes.

3.25pm

Rhys and Winifred, like many others, had tired of the event and taken themselves home. Just before half-past-three o'clock, it must have been – with Rhys claiming he had some important business to attend. And, as Wyn had lagged behind to say goodbye, she gave Cari a smile which would have graced a martyred saint.

'The Lord tells me to honour my husband in all things,' she'd said.

'What was that?' Nesta asked, after Wyn had gone.

'Nothing, Nessie. Nothing important. But have you seen Amos and the lads? I thought they might have been here.'

She was being slightly disingenuous, for she'd seen several black faces in the crowd, though none she recognised. And she wondered.

There might be a sectarian amnesty this day, but did it apply also to the Kru and whatever faith they might follow? There had been a moment in the speech delivered by Joe Cotter, from the ships' cooks and stewards' union – about Elder Dempster. Some sort of offer, though Cari hadn't caught the details.

'Over by the fountain,' said Nesta.

'Cooling down?'

'The opposite,' she laughed. 'All got their overcoats on. Trying to stay in the sun.'

Cari remembered her stupid image of the Africans' homeland but – well, maybe it wasn't so daft, after all.

'Happy with the way it's going though, are they?'

'They're managing. I collected a couple of guineas for them too.'

'Good of you, Nessie. But where on earth did you get it?'

'Here and there,' she shrugged. Cari wanted to press the point but didn't dare.

'But no agreement on their pay?'

'You think anybody's worrying about a deal for the Krooboys, Cari?'

Cari supposed she must be right. No doubt that, when the rest of it was all over, Amos Gartee's black seamen would benefit no more than the pit-brow women. Probably less.

'Though I heard someone mention Elder Dempster,' said Nesta. 'We should ask Amos if he knows anything.'

So, Nessie had been paying no more attention than Cari herself.

But then they spotted the fellow with the motion picture camera, the apparatus set up between Lime Street's currently redundant tram tracks. There was a steadfast wooden tripod bearing a small banner: *Pathé's Animated Gazette*. The machine itself dwarfed its operator as he gently cranked a handle at the tripod's steel top, caused the camera to smoothly and slowly revolve, to capture the entire panorama. When he paused, Nesta grabbed Cari's arm.

'Come on,' she said, and dragged Cari through the crowd, straightening her *Votes for Women* sash as she went.

'Hang on, Nessie,' Cari said to her. 'Is this wise? The bobbies…'

They'd already had their picture taken by Mister Mills – Gwilym, he insisted they call him – another of their father's countrymen and associates, from Llanidloes originally, and a regular member of the chapel's congregation. He now owned the Carbonora Photographic Company, on Wilde Street. Yet this business with Pathé seemed a different matter entirely.

'By the time Sergeant Ladysmith gets to see this,' Nesta laughed, 'I'll be long gone. And just imagine how furious he'll be when I pop up on the silver screen, right before his eyes.'

'Long gone?' Cari repeated, stupidly.

'It'll be two weeks before anybody sees this, you goose. I'm hardly likely to still be hanging around on Lime Street waiting for him to cart me off to the Bridewell again, am I?'

Cari giggled at her own foolishness. Yet it was a fine day, and the devil was in them, she thought. Cari in the same white frock they'd made for the Coronation Procession in London, the same flower-strewn white hat, and Nesta in her best fawn hobble skirt and high-necked blouse, her boater with the WSPU ribbons. They turned heads and, exactly as Nesta had intended, they also turned the camera. And each flirted with the sashes they wore, displaying the wording for the whole world to see, drew some shouts and whistles from the men around them.

3.30pm

'My favourite cousins!' Tom Priddy shouted, as the camera operator scribbled the girls' names in his little notebook.

Tom thrust his hands deeper into his pockets, strolling along as though he'd not a care in the world. 'Where's young Winifred, though? Make the prettiest picture, it would. All three of you together. Fashion photographer's dream, like.'

The Lord Jesus was within him, and while others might choose to see this as their Cousin Thomas at his supercilious worst, honeyed words drawling from a face that looked like the epitome of morbidity, in truth he meant every syllable.

'Rhys had business to attend to,' Nesta growled at him. 'Left a while ago.'

At least the Dumpling had spoken, though almost as if she'd forgotten not to do so. She looked up at her sister in some confusion.

'Business?' he grinned. 'On a Sunday? Yes, I suppose he might.'

He had his suspicions about Rhys Gateman. Well, more than just suspicions. But by then he'd dug out some small change and was jingling the coppers in his hand.

'Perhaps I could buy you both a drink?' he said.

There were vendors everywhere. Small handcarts. Barrows. Or trays slung from their necks. And offering everything from bottled lemonade, peppermint water and ginger beer to pork scratchings, pickled whelks and punnets of fresh blackberries. There were even some of the Italian hokey-pokey men selling shaved ices, and he was cut to the quick, genuinely hurt, when both of the girls demurred.

'Needn't bother,' snapped Dumpling Nesta.

'Speaking of business though,' said Cari, 'it was interesting, meeting Mister Hughes earlier.'

'Mister Hughes?' asked Nesta, sharply, and Tom saw the Beanpole link her arm, feeling safer this way, perhaps, as they began to edge their way back along Lime Street.

'A new partner of Tada's,'

'And mine, Beanpole,' Thomas smiled. 'And mine.'

Yes, he had certainly wormed his way into their business.

'By huge coincidence,' the Beanpole smiled serenely, 'this Mister Hughes has an office on Rathbone Street, Nessie. Just along from the boozer where Theresa MacKenny worked. And Cousin Thomas a regular visitor there, aren't you?'

It was the thing he admired about her. Quick, she was. Didn't really miss a trick, like.

'To the office, Beanpole,' he said. 'Only the office. Never to the public house, naturally. But why should this intrigue you so?'

'You really didn't know who she was? When you saw her after the accident?'

The tone of her voice. A challenge. A confrontation. It troubled him – though not much.

'I would have said so,' he replied. 'Why would I not?'

'I keep asking myself the same question,' said the Beanpole.

'Tragedy, it was,' said Dumpling Nesta, though careful to direct the comment towards her sister. Trying to ignore poor Tom, he thought. See? Still not learned her lesson.

'But maybe a silver lining,' said Nesta, 'if, at the end, Tada and

Taffy can bury their differences.'

'My thoughts exactly, *cariad*,' Tom smiled at her, lying through his teeth. 'Really. Bury their differences.'

He'd not really intended a pun, decided the Lord Jesus must have put the words in his mouth. He saw the Beanpole wince.

'And must be your hope too, Beanpole, isn't it?' he pressed on. 'Blood thicker than water, eh? Sometimes the Lord Jesus needs to give things a little push. See?'

He felt the muscles of his face turn to harsh granite as he pushed her, also. A gentle pressure, his two hands against her upper arm, but enough to make her stagger backwards. They'd almost returned to the bottom of Lord Nelson Street, where the elegant station hotel side windows gaped across to Silverman's and the theatre's red brick flank beyond. There was a shout.

'*He, Sie da!*'

It was the German wretch, Ernst Jurks, balancing with some others on one of the stone window ledges and, therefore, with a fine view over the heads of those at street level.

'You good, Cari?' the German yelled.

There was a look of stupid concern on his face and he must surely have seen Tom set hands on her. Not that Tom was greatly troubled, of course. For he narrowed his eyes, flashed the Beanpole a message with his eyes she could not possibly mistake for anything but a serious warning.

'Yes,' the Beanpole cried back. 'Good. Thank you. Just...' She seemed to struggle for a word of easy explanation. 'A game. Yes, a game.'

How she must wish she could tell the truth, though. A vision of perhaps seeing the big German bound across and give Thomas Priddy a good thrashing.

But Tom was waving up at him, a benign smile on his cadaverous lips. He supposed the Beanpole would have left matters there but Dumpling Nesta had already launched into a tirade.

'What *do* you think you're doing?' she shouted at him.

Tom thought things could hardly get any worse when he saw the brother, Taffy, pushing his way through some dockers, just beneath the German's perch and out of Lord Nelson Street itself. If Daft Taffy got the wrong end of the stick now, if the Dumpling couldn't hold her tongue – well, with Taffy's quick temper…

Yet, just then, he saw their German friend turn his back, as quickly as he was able, leaning out as though from the rigging of his ship, clinging to another fellow for support, and peering at something further up the side street. He spun back again, almost lost his footing from the ledge. His companion steadied him, and Jurks was shouting. At the Beanpole? No, at Dumpling Nesta. His one free hand was cupped around his mouth, and the mouth wide.

'Run, girl. Run!' There were hands grabbing at his legs, jostling and shouting among those gathered beneath him. Blue-uniformed arms reaching for him. 'Run!'

A scuffling melee. Bobbies trying to force their way through the dockers. Truncheons rising and falling. The first bloodied heads. Screams and furious bellowing. A curious toilet smell he'd not noticed earlier.

And that sergeant, Ladysmith, of course. About time, as well. Tom had given him enough notice she'd be there, after all. Ladysmith's whistle was between his teeth with its strident call to arms.

Tom Priddy watched as the Beanpole looked around for her brother, but she couldn't see him anymore. Made himself scarce, just as Tom had hoped he might. And there was the suspicion painted all over the Beanpole's face. Not a second time, he imagined she'd be thinking. A second time Daft Taffy had betrayed Dumpling Nesta to the police. Priceless!

3.45pm

'No nonsense this time about giving yourself up, girl,' Cari yelled. 'Now go.'

'I'll take her,' Cousin Thomas volunteered, and Cari reluctantly nodded her agreement, uncertain why she'd not simply led Nesta to safety herself. Not sure if she was any more secure with Tom Priddy than with Sergeant Ladysmith, for she saw the expression on her sister's face at the suggestion. Fear? Loathing? Fury? But the next moment, she was gone, dragged by Cousin Thomas into the crowd.

Perhaps it was irrelevant anyway, for the policeman was in hot pursuit of his prey, knocking folk aside as he went, and two of his men striking out with their truncheons to clear a path. There was, at first, something of the comedic about it, for they were plainly inebriated, their truncheons often flailing wildly against thin air for the most part, and they were so outnumbered it could only end badly for them. Yet, whether Taffy was somehow implicated or not – though Cari was sure he must be – this pursuit of Nesta, fugitive felon though she might be, seemed a strange obsession to follow on a day such as this.

Yet there is some saying about the long-term effects from moving a single grain of sand and this, it seemed to Cari, might illustrate the point perfectly. For, as the scuffle continued at the corner of Lord Nelson Street, and as Sergeant Ladysmith was stopped in his tracks by a dozen belligerent dockers, there was a new commotion, away behind him, further up the side street.

Reinforcements, of course. She could hear their boots on the cobbles, the rhythmic stamp of their feet echoing between the station walls on one side and the high theatre building on the other, and the sound split by a train signalling its departure to the world. A cloud of coal smoke was carried on the breeze and, while the seagulls wheeled and screeched above, a child's ball bounced past, its small owner being dragged away by his mother, her face riven with fear and premonition.

Men were running, dozens of them pouring from Lord Nelson Street like stampeding cattle, some tripping and falling, a few pausing briefly to howl insults over their shoulders at their pursuers.

Cari looked for Ernst, but couldn't see him. She tried to push her way against the tide, making for the corner where she'd last seen him. Yet it was impossible. There was blind panic there, and she was pushed aside several times without thought and nothing more than the occasional 'Sorry, luv.'

The bobbies, by contrast, were consideration itself. To Cari, at least. And only then, in that moment. For there was soon nothing between her and their advancing solid ranks. Fifty of them? A hundred, perhaps? But they parted smoothly around her as they hit Lime Street, formed a cordon there. A few of them remained near the station gate, hustling away those men already arrested. Yet still no sign of Ernst.

Cari spun around, saw the policemen drunkenly set about anybody who came within range of their sticks and then, just as rapidly, they were moving backwards up the street. One of them took her arm and, for an instant, Cari thought she must also be arrested. But he simply gave her a look of stern reproach, glanced at the sash.

'Shouldn't be here, miss,' he said, and Cari realised he had a Birmingham accent. Strange, she thought, as he guided her across to the pavement. 'Off you go, now. There's a good girl.'

The words, the tone, grated. She didn't go, of course. Merely slipped back around the corner, onto the main road again. Men were down. And an older woman, sitting with her legs all a-kimbo and nursing her head, sobbing violently, so that Cari went to kneel beside her, tried to comfort her while a young man squatted at the side, her son perhaps, trying to hold back his own tears.

There was a fellow being carried away by friends, his head lolling back as though he were dead, and his arms and legs all dangling, lifeless – and Cari prayed he was simply insensible. Personal possessions scattered the ground, and there were the first signs of ferocious anger among all the confusion.

Somebody was shouting.

'What the bloody hell happened? What?'

The cry was taken up by others, and Cari could hardly explain it was all her sister's doing. Or her brother's perhaps. Or maybe the fault of Ernst Jurks.

3.50pm

Amos Gartee and his brothers heard the whistles. From their place by the fountain they could see the ferment as well. Yet, elsewhere, the afternoon seemed simply to be following its course, largely heedless of this new development. At the speakers' platforms and among the denser crowds over on St. George's Plateau itself, faces turned momentarily that way. But then the speeches began afresh. It seemed to be the way of these things. A closing resolution to strengthen the strikers' unity. Folk checking their watches so this resolution thing might be read at precisely the same moment at each of the speakers' platforms. A wondrous thing. Yet a few folk drifting towards the developing disturbance, crossing Lime Street and asking people nearer to them what might have happened.

There seemed to be people injured as well. And in their midst, one figure stood out from all the rest. It was some distance away, yet he was almost certain – yes, it could be nobody else. A woman, tall and slender, white dress. A sash of purple, white and green. Missee Coconut Palm, surely. Surely, if one sister was there, this strange and dangerous afternoon…

'This will not end well,' he told the others, as he sniffed the air. 'Not a good place for us to be, I think.'

If these po-leese were attacking their own, what chance might there be for themselves who could so easily attract animosity even when blood was cool?

'Better leave now,' he said. 'Find safe way. Back to Sailor Town.'

He pointed away from the direction by which they'd arrived, to the slope down past other magnificent temples, past the trees and gardens behind this Hall of St. George, down towards the river, he was certain.

'That way.' He glanced up at the afternoon sun. 'West. Then south until you see great House of God on the hill. Stay together.'

'And you, Amos?' said the Guere, George Sanjay.

'Me?' Amos replied, and glanced back towards Missee Coconut Palm. 'Goat has things to do,' he smiled.

They followed the direction of his gaze, Barkuh Togba smiling in his turn.

'*Ene?*' Barkuh laughed. Is it so? 'Then we shall stay also.'

They would not be shaken in their loyalty to him, but at least he persuaded Jonah Samba to lead his Mende men, the few Mandinkas, and most of the Kru brothers to safety.

'Come then,' said Amos to George, to Barkuh and to Samuel Nimene. 'But keep away from any trouble.'

Yet as he began to lead them through the crowd, like forcing their way through a jungle, his heart sank. The merest glimpse. But certainty. Miss Nesta, to be sure. In the company of a man. Or was it? A white man, naturally. Not the Germany fellow. No, this one wore the whiteness of death. The wild eyes of a demon. Like the white spectres which haunt the Kpelle forests. And, like the white spectres drag prey to their doom, this demon seemed to be dragging Missee Nesta behind him.

It frightened him, but by the time they'd managed to cross the intervening space, the demon and Miss Nesta had simply vanished.

So, it was to Missee Coconut Palm's side that Amos went. She was kneeling by an old woman, while a young man squatted at their side, trying to hold back his own tears.

Nothing more. Until the young buck – Amos imagined he might be the injured woman's son – snatched up a fallen placard and wrenched its message board free, leaving just the stave in his hand. And, fury replacing the tears, he stamped towards the police line now stretched across the side street from the station gate – and it was a line which, to Amos Gartee's eyes, seemed to be swelling in number by the minute.

'What the fuck were you doing?' he heard the fellow yell, then smack the stave repeatedly against the open palm of his free hand. He shouted something else, but Amos couldn't make out what he said.

'No,' the old woman shrieked. 'Jimmy!' Then she turned beseeching eyes at Missee Coconut Palm. 'Don't let him, luv.'

Too late though.

The po-leese surged forward again, a moving wall hitting Amos and his brothers like a stampede of raging rhinos. He had no idea what happened. One moment about to ask about Miss Nesta, the next a hammer blow to the side of his face which rattled the teeth in his jaw. He was falling, his nose pressed into the cloth of his greatcoat until his head hit the ground. He cried out as the stampede rolled over them. From the corner of his eye he could see Missee Coconut Palm throw herself upon the woman, trying to protect her as blue trouser legs ran past them and Amos Gartee's nostrils were filled with the smell of them, sweat-soaked serge and hot boot leather.

He glimpsed, merely glimpsed, his brothers and bystanders alike, being punched, kicked in the groin or beaten about the head with batons. It seemed like hours but could have been no more than minutes, before the po-leese had fallen back once more and it was all over.

Again. All over, except for the groans of the wounded and, incongruously, a little man with a moving picture machine on a tripod, cranking its handles. Close to him another fellow, with a camera, changing its photographic plates as quickly as he was able. In all this chaos, those two alone seemed unscathed.

Thank the Lord, Amos thought, there will be a record of all this.

Yet perhaps he was being naïve. To believe that those bold policemen, the so-called protectors of *poto* laws and justice, would ever allow those images to be seen!

At the time, however, Amos was more concerned with the injured. With his friends. So much blood. And the stink of it. Like a butcher's shop. The debris of this one-sided battle also.

4.10pm

Cari looked down at the skirts of her Coronation Procession frock, saw a rip already in the hem and used it to begin tearing away strips of the cotton fabric. She hadn't even seen Amos Gartee's arrival, yet he was here now, trying to lift himself from the ground, blood dribbling down the side of his face and running around those strange, raised scars.

'Mister Gartee,' she gasped. 'Amos. What on earth...?'

He replied, but in a language she did not understand. Poor man, she thought, he must have lost his wits. Yet then he rallied, sat upright.

'Fine-fine,' he said. 'I am a'right.'

He wiped some of the blood away, stared at the fingers, then around at three others of his fellows. Cari vaguely recognised them. Each had his own injuries, though she thanked heaven they seemed not too badly hurt. Not like others.

'Forgive me,' she said. 'I have to help.'

She ran to a man crawling in the gutter, his nose entirely smashed to pulp and his eyes swollen shut from the hammering he'd taken.

'Water!' she shouted, for she knew it was necessary to bathe the wounds before applying her makeshift bandages. 'Anybody got water?'

She looked imploringly over towards the Italian hokey-pokey man with his ice cart, but he seemed transfixed, wiping his hands repeatedly on his white apron as though it would help to make this all go away.

'Water,' she screamed again, knew she was being hysterical, though couldn't help herself. 'Water!'

Then Amos Gartee was at her side. She had no idea how he had managed the feat, but he was carrying a bobby's helmet – a helmet now filled indeed with water. Yet, before she could make use of his gift, another charge, only a heartbeat later. She had the stupid feeling that, somehow, her shouting might be to blame. For triggering the attack.

The thunder of their boots again, and Cari turned towards the Plateau, unable to properly comprehend how this could be happening, saw that this time, at least, the main crowd seemed to be dispersing, streaming towards London Road, Islington and this little skirmish ground, yet still huge numbers on the steps. And this was when it changed. When the whole world changed.

Cries of protest from the steps themselves, then khaki and dark blue uniforms surging out from the building's wide doors. She thought she saw the flash of bayonets – though she might have been mistaken about that. Yet, one way or the other, these new hordes of policemen and soldiers could plainly be seen, bludgeoning their way down among those gathered on the steps and towards the main speakers' platform. Or forcing men, women and children towards the southern extremity of the Hall, where there was the huge drop, twelve feet or more, down onto St. John's Lane. And those hapless spectators were tumbled over and through the protective railings there, over the edge, like water pouring from the lip of a cataract.

From St. John's Lane, as well, came the sound of horses, the ground quaking beneath her. Charging horses, as the mounted police swept up and round the corner, their long sticks, like sabres, hacking and slashing at anything in their way.

4.25pm

Two young women came, dressed in the same way as Missee Coconut Palm. They looked askance at Amos, unsure quite how to deal with the scene. He and his small band of greatcoat-clad warriors standing guard around her where she sat weeping among the hundreds of wounded. Among the ambulance wagons which seemed only ever to come for the po-leese who themselves had been injured in the counterattacks. Among the shattered glass and broken pottery, among the lost shoes and abandoned caps. Among the splintered staves and fragments of brick. Among the lazy tumbleweed pages of a newspaper or the carpet of scattered pamphlets. And sitting among the melted contents of an upturned ice cream cart.

'He is a friend,' Missee Coconut Palm told the two young women. 'A good friend. These men have been on strike since – well, I can't remember how long.'

She thanked him. Thanked all of them, then picked herself up from among the debris. He knew they must have made a strange sight. They'd each been hit more than once. Sometimes it had seemed they were a favoured target. Bloodied heads, ripped clothes, and poor Samuel Nimene had lost several of his front teeth.

'Missee,' he said, before they could lead her away. 'Miss Nesta. Where she go?'

'I have no idea,' she told him. 'But safe. With our cousin.'

'Him devil man?'

'Devil man – well, no. Our cousin. And yet...'

'Even Germany fellow good past devil man. Germany fellow has bride price, I think.'

'Bride price,' said Missee Coconut Palm. 'You mean...? No, you're mistaken, Mister Gartee. You could not be more wrong. At least...'

But before Amos could discover what she might mean, her friends urged her away.

Afterwards? They made their way painfully back to the fountain, certain they would also be a target for arrests, as so many more of the injured were being picked up by the black carriages of the po-leese. Yet, remarkably, they were left to bathe their wounds.

'Well,' Samuel spluttered through his broken teeth and dripping lips, 'at least we have our tenbob.'

Barkuh Togba touched him gently on the shoulder and they all laughed, though it was painful to do so.

'Five months with no pay and now this,' Barkuh said. 'Next time I think I'll stay in Nana Kru. But at least our famous *krogba* has been taking lessons from the Wolof on how to defend himself – and us. Just imagine how badly they'd have beaten us otherwise.'

Yes, very amusing, Amos thought, while his brothers shared more banter. But one way or the other, they were safe. For some reason, this space, around the circle of black marble which formed the fountain's base, seemed to have become neutral ground. The damaged and the broken were gathered there, black-garbed old crones moving among them, bringing modest succour to the fallen.

The strikers, their families, had been cleared from the Plateau itself. Everybody cleared, except the merely curious, life's vultures. And hence it was to here, at the base of this tall column with the statue at its top, that a procession of dignitaries arrived. Fine clothes, heavily guarded, to read a document to them. To those who had been so brutally attacked.

It was, somebody said, a thing called the Riot Act. A warning, it seemed. Groups of twelve or more people would be considered an unlawful assembly, rioters, and would face punitive action.

Even this late in the day, Amos foolishly believed English justice might apply this law to those who had so badly run amok that afternoon, to the marching warbands of po-leese now tramping along the road, or the soldiers who followed them, with their gleaming rifle blades, or the mounted men on their white horses. But no, it was their battered victims who found themselves dispersed.

5.15pm

'How can we ever win?' Cari sobbed, as Patricia Woodlock and Mary Robson led her down the hill, past the Reading Rooms and the Museum, towards her home. 'How can we? Against that?'

'She's right,' said Mary. 'Those poor buggers just want a few extra bob. But us – well, we want to turn the whole damned world upside down.'

But Patricia simply laughed – Patricia who'd helped establish the Catholic Women's Suffrage Society.

'Ach,' she said, 'this is where Tom Mann and all his Syndicalists have got it wrong. They've not got Our Lady nor the Pankhursts on their side, girls!'

They left Cari, somewhat restored and reassured that her women's clerks had got away safely – Patricia had seen them, unharmed and undeterred by what they'd witnessed – at the bottom of Hunter Street but, by the time Cari had walked past the weighbridge office, it was clear all was not well at home either. The ground floor windows were all broken, beneath her father's business sign, which had been smeared in red paint. There was some irony though – Mister MacKenny's words earlier. *This one's high up in the glass-smashers.*

'Taffy's little mates,' Tom Priddy sneered, as she reached the doorstep. He was trying to board up the damage.

'The price we all pay for Tada printing the Watch Committee's flyers?' she said.

'Animals, they are, girl.'

'And Nesta? Did she get back safely?'

'How should I know? Went off on her own, see. Better here at home, I reckon. Snug, it is, in the paper loft. Doesn't need to be round there with those Fritzes all the time. But what about you, Beanpole? Your fine dress all ripped. And wet. *Duw!*'

His lips were wet. Ugly. And then she realised she'd lost her sash somewhere. Her fine flowered hat, as well.

'Is it where she's gone. To the Jurks's?'

He supposed so, he said, though he couldn't be sure. And not seen anything of Ernst.

'Nor Taffy,' he smiled. 'And there, you're a great one for coincidences, Beanpole. Strange, it was. The way your brother showed up just ahead of that police sergeant. Very strange, see.'

'I once swore, Tom Priddy, that if you ever called me Beanpole one more time, I'd lamp you, see?'

She knew the opportunity was lost, long ago. She knew it from his stupid grin. And she knew he was right. But she couldn't cope with it just then. Nor having to listen to a lecture from her father about the folly of the day's events. He'd not stopped ranting since he'd got home – and now gone off yet again to find a bobby. To complain. About the damage to his property. Well, good luck with that!

So she went round to the court, picked her way through the filth, past a rank midden. In the courts, they said, everybody's business was nobody's business. But when she reached the narrow cottage occupied by *Herr* Jurks and his family – and used as a hideout so often by Nessie – the whole household was in a state of some distress. Conflicting rumours. Ernst had been arrested. Or worse, he was now up at Christian Street, with some of his friends. German friends.

Nesta came to the door, and she looked far from pleased to see her sister.

'Christian Street?' said Cari, though she could plainly hear the sound of not-too-distant discord, which should already have given her the answer. 'What's happening on Christian Street?'

'Barricades, Cari,' Nesta told her, as though she was stupid not to already have this information. 'Barricades. Bobbies and the Tommies have marched up as far as Islington. Lots of the lads building barricades. Stop them getting any further.'

'It wasn't me who sent them there, Nessie. Why so cross, like?'

'Really don't understand much, do you?'

In truth, no, she didn't.

'And hasn't there been enough blood already?' said Cari. Her hands, her sleeves, were still smeared with it. 'But if Ernst is up there, maybe we should go. See how the land lies. And do you know Amos Gartee came to look for you?'

She saw the change come over Nesta's face. Concern in place of strife. She shouted an apology, an explanation – neither of which he understood – over her shoulder to Ernst's uncle, somewhere back within the house.

'He wasn't hurt, I hope?' said Nesta, once they were outside again.

'Hurt, yes, Nessie. He and a few of the other Krooboys. They stayed to protect me. But it was you he was concerned about. And he seems to think – well, that you and Ernst...'

'Silly man,' said Nesta. 'You think it's sinful, Cari? How I care for Amos so much?'

They lingered briefly outside the cottage in the gathering gloom. Cari considered Nesta would perhaps fare better if she were honest with Mister Gartee. Yet she feared for her sister. For where her affections might lead her. And she decided to avoid the question.

'Cousin Thomas managed to lose you, then?' she asked, instead, as they headed up the hill.

'You have no idea, Cari, do you?' Nesta snapped back at her, halted Cari in her tracks, astonished at the vehemence of her words. 'You put me in the hands of that creature. Again.'

'Cousin Thomas?'

'Cousin?' Nesta spat the word. 'What kind of cousin would try to do what the filthy swine did to me in the paper loft? Why, Cari? Why, in the name of our Lord, d'you think I couldn't stay there anymore?'

'But you never said...'

'Who'd have believed me? You, Cari? You still think I took the money from the café, don't you? Or Tada? Think he'd hear a word said against precious Tom Priddy?'

'And what…?'

'Want me to paint you a picture, Ceridwen?'

9.30pm

At the Rotunda Theatre, Tom Priddy was back on cloakroom duties. *The Love of the Princess* required few scenery changes, and the travelling troupe was mercifully intact, no stand-ins required. It was a woeful little play, anyhow. Not even a competently scripted farce. But no mind. It had already been an eventful Sunday. Enough excitement for one week.

His customers at the cloakroom desk were full of it, of course.

'Riot Act?' they said. 'Those hooligans should be hanged.'

Or, 'Communists, the lot of them. No more theatres if the communists take over.'

Or, 'Revolution. Nothing short of an anarchists' revolution.'

Or, 'All the fault of foreigners.'

Or, 'It's the Germans, of course.'

Tom Priddy agreed with each and every sentiment. Yet, while he hung their summer coats and hats, his thoughts turned more towards the girls. He'd hoped that leading Dumpling Nesta home from the chaos on Lime Street might present an opportunity. A further opportunity for – well, it hadn't happened. Not a word had passed her pretty lips and they'd only been halfway down William Brown Street when she'd struggled free of his grasp and run. To the Fritzes, of course.

Nine lives, our girl, he decided. And the useless policeman, Ladysmith. How could anybody be so incompetent? How many times must Tom bait the trap for them, only to have it sprung, time and time again. Still, it would have been far less entertaining if they'd simply caught her. All this collateral bloodshed. Priceless! Yet he hadn't been about to hang around in its midst to give Ladysmith a further opportunity. No, that bird had flown.

'But not the point,' he said to himself. Or, rather, to the Saviour who dwelt within him.

No, not the point.

Here at the Rotunda. Plans for the bioscope. Moving pictures. No passing fancy, as Mister Clamp had once insisted. Not at all. It was the future, like, Tom was sure.

And so he had come across the Beanpole and Dumpling Nesta, flaunting themselves for the camera like a pair of scarlet whores. Flaunting themselves. Well, they wanted their moment of notoriety? Perhaps he should accommodate their ambitions.

Besides, the Beanpole in particular was getting just a bit too close for comfort. Her questions about the lottery scheme. And prying into the Catholic girl's death.

For now, however, his customers were right. Revolution, a rebellion to be quelled. And the brother, Taffy, to be put down at the same time. So, as the performance began, the foyer now empty, he picked up one of the flyers from the counter. From the Liverpool Watch Committee.

Volunteers Required. In the face of continuing civil unrest within the city and to ensure that our citizens should be adequately fed, supplies of comestibles and other provisions to reach our warehouses and retail outlets, experienced carters, or those with similar freight and transport skills, should report…

Yes, thought Tom. How appropriate, like.

11.35pm

Despite Cari's misgivings, and despite her revulsion at Nessie's revelation about Tom Priddy, they headed up the hill. And they helped. Both of them. To build those barriers of dust bins, upturned carts, mattresses, barrels and barbed wire. Afterwards, the papers could call the rioters all they liked. But this was no riot. Oh, there may have been some – there are always some, after all – who seized the opportunity for a bit of looting. Though the rest? This was their home, whether they lived in Little Italy or here on its fringes.

So, regardless of whether they were from the more salubrious stretches of Hunter Street itself, or the warrens around Gerard Street, Fox Street and Soho Street, this was home. They would defend it. All through that long evening of skirmishes with the soldiers and the police, when they tried to break through the barricades, the girls lobbed half-sets with the best of them and helped their wounded as much as they were able.

Many times, Cari's thoughts turned to Amos Gartee and his fellows, knew Nesta must also be wondering about him, hoping he was safe.

The battles raged all through the night, with rifle shots echoing in the distance. And, in those same hours, just before midnight, several things were resolved in Cari's mind.

'Here,' said Nesta, during a lull in the fighting. She was still abrupt, still more than simply vexed. Wounded, she was, Cari now understood. 'Have some water.' She offered a military canteen with only a few drops left in the bottom. 'Spoils of war.'

'I need to tell you something,' Cari told her, and put an arm around her shoulder. 'You know how much the family means to me, don't you?'

'This about Taffy? I don't want to hear it, Cari. That slimy cousin of ours already tried to put the worm in my ear. It's coincidence. Nothing more. Taffy turning up just ahead of Ladysmith, like.'

'Except it's not the first time,' Cari murmured. And then she had no choice but to explain that morning at the station, on their way to London. One good turn deserved another.

'And you didn't think to tell me this before?'

'Didn't want to believe it myself. But now...'

'You let me go through all this?' Nesta snapped. 'Pandering to Taffy's nonsense about looking down our noses at Theresa. Making me put up with his stupid prejudices about coloureds, about Amos and the Krooboys. Handing me over to Priddy. Again. For what, Cari?'

'For the family. What else?'

'Then you're a bigger fool than I thought, girl.'

It stung, but Cari couldn't control her tongue now. Anything to defend herself.

'There's another thing, though,' she said. 'All this about Tom Priddy.'

'What?' Nesta sneered. 'You're going to tell me we should maybe cut Taffy some slack because you think that little toad pushed Theresa from the tram? Oh, I can read you like a book, Cari Maddox.'

'I'm sure of it. All his business on Rathbone Street and never knew she worked at Penny's. Never seen her? Saw her being taken away but reckons he didn't know who. He must have known. So why pretend he didn't. And such a liar. Besides, you saw him this afternoon. The way he shoved me. It was a warning, Nessie. To make me keep my mouth shut.'

'Shoved you?' said Nesta. 'Shoved you?' Her anger was somehow punctuated by the sound of a rifle shot – Cari was certain it must have been a rifle shot – a flash of light in the night sky. Then silence. 'I already told you what the filthy pig tried with me, Cari. I'd believe almost anything about Tom Priddy. But a long stretch from thinking he might have killed poor Theresa. Or anybody else, you goose,' she said. 'Time we went home. You're all shaken up. From this afternoon. And things have quietened down now.'

But they hadn't. And, as they made their way back down the street, past the darkened façade of the Friends Meeting House, there were renewed shouts behind them, a couple of screams, breaking glass again, two shots which lit the blackness, more running feet, and the now familiar thump of hobnailed boots on cobblestones. Nesta pulled Cari into the Friends' gateway as six or seven men raced past, then tried to get into Ma Sanguinetti's. But the bobbies were right on their heels, caught them and began to beat them without mercy.

'Nessie,' said Cari, unable to watch anymore. 'Has the world really changed so much? Or has it always been this way and I just never saw it?'

'Neither of us ever saw it. Nor all this about the family. So about time we took the blinkers off. Both of us, girl.'

Maybe Nesta was right. About Tom Priddy. The events of the day had perhaps made Cari more fanciful even than usual. Yet she remembered the poor souls who'd fallen from the edge of the Plateau earlier. Children among them. Lots of children. And she felt her heart harden, something turn to ice within her.

Teach me to savour wines of memory,
For women beaten by those lawless clubs.

Cari forced herself to watch again. Watch as those men were beaten into submission, then handcuffed and dragged back up Hunter

Street. Up and past the gateway so that, as the procession came alongside, she saw one of the prisoners turn his bloodied face towards her and smile. It was Ernst Jurks.

'I'm going to make sure we do it,' she murmured. 'Like Mary Robson said. Turn the whole damned world upside down. Pay them back for all this.'

Chapter Eight

Wednesday 23rd August 1911

10.00am

'They can shoot. They kill people. And nothing happen?' Ernst was incredulous. And Cari wished she could throw her arms around his broad shoulders across that table in Walton Gaol's cold visiting room.

A dozen such tables in there, and each of them occupied. Husbands and their wives for the most part, some with small children come to see their imprisoned fathers within those drab green walls. Yet this didn't seem right to Cari. If Ernst was my husband, she thought, I should not let his children see him in this place.

She and Nesta had been helpless once Ernst and the others had been hauled off to the Bridewell and, again, when they'd appeared the following morning at the Dale Street Police Courts. Sentenced to two months on a charge of assaulting a police constable in the execution of his duty. And he'd been held in the cells all that day while street battles continued to rage.

'Nothing,' she replied. 'A couple of protest meetings. Statement from the TUC. But otherwise, nothing.'

Nothing. Or not much. At least, from the strikers' side. Though Home Secretary Churchill had, indeed, sent navy ships into the Mersey to threaten them, and filled the entire city with thousands of extra soldiers so every district was like an armed camp. Well, gunboats on the river? It rather wiped the eye of Rhys Fingers.

Not just Liverpool either, but London and Hull as well. One or two commentators had tried to draw parallels between the events on Liverpool's streets and those back in January when the same Home Secretary Churchill had been so directly involved alongside the military through that gun battle in the East End of London. Stepney.

Against the Latvian gang from the jewellery robbery. Houndsditch, wasn't it? The shooting of three policemen. Anarchists, naturally, those Latvians. Revolutionaries, maybe. Socialists? Oh, very likely. Foreigners, certainly.

And Pathé there, on that occasion also, to make a cinematographic record of the Sidney Street siege. Unlikely, though, for any of those particular moving pictures to have disappeared as so much of Liverpool's own had seemed to do. It was Taffy who had given Cari the news. A brief encounter on the street. Not even an enquiry about the wellbeing of poor Ernst. Simply full of fury that the Strike Committee was supposed to see the thing in the days following the demonstration – but shown only a version with, of course, all the incriminating evidence removed.

'One day, Cari, some will ask. Want answers. One day.'

'We'll keep trying, Ernst.' She reached out to touch his hand, and a pinch-faced, whiskered warder slammed his truncheon down upon the table, no more than a foot from her fingers.

'None of that!' he yelled, as she jumped in her seat.

Cari glowered at the man, turned back to Ernst Jurks.

'But yes,' she murmured. 'We'll keep trying.'

Nesta and Cari had followed the arresting officers and their prisoners all the way to Christian Street – a battlefield in every sense of the word by that hour of the morning – and then onto Islington, where lanterns were burning, cavalry units and rows of hurry-up wagons waiting to cart off the captured. They'd risked being taken on more than one occasion, unable to restrain themselves from hurling insults at the bobbies, despite the foolish risk for Nessie in particular.

'But Parliament?' she said. 'They'll avoid any more embarrassing questions.'

Ernst nodded, though Cari wasn't sure whether she'd made herself clear enough. 'You understand, Ernst?'

'*Ja*, Cari. Understand. Politics it is. Your Churchill, he want to paint all white.'

'Whitewash,' she said. 'He'll want to whitewash the whole affair. I just thank the Lord Jesus you weren't hurt too, my friend.'

He smiled. A cynical smile and, Cari thought, not for the first time, he must surely be a non-believer. Yet how could this be?

A non-believer but also a good person?

'I had fear. *Verstehst du?*' You see? 'Big fear. When shooting start.'

Yes, Cari thought, the shootings.

10.00am

Tom Priddy decided that volunteering might not have been one of his better ideas. Yet he'd been there, the day after Riot Sunday, to sign upon the dotted line at the temporary and heavily guarded office set up by the Watch Committee. He'd listed his experience – the carriage service for the Llewellyn Hotel, his work in the stables at Waugh's. Old Waugh had even given him a reference, agreed that, of course, his position would be held open for as long as Tom needed to fulfil his patriotic duty. A special constable. Better title than *scab* or *strike-breaker*. Yes, eminently qualified for the task at hand.

He'd even managed to persuade them he should be allocated to specific duties. At the South End. For, whilst he had no fear of Taffy and his mates from the North End docks – he would almost have relished the prospect of rubbing Taffy's nose in it – Tom had other intentions.

So, by the Sunday, he'd turned up before dawn, as required, at the stables and warehousing they'd established at the old Corporation Depot in Lavrock Bank. They allocated him a cart, a couple of tired nags called Lucky and Jim, with which he joined the convoy heading down past the Mersey Forge and the gasometers, swung right along Caryl Street, just ahead of the Horsfall Street railway bridge spanning the Brunswick Goods Yard, until they came to the goods station itself.

It was a fortress, the place where those troop trains so often arrived, avoiding the demonstrations which would have been inevitable if they'd run, instead, into Liverpool's Central Station, for example. And the warehouse so enormous, the facilities so extensive, it had been easier to unload the horses of the cavalry detachments here.

'Reckon you're mine, lad,' a fellow had yelled up to him as Tom and his team moved forward in the queue to be loaded.

He'd been watching the routine. Each cart reaching the freight platform received its share of barrels, crates and hessian sacks. Hardly the smoothest of operations, though. Some of these blokes must never have handled a proper team in their lives. Horses screaming whenever their drivers roughly handled their reins. Or a cart slewing one way across the loading bay's grey cobbles, the other way, wheel rims grinding and sparking against the platform's brickwork.

But at the point of loading, each wagon received an additional passenger. A second hand. Somebody, Tom decided, to ride shotgun. And hence, this ruffian.

'Yours?' Tom laughed. 'Think you can handle the job, like?'

The man was stocky. Broken nose. His face unshaven and riddled with eruptions. Sparse hair straggled in tufts from beneath his tweed cap as he pulled himself up onto the driving bench. He slid along, slammed into Tom's side. Deliberate, it was. The man hawked and spat a gobbet of phlegm down onto the ground.

'The job, sure,' he grinned, and Tom struggled to place his accent. 'Any of those bloody strikers what get in our way, too.'

Tom was given the go-ahead, following the previous wagon out through the cavernous mouth of the goods station with its mingled odours of coal smoke, horse dung, cooperage and rope.

Out onto Sefton Street, the dock road, where the convoy itself was formed. Up ahead, mounted policemen, soldiers' khaki caps and bayonets just behind them. Then the line of carts, with more squads of soldiers on either side.

'What d'you do?' said Tom, as they'd moved off, following the Overhead Railway's stanchions northwards past the stockyard and the next goods station, this one for the Lancashire & Yorkshire, its woodwork and signage all pale green and mid-brown. 'When you're not doing this, like?'

'You stupid or somethin'? Copper, that's me, lad. Over in Lincoln. Drafted over 'ere for this little bit of delight, see. Extra pay. An' you? Christ, never seen anyone as pale as you what wasn't dead. Undertaker, I'm guessin'. Am I right or am I right?'

'Should have been a detective, you should,' said Tom.

But that was when the first bottle hit them. The Brunswick Dock gate, just this side of the Granary tower. Bottles and bricks from the crowd of strikers. And from then it was running the gauntlet. All the way to their destination, the warehouses just past the Mersey Engine Works and the other side of Stanhope Street.

Well, it had been his first day, more than a week previously. Tough enough. But when he'd finished his shift, headed to the Rotunda, the whole place was buzzing with the news.

Just a little earlier, that same Tuesday evening. A convoy of prison wagons and Black Marias had been organised and set off for Walton, accompanied by a magistrate with a now well-rehearsed copy of the Riot Act.

Everybody, it seemed, knew the story. Protestors on Vauxhall Road. Stones thrown at the horses – both those pulling the wagons and also the mounts of the 18th Hussars who formed the escort.

Horseshoes skittering on the cobbles, somebody said. Panic. No reading of the Riot Act by way of warning. Just the Hussars' rifles and bayonets as a response. People indiscriminately shot or stabbed. Two men shot dead. Bloody Tuesday therefore following close on the heels of Bloody Sunday.

Bloody Tuesday, eight days earlier. By then, the entire city at a standstill. All of it. Then the railwaymen's strikes, the threat of a national stoppage. Not just localised anymore. No longer unofficial. Spreading like wildfire, seemingly within hours, so that, in just a few short days, the whole country would have been in a state of collapse, brought to its knees, station gates and entrances secured, nailed shut with wooden boards. Home Secretary Churchill forced to instruct the railway owners they'd no choice but to surrender. Now, the strikes all but finished, everybody expecting a general return to work within days.

A pity, thought Tom. But the convoys – and Tom Priddy – for now, still sometimes running the same gauntlet. The shipments of food into Liverpool still necessary, for the strikes had demonstrated how inadequate were the stocks normally held within the city, how quickly they'd been exhausted. And wherever there were convoys, it seemed to him, there would always be hooligans willing to attack them. Of course, it was possible for the authorities to seek a Strike Committee Permit to shift essential goods. Yet so much confusion about what qualified as essential. And sometimes merely stubborn pride the obstacle to kowtowing before the damned strikers. Better now, of course, the strikes largely settled, the escorts mostly a token gesture. He just hoped today might be another of the quieter ones.

*

10.20am

'I still can't believe it's happened,' said Cari.

Two men shot dead. Two Catholics, so no sympathy from either her tada nor Cousin Thomas, the devil take him. Neither of the victims involved in anything even vaguely riotous. The youngest, just nineteen, killed by a stray bullet in his new house on the corner of Hopwood Street while putting up some shutters. The other, a docker, shot twice in the chest while watching the commotion. A dozen injured. There'd be an inquest, of course, but nobody believed there was any chance of an honest verdict.

Both men buried a few days later at Ford Cemetery. The end of last week. John Sutcliffe. Michael Prendergast. Both Cari and Nesta had made the long walk, the funeral procession, to be there – along with eight hundred more. And the sisters had proudly marched close to the banner of the Netherfield Road Protestant Reformers Crusade. It was certainly not a day for sectarian divide. And shame on their father. Tom Priddy too.

Meanwhile, a couple of days before the funerals, news that two more unarmed protestors shot and killed in Llanelli.

'No,' she repeated. 'Just can't believe it.'

Though, of course, she did. It had happened before, naturally. Belfast, four years earlier.

'But believe I can,' Ernst told her. 'And understand. Because us they fear as well, Cari. Fear Tom Mann. Others like him. Jaurès in France. In my own Germany. America too. International Workers of the World.' He pronounced the words slowly, carefully, proudly. 'In Russia – *Na dann, Russland ist Russland.*' Well then, Russia is Russia. He shrugged. 'But they must stop us. And shoot us. That is only way for them. On streets. Or in war. They do not care.'

'Yet we are very many, Ernst,' she said. 'Even with a war, they cannot have us all shot.'

He shook his head.

'*Nein*, Cari. You it is, not understand. War that comes, it will be not war like other war. This war, all we *will* be shot. Millions maybe. This they want.'

He wiped his hands together slowly, as though removing something noxious from his palms. And Cari asked herself how he could be so certain.

'All the same,' she said. 'I am resolved. Determined. I shall help to turn their world upside down.'

'And your sister? What happen with Nesta?'

Before she could answer, the warder shouted across the room. Five more minutes. Five minutes only. A tearful young woman on the far side of the room couldn't contain her emotions, flung herself across the table to embrace the lad who, Cari assumed, must be her husband. The warders leapt into action, one dragged her back, the other struck her with his billyclub.

And Cari, appalled, jumped to her feet as well.

'Stop!' she cried. But, by then, the woman had been pushed weeping out through the visitors' door, the young man off towards the cells. And another warder was advancing towards Cari, smacking a truncheon into the palm of his hand. The message was plain and she sat once more.

'Five minutes, Cari,' said Ernst. 'Five only. So, tell me – Nesta?'

'Working again,' Cari murmured, trying to pull herself together. 'Your pa said it was payment for her looking after him while you've been — here. Anyway, work at the Vienna Bakery. They've opened up again, at last. Some connection of your father's.'

The Vienna Bakery wasn't Viennese at all, of course. But Mister Kirkland, the owner, had the notoriety of having been, officially, Baker to the Emperor of Austria and, whether for commercial reason or not, several of his staff were German or Austrian. Like all the other bakeries in town, it had been closed for weeks. So many people going hungry. Near to starvation.

'Hours are perfect for her,' said Cari. 'She begins at three every morning and home again by seven. Far too early for Sergeant Ladysmith to be on the prowl.'

'You must not let her come to this place, Cari. Not here.'

She needed no encouragement in that regard, for Cari had been there herself back in January, of course. Outside anyway. The protest against forced-feeding of their women. Yes, she knew what happened to women inside these walls.

'You care for her, Ernst?'

'Your sister, she is. Your sister. How can I not care?'

He tugged at the white uniform jacket with its black arrows, straightened it.

My poor Ernst, she thought. They have branded you with their Broad Arrows. Marked you now as property of the Crown. And what would she do if, as they'd threatened, the powers-that-be decided to send him back to Germany.

'Yes, but you are fond of her,' she said, and held her breath.

'Fond.' Ernst rolled the word around his tongue. Then he smiled. '*Ja*, fond. But, Cari, not fond like I am fond for you.'

11.00am

The Elder Dempster vessel *Mendi* had berthed in the Harrington Dock. And Amos Gartee found himself in a difficult position. The seamen were mostly back in work, once more. The strikes all but over. A final meeting with the shipowners' bossmen due to take place. But no chance the Elder Dempster offer would get any better.

So, when the *Mendi* had arrived, its Kru sailors discharged and now accommodated in the reopened hostel, the bossmen's agent had set up shop in one of the Harrington warehouses, offering berths for the return voyage to Freetown.

'What shall we do, brother?' Barkuh Togba and the others had asked him.

'You want to go home?' Amos had replied.

Of course, they did. And so they were lined up, before the table in the open space at the centre of that half-empty, rat-riddled, red-brick warehouse, each with his kitbag, waiting a turn to give his name, to sign or make his mark.

'All Krooboys,' asked the agent, taking a puff on his pipe.

Amos glanced from head to head along the queue in front of him. Jonah Samba and the Mende men. The Mandinkas. His own brothers.

'For true!' he lied. 'All Kru men.'

Then he waited, thinking about Miss Nesta.

For a few days, all had seemed perfect. She was working at the place of baking bread. He'd made the plans with her, passing through the city in the dead of each night to reach the house where she was sheltering. He faithfully escorted her back to the bakery, then found a hiding place where he might wait out the three hours during which she laboured at the ovens. He waited, wrapped in his greatcoat, until first light broke and they could repeat the journey, delivering her home once more.

She'd praised him for standing with her sister on that dark day of the previous week. They had spoken of the Germany man, now in their prison, and they had spoken of Miss Cari Coconut Palm's distress.

'And what shall you do, Amos,' she had said, on their first walk together, three nights ago, 'now you have won your victory?'

'The tenbob? Some thing, it is. Yet victory?' He still wasn't sure. 'And Germany man,' he said. 'Sister will be him bride?'

She had laughed at him.

'Poor Ernst. Yes, I fear it might be so.'

'Fear? Not want this?'

'Amos, I want it very much.'

And over the intervening nights that simple conversation had grown into something much more. A cautious courtship dance. Not even a mention of bride price. Just the first imaginings of a possible future.

'Tell me about Nana Kru,' she'd said, though Amos understood very well that this was, in truth, a complex question.

'You mean,' he whispered, 'Nana Kru for home?'

There might not yet be much light but he could still see the way her *poto* skin flushed red. He would never have been able to find the words. Yet imagine, he'd thought. How could she ever survive – as his bride in Nana Kru.

'Better,' he said, 'go to your Wales.'

They had spoken about this Wales. It wasn't easy to pronounce, but he had practised.

Indeed, from the highlands of this Liverpool place, on clear days, you could see those distant and misty mountains. Liverpool's highlands, yes. For the Wolof, Charles Tuohey, had explained to him how this Liverpool place was like another great city called Rome. Another city built upon many hills. And the ancients of that Rome place had once, like the *poto* English, marched their armies across the world to enslave whole continents.

Was that not, the Wolof had insisted, precisely what the English had done? When they had no longer been able to trade in slaves taken out of Africa, they had come up with a superior plan. Why not simply enslave all the Africa people where they stood? Enslave all Africa.

Amos had never quite thought of it this way. Yet it was those Rome people who intrigued him. An image of them striding across the world, spanning the seas, dressed in their iron clothes and iron hats, singing a song which, if he'd caught the Wolof's words correctly, made little sense. Very, very itchy! Was that not the way it went?

Yet this was another thing. And this Wales? She did not say so, but he could see she was thinking the same as he had thought about her. That he could no more find a home in this Wales than might she in Nana Kru. No, they had decided, there must be a better solution for them.

But, this morning? He was forced to break the news about the *Mendi*'s arrival, the possibility that, with the strike settled, he might be called back to sea, return to Nana Kru with his brothers. It had taken him the whole walk from her house to the place of baking bread. There had been misunderstandings, many of them, though he had finally made her understand.

'I'd thought...' she'd said, tears running down her cheeks, face crumpled like a discarded polishing rag. 'Amos, you cannot. My dear...'

He could see her, even now, as he neared the bossman's table.

'Name?' said the agent.

'Gartee,' Amos replied. 'Amos Gartee.'

The fellow looked up at him, checked a piece of paper at his elbow, then grinned and shook his head.

'No, lad,' he said. 'Not you. Now, on your bike.'

'Brother, what happen?' said Jonah Samba. And when Amos explained, it was the Mende man who protested. If their *krogba* did not sail, none would sail. It touched him. Jonah Samba, of all people. Yet he quelled it quickly, confronted one declaration of loyalty after another, remonstrations. How could he possibly stay alone? How could they possibly sail without him? But when all that turmoil finally abated, there were the farewells, the emotional farewells.

Amos stood at the warehouse gates a long, long time – until they were gone. All gone.

Alone, he wandered back onto the dock road. How would he explain to Missee Nesta? Her tears. And now he had not gone after all. But was it too late? He needed time to think, determined he'd try to find the Wolof, Charles Tuohey.

Ahead of him, turning onto the road was a convoy of food wagons. The convoys still had escorts, but only a few of the po-leese. And as he slowly overtook them, his eyes turned to one of the drivers. A white man, naturally. Usually difficult enough to distinguish one *poto* face from another. But this fellow was *white*. The whiteness of death. The wild eyes of a demon. Like the spectres haunting the Kpelle forests, as he had thought before. The same devil man he had seen leading Miss Nesta away on the day of darkness.

12.20pm

She knew she should have gone straight back to work, but Cari had made up her mind. To confront Cousin Thomas about whatever might have passed between him and Nesta. Her sister's lips remained sealed, so it had been left to Cari's imagination, trying to fathom the truth. Her thoughts had been lurid. So lurid, she had no idea from whence they could have originated. She was no prude, though her experiences of a – well, of a physical nature – had been limited in the extreme. Her reading of romances had given her little clue also. Yet the words ran through her head like a torrent. Ravishment. Violation. Seduction. Deflowerment. Could it have been?

'You stink of that place, Ceridwen,' shouted her father over the clatter of the machine.

She supposed he must be right, for she'd been able to smell the prison on her own clothes all the way back on the tram. Though how he could discern any of that particular stench among the chemical and paper odours of the print shop she had no idea.

'I only came to look for Cousin Thomas,' she called back. In truth, she also wanted to change into her other work skirt and blouse.

'And why not at Kaplan's? Think we're made of money?'

He worked the bar on the jobbing press, back and forth, so the rollers might evenly spread the fresh ink he'd just dabbed all over the plate, ready for his next batch.

'Make up my hours, I do, Tada. You know that. And I thought

those things were supposed to make us a fortune.'

She pointed at the lottery tickets he'd already churned out.

'Early days, girl. Early days. And you'd not need to work extra hours if you didn't waste so many of them on that Fritzie. Communist too, I reckon.'

He moved to the front of the Cropper, reset its counter, while Cari picked up one of the tickets, pretended to read some of the small print. Ernst a communist? Yes, she had no doubt. But what was wrong with that?

'And Cousin Thomas,' she said. 'The prodigal son. Not here, then? Not much use as a printer's devil, like. Leavin' you with all this.'

Her father stopped short, on the verge of touching the wheel, about to set the machine in motion, but at once alert, wary.

'Why'd you say that, *cariad*?' he growled.

What troubled him so much? The bit about a printer's devil. Or… The letter. Matters concerning Cousin Tom's mother. Why had Cari not been able to ask him? Would it be so difficult to admit she'd been prying? Perhaps, but she still wanted to explore all this herself. And *then* she'd speak to her tada. But meanwhile she'd never quite found the time, one thing pushing out another.

'No reason,' she said. 'But been keeping strange hours, he has. Smells different, too. Don't you think, Tada?'

Yes, different. Less embalming fluid, more – well, horse dung, if she was honest. But her father simply shrugged.

'Heard the good news?' he shouted, finally sitting at his small table in front of the printer. He began feeding the bed with sheets of paper, fell into the rhythm. Feed. Print. Remove. Feed. How old *was* the Cropper, with its flaking emerald paint? She'd known the monster all her life, but it was considerably older again than Cari.

'News, Tada?'

'Tram workers, girl,' he called back, his words almost keeping time with the tempo of his task. 'Council agreed to reinstate them. As and when required, whatever that means. But strike's over.'

And in a few days, Cari supposed, there'd be a general return to work across all the unions.

'Communists as well, Tada – them tram workers?'

'Course not,' he replied. 'Just dragged into all this nonsense by your communist friends. Taffy and his mates, as well.'

She left him to his work, changed quickly and was back outside again, not even bothering to tell her father she was leaving. The street door. And there, to her astonishment, was her brother.

'*Duw Annwyl*, Taffy. Come to see Tada?'

She hoped so, for it continued to eat away at her, this fracture within her family. On the other hand, apart from Cousin Thomas, she'd been looking for a chance to confront Taffy as well. Turncoat. Squealing to the police about Nesta. And not just once. But the expression on his face – worry? Fear, maybe. He shook his head.

'No,' he said. 'You, Cari. Come to see you, I have. Trouble, see?'

'Can it wait?'

Oh, how she wished she'd not spoken those words. The change in his expression. Anger again. Fire in his eyes.

'Too busy, is it?' he snapped.

She apologised, gripped his arm, explained how she'd been at the prison, now late for work. Very late.

'So, walk with me, Taffy. Tell me about it.'

They walked. And yes, Taffy explained. Didn't even bother to ask about Ernst. Strike fund, he said. Apart from the main one, the North End dockers had made their own collections. No, of course that wasn't precisely how things were supposed to work. But just a small kitty. In case, like.

'Supposed to look after it, I was,' he explained, as they crossed that recent battlefield, the Plateau. 'Kept it hidden at the MacKennys' place.'

He was still living at their house, of course. Theresa's mother wanted him there. Clinging to the link with her lost daughter.

'You lost it?' she said. 'Tell me you didn't, Taff.'

'Lost?' Taffy looked stricken. 'I suppose – listen, Cari. That night when you was there. Before Theresa...'

He almost choked on the girl's name.

'The Finny 'Addy,' she said, and he nodded.

'The priest came in. Remember? Picked up his shilling and went again. But then the real Father Doolan arrived later, screaming and shouting about imposters.'

'Sacrilege,' said Cari. 'Wasn't that what he called it?'

'Well, it's bloody happened again,' he said. 'I can't be sure, like. But...'

12.30pm

The fellow had followed the convoy all the way to the warehouses. Rather, he'd followed Tom Priddy's wagon. Tom couldn't be sure it was Dumpling Nesta's Krooboy, but he had a sneaking suspicion it might be him. There'd been no sign of him, however, on the return journey back to the depot on Lavrock Bank. But yes, he was fairly certain.

His little network of spies had brought him the news soon after the Dumpling had started work at the bakery. Tom Priddy's Hunter Street Irregulars, as he'd styled them. A few of old Huw's Points Boys and Post Boys, as well as several ne'er-do-wells from the local drinking dens. Tom's temperance and the Lord Jesus prevented him from entering those iniquitous places in person, of course, but needs must, as the saying went.

Helpful, and so much intelligence soon reaching him that he'd been forced to keep a small journal. A black journal, naturally. Separate sections for each of them. The Beanpole and her visits to see the Fritz. Dumpling Nesta. Daft Taffy. Wicked Wyn and her reprobate husband Rhys the Gateman. It helped him keep track of where the Dumpling might be lodging, since the Beanpole certainly refused to tell him. He'd thought he began to see a pattern, and when the time was right...

The problem, however, was that the police sergeant, Ladysmith, seemed to have lost interest in the girl. After Riot Sunday. It hadn't worked out the way Tom had planned things, of course. All seemed so simple. He could read them like a book. He'd told Ladysmith precisely where to find them. All his men had to do was – well, pick her up. But then, it had all turned into a pitched battle. All that blood. Ladysmith had avoided him ever since. And when the Points Boy had brought word about the companion he'd seen with the Dumpling on her way back towards Little Italy before dawn – crossing the lines at Norton Street's Islington junction – Tom had been pitched into a cauldron of conflicting emotions.

He'd known about her misplaced support for the Krooboys, of

course. It had caused enough rows. But this! And the fellow who'd followed the convoy? Heathen scars on his face. Army overcoat. Kitbag over his shoulder. Yet it was the darkie's trousers which had caught his attention. Striped. Looked expensive.

Anyway, one day there might be a trap to spring. He could just imagine the look on old Huw's face. His fine daughter – and a Krooboy. It would probably kill him.

For now, though, he needed to get the wagon back to the old Corporation Yard. He didn't imagine he'd have many days of this work left. And he'd miss it. The cart and the horses. Attached to them, he was.

Lucky, the bay mare of the pair, lifted her muzzle and snorted, nostrils flaring and lips quivering as a train rattled past on the Overhead.

'There, girl,' he said to her. 'Miss me, as well, you will. But what will I do, like? No more Special Constable duties, either. Shame, that'll be. Real shame.'

He'd rather hoped he might be able to make the arrest, see? Daft Taffy. For the Hunter Street Irregulars who frequented the Byrom, Mad John's, had brought him that interesting snippet. Taffy drunk, of course. Bragging about how clever he was. Strike Fund. Hidden in an old bread jar. Dough, the fool had joked. Dough, see? Bread jar – get it?

The gasometers came back into view. Stinking today, like rotten eggs. It made him smile.

12.45pm

It was strangely quiet. Another hot day. The tram strike might officially be over but there weren't many running. Only one Bellamy rumbled past as Cari and Taffy crossed the Haymarket and over into Queen Square, past the Stork, the waiting carts, the crates of caged chickens, and Black Joe the banjo player.

'The priest?' she said again. 'And what? Drops in to pick up his shilling and just finds the strike money on the shelf as well?'

'Don't be so bloody stupid, girl,' he snapped back. 'Hidden, it was.'

'At the MacKennys? Those kids? They must all have known. Could have told anybody.'

He shook his head.

'Nah. Just me and Ma MacKenny. A bread jar. And underneath a little sack of flour.'

They crossed Roe Street, the tramlines, past the soot-stained brick and stonework of the market's rear façade. Then Brythen Street's alehouses and Cold Storage, where two leather-gloved workers were manhandling ice blocks from the loading bay onto a wagon. All the time, Taffy blathering about how carefully the money had been hidden. And the priest. That damned priest.

'And the boozer, Taffy,' she said, as they reached the bottom of Basnett Street. 'You didn't mention this to anybody in the boozer, like?'

Cari spotted the way he avoided looking her in the eye, glanced instead across to the Baroque bulk of St. Peter's.

'You think I'm stupid?' he said. 'Think I'd announce to Mad John's how there was a small fortune hidden in Ma MacKenny's bread jar?'

'I've got to go,' she said. 'We'll need to talk about this later.' She pushed at his arm, picked up her skirts and began to run. Towards Post Office Place, shouting back over her shoulder. 'And yes, Taffy, that's exactly what I think.'

Through Brooke's Alley and into Hanover Street. The newspaper kiosk again. The billboard.

Garston Dock Strike Over
Churchill Orders Troop Withdrawal.

The newspapers. Their coverage of Bloody Sunday had been outrageous, naturally. The *Telegraph* and the *Mail*, both clamouring about "mob rule" in Liverpool. Deaths and the bloodshed blamed entirely upon the strikers or, more simply, "Liverpool hooligans." And Home Secretary Churchill? Darling of those same newspapers, of course. His escapades at Omdurman. His escape during the Boer War. But to Cari? A Home Secretary who claimed to support votes for women – but had delivered nothing. And his heavy-handed response to the South Wales miners? Well, heavy-handed hardly did it justice. And now? The man who'd brought martial law to her city. The man who'd sent HMS *Antrim* to the Mersey, its big guns trained on the city centre.

She thought about it all the way round to Seel Street.

The powerful and famous, she supposed, were simply human beings, after all. The same person capable of good deeds *and* bad. She was no great student of history, but she always thought of Cromwell. Depending on the eye of the beholder, either saint or devil. Why not both? Were people so stupid that they had to see everything as either black or white when, in truth, there were merely shades of grey. Cromwell? Churchill? Nothing worse than putting people on pedestals.

Yet, mingling somewhere within her thoughts, the memory of the words Taffy had yelled after her when Cari had run from him on Church Street.

'You don't understand, girl,' he'd yelled. 'They find out it's missing, I'm a dead man.'

3.15pm

The devil man. Miss Nesta had spoken of him – but only a little. A cousin, she'd said. Yet hated him. Fear hanging from her words, even though so many of the words themselves were lost upon him.

He'd tried to imagine the nature of her fears. And he was no fool. He knew what sometimes transpired inside families – wherever in the world you might happen to be. So, if Missee Nesta needed an avenging angel…

Yet here was the devil man driving one of King Billy's carts. No button, though. Not a union man. Po-leese with the wagons. A scab, then. Blackleg. Useful words within his new vocabulary.

Did they know this thing – Miss Nesta and Missee Coconut Palm? That the devil man cousin was a scab?

Perhaps, he said to himself, I should find the Wolof later. Find a place to stay, as well. For now, see where the devil man takes me.

Therefore, he waited, watched and followed – though keeping always to the shadows, keeping his distance. Back along the dock road, towards the Harrington Dock where he'd so recently and so painfully bidden farewell to his friends. He wondered, even now, whether it might not be too late to give this up, to join them. If the bossmen might be persuaded to allow him. Yet he knew in his heart he had burned that particular bridge.

He passed the towering goods station again and, just beyond, the brick wall where he had stood so often over these past months, peering over the parapet, down into the darkness of the wide cutting, a brick-lined chasm carved into the sandstone upon which this Liverpool place had been built. A chasm with its elegant criss-cross pattern of railway tracks and sidings, smoke-belching engines shunting endless lines of screeching trucks back and forth.

Yet always he kept the devil man in sight. Even through the smog and fumes where the street climbed up over the goods yard with, on every side, ghosts of the chimneys, the furnaces, the boilers, the scrap heaps, the steam engines and the forge hammers which, according to the Wolof, had previously been the greatest iron works of the world. It must once have been another miracle, though some traces of its former glory remained. Smaller smithies still working. Men and boys, glistening with sweat, where the gateways allowed him a view inside.

In one of the gateways, three fellows who seemed not to belong. Smoking cigarettes. Furtive in their behaviour as the devil man drove past them. Hyenas, Amos decided. And, sure enough, up ahead of him, they also began to follow the wagon, though making a great play of not doing so. In like fashion, they loitered near the yard into which the devil man had driven his team.

Ten minutes later and the devil man emerged again, jacket slung over his shoulder, heading up the slope towards the road where the tramways ran, and through the densely packed narrow houses. The three fellows dogged his steps, and the devil man seemed not to have noticed them.

Amos watched, still keeping his distance, as they moved more quickly, getting closer to a narrow alley running between some of the houses.

They drew alongside and, as though they must have practised this thing many times, they pushed the devil man into the alleyway. Nobody else in sight. Scab, Amos heard them say. Bloody, pissing scab!

The devil man shouted back at them, though Amos didn't catch the words. And then they were shoving him. Back and forth. One of them slapped the devil man's head.

A dilemma. What would Miss Nesta wish him to do? Leave the devil man to a well-deserved beating? It was tempting. But not in Amos Gartee's nature.

But there were the trousers to consider. The trousers he'd been gifted by the Wolof, Charles Tuohey. Striped trousers. His pride and joy. Too precious to be risked. He remembered the pair so badly ripped when he'd been attacked that day by the straw-haired men. Again, when the po-leese had beaten them so recently. Thus, he leaned against a wall, slipped off his boots and reached inside his overcoat, unclipped the braces he wore on top of his woollen gansey.

As Amos started to step out of the trousers, an old *poto* woman came out of the house just alongside.

'Mary, Mother of God,' she said, saw Amos, now stripped to his long johns, then glanced across to the alley. 'Hey, you lot!' she yelled.

One of those fellows shouted back to her.

'Bloody scab, ma. See?'

The woman nodded, gave Amos a final puzzled look, and went back inside, while the devil man's attacker now also noticed Amos. His two mates had the devil man up against the wall, one holding him, the other searching through the devil man's pockets. But this third ruffian, he must have been trying to work out what he was seeing. A black man, trousers folded over his arm, long johns, barefoot, carrying his boots.

'Hey,' said the fellow, 'look at this, lads.'

'Brothers,' Amos shouted, 'you must let him go.'

Oh, the abuse with which they showered him. Much of it he did not really understand.

Hyenas, he'd thought. Yes, hyenas. But like all hyenas, when you examined them at closer quarters, always those distinguishing marks to differentiate one from another. And these, the same. Mister Crater Face, still holding the devil man by the throat. Mister Ginger Bristle, advancing across the street towards him. Mister Egg Nose, moving to join his friend.

Amos carefully laid down the trousers, took up the stance Charles Tuohey had taught him. Weight slightly on his back foot, right fist tucked into the centre of his chest, left arm extended, head held back. He was confident of being able to slip, feint and block anything aimed in his direction and return fire with a punishing left jab. The fine art of hitting without being hit in turn. Impossibly difficult. Yet it was, Tuohey claimed, precisely the way an American, Jack Johnson, had become such a champion. But that, of course, was in a boxing ring. There were rules, in a boxing ring.

'You taking the piss lad?' Mister Ginger Bristle laughed. 'Come on then, monkey boy, let's see what yer've got.'

Well, Amos thought, now we shall see the quality of the Wolof's lessons.

Chapter Nine

9.35am

'What d'you reckon, then?' Tom Priddy asked Mister Waugh. 'Tomorrow, like.'

'Villa? Away game?' the funeral furnisher hissed through his teeth, shook his head. 'Not sure I like our chances.'

Like old Huw Maddox, an Everton supporter. And so, in their company, Tom Priddy extolled the team's virtues as well.

'Fingers crossed, then,' he said.

The season had started reasonably enough. Everton's first match against Spurs a draw, then two away defeats against Newcastle and Man. United. But last Saturday? The glory of a home Derby victory against Liverpool.

And now the football banter would have to wait as yet another bereaved family was ushered into the reception parlour. For the most part they were just another identical bunch of mourning relatives, embarrassed by their loss, by the strangeness of their circumstance, exuding just the level of sadness they believed might be expected of them. All but one of them, at least.

Alongside the sorrowful widow, the downcast and confused children, an entire company of their relatives, was an Uncle Jimmy. Irrepressible. One anecdote after another about his deceased brother Johnny.

'Hey, mate,' he said to Tom Priddy, just after the introductions. 'You the fella what knows all the hymns?'

'I can help with suggestions, see,' Tom told him, fearing yet another challenge. 'If it's what the family needs, like.'

'No, mate,' Uncle Jimmy told him. 'Our Johnny, see. He 'ad

a favourite. Bet you don't know it, though.'

Yes, another challenge. It was becoming tedious.

'Try me,' said Tom.

'*It Is Well With My Soul*. That's the one.'

'If it's an American hymn…' Tom Priddy assumed his most apologetic and puzzled expression. Uncle Jimmy's tobacco-stained and spittle-smeared teeth responded with a grin of triumph. Tom allowed him to savour the moment, though not for too long. Then he raised his countertenor's voice to the parlour's ceiling and sang.

When peace like a river, attendeth my way,
When sorrows like sea billows roll;
Whatever my lot, Thou hast taught me to know
It is well, it is well, with my soul.

'How d'you do it, Mister Priddy?' said Waugh once the arrangements were all agreed and the family had filed out once more.

'Plenty of time to practise, see,' Tom replied. 'On the convoys, isn't it.'

Still work for the Special Constables. The backlog of supplies piled even now in the goods stations. But not for much longer, Tom supposed. He'd miss it. Already missed the soldiers. The Scots Greys. *Duw Annwyl*, had he missed his vocation in life? Soldier. And if he'd been a soldier, he'd have sorted out those strikers. Damn them. Like a cancer. There'd even been news boys on strike at the end of August. The tramworkers, as well, of course. Eighty of them still not reinstated. Tiresome protests everywhere about Riot Sunday. Now, drillers at Cammell Lairds. Didn't seem to matter where you looked. Strikers.

'Heroes, all of you,' said Mister Waugh. 'Heroes. Where'd we have been without our Specials, eh? Anarchy, that's where. And now – this with the schools.'

It was true. Strike fever even in the schools. Boys mostly. No more caning, they'd demanded. Less hours. Started in Edgehill and spread like wildfire. Even their own strike committees in some places. Tom recalled his horror at arriving in Liverpool early in the year and discovering that here existed a flourishing Anarchist-Communist Sunday School, run by a heretic called Jimmy Dick.

Somewhere within Tom Priddy, his personal *Iesu* spoke to him: *Suffer little children, and forbid them not, to come unto me: for of such is the kingdom of heaven.*

'Suffer little children?' said Mister Waugh, as though he'd heard the words of Jesus also. 'I'd make the little devils suffer. Need a good beatin', eh?'

A good beating, indeed. Tom just wished there were better punishments for the rest, as well. It had been his fervent wish, for the Beanpole's Fritzie sweetheart to find himself sent back where he belonged. Germany, see. But then some bunch of Irish do-gooders – yes, papist Irish – had persuaded the Home Office to offer clemency to the rioters already in prison. Even the Fritzie, it seemed. So, no deportation, after all.

'Where will it all end?' said Mister Waugh.

'You think it *will* – ever end?'

Tom Priddy thought it might not. That this city might have been changed forever. That it would now always be this way. Yet he'd do his best to prevent it. His own modest contribution? The business with Taffy Maddox.

All things considered, the Dumpling's Krooboy hadn't done too badly, like. A month ago, but Tom still enjoyed the memory. Proper pugilist, he'd turned out to be. Floored two of them, sweet as you like. Fuzzy-wuzzy, they'd called him. Teapot. Monkey boy. But jab, jab – down they'd gone. And the strike fund money still safe in Tom Priddy's pocket. If they'd finished searching him...

'Why did you do it?' he'd asked, when the third of those ruffians had helped the other two stumble away and the Krooboy had retrieved his trousers.

'Lord Jesus Nyesoa,' the Krooboy had replied, 'tell me it right.'

The fellow hadn't seemed too certain. But Tom didn't care. He was simply confused. The Krooboy and Lord Jesus? Not a heathen? Was it possible – for his own Lord Jesus to live inside the Krooboy as well? It must have been true, for the Lord Jesus had spoken to him then. About the strike fund money. He'd not been entirely positive before, but now...

Let him that stole steal no more: but rather let him labour, working with his hands the thing which is good, that he may have to give to him that needeth.

Ephesians. It had helped to make up his mind. Sergeant Ladysmith, of course.

1.05pm

'I'm sorry, Mister Kaplan. I had intended to be back earlier.'

Cari had thought it best to pop her head around his office door rather than wait for his admonishment. Part of her intention, in future to confront issues more positively. Bull by the horns, sort of thing.

'What's that, Miss Maddox?' He barely raised his head from the newspaper.

'Five minutes late, I'm afraid. But I'll make up the time later.'

'Time? Yes, of course.'

She turned to go, more unsettled by his seeming indifference to Cari's misdemeanour than any scolding could have made her. But he'd not finished with her, after all. 'Have you seen?' He held up the headline. 'Even here,' he said. 'Even here.'

Jewish families evacuated by special trains from the valleys of South Wales. Anti-Jewish riots. Attacks on Jewish property, against Jewish women and children. They had swept Glamorgan and Monmouthshire. Yes, she said, she'd read the papers. Shocking.

'It was the same,' he told her, 'when I was a boy. Close to Lemberik. We had nothing. But we all lived together in the same village. Jews. Non-Jews. Then, one day – some pogrom. They forced us out, onto the road. And those who'd worked with us, shared our food, been our friends, they spat on us, chased us with sticks. What happens to people, Miss Maddox?'

She wasn't entirely sure why he should seek her opinion, for it was a rare intimacy.

'My father believes some collective madness has gripped the world recently,' Cari told him. 'Like an infection, which will pass in time.'

'I sometimes think my people must carry this infection within us, my dear. For it follows us wherever we go. And has done so through all the ages. But I'd hoped to dare that here, at least...'

She had no answer for him. Not really.

'My father tends towards the optimistic,' said Cari. 'A favourite line from *Great Expectations*. About how, when we are bent and broken, it is always into better shape.'

'Bent and broken? My people for sure, over the centuries. But better for it? *Feh!* He must be a good man though, your father.'

Good? Yes, she supposed so. His days recently filled with the task of raising relief for the Post and Points Boys. Some of the tram workers still locked-out and, though most of the soldiers now gone, convoys continued to move goods and supplies around the city – greatly smaller escorts than at the height of the strikes.

'I never heard him utter a bad word about your people, Mister Kaplan,' she said.

Unlike Wyn, Cari thought, whose nineteenth birthday they'd celebrated four days earlier. Though little of real celebration about it. Simply another fractious gathering. No Taffy, of course. The lost funds never recovered and yes, he'd taken a beating. But worse, since then he'd never once got the tap. Not a day's work in almost a month.

'And how is your father's business, Miss Maddox? Prosperous, I hope. Despite all this unrest.'

Tom Mann's call for a general transport strike had not entirely come to fruition – except here in Liverpool, perhaps – though to all intents and purposes the result had been the same.

'I suspect my father's definition of a prospering business might be somewhat similar to Wilkins Micawber's recipe for happiness,' Cari told him. 'He calculates his income, then spends all but the last penny, usually on one or other of his favourite philanthropies. The young boys who work for the Corpie trams. And now Welsh orphans in the city. A scheme to provide them all with new Blucher boots through the sale of lottery tickets.'

'*Azoy?* This could turn him a pretty penny. And those orphan boys. Always plenty of land agents about, happy to pay a premium for young ones who can be persuaded to work the mines of South Africa. Or herd sheep in Australia. Or chase cattle around the Canadian Prairies.' It sounded a little too much like selling them into servitude, but Cari let it pass. 'Yes,' Mister Kaplan went on, 'he sounds like a shrewd fellow, your father.'

'I never thought of him as shrewd,' she said. 'And, at the moment, anything that goes wrong seems to be the fault of the railwaymen. Or the carters.'

At least by now the last groups of dockers had returned to work, victorious for the most part. Only some groups of tramway men still fighting to be reinstated. The streets were therefore now being scavenged again, much of their noxious odour disappeared, along with the stranded travellers and armoured police trucks.

'And you, Miss Maddox. You have a young man of your own, I suppose?'

It was kindly put, though Cari suspected Mister Kaplan might simply be trying to calculate how much longer he could rely on her services. Before she ended up in the family way.

'As it happens,' she smiled, 'a certain young man has recently confessed to being particularly fond of me.'

'Well, I'm pleased for you, of course. But perhaps not a good enough reason to be standing around like this when there's so much work to be done. Here, at least.' He glanced at the wall clock. 'Much more than five minutes to be made up now, Miss Maddox.'

1.30pm

'This is him,' King Billy shouted down into the gig boat. 'Amos Gartee.'

It was a handsome enough craft, Amos decided. Twenty feet? No, more. A mast, its red sail furled on a lowered gaff. Three forestays, each with its own headsail. Oars shipped.

'Then step aboard, Mister Gartee,' called the *poto* seaman from the boat. The fellow wore a skipper's cap and a once-white, oil-stained, woollen gansey.

'Good luck,' said King Billy and turned away, left him there.

Amos mumbled a word of thanks and climbed down the ladder, jumped nimbly onto the centre thwart. Good to be back on the water. The Coburg Dock.

'Coleman,' said the man, offering his hand. 'Tom Coleman.'

Amos shook the hand, shook it with grateful enthusiasm. Then clicked his fingers, equally exuberant.

'What d'you think of her, Mister Gartee? Billy says you know your boats.'

To be fair, King Billy only knew this because Amos had told him so. But he'd known how much Amos wanted work – seamen's work. And he had this friend, Coleman. Unusual, King Billy had said. These gig boats. Families. Generations of the same families. Yet this one, this Coleman family. Two sons lost and in need of a good hand.

'Fine, she is,' said Amos. 'Fine past all these others.'

He looked along the line, the other gig boats moored at the wharf.

'But how will you handle her?' Coleman asked him. 'The fastest tidal run in all Europe. Understand – tidal run?' Yes, Amos understood. 'And the highest tidal range in Britain. You ever sailed anywhere like this?'

'At Bissau, same. Will be a'right, skipper.'

He knew he was being a big rusty man. An exaggeration. For the tides at Bissau were only half the height and strength of those here on this Mersey river. Still fast and dangerous, though. And the Kru boats only half the size of this one.

'Then we'll see how you get on, Mister. Welcome to the Mersey Watermen's Association.'

Was this it? No ceremony or initiation? King Billy had taken him before some elders, of course. Their *krogba*, an ancient named Anderson. And that, it seemed, had been enough. A member now. The close association of watermen responsible at times for ferrying passengers or crew ashore but more importantly for carrying lines to mooring dollies, or inshore pilotage. Without such watermen, shipping could not function in a place like this.

So, Amos felt at home. For his people had been masters of this trade all along their own coast as well. He would tell Miss Nesta. And perhaps, in the telling, it would restore their friendship.

She'd been distant with him since the day he had saved the devil man.

'Did I not do right?' he had said when he'd seen the look of dismay on her face.

'The right thing,' she'd told him, 'would have been to drag that creature down to the dock and drown him.'

5.15pm

'It's a trick!' Cari yelled. 'Another trick. And we're too blind to even see it.'

'Perfectly normal parliamentary procedure, Miss Maddox,' Alice Davies was insisting, even before Cari was finished speaking. Yet it was, to be fair, the third time Alice had tried to do so.

'Widening amendments?' said Cari. 'To a Conciliation Bill we'll be lucky to see supported even as it stands.'

The weather had cooled towards the end of August, then turned torpid once more as they reached the middle of September. Somewhat akin to Tom Mann's revolution, now she came to think of it. All the fervour about social injustices simply evaporated in the heat once the pay deals were settled. But, one way or the other, they seemed to have brought the heat of this Indian summer – as the newspapers were already calling it – into the evening's meeting. Another room hired in the Ranelagh Street hall and they'd barely managed to maintain civility even during the minute's silence. Mrs Ramsay MacDonald. NUWSS, of course, and certainly no supporter of the WSPU goals. But blood poisoning. And only forty-one.

'We can hardly suspect the motives of those proposing amendments,' said Florrie Thompson-Frere, 'when they are so evidently our allies. Like it or not, our allies.'

'Because one or two may emanate from the Independent Labour Party,' Cari argued, and inevitably thinking of the recently bereaved Mister MacDonald again, 'doesn't mean they're not misguided.'

'They are amendments, Miss Maddox.' Alice was losing patience again. 'If they fail, the substantive vote will still take place on the Bill as it stands.'

'Oh, ladies,' said Cari, turning theatrically to embrace the entire gathering, then holding up her hands in apology to the fellows from the Men's League, 'I sincerely regret my ignorance on these constitutional issues. You see, I was foolishly wondering why some of these harmless amendments are so plainly being formulated, not by our friends, but by our bitterest enemies.'

The Anti-Suffrage League, they'd been told, had been especially active these past few weeks.

'Yes, our enemies,' Cari repeated. 'And, of course, I was also labouring under the impression that, in the House, amendments to proposed Bills are taken on one day, and the Bill itself, amended or otherwise, on another. So, simpleton as I am, if I wished to wreck this

Bill, I should simply arrange for a few friends to put an amendment – let's suppose an amendment proposing the vote for every male and female over the age of ten…'

'Oh, this is quite absurd,' protested Mrs Little Crosby, waving her cheroot impatiently in the air. 'Quite absurd.'

'I agree,' said Alice Davies. 'Time to move on to other business, I believe.'

'I'm sorry,' Cari cried, 'but I haven't finished.'

'Let her speak! Let her speak!' A chorus of voices from her women clerks. From Mary Robson, as well.

'I know the example is a foolish one,' Cari apologised. 'But I was exaggerating for effect. Though I think you all take the point. Some amendment that really is absurd.' She glanced at Mrs Little Crosby. 'Quite right. Absurd,' Cari said to her. 'Yet then the Chamber deliberately empties when this absurd amendment is proposed. And, for lack of numbers except those mischief-makers putting it to the vote, it gets passed. And therefore makes a laughing-stock of the amended Bill so that, when taken in its turn, it falls. Though, as I say, you must forgive my foolishness for thinking such a thing to be possible.'

Cari sat down to a ragged round of applause from her friends.

'I doubt even Niccolò Machiavelli could have invented your scenario,' Alice smiled. Condescending creature, Cari thought. 'But we do really need to plan for a more likely outcome. Emmeline believes there will, indeed, be waverers.' Emmeline again! 'And we'll need a show of force on the day of the vote.'

'London, I suppose,' said Cari, in a stage whisper to those around her.

'Nicole O'Who?' murmured Mary Robson, and Cari wondered for a moment what she was talking about.

'No,' Cari told her, when the penny dropped, 'not Irish. Italian. Wrote about the art of cunning in politics.'

'London is where the decision will be made,' Alice explained, very slowly. 'And Emmeline – Mrs Pankhurst – has been explicit about the need for an impressive demonstration.' Cari knew this, of course. Mrs Pankhurst had been touring Scotland, speaking to packed crowds. 'Impressive,' Alice emphasised. 'And hopefully without incident.'

She looked straight at Cari, exactly as Cari had known she must. For she'd made a point of pulling her to one side just as Cari arrived. Another inquiry, this time from Mrs Pethick-Lawrence, about the alleged assault during the Coronation Procession. Three months earlier, for goodness sake. Though apparently the "victim" was some person of note. Anonymous, though of note. Yet Alice, for whatever reason, had chosen to ignore the earlier query. Hardly a desire to protect Cari, she thought. More likely some embarrassment in explaining that the deadly missile had, in fact, been nothing more than a Bramley apple.

'Without incident,' Cari concurred. 'So long as it goes through. But it's more faith than me you've got, Alice. This Bill's already been pushed back to the autumn. And it'll be any excuse to stop it. Whether it's widening amendments or something else.'

'I'm assured,' Alice replied, 'the whole issue of these amendments will be explained in tomorrow's edition, Miss Maddox. Now, the demonstration.'

5.25pm

'Yes, certain, it is,' Tom Priddy told the sergeant. 'The darkie dropped it. *Duw Annwyl*, how many Krooboys have you got in this city?'

Ladysmith had been waiting for him at the Rotunda when Tom had arrived in time for the evening performance.

'Tell me again, Mister Priddy. What happened?'

'Sergeant, I have scenery to shift. An' I already told you this story twice. For pity's sake, it was weeks ago. But if you insist...'

Attracting attention, they were. The manager, Mister Mantlemere. Early customers for the ground floor café and the billiards hall.

Tom glanced at the foyer clock. Not much time – though for another reason. The summons he'd received to meet Lewis and Rees at the Temperance Hotel. He didn't like it, see. Trouble, like. He could smell it. His own Lord Jesus could smell it, as well.

But he dutifully led the sergeant into the comparative privacy of the cloakroom, Ladysmith picking up one of today's programmes from the foyer's desk as they passed.

'*The King's Romance*,' said the policeman. 'Any good?'

'Another farcical comedy. Seem to show little else, we don't. But that's life, I suppose. Farcical comedy, like. This one? Ruritania. Some baron poses as a prince so he can elope with an anarchist's daughter.'

'Anarchists,' said the sergeant. 'Get everywhere these days. And your attackers, sir – anarchists too, d'you think?'

'Very likely, see. Just returned my rig to the yard, I had. Walk up Harlow Street to catch the tram, I do. Next thing I know, I'm getting pushed into some back jigger – it's what you call them here, like, but Welsh word, it is. Did you know that, Sergeant? Jigger, see.'

Tom began to tidy some of the hangers on their rails. He was proud of the way he'd got to grips with the local jargon.

'And how many of them, did you say? Four?'

'*Oedd*, there were four. Three white boys and the darkie. Scars across his face. Like…'

He ran his fingers across his own face, a crude imitation of those raised patterns on the Krooboy's cheeks.

'And you fought them off?'

'I can look after myself, see. Knocked one of them on his arse and the others…'

'You'll forgive me for saying so, sir, but the intelligence you've given us in the past, about Nesta Maddox – not always much use.'

Cheek of the man.

'The intelligence, Sergeant, has been fine, see. It's been your men, I reckon, who've managed to make a mess of things. And, like I say…'

'Only, it's strange, Mister Priddy. Woman across the road. Came forward to report a black man she'd seen. Fits your Krooboy's description. Says he was parading around the street in his long johns. Then a boxing match in the street. Against three of four other fellas. Does this ring any bells, sir?'

5.30pm

In the Ranelagh Street meeting hall, the following half-hour passed with all the normal turgid details of travel arrangements, dress requirements, complaints from Mrs Avery about something-or-other. And Cari with time, at last, to think about Ernst Jurks. Fond. Since that first time, weeks before, he'd repeated the word often enough.

What had he meant, exactly? His grasp of English was good. But far from perfect. He had seemed to wish his fondness to imply something special. Yet how special? She could picture him again, in his prison uniform, those demeaning arrows. Still, it seemed he would not face deportation, as they had each feared. The Home Office. Home Secretary Churchill. Well, she had to give him that one, at least. Shades of grey, indeed.

But Ernst? Hardly anybody's image of a typical German, she decided. Perhaps, however, he was characteristic of the area from which he came. Rostock, on the Baltic Sea. Pale, for a seafarer. But then he seemed to have travelled no further than the Russian ports in one direction, England, Ireland and the Low Countries in the other.

Once, on the hottest of those August days, she had seen him at the fountain without his shirt, sluicing water over his shoulders and chest, his right upper arm marked by an elaborate tattoo – ropes and crowns and anchors. And the single word, Rostock, beneath. He had quite taken her breath away.

So, fond it was. She turned it over. English and then Welsh. *Hoff*. She wondered whether the German word in Ernst's mind might have some deeper significance than the blandness of *fond*. And was she fond of him in return? Certainly. Something deeper than mere friendship. But did she love him? And now she found herself struggling with yet another simple word, the meaning of which had more tentacles than an octopus.

Love? For goodness sake. Not this nonsense of Wyn's, that was certain. Cari loved her family. She loved the Lord Jesus. But this with Ernst? It felt as though it belonged in a separate compartment entirely, one on which she would need to keep the door fixed ajar. Plainly not shut in his face, but not fully opened either. To be controlled. Measured and monitored against developments, she hoped. So that perhaps, when he was at liberty once more, they might discuss the thing with a wider vocabulary. So she could explain. That, yes, she might contemplate marriage if she should ever be asked. And Cari imagined those strong deckhand's fingers touching her cheek, his lips brushing her own, the door to her secret compartment slammed open with the wind which followed. A wedge needed against such eventuality, therefore. For she would be no man's slave.

Slave. The word bounced back at her from within the hall, brought Cari shockingly alert once more to her surroundings.

'Slavers!' Mrs Little Crosby was saying. 'You must all have seen it.'

Last week's edition of *Votes for Women*, Cari recalled. A somewhat confused letter to the editors, asking the WSPU to perhaps highlight the dangers of this apparently growing phenomenon.

'There doesn't seem to be much evidence, however,' said Alice Davies. 'Apart from some hysteria in the *Daily Mail*.'

'Oh, really!' Mrs Little Crosby was on her soapbox now. 'There are many accounts, Miss Davies. Young white women taken from the streets. Sold into the most unspeakable situations. In Barbary and such. By all manner of undesirables. Lascars. Darkies. Chinamen.'

'Germans?' said Cari.

'All those denizens of Sailor Town and Dark Town, I fear, Miss Maddox.' Mrs Little Crosby sneered at her. 'So yes, Germans too, I suppose. It is a vile trade. And they are a nation who would stoop to anything that might advance their wealth, expand their empire.'

'But not an issue we can influence, my dear.' Florrie Thompson-Frere patted the ridiculous woman's arm. 'I'm afraid not. And how did we get onto this subject anyway?'

'Miss Robson's question,' said Alice, plainly unhappy about having to re-open the debate. 'The paper's apparent ambivalence towards the crisis here in Liverpool – though I don't share her view. We gave support to some elements of the strikes in a measured way, but never allowing it to divert attention from our main focus. This is the correct approach. Would you not agree?'

'Mary's right,' Cari told her. 'There's been barely a mention. It's a disgrace.'

Even the pit-brow women seemed to have slipped from the pages. And each of Cari's own letters, an entire article, as well, which she had written, had been roundly ignored. It still stung. Badly. Those images of women and their children crashing over the precipice of St. George's Plateau. Heaven alone knew what injuries they'd suffered at the hands of those brutes – those men who were a disgrace to the very cause of law and order. How could this not be an issue for her WSPU? How not the very embodiment of women's repression by a male establishment?

'Purely a matter for the editorial team,' said Alice. 'Unless the meeting wishes me to submit a formal letter of protest?'

'Well…' Cari stood to speak, but then saw that most of the members were shaking their heads. Alice had read them well and Cari knew it was a lost cause.

'Good!' Alice smiled. 'The editorial team have a difficult enough task already. Mrs Pethick-Lawrence and her husband devote so much of their lives to the paper's production. It would seem like a total betrayal to criticise their efforts. A betrayal of the paper itself.'

And Cari began to feel the jaws of a trap closing around her.

'I understand also, Alice,' said Florrie Thompson-Frere, 'that tomorrow's edition carries an amusing piece about the mess into which the Antis have got themselves over the municipal elections issue.'

'It promises to be excellent,' Alice replied. 'Front page cartoon. Quite clever. And you're very well-informed, Mrs Thompson-Frere. Finger on the pulse, as usual.'

Cari could feel it closing, the trap, but still refused to believe. She'd been Acting Secretary for Liverpool North all those months now. Sales were excellent. The rounds well organised. And yes, Florrie Thompson-Frere played her part admirably for her own corner of the district. But with the Secretary's position due to be formalised at tonight's meeting, Alice surely couldn't be intending…

'It's an important point though,' Patricia Woodlock was saying. 'The Antis may have shot themselves in the foot.'

The Anti-Suffrage League had set up their own Local Government Committee, with the aim of showing how, contrary to the WSPU's own claims, it was relatively easy for women to stand in municipal elections.

'Easy, they say,' Patricia went on, 'for women to stand. And then what? The very first candidates they put forward run into all the brick walls we've been fighting against. And they have the nerve to be outraged because of it. It's perfectly hilarious. But this shouldn't prevent us from thinking about developing some candidates of our own for the next elections.'

'Well,' cried Mrs Little Crosby, 'I think Mrs Thompson-Frere would make an admirable candidate.'

And Florrie Thompson-Frere was on her feet immediately, nervously fingering the same gold watch with the dragon motif, which Cari had first seen her wearing on Census Night. It seemed such a long time ago.

'It's very flattering,' she smiled. 'But my ambitions stretch no further than fighting for the cause, and this alone. Happy to devote myself full-time, body and soul, so to speak. If necessary. To the promotion of our work.'

How the members loved it! And it was through this clever piece of pantomime that she stood against Cari and carried the vote, twenty minutes later, to be officially elected as *Votes for Women* Secretary, Liverpool North. All over too quickly for Mary Robson or the women clerks to assist very much, yet Alice must have worked hard to make it happen. Machiavelli would have been proud of her, Cari decided.

5.45pm

'You'll do for me, Mister Gartee.' Skipper Coleman, alongside him at the *Otter*'s tiller, slapped Amos on the shoulder.

The tide was rising fast. Very fast. And a steam tug with a buff-coloured funnel had brought the square-rigger along the wall to the Coburg Dock's entrance. Seventy feet wide, unless Amos was mistaken. Deep, as well, Coleman had told him, as Amos deftly caught the heaving line, coiled it and began to haul in the hawser to which the line was made fast.

'See how she's stemmed the tide?' Coleman shouted, while Amos took a couple of neat turns of the hawser around a stern clean to secure it.

A second gig boat, the *Freedom*, had already taken one line ashore, aft, allowing the ship's stern to swing out, a breast line keeping the vessel from drifting further downstream. Easy enough today, though Amos could imagine how this might be in strong winds, the Mersey river's ripping tide and steep seas.

Above them, the dock gatemen had rigged a huge pudding fender of knotted hemp at the knuckle of the entrance, and Amos remembered how Miss Nesta had told him about another sister whose husband was just such a man. A man of substance. A gateman.

'Forrard now, Mister Gartee.'

Skipper Coleman pointed the *Otter* up into the wind, and Amos took the coiled heaving line towards the bow, over the centre thwart where another of the crew, Dainty, was bringing down the mainsail's gaff.

For a moment, as he hung the coiled rope temporarily over a belaying pin, Amos imagined one of the gatemen here might be the same fellow. That he might tell his wife, and that the sister-wife might tell Miss Nesta.

'Ay-yah,' she would say. 'My husband tells me there was this fine sailor today. A Kru sailor. A sailor fine past all the others.'

Amos Gartee smiled, happy to be back on the water. Happy to be a fully-fledged member of the Mersey Watermen's Association. A gig boat man.

'Look lively now, boys. And you, Mister, if you please. As before!'

He'd shown his skills earlier, out on the river, and now repeated his magic. Two of the jibs already furled and the foremost jib topsail hanked down, leaving just the clew free to be played. And Amos played it to perfection, catching the breeze in little more than a towel-sized stretch of canvas, powering the *Otter* just enough to see her through the entrance.

His eye was caught by a group of naked boys, milk-white, near the dock's moored barges – probably the children of the bargees – taking turns at jumping into the water, enjoying the sunshine. For the Wolof had told him the weather was exceptional for this Liverpool place. Unseasonably hot, he'd said, though Amos failed to see how any sane person could think it so. Still, the scene reminded him of home, pleased him even more.

'What the hell are you waiting for?' yelled Skipper Coleman. Amos awoke from his reverie in time to realise they were almost past the steps.

He grabbed for the coiled heaving line and jumped. A magnificent jump into the seaweed slopping around the waterline of the granite staircase. Up the steps and dragging the hawser which Skipper Coleman had unhitched from the cleat, Amos passed the dripping rope to the shore gang.

Yes, he thought, as the square-rigger was warped into the Coburg Dock, a sailor fine past all the others. A sailor who would soon have the bride price. A man of substance.

*

6.00pm

Cari was still licking her wounds, wondering at the pettiness of it all, and had already passed the station's front entrance, heading for the corner crossing of Lord Nelson Street – that fateful location which would, forever, associate itself in all their minds with the carnage of Bloody Sunday. Riot Sunday, as the papers preferred to call it, disparagingly.

Taffy – if such a thing was even possible – was now more resentful towards them than previously. They'd gone to visit him at his new lodgings, a dosshouse on Duke Street.

'Why not just come home?' Cari had said, just after he'd moved in, as she and Nesta tried to bring some order to the place. It might have called itself a boarding house, but this room – a cubicle, more like – was barely large enough to accommodate the two hammocks. Though, fortunately, the second hammock presently had no occupant, Taffy having the room to himself. The pink paint on the walls flaking away, cobwebs in all the corners. On the floor, the remains of the slops their brother had been served for his dinner.

'Home,' Taffy had sneered. 'I had a home at Theresa's.'

Ma MacKenny had done her best, Cari supposed. But once news of the missing strike fund had spread, and after some of the younger dockers – the worse for drink, of course – had turned up at the house, threatening to "kick his head in", there'd been no choice. He'd had to move out.

'Shouldn't have been so bloody careless, then,' Nesta had murmured. 'Lost the fund.'

'Lost, Nesta? Lost? Know what I heard, girl? The latest? That the bobbies are lookin' for some darkie they think might have nicked it?'

Cari stopped to look at the Empire's theatrical posters, remembering the moment. Preposterous. If the cash had been so well hidden, how on earth, did he think…? Yes, preposterous. But this hadn't stopped him. And, slowly, for Nesta the penny had dropped.

'Wait,' she'd said, at last, 'you're not thinking…'

'Well, wouldn't you, Nesta? For your precious Krooboys? A going away present? Not as if you haven't got form, like.'

Nesta had been too flabbergasted to respond, and Cari had feared this moment more than any of the other rifts which had appeared in the fabric of her family.

'Taffy,' she'd said. '*Iesu*, are you mad? Wasn't it you who made such a big thing about nobody knowing? Nobody. Not me. Not Nesta.'

'Well,' Nesta spat at him, 'at least if the bobbies are after this *darkie*, like you say, they might leave *me* alone. Unless you've snitched to them again.'

'Snitch?' he'd yelled at her. 'You think I'd snitch to those mutton shunters about my own sister? About any bloody thing?'

And on it had continued, him ranting at her, and Nesta countering that it was all well for him, though, to accuse his sisters of looking down their noses at Theresa MacKenny. Or of somehow helping to steal a strike fund they knew nothing about.

'You think it's the same thing, Nesta?' he'd bellowed. 'And isn't it the truth anyway? After all you did. Blathering to Pa about her. About Catholic girls, as though they were...'

He'd stopped himself in time, apparently, from repeating whatever docker's language was in his mind. Yet it had left poor Nessie in floods of tears, inconsolable, blaming Cari, of all people, for putting suspicions about Taffy into her head.

Well, Cari was right, wasn't she? Wasn't she? It didn't matter, though. Of course, it didn't. And each time Cari had tried to see her afterwards, she'd been greeted with the news that she was off supporting Amos Gartee's Krooboys – food parcels and strike funds. Yes, strike funds. An unfortunate coincidence. And it was, wasn't it – a coincidence?

This was all before their strike came to an end, of course. Before the rest of the Krooboys had sailed home again. But money? Cari wondered again, as the names on the Empire's theatrical posters finally came into focus. The Paxton Trio. Burley and Burley. Bessie Butt.

Money, she thought. Money, from where? She hoped against hope, of course, that its source hadn't been Nesta's new employer, at the Vienna Bakery. Surely she wouldn't be so stupid.

6.00pm

'Here?' Tom Priddy gasped and collapsed into one of the Cocoa Room's green leather armchairs. He'd missed his stop, already late for this meeting he didn't want to attend in the first place. Had to run all the way back from the Haymarket. 'What happened,' he said, 'to not being able to meet in Liverpool, like?'

'That was then,' Rees replied. Not even a pretence at affability today. 'Before you forgot about our little arrangement.'

The Temperance Hotel and its Cocoa Room, right next to Mad John's – literally a stone's throw from the printshop. It wouldn't help if any of old Huw's brood spotted him with these two. More questions to answer. And he'd had enough questions for one day. Ladysmith and the nosey biddy in Harlow Street. Dodged it, though, he had. What? A darkie in just his long johns? He'd laughed. Had Ladysmith smelled her breath? Gin, maybe? And there it had hung. But now...'

'Could have met at any of them,' Tom growled. 'Know how many temperance places there are? St. John's Lane. Laurence's on Clayton Square. The Shaftesbury. But here? What if the old man himself walks in?'

'I suppose you'd have some explaining to do,' said Rees, spinning his flat cap around on his fingers. 'And hey!' he yelled at the white-aproned waiter leaning against the counter, chatting with the barman. 'We get service here, or not, like?'

The fellow sidled over, jerked his head back by way of taking their order. But not a word. Still, ginger beer for Rees, lime cordial for Lewis, tea for Tom Priddy.

'So,' said Lewis, 'why've we not heard from you, Tommy boy?'

Cordial. This was the way Lewis spoke, as well. But cordial so Tom Priddy knew it was also menacing. A cordial kind of menacing. Not that Tom Priddy took too readily to menaces. No, these two didn't frighten him. Not really.

'Better ask whoever you've got selling the things,' Tom Priddy told them. 'Just not as much coming in as we thought. Your boys, after all. Check, you could.'

'Listen, Tommy.' Lewis shifted his armchair nearer to Tom Priddy's own, leaned still closer. 'We asked you to get the start-up money – the business capital, let's call it. An' we used it to hire some likely lads, here in Liverpool. All you had to do was provide the tickets. Those lads of ours, they know which side their bread's buttered. They know what happens if their books don't balance.'

He glanced at Mister Rees, who carefully turned his cap so Tom could see inside the peak, to the single-edged razor blade concealed there. Not very subtle, like.

'Understand?'

Tom Priddy understood perfectly.

'And the cash,' said Rees, folding the cap into his hands once more, 'has to all come back to you, boyo. To go through old man Maddox's accounts, like. On paper. A few prizes. The rest – on paper, like – to the bloody orphans. Only...'

The waiter was back. But Tom wasn't sure he'd be able to hold the cup. They waited, in silence, for the drinks to be poured and, during this brief respite, Tom Priddy asked his Lord Jesus how he'd managed to make such an error. He'd brought cash for these two associates, yet knew it would never satisfy them.

On the other hand, he'd surrendered the strike fund money to the police. He could have used it now. But instead his Lord Jesus had come up with the other plan – a plan to shake up the Dumpling's dangerous little liaison with the darkie. Never occurred to him the police might not relish the chance to lock up a darkie. For pity's sake...

'Well?' said Lewis, pursing his lips at the bitterness of the lime juice. 'The money, lad.'

Tom reached inside his pocket, reluctantly took out the manila envelope, slid it along the arm of his own chair.

'This it?' Lewis was incredulous, threw the envelope to Rees. 'Really?'

'You're takin' the piss, like,' said Rees, peering at the envelope's contents.

'Told you,' Tom Priddy hissed. 'If your lads don't sell...'

'You stupid?' said Lewis. He took a handkerchief from the pocket of his flannels, blew his nose. 'If the lads aren't sellin', you'd better find them more punters. Or get sellin' yourself. Otherwise...'

6.15pm

Cari remained standing in front of the Empire's posters.

'They're much more amusing on the stage, Miss Maddox.'

She spun around, found Mister Mills the photographer standing behind her.

'I'm sorry?' she said.

276

'Passmore, Danvers and Fraser,' he explained, nodding towards the poster. She'd been staring at the thing but not seen it. Twice nightly: their music hall farcical sketch, *Sweet Williams*. I could get tickets, if you'd care to see the show.'

He was a good-looking fellow, she had to admit. Older than Cari, of course. Dapper, she supposed you would call him. Summer suit, with the jacket folded over one arm and a flat, black case tucked under the other. A wide fedora hat.

'Well…' she hesitated. She didn't really know him, after all, this Gwilym Mills. Tada would approve, naturally. Welsh. With his own thriving business.

'Please,' he smiled. 'You must say yes. An omen, see. Meeting you here.' He took the case from under his arm, opened it once he'd struggled a moment with the jacket, then let her view the contents. Photographs. What else would they have been? And there, on the top, Cari and Nesta parading themselves and their WSPU sashes before the Pathé moving picture camera.

'That terrible day,' she said, and looked over towards the Plateau.

'Terrible. Indeed it was.'

'Your photographs, Mister Mills. Gwilym,' She corrected herself, and felt a surge of hope. 'You must have evidence of the brutality. Surely…'

'I'm afraid the authorities had the same idea. Anything they thought might be incriminating – well, they came to the shop, examined all the plates. Confiscated almost twenty. Not a penny compensation either.'

'Was their financial value your only concern, then?' Cari snapped, without meaning to do so.

'We must all eat, Miss Maddox. But perhaps you could think about my offer? The tickets?'

'And the photograph of me and my sister?'

It was rude of her to simply ignore his question, and she could see from the disappointment on his face, he thought so, as well.

'Ah,' he said, after a moment, 'I shall take that as a gentle rebuke. And a rejection. But this? I was planning to see whether J.H. might be interested.'

It was a very Welsh pronunciation. *Je Aitsh*. John Herbert Jones.

Known everywhere simply by his initials and editor of *Y Brython*, their very own Liverpool weekly.

'This has been a difficult day for me, Mister Mills. Gwilym. I apologise if I seemed abrupt. Your offer was very kind.'

'Difficult in what way?'

It seemed impudent of him to ask – though it might have been good to share her ire with somebody. But how could she have explained? She had put such effort into selling the paper. And she blamed so many for the shabby way in which she'd been treated. Florrie Thompson-Frere and Alice Davies at the top of her list, of course. Those upon whom Cari thought she could also rely for support. For their votes. Those two fellows from the Men's League. Patricia Woodlock, for reasons she couldn't fathom. And Nesta. Because she hadn't been there.

'To do with this, I suppose.' Cari touched her finger to the glossy image of their sashes. 'But nothing to trouble yourself with. Truly.'

'And my offer?'

'If I were to be perfectly honest, the line-up of artistes does little to tempt me.' He was crestfallen, yet again. 'Though I must confess to being intrigued by the Kinemacolor showing. Is it as good as they say?'

The theatre had recently been equipped with one of Mister Urban's bioscope projectors, and the newspapers had been full of it. Moving pictures, in colour! Shown between the main attraction and the supporting acts.

'You should judge for yourself, of course, Miss Maddox,' he said, though he sounded less than enthusiastic about it all.

'Then perhaps there is a deal to be done. Might it be possible to lend me your copy of the photograph? So I could show it to Tada, and to Nesta also.'

A way to thaw the ice between them, she thought. How could Nesta not be amused by the image?

'In exchange,' she said, 'I shall accompany you to the theatre, as you suggest.'

After all, she would now have considerably more free time on her hands. There was a momentary guilt, of course. That she should be gallivanting about with another man while poor Ernst was languishing in Walton. But where was the harm? Mister Mills a friend of the family, after all. And the photograph? Worth the sacrifice, surely.

'I should have preferred the offer to be accepted for its own sake,' he smiled. 'But – here, please accept this as a gift. A token, even. I can easily make a further copy for J.H. So long, of course, as you would not mind him reproducing the picture for his paper. And listen, Miss Maddox, perhaps the theatre might wait until a later occasion. I am guessing you're also a young lady who enjoys fine art. Am I correct?'

Cari wasn't quite sure. A few visits to the gallery there, just across the road, certainly. Some favourite paintings. But otherwise? She'd become completely lost on a couple of occasions when Florrie Thompson-Frere had tried to engage her in discussions about her latest artistic passions. Florrie had once used the word *avant-garde*, as though it were also new to her. And then the term *Pre-Raphaelite* in almost the same breath. She knew little of the world dominated by William Morris or Rossetti and her tada had always rather looked down his nose at such things. Yet she now found herself with somebody else's words in her mouth.

'*"We have art so that we shall not die of reality,"*' she quoted. Ernst had taught her all about Nietzsche during her visits to the gaol. Dangerous things. About Christian morality as an expression of power.

'Precisely,' said Gwilym Mills. 'And you know about the exhibition, of course?'

She did not, but she glanced across at the gallery and there, between its columns, above the wide entrance steps, hung a banner. *Autumn Exhibition of Modern Art: The Forty-First.* But from this distance she couldn't quite make out the dates.

'At the Walker?' she said. 'Yes, of course.'

'Opens tonight, as you'll know. Though not for the general public. No, tonight is the inaugural banquet. A glittering affair, I imagine. And – well, I have an invitation to attend though, sadly, nobody with whom to share its pleasures.'

6.45pm

'Think she'll forgive you on the strength of a photograph, Beanpole?'

Tom Priddy made himself comfortable at the kitchen table, copies of the *Daily Post* and *Y Cymro* spread before him and his feet up on another of the chairs, toes wriggling through the holes in his socks.

Shirt sleeves and braces. Not quite the image of himself he normally liked to portray but – well, this was home. For now.

'Between me and Nesta,' the Beanpole told him.

'*Duw*, there's tetchy, it is,' he drawled, and knitted his fingers together, deliberately popped his joints in the way he knew annoyed her so much. 'What is it, Cari? Come on, you can tell Cousin Thomas. Those women you call friends, let you down, have they?'

He saw her puzzlement and laughed. Wondering how he knew.

'Like a book, Beanpole. You went out with your satchel. Came back without it. *Votes for Women*, indeed! What happened? Gave you the elbow, did they?'

'It was taking up too much of my time. Other things to think about, just now.'

'That German, I suppose. In gaol, where he belongs, if you ask me. But, ah, the unsinkable Cari Maddox. You'd better watch out though, Beanpole. Those as think themselves unsinkable are often in for a nasty shock.' He drummed his fingers against a quarter-page grainy picture in the *Post*, and thrilled as Cari looked over his shoulder. Close. So close.

The picture. The White Star liner, *Olympic*, in collision with one of the navy's cruisers. A huge gash ripped in her side. My goodness, such a gash! Her so-called watertight compartments flooded. Well, it was to be hoped her skipper – Captain Smith, said the papers – might have learned some lessons from the episode. Would Cari catch his drift also, however? This was the question.

'You see, Cari? Accidents happen.'

She pulled back from him. No fool, this girl.

'Like I said, Cousin,' she replied. 'More time to myself now. I'll have to avoid all those pitfalls, eh?'

The Beanpole could have no idea, though. Pitfalls? No idea, at all.

'Go on, Beanpole,' he grinned. 'Tell me who's upset you.'

'Florrie bloody Thompson-Frere,' she spat, seemingly unable to contain herself. 'That's who. Waterloo snob. Posh house on Haigh Road.'

'Never mind, girl,' he said, and turned the page. 'Bet she'll get what she deserves for crossing you.' The idea amused him. But maybe this would be something for later. 'And this?' He nodded towards the paper. 'What would Nesta say about this, d'you think? Encouraging those darkies, the way she did.'

'The fight?'

'Of course, the fight, girl.'

'Speaking of which,' she said. 'Nesta tells me her friend, Mister Gartee, had cause to rescue you from some ruffians. But he wasn't very forthcoming about the details, she said. Is it true?'

He was surprised it had taken them so long. He'd expected for weeks to be challenged on his role as a Special – a scab, he thought she'd say. But nothing. And yes, he still recalled the darkie's pugilistic skills. Astonished, he'd been. Yet, not very forthcoming – what did it mean? He wondered, also, what Dumpling Nesta had *actually* told the Beanpole. Probably wished the Krooboy had used his fists on me instead, he decided.

'Rescue is cutting it a bit strong, like,' he laughed. 'Tom Priddy never needs rescuing, girl. No, I'd already sent them packing and along comes this darkie. Never introduced himself, though. Why would he? Doesn't know me from Adam, see. An' you're sure – it was him?'

She was sure. But he could see from her eyes she knew this wasn't going anywhere.

'So,' he said, 'this Jack Johnson fight.'

The newspapers had also been obsessed with this. He knew she'd have no interest in pugilism at all – even leaving the Krooboy aside – but it would be hard, even for the Beanpole, to avoid this particular proposed bout. A world championship heavyweight match at Earls Court between black American titleholder, Jack Johnson, and white British contender, 'Bombardier' Billy Wells.

'Barbaric sport,' the Beanpole told him. Predictable, she was. 'Enough reason to ban the thing on those grounds alone.'

'A sport for white men, Beanpole. Decent white men, too. You don't agree with the way he lives, Cari, surely?' He meant Johnson, of course. 'All the white women he keeps in tow all the time, like – well, you know like what, isn't it? Fast motor cars. Fast women.'

'Sounds like jealousy.'

'*Nac oes*. I'm a man of simple pleasures, Beanpole. You know that!' He leered at her. 'But those riots in America last year.'

Johnson had successfully defended his title the previous year and the papers had been full of the anti-black riots which had followed. Many people killed in the clashes.

'The same thing could happen here,' he went on. 'There's another reason for the match to be declared illegal. Country like a keg of powder as it is. Hooligans still all over the place. Here. Yorkshire. Dublin. This boxing match could be the spark, see?'

'Nothing to do with everybody knowing Johnson would win?'

'That's the worst thing,' he said. 'A fight between white and black. And black likely to be the winner? I'd certainly not waste a penny betting on Wells. Stands no chance. And what sort of message would it send, Beanpole? Black beating white. Darkies all over the Empire watching. Calvary Chapel have got it right.' This time he slapped the copy of *Y Cymro*. 'The result of this one could bring revolution to the Empire. Darkies rising up against us at the drop of a hat.'

'Really?' Her turn to laugh, though he was certain she couldn't be without similar thoughts herself. Inherited from years of old Huw's views about the relative intelligence of coloured folk. Thoughts she'd need almost physical effort to suppress.

'You think so?' she said. 'Well, why don't they go the whole hog and press for a colour bar in boxing matches? Pass a law to stop black men competing against whites?'

He knew she was being sarcastic, but he'd let it pass.

'First sensible thing I've heard you say, Beanpole,' he told her without any hint of irony. 'And exactly what everybody's clamouring for.'

'But you're right,' she said. 'Far more likely to break the ice with Nesta if I chat with her about this silliness. Shame to waste the photograph, though.' The Beanpole threw it on the table in front of him. 'D'you know what time Tada'll be back?'

'I'm not his keeper, girl. Meeting some of the tram lads, I think.' Then he slid the picture towards himself. 'Nesta,' he grinned. 'Good-looking girls, all of you. Especially young Winifred. Apart from the...' He dug his fingers into the side of his face, the places where Wyn's smallpox scars might be. 'You seen her, by any chance?'

'Not since Sunday.'

Rhys Gateman had been marginally more civil, back in work

again. Though, he'd still not a good word to say about Taffy and the dockers. Especially now. The strike fund. And refused point blank to help stupid Taffy get the tap again. Yet, a grudging acceptance that, for the moment, at least, there seemed to be work for all, getting the city back in order after the strikes.

'Only I was thinking, see,' said Tom. 'Must all take after your mam, I suppose.' Did they? The others all had old Huw's stocky build. But facially, the Beanpole? 'Shame,' he went on. 'About your mam. And he doesn't talk about her much, girl.'

'Talks about her every day,' the Beanpole retorted. 'Maybe not to you, though. He loved her very much.'

She spat out the words. Almost defensively, causing him to put up his hands.

'Steady, Beanpole,' he protested. 'Suppose you must be right. About him loving your mam. But I was wonderin', like. Whether you all ever remember her together. Her birthday, or something.'

It was a pure guess. That they never had. And from the look on her face, he saw he was right. Cari appeared to have no idea when her mother's birthday might even have been.

'Only a shame, it is,' he went on. 'You all at odds with each other. Family should be family, after all.'

He could also see she must be thinking he might have a point. Her excuse to bring everybody together. An invitation none of them could refuse.

'I can hardly ask him,' said the Beanpole. 'He'll want to know why. And unless we make it a surprise, he'd never agree.'

'Must be some way,' he replied, then made a show of biting his lip, as though searching for a solution. 'Well,' he said, 'what about Uncle Huw's old box? Something in there, maybe, see.'

The mahogany tea caddy. That solicitor's letter, asking her father to confirm his identity. And matters concerning Tom's own poor dead mother. She'd settled, of course, for the obvious explanation. The family connection. A request for her tada to act as their cousin's guardian, in some way. But he thought it must still plague her. The box.

'If he comes back,' she said, 'he'll not be happy about me rummaging around among his papers.'

'You're right, Beanpole. Have to think of something else,

I suppose.' He remained quiet for a moment, then tapped the photograph again. '*Duw*,' he said. 'Just the ticket. Take the picture. Put it in the box. And if he comes back, if he catches you, tell him he's spoiled the surprise. Your lovely photograph. Gift for him. You were going to tease him. Treasure hunt, something of the sort.'

7.00pm

'There,' said Charles Tuohey. 'Now perhaps I can have my sofa back.'

The Wolof had been kind, taken him in and given him a home, showed him how it was to live, as a free man, in this Liverpool place. But now, as a man of substance, it was time to move on. And some acquaintance of the Wolof had a vacancy, here in this rooming house. Duke Street. Not far from the spot where those straw-haired fellows had once given him such a kicking, and from whose clutches Charles Tuohey had first come into his life.

'Norway men, them still here?' said Amos.

'Why should you care? Look at you. The very picture of a Liverpool gig boat man. And they'd be sorry if they tried to get the better of you these days, Amos Gartee.'

He'd told the Wolof his story, weeks ago, about the devil man. And the Wolof had agreed with Missee Nesta. Should have thrown him in the dock. Well, perhaps. But it was all complicated. Miss Nesta and the devil man. The Doitshee, as well. And yes, he knew the difference now – just about – between Dootshies and Doitshees. He thought he understood that the Doitshie in whose house Miss Nesta had been living was actually the sweetheart of Missee Coconut Palm, though this Doitshee was, of course, now in prison. So many troubles in the world.

'Yes,' he said, and stamped his foot on the floorboards. 'Solid bottom. Like Coburg Dock.'

Sand and rock, Skipper Coleman had told him. Good solid rock. Though not so good if a skipper overloaded his deep-draft steamer. Danger of grounding at neaps.

'Good foundation for the start of a new life,' said Charles Tuohey. 'You're right.'

The room possessed a bed, an ancient sea chest – empty, yet covered in labels.

'This fellow, he seen the world.' Amos admired the box. Great Eastern Hotel Ltd, Calcutta. Pera Palace Hotel, Istanbul. Hotel Majestic, Paris. He imagined himself, one day, with Miss Nesta on his arm, strolling down that great thoroughfare in Paris he had once seen in a picture. And their great tower of iron.

'Now all you need to do is fill it, brother. And this, too.'

The Wolof had opened a drawer of the only other piece of furniture. A tallboy, also empty, though a single candlestick stood upon its polished and pitted upper surface. The walls were papered, green leaves and tiny pink flowers. On one wall, a gas mantle.

Amos opened his kitbag on the bed, lifted out some of the spare clothing Skipper Coleman had gifted him.

'Tell me,' he said. 'Them Doitshees. Germany men. Newspaper, he say Doitshees no good. All evil.'

'You've been reading the *Daily Mail*, Amos. I've told you, the *Daily Mail*'s owners believe it their duty to stir up hatred against just about everybody. Women fighting for the vote. Immigrants, and especially Jews. Our strikers. And yes, Germans. Their readers, as always, will follow them like sheep – though, in most cases, the *Daily Mail* is simply printing stories reflecting the views their readers already hold.'

'Do not think for themselves? These England people?'

'Oh, indeed,' the Wolof lies. 'They form strong opinions about this or that. And, once formed, they will never allow any quantity of opposing evidence to shake the belief. Hence, they turn to the *Daily Mail* to reassure them, on a regular basis. To show they are, despite all evidence to the contrary, still correct. Take, for example, this upcoming fight.'

They'd talked about this before. A black American fighting a *poto* English fellow. And all the world, it seemed, up in arms about it. He decided he would speak to Miss Nesta, when he was able. Ask her to explain.

7.30pm

Cari had found herself falling in with his scheme. Well, to be honest, she hadn't needed much encouragement. Maybe another peep at the solicitor's letter. See if she'd got it right. So that, five minutes after they'd discussed it, she'd been in her tada's room. At the box again. By then, she'd come to her senses. Who cared about the solicitor's letter anyway? And spying on her own father? She was ashamed for even thinking about it. So she'd opened the lid with no intention except to deposit the photograph. No more. But he'd baited the thing cleverly, Cousin Thomas. Creeping Tom Priddy. Another envelope, sitting in plain sight at the top of her tada's documents, the words beckoning to her.

Marriage Certificate. *Tystysgrif Priodas.*

She'd opened the envelope and took out the document.

The year, 1893, screaming for attention.

Marriage solemnized at the Seion Chapel, Bousfield Street, Kirkdale. The full date. Saturday, 30th September, 1893.

Her tada's details. Huw Maddox. So he'd used his adopted name.

Age, thirty-eight. Bachelor. And the profession correct. Printer. Address, Hunter Street, Liverpool.

Father's name, Tecwyn Priddy. Must have raised an eyebrow, surely? Father's name different to his own. And father's profession: Deceased.

Underneath, her mam's details. Nerys Davies. Age, twenty-six. Spinster. Profession, barmaid. Address, Bootle Lane, Kirkdale. Father's name, Mervyn Davies. Father's profession, licensee. All looked straightforward enough. Signed by a Superintendent Registrar and witnessed. Names which meant nothing to Cari.

Then the date again. Saturday, 30th September, 1893. Could this be right? Only weeks after Winifred was born. Winifred, the youngest of them that had survived. And how would Cari tell them? Especially God-fearing Wyn. How? How they, all of them, were – she'd hardly been able to bring herself even to think the word. Bastards. Illegitimate. All except poor Pryce, who hadn't survived to appreciate the joke.

It plagued her all through the banquet. She'd almost determined to give the event a miss. This news. And besides, there was Ernst to consider. It couldn't be right, could it? Languishing in Walton Gaol and she out gallivanting with another man. But what could she do? Simply fail to attend? Leave Mister Mills – Gwilym – in the lurch? No, this wouldn't serve either.

'I'm so glad you decided to come,' he said to her, as the soup was served. *Consommé Doria*, the souvenir menu named it. A thin stew of chicken, with bits of pale pasta and colourless cucumber floating on the surface. 'And the dress, new I perceive.'

It had taken every penny of her tenuous savings. But she'd needed something of note. The one she'd worn for the London procession still lay folded in her clothes chest, the blood stains from that terrible Sunday finally removed, the rips repaired, though it would never do – not for something so grand. And there'd been a sale. At George Henry Lee. In the sale, she guessed, because it had been made bespoke, and then rejected. Some woman as tall as Cari herself, and difficult to sell. High neckline, which would not shame her inadequate bosom – though she'd managed to pick up a modest bust enhancer and some hip padding at the haberdashery department almost for a song.

The dress itself, Nile-green French voile, with dainty touches of all-over lace and banding on the waist portion. Elegant, yet serviceable. A simple flower pinned into her hair. No jewellery, of course, apart from the small mesh purse she'd had as a child and still a prized possession. And she'd found, among the things Nesta had left behind, a simple feather boa. Goodness knows how she'd acquired the thing, and thank heavens the weather was still warm, that she did not need anything more elaborate. Yet she could easily have wished for a few additional luxuries.

> *Drown me in perfume from Fragonard.*
> *The smoothest satin silks of Luberon.*

'I couldn't *not* come,' she said, with the soup spoon halfway to her lips. 'And miss all this? But the dress – how did you know?'

He leaned across to whisper in her ear.

'*Cariad*,' he said. 'There's a label.'

She almost dropped the spoon, felt the red rash of her embarrassment creeping up her neck.

'But I don't believe anybody else can have seen it,' he went on. 'And if you might allow me…'

His head was still close to her own, but he turned his face to gaze up at one of the paintings hung here in the Grosvenor Room for the occasion. He pointed at the picture, as though they were discussing its composition, and she felt a sharp tug at her shoulder.

'There,' he said more loudly. 'Almost a caricature, don't you think? Lyons. I admire his work very much. And this sherry – just perfect with the consommé.'

He'd taken his hand away from her shoulder, reached for the tiny glass, crunching up the offending price tag and dropping it onto the table, beside her purse. She turned to thank him. Great heavens, he was indeed good-looking. And in his tuxedo, his hair so carefully oiled. But this wasn't her world. Here, among the great and the good. The Lord Mayors of Liverpool, of Manchester, and everywhere between. Members of Parliament, Challoner, Scott and the rest. Even O'Connor from the Irish Parliamentary Party. The Levers. The Bowrings. All their fine ladies.

'You're uncomfortable, my dear,' he murmured.

'I already told you, I wouldn't have missed it. At least...'

'The exhibition. You wouldn't have missed seeing these wonderful example of modern art. But the banquet...'

The second course. *Suprême de Turbotin Cardinal.* Turbot, she had never tasted. And the sauce – goodness, she licked it from the tip of her fork, closed her eyes in sheer delight.

'Béchamel,' he said. 'Lobster butter, Cayenne pepper.'

'You see?' she smiled. 'Fish and chips is my usual for a Friday night. Still, you're right about the pictures, like. And not just the pictures, either.'

She'd so far only seen the exhibition's first gallery, on the way to the Grosvenor Room. The last time she'd been there, that gallery had boasted a colourful ceramic fountain at its centre. But the fountain had gone now, replaced by a collection of sculptures. A bust of poor dead King Edward. A statue in tinted plaster – a statue simply called *Sleep.* On the walls, all was gaiety. The men, of course – Moser, Collier and the rest.

'Though they should have had some photographs,' she said. 'Don't you think. Like your photographs. Those are modern art, as well, aren't they?'

But it was the women's work she'd admired. Miss Hope. And Laura Knight's *Daughters of the Sun.* Two young women, a beach by the sea. Full of light and hope, though entirely shades of grey and white. Yet the two women naked. Or almost so.

Then walk I shall upon the Seaforth strand,
No beach tar on my soul to spoil the steps.

Something haunting about the image and, as often happened when her emotions were raw, she imagined she saw little Pryce running across the adjoining doorway.

'You flatter me, Cari,' he said. 'But yes, I like to think of them as works of art. And perhaps, apart from the Kinemacolour adventure, we should return here without the banquet. Spend more time studying these splendid exhibits.'

'Well, we shall see. But I am perfectly occupied just now. Family business, see. Which reminds me, Mister Mills…'

'Gwilym, *cariad*.'

'*Duw Annwyl*, I don't think I shall ever – but yes, Gwilym. Anyhow, I was wondering. The Seion Chapel in Bousfield Street. You know it by any chance? And a Welsh family there? Davies, their name.'

Yes, there'd been Ernst to consider. And no, she could never have left poor Mister Mills – Gwilym – in the lurch. But above all this, there'd been her hope that, somehow, she might just be able to get some more information from him.

Chapter Ten

Friday 20th October 1911

10.15am

Tom Priddy drew the scent of her deep into his nostrils. He sat on the edge of the Beanpole's bed, lifted the soft hem of pale blue-green material to his nose. The new dress, the one she'd bought for last month's assignation with the photographer. As usual, her fragrance made his passions rise, and if his Lord Jesus hadn't been standing on the other side of the room, watching him…

Still, a busy day ahead.

Old Huw Maddox was below, busy at the Cropper already. He could hear it, even from upstairs. Feel it, rather. The stamp and go vibration in the walls. And the smell of the ink seeping through the doorway. Tom would need to go and check on him soon, make sure he got the numbers right. And later send some of his own Hunter Street Irregulars out on their new rounds. The lottery tickets around all the Welsh streets. Why Rees and Lewis hadn't thought of it, he had no idea. Welsh orphans, after all. Wasn't this the whole point? He just hoped the sales would come up to expectations. For when he met them later. Get them off his back. Otherwise – well, he'd worry about otherwise in a while.

For now, he lifted the rest of the dress carefully from the Beanpole's clothes chest, laid it on the bed. Then some of her other garments. The heat again. But the words of his Saviour, whispered across the space between them.

'*And lead us not into temptation, but deliver us from evil.*'

'If You say so, Lord,' Tom replied, delving further into the chest until he found the older white frock she'd so carefully repaired. He lifted the linen shoulders with care, and placed within the folds below, first, the small accounts book and, second, the engraved watch. With equal attention to detail he restored each of the other garments precisely as he'd found them.

The Beanpole had been out of the house early. Though not on her way to Kaplan's, he'd decided.

No, he thought. Today she's finally going to take the bait.

But what had taken her so long? Fear of discovering the truth, he decided. And fear was good.

She'd been different with him, as well. Since he'd led her so cleverly by the nose to find the marriage certificate. Different, yes. Yet not what he'd expected. Tom had supposed there would be some rage, at being played that way. Instead, she'd almost seemed grateful. More amicable, somehow. Gratitude – which had cooled much of his passion for her. Spoiled things a little, if he was honest.

A change of plans, maybe. At least, a minor adjustment.

For the rest, however, his schemes remained largely intact.

It all hinged on tonight, he supposed. The Beanpole's clever plan – thanks, once again to the marriage certificate – to bring her precious family back together again.

Though what about *his* mam?

No, tonight would be about Tom Priddy's mam. And about the Beanpole's intentions all going up in flames. He could see the blaze even now. Surprises all round for the whole bunch of them – for the Beanpole herself; for Dumpling Nesta; for Daft Taffy; for scar-faced Winifred and her depraved husband; and, most of all, for old Huw Maddox, God damn his soul.

He stroked his fingers against the Nile-green voile of the Beanpole's new dress and closed the lid once more.

10.50am

Cari didn't really know Bousfield Street, though they must indeed have been to the chapel there a few times when she was small. Once for Wyn's christening, it would have been. Cari no more than three. Presumably with Taffy and Nesta in tow. Her tada, of course. Tada as she loved to picture him, a sweet suet pudding of a man, full of life and a smile as wide as the Mersey Bar.

Her mam, by contrast, she could only bring to mind through

a series of fog-shrouded sensory recollections. Movement. Swinging on her mother's arm perhaps. The kidskin scents and liquid touch of leather gloves borrowed perhaps for the occasion. The mingled scents of violets and carbolic soap. The slender warmth of her woollen skirts, to which Cari clung so hard – or thought she did. Very tall. Very slim. Like herself, she supposed.

But when would this have been? Winifred still a babe in arms, so no more than a few weeks after she was born. Ninety-two, then. Mid-September? But then they would have been married in the very same chapel only weeks later, at the end of September. What pastor in his right mind would have married them in the same chapel knowing they'd just had a child? And three more besides. Or had they somehow deceived him?

Then perhaps a couple of further visits. Other family events, she'd supposed. Until the time when, not too long afterwards, Cari saw a different Tada, bloated with fury and red-faced, roaring and shouting against – well, something or other. Yet it couldn't have been the wedding, of course. She would have remembered a wedding. And not Pryce's christening, certainly. That one was printed on all their memories. Cari five by then. Their mam already taken from them. Victoria Chapel. More tears than she would have thought possible.

A family connection, she was certain, though Cari had no idea why she was so convinced. Now, however, it seemed to make sense. Her mam's address given as Bootle Lane, close to the Seion Chapel.

So, she caught the first tram that would take her out past the Rotunda to the Fonthill Triangle, and jumped off there, then nipped across the road to the chapel itself. She was lucky to find the pastor about his duties, though he couldn't help much – only been there seven years, as Gwilym Mills had told her, and the pastor's first task had been to transfer all the records to the County's Records Department. The Marriage Act to blame, apparently. She could search there, maybe, he suggested. But Cari knew it wouldn't help and, at best, would only provide the same intriguing details she'd found on the marriage certificate. Yet before she could leave, he called her back.

'Bootle Lane, you say?' he asked. 'And what was it again, your mother's maiden name?'

'Davies,' she told him. 'Nerys Davies.'

'You might try the paper shop then. Dai *Papur*. He's a Davies, see. And Bootle Lane. Never know, do you?'

It was due to be her next port of call anyway, as it happened. For Gwilym had also known about the shop. And no, she thought. Indeed, you don't ever quite know.

11.05am

'What the hell…?' yelled Skipper Coleman.

They'd been working the Salthouse Dock this morning and Amos had already made one mistake while they were helping the *Garthpool*, another square-rigger, navigate the Canning's half-tide dock.

Now, as he made the familiar leap to the steps below the Salthouse mooring posts, he felt his feet slide from beneath him.

He grabbed for one of the iron rings along the dock wall. Missed it. Hit the water. Cold. Cold. The chill bit into his skull, though didn't yet penetrate his canvas smock. But his ears filled, his eyes almost blinded in the murky depths. Bubbles of precious live-giving air erupting upwards from all around him. And the heaving line, so carefully coiled, had now unravelled and, in the way of ropes everywhere, developed an intelligence of its own, finding every feasible way to entangle him.

His own fault. His mind elsewhere.

Was this his punishment? How could he have done it? So heinous a thing?

Yesterday had seemed so fine. Amos and Nesta at another great meeting. Jocota there, as well. Joe Cotter, of course. He must remember to say the names correctly. Missee Coconut Palm. King Billy, as well. To hear the fellow Nesta swore would change their England for all time. Another leader of working people. To rally folk in this Liverpool place. Elections in a few days.

Perhaps the excitement of the occasion, but she had clung to his sleeve throughout.

And when, as was his custom, he had waited for her in the early hours before dawn – dawn so much later now in this autumn month of their year – to commence their walk back from the place of baking bread, they had talked about the meeting some more.

Though only after he had checked they were not being followed.

For there had been many times when he had seen some fellow from the corner of his eye. In the shadows. Always in the shadows. But yes, following them. Yet, this morning, Amos had been certain they were not pursued.

Still, he'd remained alert, even when their chatter turned to the boxing fight which had not happened. Amos had already discussed the matter with the Wolof, Charles Tuohey, so some of the English words were still fresh in his mind.

'How can it be?' he'd said to her. 'Against your law?'

The Wolof had tried to explain. A danger to public order, its opponents had argued. Afraid of riots if this Jack Johnson won the bout. If the black man defeated the *poto* boxer. There'd been a picture in the newspaper. A courtroom packed with people. An injunction, that was the word.

'Yes,' Miss Nesta had replied. 'But there were those campaigning for the fight to be banned purely because the sport, Amos Gartee, is barbarous.'

An argument had developed. Not at all what he'd wanted. Both lost their tempers, it was true. But, even so…

He seemed to have been sinking into the depths of the Salthouse Dock for a long, long time. The last of his breath escaped from between his lips.

Amos Gartee remembered the place where it had happened. He had pressed her into the remnants of the old churchyard. The church, now largely torn down to make way for an extension to the big hotel in the shadow of which it had once stood. The church, she had told him when they'd passed previously, of St. David. The church where only the Welsh tongue of her forefathers had once been spoken. Yes, it had seemed the right place.

He could see it, even now, as the boathook caught in the canvas of his smock.

11.10am

Cari had thanked the pastor, then slogged her way along Barlow's Lane before turning up the hill towards Bootle. The road in question had been named anew – Westminster Road now, rather than simple Bootle Lane, and she could have caught the tram again, up towards

Walton, for it was cold and drizzling. The weather had turned, finally, after all those months, but she had her battered old rain napper and needed time to think.

First, about Nesta herself. Not just the christening, but wondering what she was up to, why she'd not gone straight back to the Jurks place after she'd finished work. But they'd not seen her. Cari had intended to share some of this with her sister, suggest they might investigate together. Another peace offering now gone awry. Perhaps if she'd struck while the iron was hot, when Cari had first seen the marriage certificate. Several weeks of excuses. Too busy. Ernst to worry about. And meetings – all those meetings. Next week's elections. Keir Hardie yesterday. But the truth? Half of her simply feared what she might discover.

And Nesta? Thinking of Nesta and the Vienna Bakery caused her to consider Old Man Kaplan, about how furious he'd be that she'd not turned in herself but, rather, arranged for one of her tada's post boys to deliver a message. Sick, she'd claimed. Violently sick. Though she knew he'd not believe her and this could be the last straw.

Yet there was so much to do today. Ernst's release from Walton at noon, and her promise to his uncle, *Herr* Jurks. Yes, she'd be there to meet him. Most of all, she needed to get her head around the questions she must ask if, indeed, Dai Davies at the paper shop turned out to have any connection whatsoever with her puzzle.

It stood next to the pub on the corner of Leighton Street, just past the entrance and long driveway to the old Ragged Union Industrial School, on the opposite side. The school had closed a few years earlier and was now a home for the old and infirmed, some of whom were in evidence being wheeled around the grounds, rain or no rain, and watching them gave Cari an excuse to stand outside for a few moments, sheltering beneath her napper and trying hard to steady her nerve.

In the end, though, she could put off the thing no longer, pushed open the door, shook the umbrella dry behind her, and saw the slender man behind the counter look up as the bell above tinkled its warning-cum-welcome. Cari offered him a good morning as she gazed around his confectionary jars and stacks of newspapers, journals and the like – though no greeting in return.

'What are you doing here?' he said, and Cari found herself caught like a butterfly in a collector's bottle, the wings of her words flapping feebly against the glass walls of bewilderment but the rattling rhythm of her response signifying both panic and anger at the same time.

'Really?' she managed, then: 'Really!'

'I know who you are.'

'Then a fine welcome for family, Mister Davies.'

It struck Cari her mam wouldn't have been much older than Cari herself when she was wed. Yet did they look alike? Perhaps. And this Dai Davies, perhaps ten years older, or more. He'd remember her this way, surely.

'No family to me, girl. Disgrace, it was. Still a disgrace, if you ask me.'

'Quick with your judgements then. That's what I'd call a disgrace. And any disgrace can hardly fall on my shoulders if I've not a clue what you mean.'

'You'll be wanting it back, I suppose?'

She dared not ask the obvious.

'Well,' she said, 'we must be cousins, I suppose. Mam's tada, Tecwyn Davies. And his brother...'

'Just turning up. Out of the blue. Feels like yesterday. Disgrace. Married, she reckoned. Then the christenin', an' all.'

Only yesterday? It had been seventeen years and more. *Duw*, it must have been the scandal of the decade, filled their narrow little lives for months on end.

'That would have been Winifred,' said Cari. 'The christening.'

'You and the rest of her filthy brood.'

'Hardly our fault. Just children.'

If she'd not been so keen on gathering information from this mean-spirited character, she would have had different words for him entirely.

'*Visiting the iniquity of the fathers,*' he was saying, '*upon the children unto the third and fourth generation.* And he had the brass neck to tell you, did he? Maddox. About them living over the broom. Living in sin. Laughed about it, did he? How did it feel, knowing you were all his little bastards?'

Good question. How had it felt? How did it still feel? There'd been a few weeks for Cari to get used to the idea. Yet it remained a burden. And a shameful one she'd not yet been able to share. Coming there with Nesta might have helped her do so but, for now, she was still bearing the load alone.

'Found their wedding certificate, I did. Only reason I came. Tada doesn't know.'

'Wedding!' She thought he was going to spit on the shop floor. 'Old Reverend Williams said it was for the unborn one. At least one of you should be legitimate, he said. In the eyes of the Lord, that is. None of us went though. Travesty of a ceremony. We all knew by then. And no surprise to find she'd died. God's punishment for them both, we all reckoned.'

Cari wanted to tell him her father and mother hadn't been entirely abandoned. The witnesses. But then it wasn't uncommon to simply find witnesses, total strangers, off the street.

'But the baby survived,' he said. 'Or so they told me. You see? With the blessing of the Lord Jesus.'

'He died too,' said Cari. 'The baby. When he was nearly three.'

Those painful memories again. Little Pryce by her side, gazing up at the sweet jars. But Cousin Dai simply shrugged.

'I didn't know,' he said. 'But they took your tada in at the Victoria Chapel, did they not? I remember somebody saying. Take anybody at the Victoria, though, I suppose. Not proper, see, is it?'

Her tada always spoke of the Welsh community in Liverpool as though it was a single entity, but Cari knew it was no such thing. For the most part it was no different than it must always have been. A series of insular villages back in Wales itself, each one closed from the others. Oh, they might come together on occasions. For performances of Frank Evans's Liverpool Welsh Choral Union. Or the famous occasion when the Eisteddfod had been held at the North Haymarket to celebrate the new century. But, other than those, the city's Welsh community was divided as effectively as it might have been by the mountains of Snowdonia.

Yet, even in the valleys, gossip managed to travel. So, Cari could scarcely believe there weren't those among the Crosshall Street congregation who wouldn't have known about her tada's history.

A minor miracle, therefore, that Rhys Fingers knew none of it. At least, she assumed he didn't know.

'Pastor Jenkins is hardly the most forgiving of men,' she said.

'My own tada always said Huw Maddox had a certain reputation. A way of paying for his sins.'

'Been a good father to the rest of us, he has,' said Cari, and turned to leave.

'If you say so, girl. Maybe better if you didn't come here again, though.'

She stopped in the doorway, recalling his earlier words. About wanting something back.

'The wedding certificate,' she said. 'It's got her address as Bootle Lane. Here?'

'You don't remember? Why would you? Too small I suppose. Fallen out about something, they had. Turned up on the doorstep one night. I was only a lad myself. Stayed a week, maybe? Before we found out, of course. About them not being married, see. So, when she left it – I remember her throwing it across the room. Furious, she was. And then we found out about them, we weren't surprised she didn't come back for it.'

'Her wedding ring,' said Cari.

'A gold ring anyway. But wedding ring? Not entitled to one, really, was she? Not then. Though I'm not sure what she did when Reverend Williams really did marry them. And then – well, I suppose she just used this address again for the sake of the marriage lines. Just one more lie, after all.'

'And how was it, exactly – you found out, like?'

'Reverend Williams got a letter, I think. My mam said so, anyhow. He wouldn't say what was in it. Not all of it. But he must have told somebody that part at least. About them not being married. And whenever we needed a lesson about God's honest truth, our tada would fetch out the ring. A lecture, see. Or a leathering. One or the other. I'll fetch it though. Don't need it anymore. My mam and tad both passed too, now. Not sure why I kept it really.'

'No.' Cari shook her head. 'I don't want it. Wasn't why I came. Take it to the pledge shop, if you like. But you said Reverend Williams had received a letter. From where?'

'Oh, I remember that. From Beddgelert, it was.'

*

11.50am

Tom Priddy's Irregulars had arrived, one after the other, at Waugh's. Noon, by the time they'd each handed over the lottery money and received their own small cut. Not a bad haul. Enough to satisfy any cursory glance from Rees or Lewis anyhow.

'You're sure?' Mister Clamp said to him. 'Can manage on your own?'

Clamp was already pulling on his overcoat.

'*Wrth gwrs!*' Of course. 'Nice and quiet, see. Just this beauty to finish.'

The gentleman customer on the table was almost done. Tom lifted the fellow's nose, used the very tip of the razor to shave inside the philtrum and wiped the soapy residue onto his towel. Just the curling irons next and he could call it a day.

'If you're sure, then…'

Clamp gave Thomas a final wave and left the Preparation Room. Waugh himself had been booked to speak at a meeting of the city's funeral furnishers. Sun Hall. Gladys, their clerk, gone with him to take notes since there were no more appointments for the afternoon. Some business about the various companies establishing trade rates. Almost a guild, a union, of their own.

No more Special Constable work for Tom Priddy, of course. Not anymore. But he feared for the city. Would it ever return to its old self? Meetings at the YMCA in support of trade unions among women. Unrest among shop assistants, tailors, telegraph workers, Garston dockers. Public protests and meetings against the capitalist classes. Protests about the police on Riot Sunday – not about the rioters! That Communist, Keir Hardie, in town – well, communists, Labour Party, all the same, wasn't it?

And now this with the funeral furnishers. Where would it all end?

Still, work to be done. Arrangements to be made.

He sang to himself as he plied the irons to the thinning hair of the deceased.

'Guide me, O Thou great Redeemer.'

He glanced up to see the Lord Jesus smiling at him. But what time? Tom wished he'd kept the pretty little timepiece now. A quarter past twelve, though, he guessed. One or other of them – either Rees or Lewis – due to be there at half past the hour. The message he'd sent. In case suspicions were aroused, he'd said. Perhaps one of them could wait in the theatre's café, just next door, Tom had suggested.

Well, fingers crossed, he thought. And just time to think about tonight. So much that might go wrong.

The bell from the street door. Somebody in the foyer. Rees, by the sounds of it.

'Back here,' Tom shouted. 'Come through.'

And, indeed, it was Rees who fumbled his way through the intervening Arrangements Parlour, then the Reposing Saloon, before coming through the door so recently closed by Mister Clamp.

Rees blinked in the Preparation Room's sudden gaslight glare.

Today, a long travelling coat of Scottish or Irish tweed, the familiar deadly cap upon his head.

'Nice job,' he said, when he saw the corpse. 'But looks more alive than you do, Tom boyo.'

Tom smiled to humour him. He had no idea how they'd managed to now feel secure here in the city. Bribes, he supposed. But their little empire had definitely grown. No longer just the towns along the North Wales coast – Connah's Quay, Flint and the rest. Wrexham as well, Lewis had boasted. And now…

'Well,' said Rees, 'where is it?'

'Our friend,' Tom Priddy replied. 'Next door, like?'

'Enjoying a mint tea. And the money?'

Tom pointed to another envelope on a footstool, against the wall, just behind him. He still had the curling irons in his hand, but as Rees passed by, brushed against his shoulder, crouched to retrieve his prize, Tom set the irons down upon the instruments tray.

Rees stood once more, glanced inside the envelope, grunted with satisfaction at the thickness of the wad, when he saw the notes within. Yet, when he flicked through the bills, found the cut sheets of newspaper just behind, his satisfaction turned to a snarl. His hand reached for the cap.

'What the…'

But, by then, Tom had picked up the larger syringe, pushed the heavy needle deep into the fellow's upper neck. The base of his skull. He'd read how you only needed a single inch of needle to destroy the brain stem. And the information seemed accurate enough.

Rees jerked upright, his back arched violently, the fingers of the hand rigid, frozen, at the cap's peak. He made a gurgling noise, as though he, also, was trying to sing. Then he fell forward, as though he'd been poleaxed.

Yes, accurate. The injection of embalming fluid an entirely unnecessary additional measure.

11.55am

Walton Gaol's fortified gatehouse was grim enough even on the rare occasions when the sun shone upon it. But that late-morning, with the wind-driven rain blowing straight up Hornby Road from the north-end docks, it reeked of positive evil. A clutch of folk there, drenched women awaiting their men's release with the noon bell. Waiting, though without comradeship, the cemetery at their backs. Simply seabirds sharing a rock in foul weather, huddled against a storm yet not quite in contact, one with the other.

Cari found herself reciting a prayer inside her head, hoping to dispel the cruelty of the warped faith in which Dai *Papur* must have revelled all his life. *God's punishment for them both.* Her mam taken from them. Could he really believe sweet Lord Jesus would have inflicted such pain on them deliberately?

Yet she knew Cousin Dai was no different from many others she'd met. Chapel mentality. Pastor Jenkins would have said the same. Perhaps he'd done so, only accepted her tada and their reduced family into his congregation because of the price they'd already paid for their supposed sins.

It made her think of Annie Besant's book again. She'd borrowed it from the library. *The Ancient Wisdom.* Theosophy, those core values, the mysteries of life and nature which, Besant said, underpinned all the world's great religions. The claim that, regardless of what we called it, there was divinity within each of us – the inner life, which we must all explore and understand. Self-knowledge. And the paths to self-knowledge through the physical plane, the astral plane, and much that was complicated to her. Yet this seemed like a kinder way to view and interpret Holy Scripture. Mountain pathways towards upland pastures of succour and plenty rather than slippery slopes into hellfire and brimstone.

Succour and light. The images dissolved in the drizzle as the prison bell began to ring and, from the open doorway in the gate, a trickle of the gaol's discharged inmates began to appear, each man clutching a meager bundle. She'd visited Ernst only a couple more times during his incarceration, and she was amazed to see how diminished he'd become in his final weeks. His broad cheeks had sunk into a grey pallor, though his grasp of English had, at least, improved. A little.

'You should not here come, Cari. Not today.'

She was cold, wet and disappointed by his lack of enthusiasm to see her.

'Somewhat ungrateful. Your father asked me.'

'He should not ask.'

Where had the fondness gone? That special fondness.

'Well, I'm here now. You shall just have to put up with my company.'

Cari tried to link his arm, but did so clumsily, wondering if she was being too forward, too delusional, and it gave him the chance to take a sideways step, as though avoiding a blow.

'Walking then. *Ja?*' he said, and looked around to get his bearings.

'It's a long way to walk. Better to catch the tram.' She pointed down towards the Preston Road Station and the junction with Rice Lane, where engine smoke was billowing over the fence, and from whence she could hear the unmistakable huff and puff, the clang and screech of shunting trains.

'Better to walk.'

'But it's raining,' she said, and then slowly understood. His pride. The glances he would attract, taking the Corpie tram with all these others, so evidently just released. 'And I have a plan,' she lied. 'For a treat. For this special day. We'll let all these others catch the regular, but you and me, Ernst – well, we shall travel in style! I've been saving.' Another lie. 'So we can take the blooming Bellamy.'

Poor man, he had no idea what she was prattling about.

'First Class, Ernst,' she said. Were they truly the only city with First Class trams? So the Corpie kept boasting, anyhow. 'We'll get on the posh people's tram. They'd never guess we'd have the nerve – oh, you know what I mean!'

But of course they guessed. And by the time the elegant cream-coloured car had made one of its rare and privileged stops along the route from Aintree's leafy suburbs, by the time the exquisitely uniformed conductor had taken the exorbitant first-class fare from her, by the time they'd muddied the coir carpets and soaked the plush blue seats, by the time they'd turned disdainful and whispering heads around the cut-glass lamps, Cari wished they could have disappeared behind the lace curtains of the tram's windows, or have the ground swallow them up. Though Ernst seemed to be enjoying himself.

They were trundling past the high red brick walls to the right, the ornate clock tower and the numerous solid three-storey blocks which, in total, could easily have been yet another prison.

'Hospital?' Ernst smiled. 'Hospital is good. Big.'

She shook her head, prayed that, one day, this might indeed find a better use. And, for now, she suspected its two thousand inmates would have preferred sickness in a hospital ward to their current condition.

'No,' she said. 'Workhouse. Poor people. No work. No home.'

'*Ach so, ich verstehe!*' He caught the eye of some of these first-class fellows. 'Capitalism,' he said, more loudly than necessary. 'And there are many of these in Liverpool, Cari, *ja*? Workhouse?'

'More than I could easily count, I'm afraid.' Prescot, Toxteth Park, Brownlow Hill, over the water at Tranmere, the Ragged School at Kirkdale, all the cottage homes at Olive Mount and elsewhere. Here in Walton. But were there more? She wasn't certain.

'This is what I thought. The world, it is mad.'

The very thing which had spoiled her third evening with Gwilym Mills. For the second, the Kinemacolor had lived up to all its expectations. He was wonderful company, and Cari was a captive audience when, several nights later, he offered her the chance to join him at the Electra Palace picture house on London Road. Sixpenny seats with a cup of tea thrown in. And a surprise, of course. Pathé News and the first showing of the moving images from Bloody Sunday, the audience almost coming to blows divided between those cheering the police and those hissing and booing.

But, in the midst of it all, there they were, Nesta, and herself in the same dress she'd worn for the Coronation Procession – before the dress was so shamefully ruined.

It made her blush, squirm in her seat in case she should be recognised. Oh, vanity! The film had been heavily edited, of course. No sign of the brutality as Cari and others had witnessed it. Yet when she later pressed Gwilym about his own photographs providing evidence of that police brutality, or perhaps of their inebriated condition, back in August, she'd received yet another lecture on the natural order of things. Gwilym's home-spun philosophy how the wheels of change move inexorably forward, but generally slowly, at their own pace, and rarely with any equality in the rate of their progress. Injustice, to Gwilym Mills, was simply another cross to be borne along the way. He'd asked to see her again, though. To walk out with her, as he put it, but she'd politely declined. Ernst's release had been imminent and she had hoped – well, she had hoped!

'Perhaps we can change it, Ernst.'

'Oh yes, we can change.' He nodded. 'But how is your family, Cari? Nesta is well?'

Nesta again. Why must he always ask so enthusiastically about Nesta?

'I've not seen her very much. And I tried to find her today. To bring her with me. But she must have gone somewhere. You'll see her later, I suppose. She's living at your father's house again.'

The thought would once have provoked livid jealousy within her but, as the tram travelled through Walton Village, past St. Mary's and Spellow Station, then down Kirkdale Road, he enquired politely about each of the others. Taffy. Winifred.

'And your cousin?' he said. 'Cousin Thomas. He is still your *Ersfeind*? Big enemy, I suppose. You have a word, in English?'

On her last visit to the prison, for the sake of conversation, she'd quietly shared her suspicions – that Theresa MacKenny's death might not have been quite the accident it appeared. He'd scoffed at the idea, though the story had seemed to cheer him.

'The word, I think, is nemesis,' she said. 'Same in Welsh too, now I think of it. But something else has happened. He tricked me rather badly, see. Into reading some of my tada's correspondence. Letters.

And you must promise not to repeat this, Ernst. Promise, now. Not to your father. Not to Nesta. Nobody. You promise?'

Cari believed she could trust him and, in any case, it seemed to her a secret shared would give them a certain intimacy. A thrilling intimacy. And he agreed. Yes, he said. A promise.

'Well,' she whispered, 'it seems my mam and tad were only married after Wyn was born.'

She waited for a reaction, some sign of shock, but nothing. 'And Cousin Thomas knew about it, Ernst. All of it! Then, just this morning, another cousin has told me the whole thing caused a huge rift in the family.'

Cari could see poor Ernst must be confused, his broad face crumpled in a great frown.

'Because of a letter,' she told him. 'A letter written to the pastor at their chapel. It was a letter from Beddgelert, apparently. You see, Ernst? Where Cousin Thomas used to live. He frightens me, he does. It's like having some horrible spider living in our house. Or an evil sorcerer.'

'When was this, Cari? When letter it was written.'

'Around the same time,' she told him. 'I was probably...' Three, she was about to say, then realised the stupidity of it. It would mean Thomas having been six, seven at most. 'Well, he still frightens me. And, this evening, the family's all getting together. Even Taffy, we hope. Our mam's birthday. Or would have been. Only tea and chips. But maybe you could come too. See for yourself. About Tom Priddy, I mean.'

She wished she'd given him the invitation earlier, before she had made such a fool of herself, before that look had come over his face. The look which made Cari question her own intelligence.

'I would do much for you, Cari. Much. But I think it is not right.'

There was some awful finality, a sense of her own doom in his tone. Scotland Road had given way to Byrom Street, and the Old Haymarket was looming up fast, creating its own urgency.

'Too cowardly,' she quoted, like her tada had done so many times during her life, 'to do what I knew to be right, as I had been too cowardly to avoid what I knew to be wrong.'

'Nothing to do with my own feelings, Cari. Fond of you, I am.

Very fond. But must do the right thing. To you. My work at the fruit market, it is finished now. *Kaputt*. They will not want me. After gaol. And all those others. Poor people. No work. No home. Capitalism, Cari. So, back to sea, I must go. Soon, Cari. And not right, for you to wait. If I go, possible I not come back.'

1.00pm

'So, what's this all about, then?' The gateman pointed to Amos Gartee's Kru marks. There was a fire lit in the granite cottage which sat alongside the pilotage buildings of the Canning Graving Docks. The clothes were steaming nicely, as they'd been doing for more than an hour. On a rack before the flames and Amos himself still wrapped in an old grey blanket.

Amos had other things to worry about, but this gateman fellow had cared for him. He owed him an answer, therefore, and ran a finger along the raised scars running down the centre of his forehead to the bridge of his nose.

'This,' he said, 'for Kru. Freedom people.'

Their independence.

'This.' He touched one of the clusters forming an arrowhead on his upper cheek. 'Eye of Nyesoa.'

Amos considered himself a good Christian, but his father had been a true follower of the One Wise One, the god of their ancestors. As a believer in the old ways, his father had held him down for the initiation, used a blade to open the flesh, rubbed charcoal into the wounds, while Amos had whimpered for his mother. Fortunately, those who had finally translated the Almighty's Holy Book into his own *Bété* tongue had used the word *Nyesoa* for the Christian God.

The Wolof, Charles Tuohey, of course, had patiently explained that this was the way of the Christians. When their Church had wanted to wean believers in the old gods away from their Midwinter Festivals of Light, they had appropriated the same dates to celebrate the birth of their Jesus. They had taken a story of the crucifixion and self-sacrifice of the Roman people's god, Mithras, and stolen it for their own. When they had been unable to shake the Old English people from following their goddess Eostra, they had neatly mixed the related festivals, and created Christian Easter. And when the Christian Bible had been translated into other languages, all around the world, the word *god* had often been borrowed from some prominent local deity.

It was for this reason, Tuohey had gently argued, that Islam was the only true faith, since the life of the prophet Muhammad, Blessings and Peace be upon him, were a matter of recorded and relatively recent history – and the words Allah spoke to him directly, recorded in the Qu'ran.

Yet there the matter had been left. No attempt to convert Amos from his own faith. All had therefore worked out fine. In that part of his life, fine. But what would Lord Jesus think of him now?

In the remains of the old churchyard, in this morning's pre-dawn gloom and drizzle, he had confronted Missee Nesta. About the devil man. And the things she had finally told him had brought him to a rage such as he had never known before in his life.

And now? He had to think of a new future. Not what he wanted. Not after he had so recently found this purpose. A gig boat man. He had hoped maybe even here he could become a talk-man. Improve his English. Act as an interpreter for Kru and others arriving in this Liverpool place.

Yet what might be his options? Perhaps this British Royal Navy, like his cousin at Simon's Town, far in the very southern tip of Africa. It was in their family, after all, the cousin's father having won a medal, fighting against the mighty AmaZulu people, thirty years before.

Or a return to his own lands. Not Nana Kru itself, but one of the other towns along the coast. Little Kru, Settra Kru, King William's Town, Nifu.

'Nyesoa,' the gateman repeated. 'Does it bring you luck, lad?'

It seemed not. For what *had* he done?

5.35pm

She was late. The early evening meeting at Central Hall had already begun and Alice Davies twisted in her seat, flapped her hand at Cari and displayed a beaming, hypocrite's smile to show she was pleased by her arrival. Then she was up, pushing past the knees of other audience members seated in her row and gesturing wildly for Cari to head back into the foyer. Cari did so and, moments later, Alice joined her there, breathless.

'Thank goodness,' said Alice, with a hand pressed against her heaving bosom. 'The bishop's not due to speak for ten minutes yet and I wondered – oh, Cari. You mustn't think I had any part in the vote. Tell me, you don't, do you?'

'It's not been the best of days, Miss Davies. Perhaps best to tell me what's amiss.'

She'd left Ernst at the Haymarket, assuring him that, truly, she would be sorry to see him sail away but, if such was his decision, he must of course go wherever his work took him. It was curt. To-the-point. And his expression had told her he'd expected a more mature, more honest response. The cheek of the man, to look at her with such disappointment. But too late. It was done now.

'The strangest thing,' said Alice Davies. 'It's Mrs Thompson-Frere. She took her dog for a walk on Crosby beach. Wednesday morning, I think. But she's not been seen since.'

'Two days.' It was stating the obvious. But the only other vaguely intelligent thing Cari could think to say would have been that she didn't recall her owning a dog! And then, equally incongruously, she recalled something Tom Priddy had said. *'Never mind, girl,'* he'd insisted. *'Bet she'll get what she deserves for crossing you.'*

If anybody else had made the comment, Cari would have paid it no heed at all. But from Tom Priddy...

'Exactly,' said Alice. 'Two days. Did you not see it in today's *Post*?' Cari had not. 'Her poor husband. He must be so distraught. And I'm sure she'll turn up safe and sound.'

Missing for two days? Cari thought. I doubt it very much. 'But, just in case,' Alice pressed on, 'I wondered whether I might prevail upon you...'

'The paper?' Cari replied, setting the thought about Tom Priddy aside and rather ashamed at seeing amusement in this but determined not to show it. *'Votes for Women* Secretary? But there was an election, Alice. You insisted we should have one. I lost, remember?'

'I blame myself,' she said. 'If I'd known Florrie was going to contest the thing, but – oh, bother. You know what I mean. You'd been doing the blessed thing. And brilliantly. Total dedication, that's what you showed. Real grit.'

'Miss Davies,' said Cari. 'Alice. I have every intention of remaining dedicated to our movement. To our cause. I believe it's my holy duty to do so. But I *choose* to be militant. To be active. I will not have activism thrust upon me at someone else's whim. And nor will I ever accept it as some form of second-place consolation prize.'

It gave her a modest satisfaction to leave Alice open-mouthed in the foyer while Cari took herself back into the auditorium to a rousing round of applause – not for her, she knew, but for the Bishop of London, just then taking to the podium. Arthur Foley Winnington-Ingram. A significant reputation as a social reformer and, at that stage, a strong supporter of suffrage campaigners. But this afternoon he thanked both the Liverpool Women's Suffrage Society and the National Vigilance Association for jointly hosting this event. Mrs Rathbone had plainly already spoken and so, as well, had Mrs Rose – the latter responsible for establishing the NVA in the first place.

Their crusade against white slave traffic had become a minor sensation, happily supported by all those many factions in the fight for the vote. And the bishop believed he knew the cause of this modern scourge, white slavery.

Worldwide instability, he said. Civil war in China; revolution in Mexico; conflict between Italy and the Ottoman Turks; Germany seeking to expand its empire in Africa; six years since the unrest in Russia, after their war with Japan, but still reverberations; fear and famine; political and religious persecution; intolerance, on every hand; and unprecedented numbers of transmigrants on the move. Here in Liverpool, it was young women from Ireland, or Jewish girls making the journey from eastern Europe to America. Hunted down on those very streets, said the bishop. To be trapped and then trafficked.

Foolishly, Cari imagined how Florrie Thompson-Frere might have suffered this fate, snatched from Crosby beach by some boatload of Barbary pirates and her dog now served up as a dainty morsel for the delight of her swarthy captors, while Florrie herself was forced to dance for their pleasure, discarding one diaphanous veil after another until…

So, Cari missed some of the statistics – to her shame, the number of young women helped by the Association to avoid the actual and inevitable results of trafficking by providing safe lodgings and sustenance to those at risk.

But, by then, the bishop had moved on to, it seemed, his favourite part of the lecture – the part played by women themselves in encouraging male licentiousness. Itself at the very heart of the abominable white slave trade. And, in this regard, he roundly denounced the phenomenon of the sex novel. There were gasps. Yes, the sex novel, its special crime that such filth was often written by women themselves. Greater gasps. Worse? The sex novel's most ardent readers were often – yes, women.

Ardent? Cari supposed they must be, for she could feel the heat rising in her own cheeks. But while the audience might have been stunned into silence by the revelation, personally she found the whole thing less than interesting. Not the trafficking problem itself, the cheapness of women's lives, even as a commodity but, rather, this trivialising of the problem. Besides, it was almost entirely overshadowed by her unsatisfactory hour with Ernst which should, she thought, have been so much more.

Liverpool was full of wharf-widows, those whose husbands disappeared for months on end aboard the boats owned by White Star, Cunard, the Allan Line, American or Canadian Pacific. But then their men always came back. Usually. For a while. Until the roving or boredom with life ashore took them away once more. So why not Ernst? He could have asked whether she might wait for him, and she would have said yes. Wouldn't she? But he'd not given her the option. And why should he think he wouldn't come back? By then, Cari's imagination was running wild. Did he have some other purpose in mind? A revolutionary one, perhaps. For she needed some reason. She had determined that the door to her own affection for Ernst Jurks should be wedged half-open, to prevent it flying wide in the wind of some wild passion, though she now found it firmly slammed in her face.

By then she had fully lost the thread of the meeting and rose to leave, making her way to the foyer and studiously ignoring Alice Davies, while quietly hoping Alice might pursue her. It was Friday, after all, distribution day for the paper. And Alice had nobody else on the north-end patch with any experience. So it was with a rare sense of smugness that Cari heard the auditorium doors open and close, and Alice's shrill cry.

'Miss Maddox! Cari!'

Cari turned just before the exit, but only once she'd wiped the smile from her face.

'I think I must owe you an apology, Miss Davies,' she said, before Alice could draw breath. 'As I said, not the best of days. But no excuse for my rudeness.'

'Then you'll reconsider?' Alice smiled. 'Take up the Secretary's role?'

'I wouldn't wish to be misunderstood, Alice. This fight means everything to me. I'm committed to it, see. Heart and soul. But I'm not quite so certain about our organisation.'

'Our organisation, Miss Maddox?' She had stopped smiling. 'I...'

'Forgive me, Alice. Despite what you might think, I'm no rabble-rouser. No, let me finish. I'm sure the Secretary's role is important, though many of us wonder, not just me – well, this truce in our activities, don't you think it's wearing a bit thin?'

'We've received every possible assurance the Conciliation Bill will be passed within a matter of weeks. You know that, Cari. And today's edition, the news from California – the sixth American state to give women full voting rights. Then a long article on Ireland, the Women's Franchise League demand. About the Home Rule Bill providing for election of women to any Irish parliament. If it weren't for this uncertainty about Lloyd George – but the government can't resist much longer. And the newspaper – it's vital if we want to turn the tide. The work undertaken by ladies like Florrie Thompson-Frere, or yourself, my dear – oh, whatever can have happened to her?'

The Chancellor, Lloyd George, had been playing fast and loose with one of those potentially wrecking amendments, almost exactly as Cari had predicted. The Adult Suffrage amendment, superficially exactly what they should have been fighting for, the wives of all existing electors, regardless of the woman's personal status. Far better than the proposals in the Bill itself – but certain to cause its defeat or significant delay.

'You see, Alice, it's the Bill that worries me. Such a massive compromise of our principles. Votes only for the élite. Not for working class women like me. Yet we find ourselves attacking Lloyd George for proposing more than we're seeking. Arguing for the crumbs rather than the cake. Why? Because we know very well he's only playing a politician's game, supporting the Adult Suffrage amendment so the entire Conciliation Bill, the entire cake, crumbs and all, will be lost in the process. But if we just took our blinkers off, and our gloves too, fought them head-on for full-blown women's suffrage, for the whole cake and nothing less, we could win, Alice. We could win! But not the way we're fighting now.'

'Are you not worried about her? About Florrie Thompson-Frere?'

Cari knew then. She'd lost the high ground somewhere. Winning the vote meant very little if, in the process, they did nothing to improve the lot of women generally, or if they lost their moral obligations, their human responsibilities, one for the other. But she couldn't help herself.

'Feels like blackmail, Miss Davies. I'm sure she'll be back with us, safe and sound, very soon,' In truth, Cari believed no such thing. 'Some logical reason for her absence. And I'm also sure there must be somebody else capable of looking after the paper for a while.'

'If you're telling me you wouldn't pick up the responsibility again on a purely temporary basis – well, you strike a hard bargain. But fine. If you insist, I shall make it clear your appointment is permanent.'

'No election?'

'Not necessary. As you say, we had one already. You are Mrs Thompson-Frere's obvious successor.'

'And if…when, rather…Mrs Thompson-Frere comes back to us?'

'I'm sure she'll understand, Cari.'

She forced the words through gritted teeth. But it felt like a minor victory. Helped in some small way to rub balm in the wounds left by Ernst Jurks – as well as those that were self-inflicted. And, anyway, Cari had great respect for the paper overall. For their readers also. She would not willingly see them deprived of their bulletins, regardless of any criticisms Cari might sometimes have. So, she agreed to return with Alice to the office, to pick up those duties again, though now as the official *Votes for Women* Secretary, Liverpool North. And yes, she made sure Alice Davies put it in writing. Yet, all this while, it was Tom Priddy who occupied Cari's thoughts. Creeping Cousin Thomas, and Florrie Thompson-Frere as well.

'Bet she'll get what she deserves for crossing you.'

6.32pm

The second of them, Lewis, had been even more simple. Tom was pleased with the way he'd caught him coming through the darkness of the Reposing Saloon. A slender drainage tube, fashioned into a ligature, knotted at its centre, with which to choke the rogue's life away. And Lewis much slighter than Rees. But still, it had taken longer than he'd expected. Even once he had Lewis down, Tom Priddy's knee in the man's back. Five minutes, at least. Five endless minutes.

Now, however, he had them both at the All Souls mortuary chapel. Transfer baskets. The wicker caskets they used only temporarily, simply to convey the deceased to the cemetery, for those who would be interred without a coffin. If things went according to plan, he'd have the empty caskets back in the storage room by Sunday evening.

'Late arrivals, Mister Priddy?' said the chapel's superintendent, Mister O'Malley. Another papist, of course.

'Supposed to be a quiet day, see.' Tom handed over the forged death certificates. And the notes conveniently signed by a couple of entirely fictional parish priests confirming the need for decent Catholic burials at Ford Cemetery. Sunday. The next of the three processions each week for those of their faith out to the burial ground. Since he had no intention of paying six shillings apiece for private graves, his two associates would find themselves in a more public resting place and no markers. All absurdly easy.

Only one possible loose end. Lewis, he recalled, had a brother in Cardiff. A pimp, they said. A gang of ruffians involved in everything from larceny to – well, he doubted the brother would ever make any connection.

Yes, absurdly easy.

The woman, however, had been a different kettle of fish entirely. Wednesday. And the dog. For pity's sake, the dog.

7.20pm

'He will come, Tada,' Cari told him as she shared out Gianelli's chips and cut up the pair of mysteries she'd been able to afford.

'Can't beat a good sausage, *cariad*,' said Rhys Fingers, and he winked at her as she served his portion. Yet there was something lacking in him tonight. His eyes red-rimmed. Some remnant of the fever which seemed occasionally to afflict him.

'Believe it when I see it, I will.' Her father reached across the table to help himself.

'Mrs MacKenny will make sure he comes,' said Cari. 'She promised me. He might not be living there but she still carries a lot of clout with him.'

'No need to worry then,' sneered Cousin Thomas. 'Got the word of a papist, we have.'

There was something about him tonight, Cari decided. Something different. Like elation. The heel of his shoe tapping incessantly on the threadbare carpet. And now she thought about it, where *had* he got those shoes? Two-tone casual shoes. She wouldn't be surprised if some poor fellow at Waugh's was now in his coffin sporting Cousin Tom's old work boots.

Wyn giggled at this mention of papists, and Cari saw the satisfied expression on Tom Priddy's face. It was a rare thing, the ability to incite levity in Winifred. Though it never lasted long and, sure enough, the smile quickly faded, her hand raised to her blushing cheek, covering the smallpox scars.

'I'd rather get my own, thank you very much,' said Wyn, when Cari tried to serve her some of the sausage and chips. At the same time, she took a cup from her bag, set it on the table. 'But you can pour me some tea, if you like.'

She touched the corner of her mouth, an inflamed and blotchy patch of skin merging into her smallpox scars.

'No, let me pour for you, *cariad*,' said Cousin Thomas, and made a grab for the teapot. 'But you, Rhys, saw you today, I did. Just by Grossi's. Not going in, were you?'

'Taffy will come,' Cari told them, sensing there was dangerous ground here, best avoided. She noticed the way Rhys Fingers shot daggers at Cousin Thomas, but otherwise ignoring the barb completely. Grossi's, the infamous bordello in the basement of the Hotel St. George. Wyn had picked up on it, though, Cari could see. 'It's Nesta that worries me,' she went on.

'No sign of her at the Fritz's, then?' said Tom Priddy, stuffing a couple of chips between those pasty lips.

Cari had found herself trying the Jurks place one more time, half of her not wanting to do so, the other half desperately hoping Ernst might be there, tell her it had all been some silly misunderstanding, how of course if he had to go to sea again, he'd be back, and then…

'Nobody's seen her all day.' Ernst hadn't even been at home.

'Got out today, didn't he?' said Rhys. 'Your Fritzie boyfriend?'

'*Duwcs*, Rhys,' Cari smiled at him. 'I even went to Walton. So I could be there when he was released. What d'you think about that, then?'

'Shameless, girl,' said her tada. 'That's what we think. *Nefi bliw*, I never heard such a thing. What were you playing at? Criminal, he is.'

'Not exactly got clean hands ourselves, Tada,' she snapped at him. 'Nesta still on the run from the bobbies, an' all.'

'Innocent, she is,' her father spluttered through his chips. 'Always said so, I did.'

Cari hoped so, as well, but then she'd seen Nessie try to steal the cruet from Florrie Thompson-Frere's and, at once, all the day's images merged. The Seion Chapel. Cousin Dai Davies. Ernst and Walton Gaol. The tram journey. Central Hall. The Bishop of London. Sex novels. *Votes for Women*. The paper rounds to be sorted. The missing Mrs Thompson-Frere. And this.

'Somebody just walked over your grave, Cari?' said Tom Priddy, and he gazed hard at her with those frog's eyes.

'*Nac oes*,' she said. No. And she sat down to eat at last. Not that there was much left, of course. 'Just a busy day.'

'Going to the prison, indeed!' said her tada.

Good job she had never told him about the visits she'd made while Ernst was still inside. Best to keep this to herself, made up some fimble-famble about where she'd been those days, both for the family and for Old Man Kaplan.

'I had some time on my hands,' she said, and poured herself some tea. 'And I was thinking about mam. So, I went to have a look at the Seion Chapel. Bousfield Street. You won't remember it, Wyn. All went there for your christening.'

Cari glanced at Tom Priddy, knowing she was simply falling into whatever trap he'd set for her.

'The Seion?' her tada spluttered. 'That place?'

'New pastor there now, of course,' Cari laughed. 'And all his registers gone off to the Records Office. Shame, it is.'

She saw the grin spread across Tom Priddy's ghost-pale face again.

'But why, Cari...?' Huw Maddox began, as somebody banged three times on the street door below.

'Taffy,' said Cari, for he'd always knocked this way, usually when he'd had a few beers. And Nesta normally came in through the works entrance on the other side. 'I'll go.'

She skipped down the stairs, touching a hand to her hair, hoping to look her best, hoping Taffy wouldn't be too much the worse for wear, but pleased with herself. At least, she might be on the way to bringing Taffy back into the fold. Fingers crossed. He was soaked, shrugged out of his badly patched coat. It stunk.

'I'm not sure about this, Cari,' he whispered, and lit a Woodbine as she led him upstairs. Thank the Lord Jesus he wasn't even half-rats, though she could smell the ale on his breath. And smell his dirty clothes. 'Any of it,' he said. 'And when did that bloody creature get his name on the sign?' Their father's most recent pride and joy. Above the brass fire insurance plaque. *Maddox, Sons and Nephew.* 'What the devil was he thinking?'

'Devil's about right!' Cari murmured. 'But Tada meant well. I'll explain later.' It was simple enough. He'd been moved to make some sort of memorial to Pryce and, at the same time, still harboured a private hope, she reckoned, that Taffy would, despite everything, one day relent and join him in the business. And nephew Thomas Priddy? Well, he'd wormed his hateful way into the business already. So, there he was, at her tada's right hand, in the uncomfortable moment when she shoved Taffy into the room.

'What?' Her brother broke the silence, tossing his cap onto their father's old sofa. 'No chips left for the prodigal son?'

Their father's guilty face. He could have been Pip, discovering how Orlick had murdered Mrs Joe with the leg iron from which Magwitch had freed himself – with Pip's help.

'Dafydd,' said their father. 'About your loss...'

'I came because of Mam,' Taffy told him, left it there, hanging in the air. Cari knew that, though this might be some progress, they remained a million miles from reconciliation. And the look of

316

triumph on Tom Priddy's face seemed somehow to make the point.

7.35pm

All the players here, at last, thought Tom Priddy. Apart from Dumpling Nesta, of course. But perhaps this was all for the good. Almost time for the curtain to go up. Tonight, at the Rotunda? *Bonnie Mary*. But he'd made his excuses. The performance here would infinitely surpass the theatre's mediocre entertainment.

'Now,' old Huw was saying, 'if only our Nesta decides to show up.'

Daft Taffy glanced round the room, chewing on that hare lip of his.

'Off on another crusade, is she?'

'Something.' The Beanpole smiled at him. Tom could see she was nervous. As though she sensed something was amiss. 'Nobody's seen the silly goose since she left work this morning.'

Tom watched her slide some of her own sausage and chips onto a spare plate, chipped around it's purple flowered rim. She passed the plate over pox-faced Winifred's head. He knew Cari'd been to the bakery, as well as the Jurks house. But her brother didn't seem concerned.

'Never got rid of the mice then?' Taffy sniffed at the air, slipped a piece of sausage into his mouth. But how he could discern anything over the smell of his own person? Tom had no idea. Living in the doss house on Duke Street. More drunk than sober, most of the time. His only earnings, a few shillings from cleaning spittoons.

'We must have all got used to the smell,' the Beanpole smiled at her brother, though her eyes never quite left Tom himself. Amusing. The presence of cockroaches and the stink of vermin in the house. 'Come on, sit down and eat. They'll be cold by now. Wyn, move up! At least all the men in the family have got their names over the door. Not us girls though, eh? What d'you think, Wyn?'

Tom wondered how Cari might be planning to break the news to poor Winifred that she, like the rest of them, was illegitimate. Born out of wedlock. *A bastard shall not enter into the congregation of the Lord.* Isn't this what she'd say? Deuteronomy twenty-three:two.

'*Nid aur yw popeth melyn,*' said Winifred, ignoring her brother having little or no Welsh. All that glitters isn't gold. What did she mean? Not that Daft Taffy took any notice, of course.

'Still peddling the papers, Cari?' he said.

'Sore point, Cousin,' Tom Priddy replied. 'They kicked poor Cari into touch. Though I see the light's back in her eyes. Something else happened with your suffragette friends, Cari?'

He saw the surprise on her face. She'd be thinking he couldn't know, surely. About the dog woman. '*Bet she gets what she deserves for crossing you.*'

'I was speaking to my sister,' Daft Taffy growled at him, then stopped himself, held up his hands. 'Sorry, Thomas!' And it took Tom a moment to understand. The fool hoped his dear Cousin Thomas might still have some final words for him from the girl. Whereas, he suspected, the Beanpole could just be thinking Tom Priddy the Sorcerer might have had some deeper part in her demise.

'Like you said, Cousin,' Tom replied, 'all here for your mam. And clever, Beanpole, isn't it?'

Not so very clever, though. Old Huw had been far more forthcoming about their mam's birthday than he'd been about their wedding. And no wonder.

'But Beanpole,' Tom Priddy went on, 'tell your brother where you've been today.'

Lordie, how she must want to do just this very thing. Share the secrets of the wedding, Seion Chapel, and her mam's family in Bootle Lane. But maybe it would spew out later. For now, he helped himself to a piece of bread, made a butty with the last few chips.

'Ernst was released today,' she said. 'I went to meet him.'

'The gaol?' Brother Taffy was incredulous.

'I'd never have got you the tap in the first place, *bach*,' said Rhys Gateman, 'if I'd known you were mixed up with jailbirds. Let alone the itchy fingers, like.'

Cari, Tom saw, was expecting an explosion from her brother but, once again, she didn't really understand, did she? This was a different Taffy. Almost subservient. Was he still hoping Rhys might get him back on the docks? If so, Tom knew he was going to be disappointed. Marked forever now, was Daft Taffy. The missing strike fund. Though, he supposed, not exactly missing anymore. Rees and

Lewis had, between them, been carrying a fair bit of filthy lucre. Far more than Tom had handed over to buy the time he'd needed – well, to solve his little problem.

'Strange thing,' he said. 'Bit of a confession, see. But at the end of the strikes – well, thought it was my duty.'

He paused for dramatic effect.

'Didn't want to say anything at the time, like. But signed up as a Special. Just to help get the food moving.'

The revelation silenced the table. Daft Taffy's gritted teeth. How he must have wanted to spit out the word scab. Go on, thought Thomas, I dare you.

'Kept it quiet, boy,' said Huw Maddox, at last. 'But proud of you, I am. Good for you, like. Don't you think, Rhys?'

Rhys the Gateman agreed, wiped some grease from his chin before picking up his pipe. Back at work now, and still blaming the dockers for his lay-off. Idiot, when it had been the Docks and Harbour Board which had dumped them after the strikes began to bite.

'Anyway, there was this day. Few weeks ago now. And these ruffians had a go at me. Scab, they reckoned. Chased them off, see. But one of them – some Dark Jack, scars all over his face – dropped this envelope. Full of money, it was. So, I hands it in. And after, that police sergeant – Ladysmith, isn't it – comes to see me at the theatre. Well, Taffy boyo, he seems to think it might be something to do with your strike fund, see?'

Like magic, it was. The thoughts that must have been racing through all their minds.

And Tom Priddy? Not just a printer's devil anymore. Now his name on the sign. The wrong title – *nephew*, like? Maybe. But he could live with it. For now.

7.55pm

Cari was still trying to fathom what was happening. Scars on the man's face? Surely, he couldn't mean – but there was the story Nesta had told her in confidence. She'd repeated the thing, just as Amos Gartee had tried to tell her. A bit garbled. But how Amos had seen the fellow he called the devil man attacked. Gone to his rescue. A very different telling from Tom Priddy's version. Yet this business with an envelope of money. So many conflicting images. So many unworthy thoughts.

'If that's right,' said Taffy, excitement in his eyes, 'about the money, like – well, I know exactly the amount. Kept a book, see.'

'Coincidence, it is,' Rhys Fingers was saying. He would have been mightily relieved nobody had picked up the mention of Grossi's. But this? 'Must be a coincidence, like,' he said. 'But the boys down on the south end were telling me there's a darkie working on the gig boats now. Tom Coleman's crew, they reckon. And scars, like.' He glanced at Wyn. 'Not that there's anything wrong with...'

'What?' Taffy was half out of his seat now. 'One o' them Krooboys. Hey, you don't think...'

'Reminds me,' said Tom Priddy, munching the last bit of his chip butty and licking his fingers. 'Those Krooboys our Nesta was mixed up with. All gone back wherever they come from, I suppose. Though I did hear a story – well, shouldn't gossip, like.'

'Gossip?' Her father seemed just a little too keen to hear it. And there was that smirk of satisfaction playing around the lips of Cousin Thomas.

'What gossip?' said Taffy.

'*Nac oes,*' said Tom. 'I can't, see.'

Rhys Fingers guffawed, poured himself more tea. Stewed now, it was. Deepest brown. But the way he liked it.

'Don't tell me,' he said. 'Our Nesta and one of the darkies. *Rargian fawr,* I got my reputation to think of, see,' Rhys went on, plainly thinking it was all a huge joke. 'Used to know old Reverend Williams at the Seion though, Cari. You just come to me, see. If you need to know anything about him, like.'

She wondered if this was supposed to be funny as well. And Rhys's reputation? He was grinning at her. The awful, hungry grin. And she wondered, did he know? About the wedding? Worse, for some reason it made her wish she'd not turned down Dai *Papur*'s offer to let her have the ring back. But this thing about Nesta and Mister Gartee...

'My Nesta – and a darkie?'

The horror on her tada's stricken face both appalled and terrified her. He clutched at his chest. He stared at her with accusing eyes.

'God Almighty,' said Taffy, and earned himself a scolding from Wyn for the blasphemy. 'You don't mean…'

'You knew, girl,' their father murmured, then turned towards Taffy. 'And you…'

It was likely to kill him. Taffy and a Catholic girl, bad enough, even though poor Theresa was no longer with them. But this!

'Don't tar me with the same brush, Pa,' Taffy shouted. 'A bloody darkie…'

'Yes, I knew,' said Cari. 'And this precious Tom Priddy, as well. It's right, isn't it, cousin? Because Nessie told me the story. How this Krooboy you're talking about saved you from a beating.'

'Wasn't like that, see,' said Cousin Thomas. 'Expect you know his name, though – this darkie?'

'Well, I know what he called *you*, cousin. Devil man, he said. Knew a thing or two, he did, Mister…'

She stopped. Some instinct. Taffy was still mouthing nonsense. Terrible things.

Cari feared for Nesta's safety. But Amos Gartee?

'Jumping to daft conclusions – the lot of you,' she said.

All was confusion. Of course, she knew Nesta was fond of Amos. And he plainly thought the world of her. This was all fine. But thinking of them like this. As – well, as what? Her brain wouldn't conjure up an appropriate word. Sweethearts or something? No, no, no. Then, this about the money. She needed time to think. Yes, to think.

'Not daft at all,' Tom Priddy was saying.

'You know this darkie's name, Cari?' Taffy snarled at her. 'Well, do you?'

'Mister…?' said Tom Priddy.

'Fountain,' Cari told him, the first word into her head. That afternoon. Bloody Sunday. 'He's Mister Fountain. His name. Joseph Fountain. But did you all forget so easy, like? Tonight was supposed to be about our mam. Why don't you tell us about her, Tad?' she said.

This wasn't what she had planned. She'd wanted to bring them together, it was true. And now it seemed the only thing on which they could be united was their suspicions about Nesta. That, and this passion they shared. Their contempt for folk whose skin differed from their own.

But then it happened again. Another knock on the street door.

'Nesta,' said Rhys Fingers. 'Now we can ask her ourselves. Too late for the chips, mind.' And he began to gather up the scraps and the chip papers.

'No,' said Cari. 'Not Nesta.'

'Well, go and see then, girl,' said her tada. 'But if it's anyone for me – I can't, see. All this.'

He was still holding his chest, breathing heavily. Not a good colour.

But she was right. Not Nessie. For it was the bobbies. The sergeant, Ladysmith, of course. And the other one, the same constable who'd been with him before. Cooper. When they'd first come to arrest Nesta.

'She's not here, Sergeant.' Cari feigned boredom, having given him the same answer each time he'd appeared on their doorstep.

'I'd like to speak with your father then, if you don't mind.'

'Why? What's happened? It's about Nesta?' She had a sudden sense of panic.

'In a manner of speaking.'

Cari stepped aside to let them in, convinced Ladysmith was going to give them news of some terrible accident. They certainly looked grim enough, both of them removing their helmets as they thumped their way up the creaky staircase.

'Family's all together, like,' said Cari, for want of anything better. 'Would have been my mam's birthday today.'

'Then I apologise for the inconvenience,' said Ladysmith, as he stood before the table. Then his gaze settled on Cousin Thomas. He nodded a greeting. 'Mister Priddy,' he said. 'Evening, Sir. But I've some news I thought you should all hear.'

They seemed to know each other well enough – Ladysmith and Cousin Thomas. But as Cousin Thomas had said, he'd reported his encounter with Amos Gartee, even if he'd reported the thing in his own twisted fashion.

'About Nesta?' She could hear the fear in her father's voice.

'But listen, Sergeant,' said Taffy. 'Cousin Thomas says you might know something about our missing strike fund and this darkie who attacked him.'

Sergeant Ladysmith seemed taken aback.

'Not why I came here,' he replied. 'Just following up on some enquiries in that regard, Sir. That's all I can say, I'm afraid. But yes, we've been asked to investigate further.'

'I've got the accounts book, see.' Taffy had stood from the table, moved around to the back of their father's chair. 'Know the exact amount. Can prove it, like.'

'Then if you can get it delivered to the Bridewell, I'll see what we can do. Procedures though. Strike fund, you understand. Might take some time – normally not our business, but...'

Cari saw the mixed emotions on Taffy's face. Expectation and disappointment, mixed in equal measure.

'Sergeant,' she said, 'this *is* about Nesta, right?'

'As I told you, miss. In a manner of speaking. Look, I'll not beat around the bush. There's been a development. At the Oriental. At the café to be precise. Mister Clayton called us back a few days ago. Continuing problems with the cash tin, if you follow my drift. Anyway, to cut a long story short, he caught another girl red-handed. Pilfering. And when we questioned her – well, she coughed to the lot. Including the money Mister Clayton thought the other Miss Maddox had taken. Seems your sister – your daughter, Sir,' he said to their tada, 'wasn't the only one with access to the till after all.'

'I always knew,' said Huw Maddox, and his face lit up with a wide smile, though a tear was rolling down his cheek at the same time. 'Didn't I tell you, Ceridwen?'

'But, Sergeant,' said Rhys Fingers. He was standing now, puffing. 'It seems we have another problem. Young Nesta missing.'

'And d'you mind me asking,' said Ladysmith, 'precisely how you'd know she was missing, as you say, when the family's been telling me all this time how none of you know her whereabouts. With the exception of Mister Priddy, of course. Though even Mister Priddy less helpful of late.'

All eyes turned to Cousin Thomas. But this wasn't the moment. Not for Cari, anyhow. More confusion. Half of her pleased Nesta was in the clear. But she kept thinking about Florrie Thompson-Frere's cruet. And then there was that first wad of money for Amos Gartee, the night they'd come to arrest her. Nine pounds, sixteen shillings and sixpence. Where had it come from? Now, this business with the strike fund.

'So, it was Annie Maguire, all this time?' she said, trying to hide the doubt in her voice.

Cock-eyed Annie.

'It was, miss, yes. So, all charges against your sister are dropped, I'm pleased to say.'

'But Nesta still missing,' said Cari. 'Mam's birthday, like I said. She wouldn't have missed this.'

The sergeant sighed, bored glances swapped between himself and Constable Cooper. A heard-it-all-before expression.

'How long, like? Since you saw her?'

'Never came back from work this morning,' Cari told him. She realised how feeble it must sound. 'But our mam's birthday...'

'Well,' he told her, 'like I said, just pleased the charges are dropped.'

Was this all? She could feel the rage welling up inside her. Rage and fear. She looked around at the others. The stupid grin on Cousin Thomas's face. Winifred and her filthy-fingered husband tidying plates and papers into the scullery. Her tada staring down at the table. Taffy standing, rubbing at his stubbled chin.

'Pleased?' she said. 'I'm sure you must be, Sergeant. Must have looked pretty stupid when she simply walked out of the Bridewell. Or were your men half-rats that day too? The same as they were on Bloody Sunday?'

'Ceridwen!' Huw Maddox scolded her.

'No, Pa, she's right,' shouted Taffy. 'Disgrace they are, these mutton shunters. Supposed to uphold law and order. But hound innocent girls without bothering to investigate. Then attack peaceful strikers for no reason. Put God knows how many in hospital. Women and kids too. And what about Johnny Sutcliffe? Micky Prendergast?'

'Oh, justifiable homicide, Taffy,' Cari sneered. 'Wasn't that the verdict, Sergeant?'

'And now,' said Taffy, 'our sister vanished. And some darkie taken her. Or worse.'

How *had* he jumped to this conclusion? Cari wanted to hit him. What a stupid thing to say. Except...

'I just wanted to bring you the news, Mister Maddox,' said

Ladysmith. 'And we'll investigate this strike fund business in due course,' he told a still frustrated Taffy.

Their tada thanked him, naturally. Apologised on the family's behalf. A grovelling apology. He asked Rhys to show the policemen out. And when they were gone, he blustered about how they should simply thank the Lord Jesus that Nesta's name had been cleared. Tomorrow, he said. She'd show up safe and sound tomorrow.

Cari hoped he was right. But she still had to find a way to make peace with Nesta when she finally came home. Though, at this precise moment, she had another of those visions. Baby Pryce standing before her. A sadness in his eyes which, Cari understood, meant Nesta wouldn't be coming home to Hunter Street. Not ever.

Chapter Eleven

Wednesday 22nd November 1911

9.00am

How could fog be so dense? Amos Gartee had never experienced anything like it. As though, with a sharp cane blade, he could have cut blocks as solid as the granite walls of this gateman's cottage.

'Sorry to trouble you again, Mister Gartee,' said the po-leese fellow, the same sergeant man. 'Just wanted to check the details once more.'

Skipper Coleman had come with him from the *Otter*. He sat now in the opposite corner, next to the fire, smoking his pipe. There'd not be much work done today. Not in this.

'I tell you time ago,' said Amos.

'But this Joseph Fountain,' the sergeant pressed him. 'You know him?'

'*Beuh beuh*,' Amos insisted. No way. It was the truth. Then, in English. 'Not know him, Sergeant.'

Amos still wasn't certain why Missee Coconut Palm had invented the name. She'd tracked him down as well, of course. Weeks before. Asked about Miss Nesta. He'd shrugged. A great deal of shrugging. Told her in *Kreyol* deliberately even more incomprehensible than usual he'd not seen her. Yes, he'd gone to wait for her near the place of baking bread, though she'd never appeared. And no, not since then. He'd rehearsed the story so many times, he now almost believed it himself. He knew one day Nyesoa or the Lord Jesus would punish him, but…

'There's another thing,' said the sergeant fellow as, somewhere out on the river, an anchored ship sounded its regular foghorn warning. 'Remember how I asked you last time – about Miss Maddox's cousin?

Reckoned some other darkie had attacked him and then dropped some money?'

The devil man. But attacked by another?

Yet the sergeant's question was about whether Amos believed this Joseph Fountain might have been involved.

More shrugged shoulders. How could he think anything about this, when he knew no such person?

'So, could you tell me precisely why you chose to stay when the rest of your Krooboy friends went back to – well, wherever it is, like, you all come from in the first place?'

He was tempted to give the sergeant man a geography lesson, but Skipper Coleman beat him to it.

'It might have something to do, Sergeant,' said the skipper, puffing on his pipe, 'with the fact Mister Gartee is now firmly established as a member of the Merseyside Watermen's Association. Good job, steady work. If you don't mind me saying so, it's a bloody fool question.'

The sergeant fellow's turn to shrug.

'All the same, Mister Gartee. Miss Nesta Maddox – you're sure you don't know her whereabouts?'

Whereabouts. It was a strange word.

'Not understand.'

'Do you know where Miss Maddox – Miss Nesta Maddox – might be? Now, like?'

Amos shook his head slowly.

'Not know.'

And it was true. Just then, he had no idea.

9.30am

"The restlessness of a great city, and the way in which it tumbles and tosses before it can get to sleep."

Cari read the passage over and over again, knowing she had become, herself, one of those desolate folk described by Dickens, condemned to spend each night either pacing the dark and rain-drenched streets, or tossing restless in her bed. Tormented by Nesta's disappearance. Terrified by the course upon which she was set.

'You know he wrote a lot of that,' said Sergeant Ladysmith, 'after he spent a whole watch here with our Night Patrol?'

There were few books on the shelf in the sergeant's threadbare office, but she'd been attracted to this one, *The Universal Traveller*, and had stood from the uncomfortable chair more to stop her legs from shaking than simply to peruse its pages. Meanwhile, the policeman, for his part, consulted his notebook for the umpteenth time this morning.

'Swore the great man in,' said her tada. 'Did you not?'

'Not me personally, Sir. Before my time. But there's a copy of the sheet somewhere. Special Constable Dickens. Wanted to see the city's street as we get to see them. While he was in town. Dead of night. Our little claim to fame, you might say.'

'It's been more than a month, for pity's sake,' Taffy snapped at him. 'You must have some idea what's happened to her.'

It was the smallest of blessings – Taffy back with them again, on Hunter Street. Her brother still not willing or able to share a room with Cousin Thomas, and therefore now occupying the space in the paper loft where poor Nesta had so briefly resided. But their tada somehow finding work for him in the printshop as well. A minor miracle in itself. Despite apparently having more and more work, worries about the cash receipts, problems balancing the books. The accounts, a leaky bucket. The more poured in at the top, the faster it ran out through the holes.

Cari rubbed at the windowpanes, trying to calculate whether it was the grease-stained glass or the river's fog still thickening outside that prevented her seeing the outer wall, or the light from its blue lamp, feet away across the invisible yard. And she enjoyed the curious sensation the Lord Jesus must truly be on her side to send such a gift, to aid her plan. She prayed it would last until tonight. The fog would both hide her and help to still her trepidation.

'A Bridewell that can't find a window cleaner,' she said, 'nor a decent rug to cover its flagstones, is hardly likely to find answers to the city's missing.'

'We've explored every avenue, Miss. And Argyle Street's no worse off, nor yet no better, than the others. But I've got a good team of lads here.'

'Front line too, Sergeant, isn't it?' Her father had aged ten years over the past month. 'Darkie Town. Fluke Alley. Dingle rednecks on one side. Papist Paddies on the other.' It was an exaggeration, of course. 'Must be like defending the Khyber Pass, stationed here.'

'It would help if they were sober, once in a while,' Taffy sneered. He'd already made at least three jibes about Bloody Sunday. 'And what about the strike fund money, Sergeant? You've got the accounts book now. What more d'you need?'

'Takes time, sir, like I told you. And I'll not deny, gentlemen, that whenever the Guinness boats are in the Salthouse, the bucket of the black stuff they bring up for the night boys is very welcome. And this time of year, especially. Keeps the draught at bay, so to speak.'

Taffy balled his fists, swore under his breath.

'Is this really a time for jokes, Sergeant?' Cari snapped, and put the book back on its shelf. But he simply looked bewildered. Perhaps he'd not intended humour after all.

'Anyway, the Watch Committee keeps a keen eye on us all,' he said. 'Quite rightly. And I can assure you, Mister Maddox – Miss Maddox too – my men were entirely sober on the day.'

'I could smell the beer on them,' she said. 'When you tried to take my sister. And look how it ended. Mayhem. All on your head. For what? If you'd already taken her, sent her down, would you have been so keen to accept Annie Maguire's confession?'

'She'd still be with us though,' said her tada, quietly, and forced the room to silence, broken finally by Sergeant Ladysmith's discreet cough.

'There were lads there from all over the show that Sunday,' he said. 'Can't speak for most of them but mine hadn't touched a drop.'

Maybe he was right. She couldn't be certain now. Yet there were two things about the day she was unable to shake off.

First, the recollection of how quick she'd been to believe it was Taffy who'd snitched to the bobbies about Nessie being there – when, as it had turned out, it was all Cousin Thomas's doing. Just doing his duty as an honest citizen, he'd insisted. Guilt about having deceived the police the first time they'd come looking for her.

And, second, that conversation with Nesta about the Pathé moving picture. 'By the time Sergeant Ladysmith gets to see this,' she'd said, 'I'll be long gone.' Nesta had laughed it off, insisted it would be weeks before anybody saw it, how she'd hardly be likely to still be hanging around on Lime Street waiting for him to cart her off to the Bridewell again. Something of the kind. But now Cari wondered about it.

'Every avenue?' she said, and the sergeant began to count them off on his fingers.

'The other girls at the bakery. Hospitals. The rest of the Bridewells. Neighbours. The Magdalens.'

'The Magdalens?' their father snapped. '*Duw annwyl*, what would she be doing with the nuns?' But he looked like he could have bitten his tongue as he stole a glance in Taffy's direction, even though her brother seemed content to let it pass, for once.

'Every avenue, sir,' said Ladysmith.

'And the Vigilance Association?' Taffy looked at Cari. 'My sister mentioned them. They take girls in, don't they?'

'Lost girls, Mister Maddox. She'd hardly be lost in her own town now, would she?'

'But all this about white slavers,' said Taffy. 'Can't just be coincidence, can it?'

Ladysmith sniffed at the room's cold air, something puzzling him, though thankfully not for too long.

'If you ask me, sir, the newspapers have made too much of the story. A bit of sensationalism. Good for their sales, see.'

Cari was sure he must be right. But the rest of the family had already made up their minds. It seemed to fit their prejudices. There'd been so many gatherings. So many arguments. So many accusations of blame. So many recriminations. So many tears. It had exhausted her.

'Every avenue but this one then, eh, Sergeant?' Taffy muttered. 'And like I said, not just a coincidence. Been mixed up with those darkies down at the Harrington. Makes sense doesn't it? Have you looked at the Elder Dempster dive on Stanhope Street?'

'Of course, Mister Maddox. You suggested it and we went there. But the Krooboys you mentioned – well, they all sailed home weeks ago. After the strike.'

'And this Joseph Fountain?' said Taffy.

'Yes, gone,' the sergeant told him. 'This morning we interviewed the fellow your brother-in-law mentioned. The second time. But he knows nothing. Thought he might have fitted the bill. Scars all over his face, like. But seems it's normal for lots of the Krooboys.'

The second time, yes. And Cari herself had gone to confront Amos Gartee. It had been good to see him in a way. Some link to happier days, to Nessie herself. His lack of English was indeed an obstacle to proper dialogue. But apart from all this, she'd been troubled by his apparent lack of concern. And the feeling – just a feeling – he might be hiding something. Yet she'd already created the lie. The fictitious Joseph Fountain. Told Mister Gartee she'd done it for Nessie's sake. Because, whatever might have happened, Nesta would have wanted Amos Gartee protected. This was her belief. And she'd kept quiet about Nesta's version of the Cousin Thomas story, as well. The one about him being attacked and finding the money. *Duwcs*, she couldn't talk about that without…

'Well,' said her tada. 'What else can you expect from Darkie Town? Or Sailor Town. All the same, they are. My poor girl gets mixed up with them. And this Krooboy, this Fountain, he sells her to some other heathen. For… for…' Tears rolled down his cheeks, as they'd done so many times these past weeks.

'You see, Cari,' Taffy snarled. 'See what happens when you poke your nose where it doesn't belong?'

This was the way it had been. Cari's fault. And she supposed, in many ways, they were right. Her tada had printed posters, of course, using the picture of Nesta from Mister Mills's photograph. All over the place, they were. But where could she be?

'We'll obviously continue to investigate,' said Ladysmith. 'But after all these weeks…'

'If a donation to the Benevolent Fund would help,' said their tada, 'I'm sure we could make a contribution.'

'The lottery tickets again, Pa?' Taffy snorted.

'Lottery?' said Ladysmith. 'You've a licence, sir, I assume?'

Her tada glowered at Taffy, though the sergeant seemed not to notice.

'Mister Maldwyn Hughes,' I said, quickly, 'from the Welsh Orphans' Society can vouch for my father. You don't seriously imagine he'd be doing anything illegal, Sergeant?'

'Bless you, no, miss. And don't you worry. I'm sure your sister will turn up safe and sound.'

Yet he sounded far from convinced. And, if she was safe – oh, Sweet Lord Jesu, please let her be safe – did she know how they'd been betrayed? The years fighting for the vote, for women's rights. The first tentative direct actions. Direct, but passive. Chaining themselves to railings. Hectoring politicians. Peaceful, like. But they'd been physically attacked, beaten, sent to prison. In prison, the hunger strikes.

Their response to the hunger strikes? Forcible feeding, cruel and painful. And the women's response to forcible feeding? Some modest window-smashing. More militancy. All suspended, of course, as part of the deal brokered by the Men's League and their cross-party suffrage supporters, suggesting some form of conciliation.

Not all they wanted and this Conciliation Bill should have passed last year, except for the blocking actions of that scoundrel, Lloyd George. Ashamed to admit he was Welsh, as well, she was. So, this year, a new Conciliation Bill with a promise it should be facilitated over the next twelve months. Yet had she not said they'd be fooled again? Tricked once more? Well, she'd been right.

But tonight, Nesta, she thought, as Taffy made one more plea about the strike fund, you'll be with me in spirit, at least. I know you will. And we shall join the ranks of the anarchists and revolutionaries together. The thought of her plan both thrilled her and made her quake inside, though she hoped it might not show too much.

10.00am

Tom Priddy was excited by the morning's prospects. Excited and enraged at the same time.

Daft Taffy still living in the paper loft and Psalm 109 so far not produced any benefit. He'd recited the appropriate line every morning and every night for the whole month. The curse.

"Let his days be few; and let another take his office."

It was a tricky thing, Psalm 109. So many lines from which to choose. Yet this one seemed to fit the bill. Yet a whole month. Morning and night. Wasn't this what the witch, Gwen, Uncle Owen's woman, had taught him? He'd been so young. But yes, he was certain. Almost certain, anyway.

The Cropper worked its own magic, meanwhile. The rhythm was hypnotic, Tom feeding and stacking, feeding and stacking. The programmes for the following Saturday's home match against Sunderland. This week, away to West Brom. The away games hadn't been going well, though next week, if things went according to plan today, he might take the day off. Get to see Ma Bushell's toffee shop at last.

The morning had begun with a pleasant surprise. The other three had gone off early to Argyle Street – seeking news of Dumpling Nesta. But he doubted they'd find anything new. If the white slavers had taken her, as he was certain must have happened – well, her own fault for mixing with those darkies. They'd probably arranged the whole thing. And served her right for spurning his own attentions.

But the thing worth its weight in gold, old Huw's dawning realisation his precious daughter must have been more than an ally or patron to one of the Krooboys – this fellow Fountain, presumably – but actually enamoured of the rogue. Like butter on bacon. Icing on the cake. Aged him. What – ten years? Taking more and more of the Hartley's Blood and Stomach pills. Killing him, Tom was certain.

Then, his discovery. One of his Hunter Street Irregulars had brought him word. The Beanpole – she'd not been herself for a couple of weeks. And nothing, he guessed, to do with her own filthy, monthly scourge. No, something else. The lad had spotted her slipping some street urchin a few pennies and he'd had the sense to follow. To Crown's, on London Road. A quart of paraffin oil. No more than a quart. Why on earth might she want a quart of paraffin?

This morning, with the house to himself, he'd hunted for it, found the empty Blue Ball jar, tucked away in one of the cupboards, here in a disused corner of the printshop. Empty, yes, but still traces of the oil. With it, hidden among some boxes and rags, three smaller bottles, half-pint bottles, each tightly stoppered but with the unmistakeable smell of paraffin around the neck. Three half-pints. One missing, then.

A mystery. And he was still pondering its depths when he heard the long-expected knocking at the outer door. He brought the Cropper to a halt.

'Mister Hughes,' he said, trying his best to look confused,

embarrassed. '*S'mae?*' How are things?

He knew very well, of course. It wasn't the first time he'd been around demanding the money for his blasted orphans. The plump little fellow stood in the doorway, swathed in fog, tentacles of the stuff creeping their way across the threshold.

'*Bore da*, Mister Priddy.' Good morning. 'Is he in, then?'

'Told him you were coming, I did,' Tom lied. 'But – well, had some urgent business, he reckoned.'

'Made himself scarce, more like. But I see a new title over the door as well, now. Nephew, it says. You, I suppose?'

'Just a junior partner, see. Can I help, Mister Hughes?'

The plump little fellow pushed his way past, into the printshop, lifted the cap from his head and the muffler from around his neck.

'Help?' said Maldwyn Hughes, and scratched at his dishevelled hair. '*Dwi'n gobeithio.*' I hope so. 'The orphans, see? Mister Maddox – well, you too, as it happens – promised me we'd see some results from this lottery of his. Remember? Your visits to the office. But, so far, nothing. Not a penny.'

'*Duw*, Mister Hughes. Can't be right. Seen his accounts, I have. Here, I can show you, see.'

And he did. Every entry. Every payment listed for the Liverpool Welsh Orphans Society.

'Seen none of it, we haven't,' said Maldwyn Hughes. 'None. How d'you explain it, like?'

Tom Priddy rubbed at his chin.

'Not for me to say, Mister Hughes. Though…'

'What?'

'Well, it's just – young Taffy's back, working here again, he is. Don't want to set hares running, but…'

'Taffy Maddox? The dockers' strike fund? He was supposed to make our payments? You tell them, Mister Priddy. Either the Society gets the money listed in those accounts, or I'm going straight to the police with this. You understand?'

Tom Priddy understood perfectly. And, as Maldwyn Hughes blustered and bustled his way out of the printshop again, he laughed. Time then, he thought, to bring this all together now. After all, he decided, *gormod o bwdin dagith gi.* Too much pudding chokes the dog.

Yes, you can have too much of a good thing.

Slight change of plans though, he decided. And he scuttled back upstairs to the Beanpole's room, amused himself a while rummaging through her clothes chest before finally removing the Thompson-Frere woman's accounts book and watch, moved them into the paper loft, buried them deep within Daft Taffy's belongings. No need to destroy the Beanpole, after all. She'd be perfectly capable of doing it herself.

12.00 noon

'I didn't expect you,' said Mister Kaplan. 'This filthy stuff.'

'*Duw*,' she said. 'Takes more than a bit of fog to keep Cari Maddox from her work.'

He looked at her as though unsure whether she was being ironic.

'Unless there are elections, you think?'

He had a point. A couple of days when she'd feigned sickness. Worth it, as well. She couldn't claim any major part in the victory – but victory it had certainly been. Three weeks earlier. The first of the month. Conservatives and Liberals both lost three seats each on the Council. All gains for Labour. The Party with seven councillors now. And she'd worked in St. Anne's Ward where, in line with her old promise, she'd taken some of the women to help Sexton hold his own seat.

'Don't know what you mean,' she told him.

'To be honest, Miss Maddox, I was surprised to see you here yesterday.'

A raw nerve. Yesterday. The Tenth Women's Parliament had been gathering in London. Some of the Liverpool girls there. And Mrs Pethick-Lawrence had led a march from Caxton Hall to Parliament Square. A protest march. They'd determined that the Conciliation Bill, and the fight as a whole, was now doomed to fail – unless women all showed their mettle.

Only one possible response. And today's headlines had screamed it from the rooftops. Windows smashed. Stones thrown. Hammers used. Government building windows. Home Office. Local Government Board. Somerset House. Others.

Cari had broken windows herself, of course. Like others had done before her. But she'd only done it twice. The Custom House and the Town Hall, as it happened. But this, in London, had been different. Two hotels. The offices of the *Daily Mail* and *Daily News*. A hat shop. A chemist. Lyon's. Swan and Edgar's. The war had spread. No longer purely confined to Government premises or those of the Liberals.

But there'd been a price to pay. Arrests. More than two hundred, according to the papers. Mrs Pethick-Lawrence among them. Lady Constance Lytton. And Mrs Mansell Moullin. Among the local members of the WSPU, Patricia Woodlock. Their cases being heard in a few days at Bow Street magistrates. Some also being sent for trial at the London sessions. Trials. The first time there'd been any trials. This time they meant to make an example. Anybody who'd caused more than five pounds-worth of damage, they said. Make a real example of them.

It all made Cari's own plans more nerve-wracking.

'Surprised I wasn't there, Mister Kaplan? Couldn't leave you in the lurch, now, could I?'

The main reason? Because, last night, she'd arranged to step out once more with Ernst Jurks. He was working again. Though perhaps more accurate to say he was fulfilling a duty. Debt, maybe. For Nesta's sudden disappearance had left a vacancy at the Vienna Bakery and the owner, Mister Kirkland, had been struggling to find somebody suitable. And since Ernst's father had the connection, Ernst's links to the tragically errant Nesta Maddox, and Ernst still being unemployed – well, it had all fitted together quite nicely.

So, it had been the theatre. The Royal Court. A performance of their very own suffragette play, *Outlawed*. Charlotte Despard's novel adapted for the stage by the American woman, Alice Chapin. Wonderful. During the curtain call, the entire cast had sung *The March of the Women* in honour of poor Patricia.

And much discussion with Ernst on the way there, on the way back, about those same elections. About Tom Mann having finally left Liverpool. About how he'd left Liverpool on the move towards becoming a fortress for radical change. About the continuing restless nature of the city. About the forty tram workers still not reinstated. About the National Transport Workers' Federation – all those unions coming together and, Ernst believed, never again to be split asunder.

'New age, she comes,' Ernst had said. 'This city, she follows a new path.'

Cari hoped he was right, settled into her work for her morning, though her thoughts often returning to Ernst Jurks, or to yesterday's arrests in London.

Ernst still insisted he must, eventually, return to sea. Still fearful about the war he knew was coming.

'Danger here there will be,' he'd said. 'My name perhaps will change. Mister Kirk will be. *Was denkst du, mein Lieber?*'

'The only point in changing your name,' she'd said, 'might be if you were intending to return.'

He'd smiled at her.

'*Ja.* But a story I hear. London, and men throw stones at small dog. Dachsund, it was. Germany dog. So, come back?' he'd said. 'Fond. Once before, you I told, Cari. I am fond of you.'

And yesterday? London? It seemed to Cari that not only her sister had vanished, but also the victory for which they'd fought. Well, for the latter there might at least be some revenge, and Cari stole a glance towards her bag, sitting innocently, there by the door, yet holding the tools of retribution.

1.00pm

He'd never learned to swim. All his time growing up along the shoreline of Nana Kru, his fearless years upon the waves and at sea – and never learned to swim. If the spirits of the ocean required one's soul, a heresy to deny them.

Yet, somehow, the idea of drowning in the oil-streaked, flotsam-filled waters of the Canning, Albert or Salthouse Docks could not possibly be the fate for which Nyesoa or the Good Lord Jesus intended him.

So now, sent home by Skipper Coleman for want of work, and having finally groped a path home to the new lodgings on Kent Square, here he was in the swimming cavern on Cornwallis Street.

'That's the way!' the Wolof encouraged him, his voice echoing in the mystical manner of the place.

Amos gripped the rim of the blue tiled gutter running around the pool's edge, stretched out his arms to their fullest extent, and kicked with legs and feet, just as a frog might do. Kick, kick, kick, until his thighs ached.

'Feet flat,' shouted Charles Tuohey from somewhere behind him. 'Push with your feet against the water.'

Easier said than done. Easier, surely, without the encumbrance of this woolly bathing suit knitted for him by his new landlady, Missee Mary – Mary Clarke, who could, from her features, be the Wolof's kin. But born in Bootle, Tuohey had said with great pride, and with her sisters June and Emma, this England's first women footballers. With the money Miss Mary had made from playing the football game, she had purchased the lodging house. Many rooms. Few questions.

The Wolof himself, meanwhile, seemed far better equipped for the swimming cavern. Some sort of fine canvas or heavy linen, striped blue and white from his knees to his neck, buttoned down the front, sleeves to his elbows, and an extra fold of cloth across his chest with the words *Life Guard* emblazoned there in red.

They had the swimming cavern almost to themselves, the fog having brought so much of the city to a standstill. And as they dried and dressed, each in his own poolside cubicle, Amos considered the water, the light shimmering and distorted in its tiled depths, and just two *poto* gentlemen thrashing back and forth, back and forth, expertly along its length.

'Missee Nesta one time tell me,' he said, 'how blood more thick past water. You think same?'

Miss Nesta was, as always, much on his mind. And this question important to him.

'Family ties stronger than those we choose to make for ourselves?' The Wolof's voice came to him through the adjoining cream-painted wood panels. 'I prefer the wisdom of the East,' he said, 'which holds that the blood of a covenant made willingly between two people is thicker than the water of the womb. Closer ties than those from a simple accident of birth.'

Amos supposed this must be true, remembered Miss Nesta's tales of the warfare which seemed to rage among the members of her family.

'Wisdom of East,' he repeated, working the towel across his bare back. 'Our *krogba*, Nana Kru, he say same.'

'Ah,' said Charles Tuohey. 'I have a friend at the library – the place of book wisdom. We must go there, you and me. Anyway, this friend has researched the links between the Ancient Egyptians and my own people. *Our* people, Amos. Here in England they set great store by the learning of the Greeks. Sophocles and Socrates. But the books show us how the Greeks took their knowledge from the Egyptians. And the Egyptians, in turn, from the even older civilisations of Africa. The Kush. The Aksum. Those from the Niger River whose names we no longer know. So this, the blood-thick binding of a willing covenant, it is a strong philosophy for us.'

The Wolof frequently spoke this way. Almost in riddles. If they had spoken a common tongue, it might have made it easier for Amos to follow all the threads. Yet he understood the gist well enough.

Covenant, he thought. It is a good word.

A covenant which gave him this score to settle. With the devil man. For what he'd done to Miss Nesta. The anger which had caused him – well, enough of this.

But another thing, as well. Miss Coconut Palm, when she'd come to see him – it had been difficult, lying to her so badly, allowing her to leave again in such pain – had told her about her brother's missing strike money, about the devil man's implication Miss Nesta's Krooboy might have stolen and dropped it, and thus the reason she had invented this Joseph Fountain.

'Devil man,' he said, as they emerged once again into the yellow smog, 'I must follow. Yet day no possible. Night more fine past day.'

'You must do nothing foolish, Amos. And, this particular night, we can do much better. Tonight, my friend, I should like you to accompany me to the theatre.'

2.00pm

Cari had arrived too late to qualify for a break. Anyway, not much point going out into this muck. And she'd thankfully brought some bread and cheese wrapped in waxed paper.

'Are you certain?' Mister Kaplan shouted from his own office.

'Yes,' she replied. 'Certain.'

He'd already allowed the rest of the girls to make their way home. Getting soft in his old age, she decided. The trams still running, but only just. Reduced service. Yet she needed to keep working. If she didn't keep working, the thought of her plans for tonight would fray her nerves to shreds.

'And your father? Still minding his pennies, I hope.'

Of course, she lied. In truth, she had no idea where the money was going. The harder her tada seemed to work, the poorer they became.

'Glad to have my brother in the business again, I think.'

But the same couldn't be said for Tom Priddy. Nose out of joint, see. Taffy no real threat to him, and he'd had nothing new to tell Taffy about Theresa, of course, but kept him dangling long enough while, for Cari's part, she still harboured those same doubts. Was he capable of having shoved her from the tram? Oh, she thought so.

Then there was Winifred. The number of times Cari had caught her and Tom Priddy whispering together – Wyn, of course, the most bountiful when it came to dispensing blame: Nesta's dalliance with the Kru; Nesta's attachment – like Cari's own – to what she described as "disgusting" suffragettes; and Nesta's failure to fully take the Lord Jesus into her heart. On and on.

And finally, the finances. The number of times she'd found her tada slumped over the kitchen table, poring over his invoices and receipts on the verge of despair that he would be unable to repay the loan he'd taken to start the lottery business.

She was still thinking about the irony of being there, at Kaplans, undertaking those self-same tasks but for a business which was thriving, when the outer entrance to the office swung open. A head appeared in the doorway. A head, round as a football, weathered. A head which wore its fifty or more years with distinction, though curls of unruly hair sprouting from the sides of his cap.

'Miss Maddox?'

'It took her a moment to place him. Then she remembered. Outside the Victoria Chapel, that awful Sunday.

'Mister Hughes, isn't it? Welsh orphans?'

'Like to have a word, I would. Private word, see.'

Cari set down the cheese butty. This sounded serious.

'Use the empty office, Miss Maddox,' Kaplan called out. 'Or can I assist?'

'Private matter, like I said,' murmured Mister Hughes. Maldwyn Hughes, she recalled.

'I'm afraid there's nothing we can offer you,' Cari told him – thinking of refreshments – when she'd shown him to the vacant room and closed the door behind them. But she'd been careful to take her bag with her. The bottle hidden in its depths. For tonight.

'Suppose it's the point,' Mister Hughes replied, sitting on one of the office chairs. 'Nothing to offer, like. Difficult, see. Spoke with that cousin of yours. Thomas, isn't it? Your tada not there.'

'About the lottery, I suppose. Is there a problem? Doing well, I understand.'

She stood before him, arms folded.

'Doing nothing at all. Not a thing. Promised the earth and now, not a brass farthing. And your cousin not very helpful. Showed me the books an' all. A bit hasty, I fear. Then remembered you. Remember your tada telling me you were at Kaplan's. Good girl, he said.'

He tried his best to smile.

'Hasty?' said Cari.

'Threatened to fetch the police. But that was more – well, he told me about your brother. No disrespect, like, but a small world, this little community of ours. Stories, see. About your brother. Strike fund. Know what I mean?'

Yes, she knew what he meant, and it angered her.

'But when did you last receive any of the lottery payments, Mister Hughes?'

'There's the thing. Never a penny. Not in three months.'

'Then you can hardly blame Taffy, Mister Hughes. He's only been back with the business a few weeks. And, by the way, Taffy's in the clear. Innocent. Bobbies found the money. Somebody else.'

He looked confused, stammered an apology.

'Oh, *rargian fawr*,' he said. 'Then…'

'Mister Hughes,' she said. 'Why don't you leave it with me a couple of days and I'll find out what's going on. Don't you fret. I'll make sure your orphans get their money.'

Of course, it didn't take a genius. Cousin Thomas. And he had no idea whether she could fulfil the promise. But the old fellow was grateful enough, thanked her profusely.

'Better try to find my way back to Rathbone Street,' he told her, easing himself out of the chair once more.

'Wait,' she said. 'I'm sorry but I wonder – well, another thing entirely. But your offices. Rathbone Street, as you say. I wonder, did you know the girl who worked at Penny's. Theresa. You may remember…'

'Tram accident,' he said. 'Tragic, it was. And yes, we knew her quite well. Poor child. Sometimes we'd send to Penny's for a jug of their finest. Partial to a drop of Allsopp's, I am. Though Mister Maddox and your cousin, being temperance, like…'

'Did she bring you the ale when my Cousin Thomas was there, then?'

'*Duw*, yes, *cariad*. Came a couple of times on his own, didn't he? Yes, now I come to think of it. Always had a joke to share with her, he did. Made her laugh. Bless her soul.'

3.00pm

Even the stink from the bone manure works was muted by the pea-souper. It was a short though confusing walk. From the Rotunda, back along the damp shroud of Scotland Road to Hopwood Street, down across Vauxhall Road and the cast iron canal bridge onto Lightbody Street. Last time Tom had walked this way he'd been able to see the gasometers, the canal locks and wool warehouses. But this afternoon all was hidden behind this heavy, grey curtain.

He had to look hard for the street sign, Hedley Street, which would lead him to the district's Welsh enclave – thoroughfares named for Cemaes, Snowdon, Barmouth, Menai. And yes, of course, Idris Street.

Tom Priddy knocked at number thirteen, wondering how anybody could be so stupid as to purchase a house with such misfortune attached. Not a grand house but the home of Rhys the Gateman and young Winifred. And he'd taken the chance he would find her alone. Though, if not, it mattered little. Another loose end to be tied. A knife to be twisted in the Maddox family's wounds.

'Cousin Thomas,' she said, peering around the corner of the partially opened door. 'What are you doing out in this filthy weather?'

'I was hoping to see Rhys. Thought he'd not be working in the fog.'

'He had to go to the Huskisson. Think that's what he said. But home soon. Should be.'

Tom nodded. He doubted it would be work taking Rhys from home on a day like this but, rather, the chance to indulge his venial sins.

'*Duw*,' he said. 'But you going to leave me on the doorstep, Wyn?'

The two downstairs rooms were very much as he'd imagined. Very Winifred. All prim and proper. No hiding place here for dust or germ. This, in itself, an irony, given the lightning bolt he'd brought with him. Antimacassars. Carbolic. But just a hint of Rhys Gateman's tobacco smoke. Whiskey Flake. It must be a strange ebb and flow. The husband, master of everything he surveyed when at home. Lord of the manor. She, returning the house to purity whenever he was absent. Well, perhaps not purity.

'And to what do we owe the honour, Cousin?' she said, as she poured tea.

Now, it was like it had been before. Pox-faced Winifred more relaxed with him. Almost flirtatious. He dropped a single lump of sugar into the flowered china cup.

'Today, tomorrow, closing accounts, I am.'

'Accounts?'

'With old Huw. And his family.'

He needed to prepare for departure. A new chapter to be opened. He was sure Maldwyn Hughes wouldn't go to the police just yet. But after this morning's visit – well, it had made sense to visit the bank. Withdrawals to be made. Later, he'd need to make sure all was ready.

'*Your* family, Thomas, surely?'

'Not really, *cariad*. I have to admit there were times. Always enjoyed making you laugh, I did, Wyn. Always thought you could have done better than Rhys Gateman.'

'Got substance, has my Rhys.' She looked around the room with pride, her gaze settling on a pair of porcelain dogs sitting on the mantle shelf. 'This house, see.'

'And secrets, like. Lots of secrets,' Tom smirked at her.

Her hand began to shake, tea slopping into the saucer.

'I don't want to know.' Her tone had changed. Sharper now. 'And what d'you mean – closing accounts?'

'Just accounts, *cariad*. But can't settle them accounts unless I start with you and Rhys. Curious about Rhys, see? Hair falling out. The rashes. You *and* him. And then all the time he spends at Grossi's. But not just Grossi's, is it, Wyn? Finds them anywhere, he does. Whores. And you don't mind. What was it, you said?'

She flushed crimson, up her neck, over the scars.

'It's better than...'

'So, I had one of my lads follow him. Know where he ended up?'

Pox-faced Winifred shook her head, clapped her hands over her ears.

'Myrtle Street,' he said. 'Radium Institute. Know what they do there, Wyn? Cancer. But skin diseases, as well. Diseases like – well, you know, don't you? They have this test now, see. But I'm guessing Rhys has just had the test himself. Or have you...?'

'Told Ceridwen, I did,' she protested. 'Good man, my Rhys. None better. Just – well, the way Our Lord Jesus made him.'

Tom Priddy made a point to check later. His own Lord Jesus, he'd realised, was mysteriously absent.

'Obedient, we have to be. Wives. *For the husband is the head of the wife, even as Christ is the head of the church.* You know that.'

'So, no test, then. Didn't think so. And got sores yourself, have you, *cariad*? Down – there?'

He made a point of lowering his own gaze towards her lap, had an image in his head. But she'd gasped, dropped the cup. Tea splashed all over her beautifully clean rug. Though he ignored her, pressed on.

'You know what's waiting for you, Wyn? There was this girl, see. In Beddgelert. Been given the syph by her husband. French disease, they call it. Sailor, I think. The husband, like. Beautiful, she'd been. So they said.'

She was weeping openly now, snot running from her nose, begging him to leave.

'Turned into a bag of bones,' he pressed on. 'Died from bleeding inside. Just a kid, I was. Me and my mates used to take dares. About seeing the husband. Didn't die. Not for years.'

'Get out!' she screamed. 'Get out!'

'And each year, *cariad*, a bit more of his face eaten away. Until you could see through the side of his cheek. See his tongue, like.' He mimed the action, with his own tongue. 'And mad. Mad as a box of frogs, by then.'

'Why are you doing this?' she sobbed. 'Tada's been good to you.'

'Good to me? You know what he did, *cariad*? Left *my* mam when she was dying. Married, they were. And just left. A whore of his own. Your mam, see. Left me, as well. Didn't mind too much. But *my* mam…'

'Family,' she snivelled. But no sign of sympathy. Not an ounce of understanding. 'Still family.'

'Blood, you mean? Blood sort of family?'

No response. More tears. And he saw that other room once more. At least, he thought so. Couldn't have been more than two. But certain he remembered the moment when she'd been taken from him. Thin. So thin. Ghostly pale. The cancer. No recollection of his tada, of course. The questions would come later, answered by Uncle Owen. And wasn't it the questions had started it all? The whippings. All those filthy things. Uncle Owen, now delightfully departed.

'Well?' he said. 'What will you do? Need the test, see. Treatment, like.'

But she simply told him again to get out.

He knew she'd stay, of course. Head buried in the sand. Until…

Shame. But he'd sowed the seeds. It would shatter old Huw. This was the point. His daughter dying from the syph. He just hoped the old man would live long enough to watch it happen, have her taken away from him. Meanwhile, Tom Priddy would savour the joy of knowing he'd lost the others, as well. Dumpling Nesta already gone – to heaven only knew where. The Beanpole next. Daft Taffy. Old Huw himself in gaol, hopefully.

Meanwhile, he'd done his last day at Waugh's and, later, his final session at the theatre. But where would life take him next? A funeral furnishing business of his own, maybe. Birmingham, perhaps. Or join a theatrical troupe. Change his name, of course.

After all, he'd have enough money, wouldn't he?

7.00pm

Amos had never been anywhere quite like it. Tiers of galleries rose in a semicircle about and behind them. Leaves and flowers burnt into the walls, columns and galleries. Green and gold. Above his head, the interior of an ornate gilded dome.

He was glad they had come, though the journey hadn't been easy. More fog. The tramway barely functioning. But at least they were here, and had run the gauntlet of protestors at the entrance, each trying to force paper into their hands.

'They're right, of course,' the Wolof had told him. 'Reformers. Conditions for so many in this city little better than Mrs Stowe described. Slavery, pure and simple.'

They had drawn some attention, naturally, but Amos was surprised to note they were not entirely the only black faces in the audience. Not entirely. Yet he was more surprised by the pained expressions of sympathy he'd received from quite a few folk sitting in the rows around them.

'We are black,' said Charles Tuohey. 'Those who have come to see the play believe we must need to be pitied for our plight.'

He chuckled to himself, while Amos studied the handbill, the image of another black man. In chains. Some *poto* fellow with a straw hat and a whip, raising the lash to strike.

Uncle Tom's Cabin, he read, easily enough.

Adapted – yes, that was the word. *Adapted for the stage by Mister George Aiken.*

'American,' said the Wolof. 'Aiken. He's American. The original story was written by this woman...' He pointed to the name on the handbill. 'The Stowe woman. Remains to be seen what this version's done to mangle her work.'

Amos shifted in the plush seat, uncomfortable in the clothes Charles Tuohey had lent him. He just wished Miss Nesta could have seen him – though no point wishing for the impossible.

'This place,' he said. 'So strange.'

'Is it?' the Wolof replied. 'Mask dancers. You had mask dancers at Nana Kru?'

'Of course,' Amos replied. Such a stupid question. Masks and dance. And music. To bring back the spirits of those who had passed. Great tragedy. Or simply foolish things to lift the soul and bring them laughter. There had always been mask dancers.

'You see, Amos? The Greeks had mask dancers also. The idea was stolen from Africa. And did you have sacred spaces for the mask dancers to perform?'

A more difficult question. For the mask dancers were known to come and go as they pleased, sometimes in the heart of town or village, but sometimes simply along the roads where folk travelled, or even among the market stalls and juke joints, roadhouse brothels and drinking dens.

And sacred? Those were the open spaces of the forest. Or the ones Nyesoa had scooped from the hillsides. Spaces where the words and music of the mask dancers rang from one side of a hollow to the other.

'I am sure there must have been,' said the Wolof. He waved his hand around this other great chamber. 'The Greeks, too,' he said. 'They claim Alexander the Great brought Greek theatre to Egypt. But Herodotus describes performances in Egypt at least a hundred years before. In the Egyptians' sacred places. You know what they were doing?'

Amos could guess, but he didn't wish to spoil the Wolof's enjoyment.

'Mask dancing,' said Tuohey, as the lights of the place dimmed, a broad red curtain before them lifting upon a scene of misery. And singing.

Early in da mornin'…

'Oh, Lord,' murmured Tuohey.

The story hadn't been easy to follow, the black-faced *poto* players speaking in some form of *Kreyol* unlike any Amos had ever heard before.

'Plantation talk, apparently,' the Wolof whispered in his ear.

More songs.

Round da meadows is a-ringin'
Dem darkies' mournful song…

'Good grief.' The Wolof almost choked.

Yet, in the end, it seemed the two main players had both escaped the chains of slavery. Eliza, run away to some cold place of snow. The old fool, Uncle Tom, escaped only into oblivion, whipped to death by the fellow in the straw hat.

Tom. Like Tom Mann, he supposed. And hadn't Miss Nesta once named the devil man this way? Cousin Tom.

'Saw it in London,' said Tuohey. 'At least they had the decency to employ black actors, instead of these minstrel boys.

One last song. And a chorus of performers, gathered together.

Swing low, sweet chariot,
Coming for to carry me home.

And there he was, leading the singing. A high-pitched voice. And the black face paint could not disguise him. Amos had been close enough to know him. The shape of his face. The devil man.

8.00pm

Her tada had tried to stop her. But Cari held fast until he and Taffy had gone off to Byrom Hall. A meeting for the tram workers still not reinstated. Though she was more concerned she'd not yet told them about the meeting with Mister Hughes.

It had been an eventful week. An infuriating week. A deputation of their societies meeting Asquith last Friday. His half-hearted commitment that he'd respect Parliament's wishes if the Commons approved the Conciliation Bill or a Reform Bill. Magnanimous of him. And he'd totally rejected the idea of a Woman's Suffrage Bill.

Alice had organised a meeting on Tuesday. Chaos. Half the members shouting for Asquith to be given a chance, believing the lying devil. The rest at their throats, knowing they were being tricked. There wasn't going to be any equal franchise, even a modest and unsatisfactory one. Another gathering tonight. But, for Cari, now was the time to act.

She pulled the cloak about herself more tightly and marched off alone into the fog, towards the ghostly green halos of Commutation Row's gas lights. Then the flaring barrel lamps of Lime Street's alehouses. But few people, thank goodness. And the murk seemed to be thickening. Perfect. So, a noisy entrance to the meeting, making a point of apologising to Alice Davies, ensuring others also noted her presence, but keeping to the back of the room, in the shadow of one of the hall's carved pillars.

She waited there until the debate became especially heated, then quietly slipped away. There was a chance somebody would notice her absence – it was rare, of course, for Cari to sit on her hands during such exchanges – but she hoped it would be impossible for anybody to pin down her movements with any accuracy. Besides, she intended to do this as quickly as her trembling legs could carry her. Not even certain she could go through with it.

She'd soon find out. Her nearest target? Just down the road, the one outside Lime Street station and across from St. George's Hall. It seemed appropriate. Symbolic. A beacon to commemorate those who'd suffered there so badly on Bloody Sunday. For those women and their children. Symbolic also for the potbellied crown topping the corpulent scarlet Special, one of those pillar boxes peculiar to Liverpool – or so she'd read.

It was busier there than she'd expected, though of course there were liner passengers arriving at all hours in the station, some bound first for the hotel, others ferried by cab straight to the landing stages. Yet the doorway to Silverman's on the corner of Lord Nelson Street gave her cover enough, and there she began to take out the tools of her anarchy from the hessian bag. The bent and twisted toasting fork she'd liberated from the depths of her tada's workbench in the passageway. One of the linen strips, which she carefully impaled on the fork's tines. The stone bottle from which she poured enough paraffin oil to soak the material. And her box of Swan Vestas.

Cari tried to stop herself from shaking as she peered around the corner, checked the coast was clear. Strangely silent, until a tram surged past. It was like some monster from a tale by H.G. Wells, its ghastly ray seeking her out as it loomed and clattered through the swirling greyness, and the yellowed interior lights spectral, distorted by the almost impenetrable curtain.

Her hand trembled. She barely managed to balance the toasting fork, with its dangling length of linen, in the gaping mouth of the pillar box. She set down the bag, tried the matches. Three of the blessed things failed her. But the fourth – oh, the fourth sparked and flared. It sent a tongue of blue flame spiralling up the rag, filled her nostrils with the homely aroma of paraffin.

It bathed her face in its warm glow, even as she used the toasting fork to push the flaming linen inside the post box, then dragged it out again, scraping the burning cloth from its tines to fall down inside the Special's fat stomach.

She was tempted to run. Right then. Though, she forced herself to wait. For the letters and posted newspapers within to burst afire.

Nothing! The merest wisp of smoke. Not the burning brazier she'd expected.

Cari grabbed the bag, retreated from the thing. Stupid girl, she thought, and steadied herself. It seemed like tempting fate to try attacking the Lime Street box a second time, so she made straight for the next target.

Down William Brown Street, trying to fathom what might have gone wrong. Too little paraffin? Perhaps. But she knew it didn't take much. Perhaps some science she didn't understand. Well, she'd have to do better.

Past the Haymarket and up Dale Street. A smell of sulphur on that laden air. Fog horns on the river ahead.

At last, the Town Hall, its bulk jutting out into the road, as it did. An easy landmark to help her navigate, right into Exchange Street and then left onto Exchange Flags.

Another symbolic site. The government offices. The back windows of the Town Hall — which she'd once broken, of course. And another Special. This time no interruptions. The toasting fork, the linen, a healthier dose of paraffin, and the Vestas.

Success! She'd no idea what was inside but the contents certainly blazed bravely, flames soon licking from the slit. And Cari, running like a loon, back towards the Haymarket, towards target number three, though she soon slowed to a less conspicuous dawdle.

She began to wonder. What had been in the pillar box?

Her mind worked overtime. Perhaps a completed character reference form, whose failure to arrive would deprive an ageing couple of their qualification for even a miserly pension. The money order supposed to compensate a poor workman for his crippling work accident. The final letter home from poor Eastern European emigrants bound for America who wouldn't survive the journey. A love letter without which the intended recipient might consider his or her affections unrequited and lead to their suicide. And the make-or-break donation to some especially needy charity.

Guilt. Guilt. Guilt. A woman's lot. For who but a woman could experience such guilt at her own anarchy. So that, by the time she'd got back to Commutation Row and the old fountain her nerve had entirely failed.

Well, she thought, one might be enough! It was enough for Cari, anyway. A personal declaration of war. And the thought warmed her on the way back to Renshaw Street and the meeting. Still in progress, thank goodness, though on the verge of breaking up. But an argument still running, tempers high about Asquith and the Bill. How long had she been? An hour, she supposed.

'Miss Maddox.' Alice Davies came bustling towards her. 'You're back.'

'Back?' Cari pretended all the innocence she could manage.

'Yes. The police. Interrupted the meeting. Looking for you. I told them you'd been here but must have left early.'

Her words rang in Cari's ears, and she staggered, certain she was going to faint. How? She'd been seen? Reported so quickly?

'I slipped out for a few minutes,' she began. 'Truly. A few minutes. When was this?' Cari whispered.

'Gracious, you look awful. Better sit down, my dear.' Cari shook her head. 'Do you know what they wanted?' Alice asked.

'I cannot imagine. But when?' Cari said again.

'Well, ten minutes I suppose.' A sergeant. Ladysmith, I believe he said. Wouldn't say what it was about, but he seemed – oh, Cari, I hope everything is all right.'

'Ten minutes? Yes, about right. I slipped out. To get some air. That time of the month, Alice. You know? I felt... Anyway, we met him this morning,' she said, composing herself somewhat, trying to make sense of it. 'The sergeant. About Nesta. Perhaps he has news after all.'

It can't be the post boxes, she told herself. It can't. And, if not, what else but news of Nessie. Not some other mishap, surely. Yet why would he be chasing me with this? Why not Tada? Unless – oh, Sweet

Lord Jesus, not something happened to Tada. Please…

'News? I really hope so, my dear.' Alice gripped her wrist, and Cari thought that, often, folk could say something and yet, by the tone of their voice, or the slightest of gestures, mean something entirely different.

I hope so,' Alice had said, but Cari knew she meant *Goodbye*.

10.30pm

Tom Priddy was pleased with his performance, never sung better, wiped the very last of the blackface from his ears while he waited for her in the downstairs passageway. And when she finally arrived, he held up one of the spare bottles of paraffin oil she'd hidden beneath her father's workbench.

'*Duw*, look what I've found, Beanpole.'

She shrugged herself out of the cloak, started quickly up the stairs.

'Tada,' she said. 'How is he?'

'Fine. So far as I know.' He dangled the bottle from his fingertips. 'Bed, see.'

'What's this, then?' said the Beanpole, and Tom sneered at her.

'Oh, I think you know fine well. But the question is, what for, eh?'

'Nothing to do with me, Cousin. But where's Taffy?'

'Half-rats, probably. The boozer. And I wonder why that should be, too. The police come a-knockin'. And off he goes. But the police were looking for you, *cariad*. For you, girl.'

'What did Taffy tell them?'

'There's interesting, it is. Anybody else, like, they'd have asked what the bobbies wanted them for. Not that the bobbies would say, mind. But you already know, isn't it?'

He climbed the stairs behind her, cursed himself for doing so. Time. He needed time. Room to think. He'd cleared his money out of the bank, the rest he'd been hiding under the mattress, stashed it all safely in the small carpet bag and been in the process of hiding the bag under the workbench when he'd rediscovered the bottles, moved there from the printshop cupboard.

'He'd have told them I'd gone to the meeting,' said the Beanpole, and threw the cloak onto the sofa. Her voice dropped to a whisper. 'And so I had.'

'Can't have been anything too serious, then. Or the police would have followed you there.'

'They did, Cousin. But I'd stepped out for a minute. With a couple of the girls. They didn't wait though so, as you say, nothing serious.'

'You're a terrible girl for secrets, Beanpole,' he laughed, then lowered his own voice. Time to share some of this with old Huw later, in the morning. 'One week you're sneaking off to the Seion Chapel. Then this.' He hefted the stone bottle in his hand again. 'So, what did you find out? About your precious tada? Not quite so God-fearing as you thought, maybe. All you kids, him and your mam not even married.'

'You sent me up there on purpose. I knew it. The photograph. Just too convenient, the marriage lines right there at the top of the box. What is it you're after, Cousin?'

She flopped herself down at the table, fixed him with those big eyes. Proud, she was. And her pride stirred him.

'But you're a good daughter, at least,' he laughed. 'Loyal, like. Not a word. *Duw*, I admire this in you, Cari Maddox. Heaven knows what would happen if our Winifred ever found out though. Imagine!'

'*Our* Winifred? You've some nerve.'

Tom made his way to the scullery. Hungry now. Not that there was ever much on the shelves.

'Fine girl, your sister. Shame, it is. She could have done so much better for herself. But tragic, now.'

He grinned at her, and he could see the penny beginning to drop.

'You told her? About the certificate? About…'

'And a few other things, Beanpole. Did you know her husband's got the syph?' It was like he'd punched her in the face. 'Filthy it is, like. And likely she's got it, an' all, see.'

'Wyn,' she said. 'Not Wyn.'

Disbelief. Denial. Then she sobbed. A choking sob.

'Anyhow,' he said. 'Thought I might as well tell her the rest. About *my* mam, for once. Sick of it, I am. *Your* mam this and *your* mam that. Never once thought to ask, did you, Beanpole? Told you once. I'll never be too grand for this family. Family of – well, you know the word, better than me, eh?'

Bastards, he thought. All of them bastards.

There was a bit of stale cheese left, wrapped in paper.

'Don't mind, do you, Beanpole?'

He bit into the crusty lump of Cheshire.

'The rest?' she said to him, and wiped a stupid tear from her cheek.

'Don't suppose you ever got much sense out of your tada, did you? And wrote to others in the family too, I reckon. What did you get back from them? Two lines, if you were lucky. Thomas Priddy nothing to do with *them*, though. Thank you and goodbye. Was that it? And never said anything about being *Owen* Priddy's son, did I?'

Tom watched her attempt to rally, gripping the edges of the table. He sat down opposite her.

'Then...' she began.

'Save you the trouble, I will. Not *Cousin* Thomas, Beanpole. Not his nephew at all. Huw Priddy's boy, I am. Left my mam when she was dying, see. Left me, an' all. Came here with your own tramp of a mother. You've been really busy, *cariad*. Letter from the solicitor in Carnarvon, all that stuff. But never once worked it out. Proud of yourself, is it?'

'You ever say anything about my mam again, Tom Priddy, and I swear I'll swing for you.' She sounded like she meant it, as well. 'And Nesta,' she said. 'The things you tried...'

'What – my sister? Who d'you think you are to judge me, girl? Got the Lord Jesus inside me, I have. And maybe Huw Priddy's boy. But not his son. Not really, like.'

He glanced across the room, saw the Lord Jesus smile at him, nod His head in approval.

'Tada wouldn't do that,' she said, and stood from the table, hands pressed to the sides of her head. 'He wouldn't.'

More wasted tears.

'Daft Beanpole. But you've still not told me about this.' He held up the bottle again.

'Nothing to do with me,' she murmured, but he could see the turmoil which must be racking her.

'Taffy's then, eh?' He gave her a hungry smile, set the bottle down, then crunched the bones of his hand together, popping the joints. 'Or maybe it belongs to your Fritzie friend. Interesting, it'll be. When I find out what you've really been doing. Why the bobbies are so interested in you. Once I know, well, then we can see.'

He'd been moving slowly closer to her, could feel the muscle spasm in his cheek again.

'Ernst is going back to sea,' she said.

Feeble, it was. She stood, edged away. Towards the scullery. Must hurt, he decided, thinking about the Fritzie. But it was just one more thing she'd have to brace herself for.

'Why should you care about him, one way or the other?' she said, back pressed to the doorframe. 'But Taffy. You think you've got a score to settle. Is that it? Why you pushed Theresa off the tram?'

Mad, he thought. As though she'd escaped from an asylum.

'*Duw annwyl*,' he sniggered. 'Priceless, it is. Priceless. Of course I pushed her. Papist whore. And here's the question you should have asked, girl. If your precious tada had his name on the marriage lines as Huw Maddox, does that mean he'd changed it legally, then? Must have done, I suppose. Or maybe the registrar just took his word for it. What d'you think, *cariad*? A man can get in serious trouble for using a false name on a marriage certificate. You know? Gaol, like. And then there's all this business selling illegal lottery tickets.'

'The sergeant, Ladysmith, he asked about the lottery tickets. Tada says it's all legal. Besides…'

Maybe she shouldn't have mentioned Ladysmith's name, of course. Because, as she did so, there was a hammering below, at the street door. And sometimes, when you name the Devil – well, up he pops.

'I'll get that, shall I?' Tom Priddy smirked, and he bounded down the stairs, leaving the Beanpole at the scullery door. He was sure it must be the police back again and desperate to find out what Ladysmith could possibly want from her. Yes, Sergeant. She's just got back, Sergeant. This way, Sergeant. What's this all about, Sergeant? And then, there he was, standing before them, upstairs. Sergeant Robert Ladysmith. And his usual companion, Constable Cooper. 'C' Division. Argyle Street Bridewell.

'Miss Ceridwen Maddox…' Ladysmith began.

And Tom Priddy didn't really hear the rest. His focus all on the

Beanpole herself. He was confused, saw her smile. But he heard the sergeant mention Lord Curzon. Charges being pressed. Assault. And the Beanpole almost laughed. As though she was somehow relieved.

'It was the Pathé moving picture,' she told the sergeant. An idiot's smile. 'Wasn't it? Nesta,' she murmured. 'I warned her, didn't I? Bloody Sunday. Told her it wasn't clever. The bobbies, I said.'

11.30pm

It was rather as Cari had pictured the place when she'd thought about Nesta being confined there – though, of course, Nessie had never got so far as seeing the inside of the cells. But Sergeant Ladysmith wasn't about to make the same mistake twice. This time he'd come with a hurry-up wagon and, despite the fog, the neighbours had turned out in force to watch her taken away, for the slow bone-shaking ride down Whitechapel's cobbles and across into Paradise Street, to Canning Place, before they finally reached the Bridewell.

And there she was hustled out of the back, into the building and straight into the dingy corridor with its six or seven holding rooms. Stark whitewashed walls, bare of all decoration. The inevitable bucket. A small gas light above the door but operated from outside. The plank suspended from the wall by its own chains, to serve as both bed and seat. And yes, painfully uncomfortable. The only surprise was the floors. All York stone elsewhere in the building, though seemed to have been recently surfaced in the actual cells. Asphalt, she thought. It smelt of asphalt.

Ladysmith filled the open doorway. She'd never taken much notice of him before, but now there was little else to capture Cari's attention, to distract her from the situation. And she was desperate to be distracted. Mid-thirties, dapper, his hair neatly oiled and centre-parted.

'I've some sympathy for your cause, miss. But these are serious charges.'

From one of the other cells came the sound of somebody being violently sick. In another, a man bellowing at the top of his lungs. Somebody was a whore, apparently. Deserved it. Cari dreaded to think what "it" might have been. Somehow, this brought back Tom Priddy's words. About Winifred. And the syph. Yes, she knew the word well enough. But all that rage about her tada. She didn't believe it. Wouldn't believe it. Not any of it.

'If I'd known when we were here this morning, Sergeant, I'd have turned myself in.'

It was a shabby attempt at *bravado*, made worse by the chattering of her teeth she couldn't prevent. All this. Tom Priddy's revelations. Winifred and Rhys Fingers. The thing about her father. Tom Priddy's father, she now knew. But abandoned a dying wife? She could not – would not – believe it.

And Theresa Mackenny? She'd known, of course, after her words with Mister Hughes. Tom Priddy had flirted with the girl. Knew her. The rest, all lies. Yet how in the name of heaven could she ever tell Taffy? Well, she wouldn't.

Yes, teeth chattering. But at least they'd allowed her to bring the cloak, and she pulled it about herself, huddled on the awful bench.

'Coincidence?' said Ladysmith. 'You'd only been gone an hour or so when the telegram arrived. Orders, like.'

'From Lord Curzon?'

'My superiors.' He leaned back, poked his head around into the corridor. 'Cooper!' he yelled. 'Constable Cooper. Tell that good-for-nothing excuse for a man if he doesn't shut his gob I'll come in there and dish out the same as he gave to that young girl. Can you believe it?' he said to her. 'Dock-wallopers, what would you do with them? Girlfriend jilted him so he dragged her to the church. Then beat her senseless at the church door. What's it all about, eh? Anyway, as I say, not without sympathy, miss. God knows, we've all got enough crosses to bear.'

'Everybody in the same boat?' said Cari. 'I suppose so. And shall I be represented?'

'You can afford it? Not really worth it anyway, if you ask me. The Beak will have you in and out of there in ten minutes.'

'Might take pity on me, don't you think?'

'Not with these charges. No chance. Throwing missiles? Disorderly conduct? Wounding a Peeress of the Realm? Suffragette in the bargain. They'll be throwing away the key, luv. No point beating about the bush.'

'Being a woman might just work in my favour.'

He laughed.

'After the riots, in August, the person they sent down for longest was poor Ellen the fruit hawker. Know who I mean? Six months, she got. And there was no Countess of Suffolk involved in that little lot.'

Cari remembered how her pride had been pricked when she'd seen the Pathé pictures with Gwilym. Pride, and now the inevitable fall. She and Nessie, flaunting their sashes. And those pictures had slowly done the rounds. Theatres all over the country. London, of course. London, where eventually they'd come to the attention of an American lady, Daisy Hyde Leiter, who'd identified the taller of the two anarchist women as the very same who'd struck her with that abominable missile back in June.

The lady reported this to her husband, and then to her brother-in-law, Lord Curzon.

The same Lord Curzon who'd financed those silly sandwichmen, with their boards and message from the Antis. *Women Do NOT Want the Vote!*

The same Lord Curzon who had now initiated a private investigation and finally gleaned the name of this suffragette felon from the pages of the Pathé cameraman's notebook. Since his sister-in-law also happened to be the Countess of Suffolk, and wanted to maintain as much anonymity as possible, Scotland Yard had taken the matter seriously indeed, communicated with the Liverpool Watch Committee, and the Watch Committee had – well, it was all pretty obvious.

Lord Curzon, former Viceroy of India, now prominent in the House of Lords. What was he, these days? A Baron? A Viscount? Cari couldn't recall. But he despised the women's suffrage movement, this much was sure.

'Countess of Suffolk,' she said, and feared the worst. 'I suppose you must be right. There'll be no pity for Cari Maddox. Funny though. The worst thing about that day was how the silly woman dropped her champagne bottle. Knocked some poor man senseless. Don't suppose they care about him, though.'

She remembered the newspaper reports. The poor fellow had received only the briefest of mentions in the *Daily Mail*.

'You've enough to worry about with these charges, miss. You

don't need any more. Unless you've anything to confess, of course. There was the attack on Mister Haldane back in March. I always wondered about that one from the first time I saw you. Suffragette. Tall and thin. Black cloak. *This* cloak, miss, I'm guessing. The very one wrapped around your shoulders. But not on my patch, Lime Street. Nor this latest thing.'

'Latest thing?'

He gave her a whimsical smile, shook his head.

'If anything's more serious than assaulting a Peeress of the Realm, Miss Maddox, it's probably committing an act of deliberate arson against the Royal Mail. Like an attack on the King himself, God bless him. Not my patch though, like I said.'

'If you asked my tada, he'd tell you he's always known I'd come to no good.'

'Maybe. But the pasty fellow who was with you. Cousin, isn't he?'

What could she tell him? The truth?

'Distant cousin, that's all,' she said.

'As may be, but said something interesting, he did, before I left. Asked whether the fire had been set using paraffin oil. So, I says to him: How would you know that, sir? And he says: Well, it seemed like the obvious thing. But, if so, he says, perhaps we should talk to your brother. And, while we're at it, maybe have a look through your brother's belongings in the printshop's paper loft. Why would this be, d'you think? Your brother another of these anarchists, is he? Anyway, like I say, not my patch. Not my job to do Cheapside's dirty work for them. But this, miss. Whatever made you do it? Throwing stones at a lady and all.'

'It was an apple, Sergeant.'

'Your defence, Miss?'

'From what you say, Sergeant, I suspect it's as good as any other. And at least it shouldn't take up too much of the Beak's precious time.'

But she was thinking about Nesta, and how she'd laughed when Cari told her the story. Nobody but Nesta, of course. 'You know what else is funny, though?' she said. 'When I heard you were looking for me, I imagined it must be because you had news. About my sister.'

'I wish I did, Miss Maddox.'

'You believe it, though? About the white slavers?'

'In this city, lass, I'd believe anything.'

It was only half an answer, of course. By then, the dock-walloper was yelling again and Constable Cooper was threatening him with a beating if he didn't quieten down. And, in that other cell, the fellow had stopped being sick, it seemed, but was now snoring so loudly Cari could swear he made the walls shake.

'Please,' she said, as Ladysmith turned to his other duties. 'Might the door be left open?'

It seemed he would reply but, in the end, he simply sighed, and slammed the door shut behind him. Then, a moment later, the gas light spluttered and died, left her alone in this dark pit, with its stink of urine.

Chapter Twelve

Thursday 23rd November 1911

6.00am

Before first light, Amos was out of the lodging house. Long before he needed to be with Skipper Coleman at the *Otter*.

To be honest, he'd barely slept. Last night, the temptation had been too great and, after the play had been over, he'd waited and waited outside the stage door, followed the devil man back to the house – the one which had once been Miss Nesta's house. He'd had no particular plan. Not really.

Perhaps he should have shared the thing he witnessed there. But he'd decided it would not help. A thing he must do himself. For they had taken Missee Coconut Palm away. The po-leese had done so. Why? He had no idea. And keeping the secret to himself had been an awful burden.

Yet, during the torment of his night, the Lord Jesus – or perhaps Nyesoa – had shown him the way. A way which led him, in those cold but mercifully fog-free early hours, to the yard and stables of Hatton & Cookson, African Merchants. Mersey Street. And the man he knew would help. King Billy.

7.00am

There was no sleep. The line of Dickens reciting itself in Cari's mind, over and over again. A great city. Tumbling and tossing in its restlessness.

Between the lines? Cari's woes all listed together.

The coming dawn, and some foolish waking dream of divine intervention, or a magistrate so moved by her pitiable appearance he might commute the sentence to some non-custodial punishment.

The horrors of her dream failing to find fruition, and the images of Walton's evils awaiting her.

Fears that, however foul her own future might be, it could not be worse than whatever fate had befallen Nessie.

Visions of Tom Priddy standing before her once more – his sudden vitriol towards her tada, and the threat of using the paraffin oil, or other things, as some lever against Taffy, as a way of settling whatever score seemed to obsess him.

The way Creeping Cousin Thomas – she couldn't think of him any other way – had manipulated her, led her to see the marriage certificate, to understand the hole at the heart of her family.

Wyn and the syph. This, almost the worst of all. For, though she'd not believed it when Tom Priddy spoke the words, here in the Bridewell's grim pre-dawn, it seemed all too possible.

The many questions which crawled out of the hole. About whether the marriage itself between Mam and Tad was lawful. About whether any of them were even entitled to call themselves Maddox. About whether those lottery tickets might bring the law down on her tada's own head. And about the absurd loan hanging over him.

Cari's knowledge that she might have lost Ernst Jurks through her own stubborn pride.

And her guilt. Guilt for not having believed, as her tada had done, in Nesta's innocence. Guilt at having so easily believed Taffy to be capable of betraying her to the bobbies.

Her continuing guilt at having wished poor little Pryce gone.

And her permanent guilt at simply being a woman. Guilt that, as a woman, she might perhaps, after all, truly be a second-class creation of the Almighty. Guilt that, as a woman, and as Winifred had once said, she might be betraying the Lord's purpose by not making herself attractive to men. Guilt that, as a woman, indeed, she had never known carnal pleasures with a man. Guilt that, as a woman, if He had genuinely intended women to be equal, the Lord would not have cursed them with monthly degradations to be hidden away so carefully from the world. And guilt that, as a woman, she should feel this depressive burden at all.

Yet, there was this. More Dickens. More *Great Expectations*, she was sure, though not a paragraph she could ever remember from her tada's lips. Something she'd read and remained with her. Something along these lines. About memorable days. About this being such a day. A day that makes great changes in people's lives. About how it is the same with any life. You should imagine how striking one selected day from your life might change its entire course.

And then the great man invited readers to pause, to think about the long chain of either gold or iron – she believed those were the metals – or of flowers or thorns, that would never have wrapped themselves around us, never have bound us, never have changed our course, had it not been for the first link in the chain, forged on this one memorable day.

9.00am

Tom Priddy wasn't happy. He should have been on his way by now. He could not, of course, have missed the delicious moment when he woke old Huw, finally managed to shake Daft Taffy from his drunken stupor. Broke the news. The arrest. And then, this morning, early, as old Huw fussed and fretted, getting himself ready to head for the Magistrates' Court, the Lord Jesus had chosen His moment to strike. A heart attack. Carted off to the Infirmary.

Still, not happy. Needed to know how it would all unfold. For the Beanpole. Delightful images of seeing her carted off to Walton.

Yet the Dale Street courthouses were busy this morning. Yesterday's fog had brought out felons by the score, it seemed.

He'd eventually discovered in which of the seven courtrooms her case would be heard. And yes, one of the ushers had confirmed, Ceridwen Maddox had been brought there earlier from Argyle Street. Now languishing below in one of the communal cells, Tom imagined. With the whores and thieves, where she belonged.

Hours went by, until the same usher returned to him.

'Ten minutes, sir,' the fellow told him. 'Thereabouts. Courtroom number five. But I should get in sharpish, if I were you. Full house today.'

Tom was almost tempted to offer his own services. Speak for her. He thought he'd make a good fist of it. Just a different sort of acting. But when he'd squeezed himself into the oak-panelled pews along one side of the courtroom, he saw there were already solicitors waiting to take the case. A whole team of them on one batch of the pews filling the centre of the room, each row with its own green leather writing slopes. The Prosecution, surely.

Wood panelling everywhere, now Tom came to look around. Nice. Gave the whole place a pleasant, warm feel. He liked it there.

Nearer to him, a lone figure. Thirty, perhaps. Good-looking, Tom supposed. Dark, well-trimmed and oiled hair. Thin, sharp and intelligent features. Stand-up wing collar and bright scarlet tie.

'Now, where did *you* come from?' Tom Priddy murmured.

'Quilliam,' said the fellow next to him and following Tom's gaze. 'That's Billal Quilliam.'

He spoke the words as though Tom was an idiot. But it meant nothing to him, and this neighbour had now set down his notepad, introduced himself as Patterson, from the *Echo*.

'Quilliam?' said the reporter. 'You must know him. Carters' Union. Their solicitor. The Strike Committee?'

It began to come back. The *Daily Post* had carried the full text of one of his speeches. And old Huw had hit the roof.

'Quilliam,' he'd said. 'You know who's his father, like?'

Tom hadn't known.

'*Blydi* Abdullah Quilliam, that's who.'

The story had poured forth. This particular Quilliam – this solicitor's father – had once been William Quilliam. Daft name anyway, it was. William Quilliam? But then converted to Islam. Islam! And changed his name to Abdullah. Even opened a mosque, of all things. Brougham Terrace, wasn't it? Closed now. And this Abdullah bloke no longer in England. Well, good riddance, old Huw had said.

But now? The son, here to represent the Beanpole. How...?

Almost noon by the time policemen brought her in through the side door, straight into the square dock behind the solicitors' pews. Looked dreadful, she did. Could barely stand. Kept herself upright by clinging to the brass rail topping the dock's solid wooden walls. She stared straight ahead, a wild look of crazed confusion in her eyes.

'Bet she's not slept a wink,' he said.

'Know her?' said the reporter, checking his notes. 'Miss – Maddox, isn't it? Oh, goodness. This should be interesting. Lord Curzon.'

'All rise!' shouted the usher, and the Beak entered. Little shrew of a man. Spectacles perched on the end of his nose. He settled himself at the raised bench – curved and panelled to match the rest of the décor – among his clerks and several stacks of legal volumes. Everybody else resumed their seats, except the Beanpole, of course.

'Mister Quilliam,' the Beak's voice was surprisingly strident. 'You have a petition for me, I understand.' One of the clerks handed him a document. 'Release on Own Recognisance?'

The solicitor stood to confirm, and Tom Priddy saw amazement spread across the Beanpole's face. So, she'd not expected to have a solicitor, either.

The Beak turned to the Prosecution's extensive team. Much whispering between them as though this was an unexpected turn of events.

'And this is opposed, Mister Bright, I imagine?'

It was, indeed. No prior notice of such a petition. Then the arguments presented. Such a serious offence must surely attract no less than a custodial sentence – the ultimate permissible in this court. The girl's brother a known agitator. She, herself, closely associated with those involved in the London riots earlier in the week. Active member of the Women's Social and Political Union. The most militant of the suffrage groups. *Extremely* active.

Risk of flight, as well, Bright insisted. Family in foreign parts. And known to have intimate liaison among aliens. Germans, to be precise. Yes, Your Honour, Germans.

12.15pm

Had it not been for Ernst Jurks, Cari believed she could have loved Solicitor Quilliam. Those soothing, hypnotic tones. Yet where had he come from? Had her tada somehow organised this?

'Your Honour,' he'd argued, 'if the defendant had truly intended violence, she would hardly have chosen an apple. And, at that, certainly never a crumbly Blenheim.'

A ripple of laughter, while the magistrate shuffled through his briefing papers, trying to discover whether the Prosecution had, indeed, determined the variety. But plainly not. He allowed the point to pass, as Billal Quilliam went on to remind the court how the *accident*

– he had already stressed the word several times – had occurred five months previously and, in all those weeks, the defendant had never shown the slightest inclination towards the leaving of Liverpool.

'And family in foreign parts, Your Honour? Wales, I believe.'

Further subdued laughter.

But yes, he said, a woman seeking facility, within the law, for women to enjoy the additional and modest ability to vote in parliamentary elections.

'A quest, Your Honour, which I know you will confirm to be no crime unto itself.'

He paused. A moment of dramatic effect, during which the magistrate craned forward, peered at him through those wire-rimmed spectacles. Cari suspected there might just be a skeleton in the old devil's cupboard.

'And not a single offence to her name. Not one. A young lady of impeccable character, industriously employed.'

He gave the details at length, mentioned Mister Kaplan by name. Just one more gentleman delighted to provide a reference. And, Cari wondered, had it been old Kaplan, then, who'd arranged the solicitor. If so, how?

'And her family members?' said Quilliam. 'No blemish there, either. My learned friend has cast something of a slur against the defendant's brother. Yet I have, here, a sworn statement signed by Sergeant Ladysmith – the constabulary's 'C' Division.'

A clerk took the paper, passed it to the Beak, while Quilliam explained its confirmation. There existed no criminal record attached to any member of the defendant's family.

Well, thought Cari, feeling her spirits finally begin to lift. Ladysmith. How about that? And thank the Lord he'd so recently discovered the truth about Nesta – though he must have worded the statement carefully enough to avoid mention of all the time Nessie had spent as a fugitive from justice. Poor Nesta! She felt a familiar tear trickle down her cheek.

The magistrate studied Ladysmith's affidavit, while Cari, wiping away the tear, noticed Quilliam turning to face her. He was staring at her, his thin lips pursed, sorrow in his eyes. What? Did he not think things were going well? She certainly couldn't fault him for his efforts, though she still had no idea how he came to be here. Tada? Kaplan?

'But Your Honour.' The solicitor addressed the Bench once more. 'There is, I fear, one final thing to say about the defendant's family. A matter of some delicacy since it is, as yet, unknown even to the defendant herself. A distressing matter, which I am loathe to raise.'

Cari gripped the brass bar of the dock. Delicacy? Distressing?

'A matter,' she heard Quilliam say, 'concerning the defendant's father.'

1.00pm

Tom Priddy could scarcely believe it. Things weren't going so well. An ill-wind, he thought.

And so it was, for yesterday's fog now replaced with this howling gale. Sprung from nowhere. Not unusual for Liverpool, of course. Always a strong breeze from the river. It had made things tolerable even during those many scorching months. But this was a beast. A beast from the east, he decided, pleased with his Welsh gift for poetry. Yet he struggled against its full force as he stepped out of the court, onto Dale Street, and clapped a hand on top of his head to keep the cap in place.

No, not going well.

Yesterday and pox-faced Winifred. He'd hoped for some dramatic closing scene. Rage, or something. Promise to kill herself. He could have helped her with it, see. But no, simply repeated more bits of scripture. About husbands. About obedience. Further nonsense about how Rhys Gateman was simply the way Lord Jesus had made him. How Lord Jesus would protect her. Her husband, as well. And nonsense? Of course, it was nonsense. Tom had checked. Checked with Lord Jesus that very night. Before old Huw…

And there was another thing. He crossed Hatton Garden where a tram was making the difficult turn into Manchester Street and he wondered how it could be that old Huw wasn't dead. Well, hadn't been when they took him, anyway. Taffy had run for Doctor Graham, up on Christian Street. And Doctor Graham had confirmed the heart attack. Serious. An ambulance needed. The nearest? Across the road at Mellor's Brewery where they kept a dedicated covered cart for just such a purpose, in case of industrial accident. Old Huw had been bundled aboard, in the fog, and trundled away. Still breathing, by some miracle, though only just. At least Tom had enjoyed the pleasure of seeing the effect it had on the Beanpole earlier, when that solicitor had announced the thing. Trying to play on the Beak's sympathies, of course. Shameless, it was.

Yet, maybe by now old Huw would indeed be dead. But how to find out? From Daft Taffy? From the Beanpole herself?

Outside the Red Lion, some black-garbed Bridget was being dragged from the alehouse, dead drunk and cursing like the devil. The demon drink, he thought.

And yes, Daft Taffy. There was another thing. That fool Ladysmith. Not the slightest interest in picking up the trail which would have led him to Florrie Thompson-Frere's possessions. Or the paraffin oil. It had been in the *Post* this morning. Letterbox. Exchange Flags. *Duw annwyl*, could it *really* have been the Beanpole? If so, perhaps he'd underestimated her.

But Ladysmith? Not his patch, he'd said. Well, before Tom left, he'd have to scribble a note, get it to the main Bridewell. About the lottery business, as well. Afterwards, he'd collect his things and catch the train to Birmingham. With Daft Taffy's name over the door, and old Huw hopefully dead, maybe they'd hold Taffy responsible. Or maybe the pair of them locked up in Walton. Face justice.

Around the corner into Byrom Street, the demolition site on this side of the road, the Technical School on the other. The wind even stronger here, gusting down from Scotland Road.

Yet justice? No real justice in this world, he knew. Look what had happened back there. The Magistrates' Court. Some smart-mouth, church-bell of a lawyer. Son of a man who'd chosen to become a heathen. Chosen. Convert to Islam, indeed. Might have known, Tom thought.

He stopped at Maypole's Dairy, bought himself some cheese to take on the train, and he was about to cross, waiting for a gap in the traffic – the trams, the carts, the steam wagons – when his eye was drawn towards the doorway of the Temperance Hotel opposite.

A fellow who looked entirely out of place. A nobby on his head, the Derby's brim turned down at front and back. And a double-breasted

Ulster, chequered, dull mustard. Not the sort of everyday attire you'd expect to see on Byrom Street. Expensive. Showy, like. To make matters worse, he was pretending to read a newspaper – entirely impossible in this wind – when anybody with half a brain could see he was watching out for something, or somebody.

Tom had a nasty suspicion it might be he, himself, for whom this rogue was keeping watch.

Well, the train could wait. There'd be another later. And meanwhile he'd wait until it was dark before heading back to the house. Pass the time at St. Stephen's maybe. Chat with his Lord Jesus a while.

4.15pm

It was almost dark when a boy brought the note. To the *Otter*. And as soon as she was all stowed away safely, everything battened down, Skipper Coleman invited Amos to join him at the Baltic. Wet their whistles, he'd said. Help him with the words, like – if Amos needed it.

Amos could read them just fine. But the meaning? This was another thing.

'Released on Own Recognisance?' said the skipper, wiping froth from his lips. 'Means she's been freed. No conviction.'

'Not gaol place?'

Amos swigged his own drink, took a drag on his cigarette. He'd developed a taste for porter. A taste for the Baltic, also. Common ground, it seemed, for every imaginable skin colour and creed. Like some Ark of Noah. All peoples of the world, two by two. Even the building's corner shaped like the prow of a ship. Yet, this afternoon, its windows rattled, its walls seemed to shake.

'No, Amos. No gaol place. But your mate says here she's been bound over. Twelve months. Fifty quid and two sureties. Twenty-five quid each.'

He might as well have been speaking this Greek the Wolof talked about so often. And there was much noise. Hard to concentrate. Dock men. Sailors. All seemingly shouting at the same time.

'Bound over,' Skipper Coleman repeated. 'Means she's had to agree to keep the peace – behave herself – for them twelve months. A year. If she doesn't, she'll have to pay this fifty quid. A fine, like. And dragged back to court. Face whatever charges she's managed to dodge this time around.'

'These sureties?' Amos asked him.

'Same thing. She'll need to have two other people. People prepared to promise they'll each hand over twenty-five quid if she's a bad girl.'

In the corner, a bunch of sailors had begun to sing. Men with hair like straw. Norway men? he wondered. Like the fellows who'd beaten him all those months ago? It seemed so long. Not the same Norway men, surely?

Even if they had been, Amos had different scores to settle.

First, a burden to share. He'd intended to do so last night. With Missee Coconut Palm. But then the po-leese, and she'd been taken away.

But after he'd shed the burden, there must be revenge. Yes, he remembered the verse from Jeremiah. *Do no violence to the stranger, the fatherless, nor the widow, neither shed innocent blood in this place.* But he believed the Lord Jesus Nyesoa would allow him this. Revenge against the devil man.

5.00pm

Cari reached Pembroke Place entirely breathless. Run all the way, against that filthy wind, arrived at the red brick symmetry of the Infirmary.

'My father,' she said at the Porter's Lodge. 'Huw Maddox.'

Her shoe's heel stamped involuntarily, up and down, on the floor tiles, while the porter checked the ledgers.

'Here, Miss,' he said, at last. 'Ward eight. It's...'

She didn't wait. Followed the signs instead. Up the palatial central staircase to the first floor and along the corridor to her left. An arched corridor, the walls tiled. Exotic. Like a picture she'd once seen of a Moorish palace.

Her tada! When Quilliam had told the magistrate, she'd almost fainted. Serious? It couldn't be, surely. Though enough to sway the Beak, anyway. And no, the solicitor had no more to tell her when she was finally released.

'But these sureties,' she'd said.

'You mustn't trouble yourself about those, Miss Maddox. One of them pledged by your Mister Kaplan, I understand.'

'The other?'

'Why,' he smiled, 'the Carters' Union. It seems you have friends of friends.'

There'd been no time for more. Yet she couldn't go to the hospital looking that way. Back to the house. Empty, thank goodness. Mixed feelings, however. Perhaps, for once, Tom Priddy would have been useful, known something more about her poor tada. Tidied herself, though, as best she was able. Then her footrace up London Road.

She passed through one of the hospital's rotundas, turned into the medical ward she was seeking. Past the separation room, the convalescents' dining area, the scullery and the sister's office. Thirty beds, and no sign of her tada. She stopped at one of the nurses' tables.

'Very end,' said the nurse. 'But I'm sorry, it's not…'

And there they were. Taffy perched on a chair at his tada's bedside. Her father almost unrecognisable. His bed just next to the doorway out to the bathrooms and the balcony. Cold, and somehow the combined smell of hospital cooking, carbolic and excrement stronger there than anywhere else in the ward.

'Cari.' Taffy jumped to his feet. 'Oh, thank god. They let you go.'

'How is he?' she said. But no need to ask.

'Doctor says it's a miracle he's still with us,' said Taffy. 'Massive heart attack.'

'Not woken up?' Cari saw her tada's tragically sunken features. The pallor. A hint of purple about his lips.

Then the sound of footsteps marching down the ward. Angry footsteps, she could tell.

'I believe Nurse Kelly,' the sister snapped at them, 'has already tried to remind you these aren't visiting hours. Now, if you please…'

She pointed towards the opposite end of the ward, the way out.

'Visiting hours?' said Cari. 'My tada's dying – can't you see?'

'My dear,' the sister was condescending, glanced up at the ward clock, 'if we consider your father might be dying, I can assure you we shall make special arrangements. But until then you will need to apply for a visiting card. Details on the wall, as you leave. Sundays, two until three-thirty. Wednesday, three until four.'

They were ushered back along the ward.

'Oh,' said the sister, 'and no food or drink, other than eggs and fruit – and then only if sanctioned by the Medical Officer.'

'I registered all our details last night,' said Taffy, as they retraced their steps through the Infirmary's Arabic elegance.

'Listen,' she said to him, and paused on the wide staircase, 'there's something I have to tell you...'

'Whatever it is, Cari, it can wait. How did they let you go?'

'Long story. But bound over, that's all. More or less all, anyhow. And not allowed to travel outside the boundaries of Lancashire. No more London trips for a while – thank heaven. But what I have to tell you – no, it can't wait.'

She took a few more steps down towards the ground floor.

'Tom bloody Priddy,' she said, though needing to be careful not to let her tongue run away with itself.

She repeated the tale from last night. Warned him, how he'd tried to persuade Sergeant Ladysmith to search Taffy's belongings. For what? She had no idea.

'But listen,' she whispered, 'I have a confession to make.'

The letterbox. And, more important, she feared Tom Priddy might have planted some of the paraffin oil in Taffy's room, as well.

'You?' Taffy laughed. 'The letterbox burner?'

'For pity's sake,' she snapped. 'Keep your voice down. And yes. Me. Though that's not all.'

At the porter's lodge, they picked up the forms for the visiting cards.

'Not all?' said Taffy, when they were back outside. The wind, if anything, was even stronger now.

No, she said. Not all. Not by a long chalk. She told him about Winifred. And about Rhys Fingers. About the marriage certificate. About the phoney lottery business. But it took the whole walk back down London Road, its bustling department stores now all closed for the night, before he believed her.

'I'll go find the bastard...' he began, almost choked, tried to bite back the word, then laughed. Bitter laughter.

'Need to be more careful how I use that one in future, eh? But he deserves a good hiding, one way or the other.'

A hiding? she thought. Good job I've not told him about Theresa. And nor would she. Some things better left buried, along with poor Theresa herself.

'No,' she said. 'There's one more thing. About Tada. And Tom Priddy's mam.'

'What's mad Cousin Thomas's mam, got to do with this?'

She explained carefully. Not *Cousin* Thomas at all. And, thankfully, Taffy decided at this point he needed a drink. Or two, maybe. Good, she'd said, and persuaded him perhaps for tonight he should stay with Ma MacKenny. Things she needed to do for herself. Apart from anything else, she must put things right with Ernst Jurks.

5.45pm

Tom Priddy kept to the windswept shadows. The far side of Hunter Street. Then across into Dawson Place. He checked the gate to the printshop. No sign of anybody, so back to the front door, fumbled with his keys and slipped inside.

He stood in the darkness at the bottom of the stairs, listened. Nothing but the gale, shaking the window frames.

Tom loosened his overcoat, lifted the cap from his head – the cap he'd inherited from Rees – and slipped it into his pocket, careful to avoid the single-edged Kampfe blade hidden in the peak. Then, up the stairs. From his own room, a few possessions, though not many. His bible. His little black journal. His razor. He would buy anything else he needed when he reached Birmingham. Or perhaps he would buy nothing at all. And yes, he'd settled on Birmingham. Mister Mantlemere, the Rotunda's manager, had an associate at the Hippodrome and there was every possibility of a senior position.

For now, however, there was old Huw's mahogany tea caddy. The marriage certificate. He'd forgotten to share that particular snippet with pox-faced Winifred and, somehow, he doubted whether the Beanpole could be trusted to do so. Winifred, he laughed to himself. A bastard. The knowledge, he was sure, would kill her.

Downstairs again. He pushed the old baby carriage out of the way and knelt to retrieve the small carpet bag from beneath the workbench. Hard to see without any light to help him, and his hand reached this way and that – but it wasn't there.

He tried again, fingers brushing against the wooden tray of shoemakers' tools, the cobbler's last, tack hammer, pincers and tin of boot studs. Tom shifted the tray to one side, explored the very back of the bench. Nothing but cobwebs. Something running across his wrist.

He snatched his hand back, shook it. He felt stupid. Spider? He guessed so.

But was his mind playing tricks? Where had he left it? The bag. The money. A moment of panic. The Beanpole? Daft Taffy? No, he was certain they must both still have been at the Infirmary. Then…?

Tom glanced along the darkened passageway towards the printshop. The merest glimmer of light beneath the door.

'Rise, let us go from here,' he heard his Lord Jesus whisper in his ear.

'But, Lord,' he whispered, 'today I forgot to repeat the curse.'

Psalm 109. Dangerous. Because, if the curse was not repeated, every morning and every night – well, it was likely to rebound on the curse-sayer. Wasn't that what he'd been taught?

"Let his days be few; and let another take his office."

Yet, if the Lord Jesus instructed him to go forth, who was Tom Priddy to gainsay Him? Still, better to be safe than sorry, and he bent once more to pick up the hammer.

He groped his way along the wall, the hammer hefted in his right hand, just in case. He felt for the doorknob, turned it carefully, silently, and eased the door ajar, the vertical line of meagre light widening a little. Still dim.

Tom peered into this sliver of luminescence, though it didn't help. And, from within, not a sound.

He pushed the door still wider, poked his head through the gap. And the entire world exploded in his face. Pain. He cried out. Violent pain in the back of his skull, through his open jaw. And a descent into blackness.

6.00pm

Amos had watched the devil man. Creeping round in the dark places near Missee Coconut Palm's house. Yes, he'd decided, time to make him pay.

Yet, earlier, when he'd arrived to begin his vigil, to await his prey, there'd been another.

A strange fellow, dressed – Amos could see in the brief moments when he crept into a patch of light – in a coat that might have come from a giraffe. But mostly the giraffe man remained in the shadows also, only the flapping of the coat's tails to give away his location. Finally, during a temporary break in the traffic, he'd darted across the road and into the lane behind the house.

Then, nothing.

Nothing until the devil man slunk into view.

Amos huddled in his old greatcoat, watched him unlock the street door. But now what? What was happening? Two of them inside. And while he had no fear of the devil man, that other fellow moved more with the predatory stealth of a crocodile than the elegant steps of a giraffe.

He moved from his own hiding place, behind the stone pillar, part of the gateway for the beer brewing place, a sickly-sweet aroma blowing in the wind.

Across the road. Hunter Street, Miss Nesta had once told him. And here they were. Amos hunting the devil man. But this crocodile fellow, with his giraffe-skin coat – how was *he* part of the hunt?

At the corner of the lane, he halted, listening. When his eyes adjusted to the darkness once more, he could see another door, a gate, further along, where the backstreet opened into an alleyway.

And from inside that gate, a cry of anguish.

6.00pm

His head throbbed. Every inch of him hurt. And there was a burning sensation. His neck. His wrists. He couldn't feel his ankles at all.

Tom Priddy tried to open his eyes, and his eyes filled with pain.

Through his blurred and aching vision, he saw somebody else's eyes staring back at him, the stink of onion on the man's breath.

'So, what happened to him?'

Cardiff accent. South Wales, anyhow. Not proper Welsh, like.

Tom tried to shake his head. To deny knowing what his captor was talking about. But the rope binding his neck to the back of the chair chafed at his flesh.

'Who?' he whispered through gritted teeth. And thirsty. He couldn't remember ever having been so thirsty.

'Listen shit-face. Wearin' his shoes, you are. Who the piss d'you think I mean?'

Tom Priddy could just about see the toe of his own right foot, though it nearly strangled him to twist his head so far. The two-tone shoes he'd taken from Lewis at Waugh's. Not clever, it wasn't. And he couldn't move the foot. His ankles must be tied to the chair's legs just as his wrists were bound to the arms.

The chair. The tall ladder-back chair he'd used so many times when operating the Cropper. Once again, he could just see the printing press from the corner of his other eye. On the table, next to the machine, his bag. Alongside the bag, those bottles of paraffin oil he'd discovered. A paraffin lamp also, the wick turned down low, just enough light to bathe the printshop in butterfly shadows, fluttering with the chill breeze blowing in through the gate to Dawson Place. The wretch must have left it partly open. Close to the lamp, a bunch of skeleton keys and the few possessions Tom had brought from upstairs, as well as the hammer he'd been carrying.

'Yeah, nice haul, though,' said the man, and glanced at the bag as well, while toying with an evil-looking cosh. 'Only thing I don't understand, though. How, like? Rees and brother Bob. You. A little frog like you? Had help, eh? That scabby little bastard who lives here too?'

This one had the same way of cordial menace as his brother. But Daft Taffy? Tom would have laughed if he'd been able.

'So, the only question now, shit-face, is what to do with you.'

He brushed some dust from that double-breasted Ulster, and looked around the room. Tom saw his gaze settle, first upon the guillotine, then upon the Cropper.

'Now, that would be interesting.'

Tom Priddy had the terrible thought he knew exactly what might be going through the man's mind. For he, himself, would have come to the same conclusion. You could do a lot of damage to a body with a printing machine. Yet the fellow scratched at his chin, shook his head. Instead, he took a couple of steps over to the table, set down the cosh, brought one of the stoppered bottles back and held it up in front of Tom's face.

'Money's one thing. An' I'd told brother Bob he'd come to no good up 'ere. Flint?' he laughed. 'Imagine anybody livin' in a place called Flint. Shithole. Long way from Cardiff, like. But word spreads, see. You imagine, froggy? Word that my kid brother's been scrubbed out by some useless prick like you – and guilty party not paid the price? Christ, how long before some other little turd comes knockin' on *my* door? Lookin' to make a name for 'imself.'

He pulled the cork from the stone bottle, slowly poured the oil onto the top of Tom Priddy's head. Tom closed his eyes, tight shut, felt the paraffin trickle down the sides of his face, into his ears, onto his neck. He felt his bladder spasm, wet himself and felt the warm spread of urine down his legs. Not by fire, he prayed. Please, Lord, not by fire.

'Going to Birmingham, I am,' Tom spluttered through the oil dribbling across his lips. 'Don't know anything about your brother, neither. Other part's true, though. Going to do a runner, I was. With the money, like.'

He had to spit out more of the paraffin.

'But there's more there than I owed your Bob. Lots more. You could take that an' just let me go, see.'

The man had grabbed another of the bottles, was sprinkling the contents all over Tom Priddy's coat.

'Where'd be the fun in that, froggy? Let you go? Havin' a laugh, you are. Big of you, like. Ownin' up. The money, an' all. Somethin', I suppose. So, thievin', is it? Where to start? The machine maybe. Crush one of the hands, like. An' if you won't talk about what happened to my kid brother – well...'

He went back to the table, and Tom watched him pick up his straight razor.

'Won't be needin' that tongue of yours anymore, eh?'

'Wait,' said Tom. 'There's more. Upstairs in the paper loft. Something valuable.'

The man delved into the ample pocket of his Ulster, drew out a small notebook and the Thompson-Frere woman's timepiece, dangled the watch from his fingers.

'This, you mean? Already been there, see.' He dropped the two items back in his pocket. 'No. Think I've got all I need. So, first the hand. Then the tongue. After – well, you're goin' to fry, froggy. Fry, see.'

Tom had to squeeze his buttocks together, that he might not soil himself still further. God knew he'd taken his share of lives. Yet he had never revelled in tormenting those he'd killed. Or had he? No, he was certain. But this fellow? Terrified him. For the first time in his life, terrified. And his captor had moved out of Tom's vision, to the back of the chair.

Tom could feel the rogue's hands behind his shoulders, holding the back posts, tipping him, dragging him towards the Cropper. For some reason, the feeling seemed to be coming back into his feet, but it was a minor comfort.

Lord, why hast Thou forsaken me?

But, of course, the Lord Jesus hadn't forsaken him at all. There He was, only feet away, smiling at him, as the man explored the Cropper, fiddled with the wheel until he'd worked out how to bring up the rollers, ready for the machine's bed to come crashing down against the platen. Then he came around to the front of the chair, used the razor to slice through the rope binding Tom's right wrist. But his grip – impossibly strong, pinning Tom's hand to the arm of the chair.

'Nice blade,' said the man, savouring the moment and holding up the razor, admiring its edge. 'Handy later.' He used it to nick Tom's cheek, a stinging cut, to set blood running, mingling with the paraffin oil. Then he closed the thing, one-handed, slipped the razor into his pocket as well.

'Now,' he murmured, moved his grip to Tom's wrist, yanked the hand across – Tom trying all the time to drag it back, keep it from harm. But it was weak. From being tied, maybe. It just wouldn't respond. But at least he'd keep his fist balled, he thought, as if this were some protection.

The man lifted the fist, slammed it down onto the machine's iron bed, panting now with the effort. Strong, thought Tom, but *how* strong? He tried to pull away, felt the chair tip backwards. Not much but maybe enough. The man tried a second time, and a second time Tom recoiled, tipping the chair still further. Momentum now. And as the fellow pulled him for a third time, the chair rocking forward, Tom found his feet, launched himself at his assailant, caught the man off balance, sent him staggering back.

Tom and the chair crashed onto the hard floor of the printshop.

The man pitched into the table. The remaining bottles of paraffin oil teetered from the table's edge and shattered, each in turn, their contents splashing all about.

The paraffin lamp plunged to the floor as well.

Tom's head was almost at the same level, his one free hand scrabbling at the rope around his neck and the chair's top rail. Then at the cord binding his other arm. He saw a thin and unbroken rivulet of blue flame snaking from the broken lamp, though the paraffin spilt on the floor, to the dampened skirt of the man's yellow-chequered Ulster.

He saw the fellow panic, batting his hands against the burning material, then try to stand, but stumbling over the stacks of flyers on which old Huw had last been working. The stacks picked up the flames. And the flames climbed higher.

And Tom saw the flames spread across the floor like a flood. Spread by the wind from outside. Spread towards him.

6.20pm

Amos heard the crash. He saw a thin column of light flare up at that place where the back door stood. Then a scream, followed by a second. Somebody else's scream.

He'd waited near the lane, uncertain how to proceed. He'd even walked the full circuit of the block. Fast. The rear of the house, though keeping his distance. Drawn some suspicious glances when he'd emerged from a further narrow lane, once more onto the main road, with its noise and trams. Then all the way around again. A closed bakery on the corner. Back up this Hunter Street. Past a narrow office and Missee Nesta's front door, returning to the lane's entrance.

Now, time to act, Amos Gartee decided.

He ran to that back door. Partly open, after all. Smoke bubbling through the gap. The stench of burning. More cries of pain. A blast of heat in his face as he hauled the door open. The flames inside turning to a roaring beast as the wind fanned them.

His eyes followed their path, up the back wall, along the ceiling beams and a wooden staircase, a ladder perhaps, leading to an upper floor, but all wreathed in fire.

In the bonfire and below, a mask dancer. A hellish demon, prancing, flapping arms, now wings of wildfire. Shrieking. Words that Amos couldn't understand.

On the floor, closer to Amos, near a big machine, another man. On the floor, partly tied to a chair, one arm free and smacking that hand against more flames which devoured his coat. This fellow did not shriek or scream. Rather, he wailed. As though he might be singing. Yet, through the wailing words, there was pain. Terrible pain.

All this, Amos saw in a few seconds.

The demon had collapsed to its knees now. Even the screaming had ceased. Though perhaps it was simply drowned by the bellowing of the bonfire. Beyond help, anyway. That was certain.

Amos lifted his arm across his face, ran to the man in the chair. On the floor, a shaving razor. He reached for it, though it seared his hand. Scorching. He burned the fingers of his other hand trying to open the blade. Even when he had the thing open, he barely managed to slice through the rope securing one of the man's ankles to the chair before part of the ceiling, the upper loft, came crashing down, barely feet away from them. And before more flames reached the man's hair and face.

Yet the man spoke.

'Bag,' he whined. 'Take...'

Amos tried to smother the flames blistering the man's cheek, his ear, his eye. But he followed the direction of that dreadful gaze. Sure enough, under the big machine, a bag, still safe from the conflagration.

Amos grabbed for it, knowing somehow this must be an important thing – perhaps the thing Nyesoa had sent him here to find.

But the smoke was choking him now. Thick, filthy smoke, clogging his tongue with sticky, scalding cinders. Filling his lungs. Coughing. Coughing. Impossible to breathe.

He took off his heavy greatcoat, used it to smother more of the man's flames, looking down into the ravaged face. And yes, of course, it was the devil man.

Amos considered leaving him there though, in the end, he acted more from impulse than reason. An explosion over in the corner. Slivers of glass flying through the flames.

Amos Gartee pulled the greatcoat over his head, took hold of the chair's back rails with his own charred hands. He heaved it almost upright, the devil man sobbing, one of his legs still afire. But now the gate through which Amos had come was also burning. Too fiercely for any escape. It burst outwards, though now a solid bonfire stood in its place.

He was trapped.

6.35pm

Taffy had left her just before they reached Commutation Row, heading for another of his favourite boozers. The place brought Nesta to mind once more. The connection with her and the events of Bloody Sunday. The wind whipped at Cari's hair, tore at her coat skirts. But a shiver down her spine as well. She'd wondered often about her last meeting with Amos Gartee. He'd surely known nothing about Nessie's disappearance. But there'd been something...

In any case, she believed she owed him. To tell him about the efforts made by the police to find Nesta.

Na fo. That's right. She'd tell Amos. But only after she'd settled with Tom Priddy. Yet, settle – how?

Her imagination ran riot, as she crossed towards the fountain, down William Brown Street. And there she heard the bells. Fire engine bells.

Looking beyond the roof of the Museum and the Technical School, the night sky was alight, and while she initially thought little of it, the closer she came to the Old Haymarket, the closer to Byrom Street and home, the faster her legs began to carry her. Until, with her skirts lifted, she was running, full pelt. Praying for the best, fearing the worst.

Before she even reached the corner of Hunter Street, she knew what she'd find. The whole place was ablaze, and here was Ernst running to throw his arms about her, shielding their faces against the searing heat.

'Cari,' he shouted, 'I was afraid. We did not know...'

The neighbours were all out on the street, of course. Policemen keeping them away, herding folk up the hill, and red salvage tenders – one near the court, the other outside the bakery – their teams working to stop the fire from spreading. A miracle it hadn't already done so with this wind.

But, for her house, there seemed no hope. How? The smoke filled her throat, of course. Soot billowing and settling on her cheeks. The taste of burnt embers on her lip. The incineration of her memories. Her notebooks with their precious lines of verse. The only home she'd ever known.

Three of the Police Fire Brigade's constables in their brass helmets wrestled with the heavy white hose connected to the Merryweather motor steamer, smoke billowing from its funnel. The men played their jet of water towards the flames roaring from the upstairs windows, and from the printshop's gate along the lane, in Dawson Place.

'Miss Maddox?'

Cari turned to find Sergeant Ladysmith coming towards her, his forearm raised above his eyes for a shield. He'd been talking with the fire constables' own commander.

'Sergeant...' she began, shouting over the inferno's roar. But then the tears began to flow.

'I can't begin to tell you,' he said. 'So sorry.'

'But why...?'

'Am I here?' the policeman yelled back. 'To be honest, I'd been thinking about that cousin of yours – Thomas, isn't it? I wondered what he'd been on about. Last night, of course. But now. Well,' he said, glancing across at the burning house, 'I suppose now... Anyway, saw the smoke, raised the alarm.'

'And nobody...'

'Inside?' said Ladysmith. 'Not so far as we can tell.'

There was a wheeled rescue ladder, near the corner. Three more constables, where the supply hose snaked down and around to the hydrant on Byrom Street. The hose had a small puncture, she noticed, a fine spray shooting and hissing upwards, dispersing in the tempest.

'But the fire already had a grip when the lads got here. No way for them to get inside. You'd know, though, wouldn't you? Family, like?'

She shook her head, wiped her face on the sleeve of her coat.

'If you're sure…'

He looked again towards the house.

Nobody, she thought, unless…

A crash. A splintering of timbers. The burning gate from the printshop exploded. The window from the downstairs passageway shattering. But then the front door thrown open and, through the smoke, a figure staggered forth. A figure hunched over, shrouded in a blanket. Or a coat maybe. The coat or blanket itself beginning to burn. And the figure dragging something. A piece of furniture. Burning furniture. Though not simply furniture, for it seemed to have arms and legs attached.

'Quick,' shouted Ladysmith. He'd seen it too. Of course, he had.

6.45pm

Tom Priddy could see little and hear even less. But the pain seemed to have left him. He thanked his Lord Jesus for this blessing because, moments earlier – or perhaps the week before – it had truly been unbearable.

Somewhere in his dream, there had been the darkie once more. The same darkie who'd come to his aid on some other occasion. The scars on his face. The same.

And then? He'd been dragged somehow. Past that old baby carriage. Why did his tada keep the thing? After all these years. The child certainly didn't need it. For there he'd been, the boy, waving Tom farewell from the bottom of the stairs.

It was the instant the pain had left him. Though not the smell. The salty, almost sweet and smoky scent of a gammon joint roasting in the oven.

Yet now? He was wet, lying on the cold ground. Cobbles, perhaps.

Somebody's fingers pressed against the underside of his wrist, and at last his hearing cleared, words coming to him like an echo.

'Finished, I'm afraid.'

Finished, he thought. How sad.

He imagined a tear beginning to trickle from the eye which could see nothing.

Finished. And yes, he knew they spoke the truth.

*

6.45pm

He watched the devil man breathe his last, there on the wet street, while the doctor applied salve to Amos Gartee's scorched hands, the side of his face, and the lower part of his leg.

'Hospital,' the doctor told him. 'This is temporary. Do you understand me?'

'*Aan*,' said Amos. 'Yes. Understand.'

The hurt was great. But even greater was his fear that, somehow, he might have made the fire worse. And only to rescue the devil man? Then for the devil man to die, anyway.

'Don't worry,' he heard Missee Coconut Palm tell the doctor fellow. 'I'll make sure he gets there.'

The doctor took bandages from his black leather holdall, began to bind the burns.

'But Missee Cari,' said Amos. 'The bag.'

He pointed one bandaged fist to the place close to the devil man's body. They'd cut him free from the chair, covered him with the charred remains of the greatcoat. Near the chair, the bag, also blackened.

'Your bag, Amos?' said Missee Cari, though she quickly turned away from him, arms folded, when the burning roof collapsed with another enraged roar, hurling showers of sparks, another blossoming black cloud, high into the night sky.

'Devil man, him bag. Important, I think.'

The Germany man, Missee Coconut Palm's friend, retrieved the bag, passed it to her.

'Oh, goodness,' she gasped when she opened the leather fastening strap. 'Mister Gartee, do you know much is here?'

He had no idea what was in the bag, let alone the quantity. But money, he supposed. Surely, money.

'There,' said the doctor, closing his own holdall. 'All done. But please remember, Miss Maddox. The hospital? And I'm sorry – about the house.'

The flames seemed to have abated to some extent. But what would be left of her home?

'All gone,' she said, and moved still closer into the Germany man's embrace. 'What now, Ernst? What can I do now?'

'I have this read,' replied the Germany man. 'In each life, there is one day. One day, if lost, it might be the whole of your destiny – fate – you would miss. You must again begin.'

They were words, thought Amos, which might so easily have come from the Wolof, Charles Tuohey.

'Tada so ill?' said Missee Coconut Palm. 'And Nesta disappeared.' She turned towards Amos. 'You were fond of her, Mister Gartee. I wanted to ask you…'

Amos saw her, silhouetted against the flames, the amber sky. Was this the time? For confession? He wasn't certain. But perhaps there would never be a better moment.

'Miss Cari,' he said. 'You not understand. Miss Nesta. A thing you must know.'

Chapter Thirteen

Friday 8th December 1911

12.30pm

Cari had overcome her anger. Her resentment. More or less.

'I still don't believe it,' she whispered, as they waited to sign the register. 'Me, Nesta. You didn't even trust me.'

Toxteth Town Hall. The interior walls almost the same shade of Nile-green, the voile, the dress she'd worn for the dinner at the Walker. White plasterwork garlands. The dress lost, of course, along with her other possessions, her precious hats and millinery materials, in the fire.

'*Aa dji ooh!*' said Amos Gartee. Help! He was having difficulty with the pen. His bandages? Or writing his name. Cari wasn't certain. But his best man, this fellow Charles Tuohey, intervened. In precisely which way, she couldn't see.

'Would you have kept it to yourself?' Nesta murmured, by way of response. 'From Tada?'

Cari didn't answer. In truth, she wasn't certain what the answer might have been. Almost two months. She'd been missing almost two months. All those nightmares. The speculation about Nesta's fate. And all this time she'd been living in the same lodging house as Amos. Kent Square. Yes, perfectly respectable. And there, sitting among the other guests, the landlady herself. Mary Clarke. Not as dark-skinned as Amos or Charles Tuohey. But once a footballer? Extraordinary. She wondered whether the WSPU should have a team. It might make a point. But she and Nesta both had Mary to thank for helping them find their wedding clothes.

'Don't suppose it matters now,' she said. 'And the work?'

Nesta's turn to sign the register. She stayed at the table to watch the witnesses sign in their turn. Charles Tuohey and the landlady.

'The work's fine,' said Nesta when it was all done and the registrar thanked everybody for their attendance, a polite way to tell them they'd outstayed their welcome. 'Hard. But it will do for the time being,' she told Cari as they wandered through to the vestibule to collect their coats. 'I just miss the girls – most of them, anyway.'

She'd been working at the wash house. Heavy labour. Cornwallis Street, where the best man, Charles Tuohey, Cari now knew, taught swimming to children, taught boxing to would-be pugilists. Like Amos Gartee, it seemed. And thus, it had been confirmed. Amos had, indeed, rescued Tom Priddy from a beating, rather than being one of his assailants.

Taffy was already outside, sheltering under the arched doorway on High Park Street. Smoking.

'You came,' Nesta said to him.

'My own sister's wedding? Wouldn't have missed it for the world.'

But he sounded less than completely sincere. Less than entirely sober. It had been a difficult discussion. And only a few days ago. Weeks after the fire and her own exposure to the truth. Amos Gartee's confession. She didn't want to think about Taffy's response. Those awful comments. Darkies and the rest. His initial anger. Then his grudging acceptance that, without Mister Gartee, they'd never have recovered the carpet bag with its modest hoard of banknotes and coin. Finally, his acknowledgement that Nesta's disappearance wasn't some slight against him personally, and he'd been somewhat mollified by the police finally handing over the strike fund into his care.

'Well, he's your brother-in-law now,' said Nesta. 'Like it or bloody lump it. And you owe him. You know you do, Taff.'

No time for him to answer, for the next to file out from the foyer was another of Amos's friends, the carter, Bill Jones – though Amos still insisted on calling him King Billy.

'Hey Taffy,' he called out. 'Good to see yer, lad. What d'you reckon, then? A few jars later?'

King Billy had been persuaded – by Amos, of course – to find work for Taffy. Hatton & Cookson. And their brother had moved back into Ma MacKenny's place. He was still there, while they waited to see whether the insurance company would pay up. Rhys Fingers had been certain he could get Taffy the tap again on the docks – now the strike fund had been recovered, returned to the North End dockers and apologies all round. But Taffy had always been slow in the forgive and forget department. Besides, she suspected, if he were back on the docks, he'd be worried about whether the news might break. His sister and…

So, no. Hatton & Cookson. And he was still struggling, Cari understood full well, with this new world in which they now all existed.

'A few jars?' Taffy smiled at the carter. 'The darkies' hostel? Don't think we'll get a decent pint there, like.'

Cari remembered it wasn't so long ago he'd called it a dive.

'You and Tada,' Nesta snarled. 'Tom Priddy, too. Three of a kind. Three of a bloody kind. Never learn, do you, Taff?'

'Me and Priddy?'

He was plainly shocked by the comparison. They'd talked at length about Tom Priddy. About whatever might have driven him to the things he'd done. But he was gone. A new world. But some things, Cari knew, were unlikely to ever change.

And now, here came Gwilym Mills.

'All set, Miss Maddox,' he called. 'And Mrs Gartee,' he beamed at Nesta. 'Let's hope the rain holds off. Perhaps one here. Then in front of the reservoir?'

He arranged them according to custom in front of Toxteth's town hall. Eleven of them. The bride and groom flanked by their witnesses. Behind Amos and Charles Tuohey, the gig boat skipper Tom Coleman, and Coleman's pretty daughter Beth, as well as the carter Billy Jones and his wife Sophia. Around Nesta and Mary Clarke, Cari and Ernst Jurks, with Taffy. Good of Gwilym to agree, though he'd made a point of asking, a wicked smile on his lips, whether she was still complying with the conditions of her binding over.

Yes, she thought, if it weren't for Ernst, perhaps she and Gwilym might…

I'd take your hand and lead you to a place,
Of ecstasy and pleasures long denied.

'A shame,' she said, over her shoulder, as Gwilym readied the camera. 'About Tada. And Wyn.'

'Wyn?' Taffy guffawed. 'This would kill her. Imagine?'

They'd decided very quickly to leave Winifred with her delusions. White slavers, indeed. Cari had the suspicion that, even had they told her the truth, Wyn would have chosen not to believe it, preferred her prejudice. Bad enough with Taffy, but at least he'd turned up.

'You don't think Rhys will find out anyway?' she said.

'Maybe. But that piece in the *Post*. Hard to miss 'im, like, an' all.' He nodded towards Amos, who was busy with an amorous embrace for his new wife.

Nesta looked happy. Proud, even. Good. It was very good. Her twenty-first birthday a week earlier. Thank goodness for that, also. No need for Tada's permission for the marriage. Just imagine, Cari thought.

'On the gig boats, see,' Taffy went on. 'Get around, it will. Darkie with a white wife. Suppose he'll put two and two together. But whether he'd tell Wyn – well…'

'She knows about Tada, at least.'

'An' the syph?' he whispered, just as Gwilym called for everybody to hold still. Smiles, as well, he insisted.

'With the rest of the money,' said Cari, 'I just hope she might somehow be persuaded to use a few quid and get some treatment…'

But then, how would Cari broach *that* subject? And one thing was certain. Even with this about the syph, her husband's whores, whatever other abuses she suffered at his hands – despite it all, the stupid girl would stand by Rhys Fingers.

'There,' shouted Mister Mills – Gwilym. 'All done. Shall we move up the road?'

The High Park Reservoir loomed above them, just further up the street. Solid sandstone walls like a fortress. The corner tower pointing into the December sky. It would make an attractive backdrop. Chilly, though. But Ernst came up beside her, threw a comforting arm around her waist. It wasn't far. But far enough for Skipper Coleman's pretty daughter to fall into step at Taffy's side.

'You goin' back, like?' Cari heard the girl say. 'The hostel?'

She saw her brother purse his lips, as though he was giving the suggestion serious consideration.

'Yeah,' said Taffy. 'Of course.' He turned to Cari and winked at her. 'But the money,' he shouted. 'How much is left?'

Well, she thought, there's a turnup for the books. Maybe hope for Taffy, after all.

'Not much,' she smiled. 'I paid Mister Hughes the money he should have received for his orphans – from the lottery business. I still can't believe...'

'*You* can't, Cari. I'm still trying to work out how Priddy managed to get his hands on the strike fund. That priest – remember?'

She remembered very well. Though there were things about Tom Priddy, she knew, they'd never understand. And maybe that was just as well. But Priddy. Taffy had called him Priddy. But weren't they all – Priddys?

2.00pm

Amos was still uncertain how Cookie had managed it. But here they were. Back at the Elder Dempster hostel on Upper Stanhope Street where so much of their story – his and Missee Nesta's – had begun. Yet wedding breakfast? His grasp of English was distinctly improved. Though this was halfway through the afternoon. So, breakfast? Still, it was convenient. No more than half-a-mile from the marriage place, a couple of stops on the tram along Park Road.

'This what you call food, Cookie?' he said, as he'd done so many times in the past.

'Flukey food,' Cookie replied, grinning broadly through the blue facial tattoos. 'All way from Flukey Alley. Eat, no eat. All same, dog-eater.'

'This my friend Cookie,' Amos said to his bride. 'But Amos never eat dog.'

The game they played, though he wasn't sure from the look on Miss Nesta's face whether she believed him.

'Flukey Alley?' she said.

'*Alhumdulillah!*' said the Wolof. 'Congratulations! I wish you years of happiness, love, and joy. May Allah bless you! And Flukey Alley, Mrs Gartee. Don't hear it very often these days. But top end of Frederick Street. Hawaiians. Popular with the ladies, they tell me. And what's in this, Cookie lad?'

He sniffed at a pot of fragrant stew.

'Potato. And pig,' said Cookie.

The Wolof slammed the lid down again.

A gift brought by King Billy's daughter, who worked at the bacon factory. Kind of her to come, Amos decided. Along with the others who'd not been able to be at the wedding place. The po-leese man. Jocota and his wife, Mary. Three of the women who worked with Nesta at the wash house. The solicitor, Mister Quilliam, from the inquest.

'My father became a follower of Islam,' the solicitor told Charles Tuohey, and helped himself to some of Cookie's *Lau*. Cooked fish from that wondrous Market of Saint John. Cooked fish wrapped in steamed leaves. Good food. Like Nana Kru. Perhaps he *could* live here.

'Yes, I knew him,' said the Wolof. 'Perhaps one day we shall have another mosque in this fine city.'

'And I have Mister Quilliam to thank for my freedom,' said Missee Coconut Palm. She and the Germany man were also moving along the table, gathering food for their plates.

'Well, thanks to William and the Carters' Union, more accurately, Miss Maddox,' Quilliam replied. 'And to Mister Gartee, of course.'

A modest man. And Missee Cari knew the whole story now – about how he had seen her arrested, sought King Billy's help for her. It had been some benefit, he thought, when he'd had to make his confession to her.

The story of the morning he'd been escorting Nesta home. The place, once a church, now almost torn down. A church of her forefathers. They had argued – about boxing, of all things. He'd pressed her into the old burial ground, told her about using his fists, as the Wolof had taught him, to save the devil man from a beating. And she had told *him* about the devil man. About the things he'd done.

'So how could you ever want to marry me, Amos Gartee?' she'd said.

It wasn't the way things were supposed to be. It was for him, the man, to raise the question of a bride price. To set the pace for a courtship. It had troubled him. For a long time.

But perhaps in this Liverpool place, this was how it was done. In any case, they had agreed. Made plans. Settled around themselves a feathered cloak of secrecy. One which made him guilty. For Missee Nesta had insisted her father would never accept such a thing. Because – well, just because, she had told him. Yes, plans. An exchange of oaths. To be married according to her *poto* customs.

And Amos, for his part, had set his own plans, sworn another oath. Revenge upon the devil man.

All behind him now. Their guests enjoying the food, it seemed.

Cookie had produced his small guitar, a *ukulele*, he called it.

'We all have much to thank you for, Amos,' Missee Coconut Palm whispered in his ear. Her eyes were bright today, though he knew she must be troubled. Their father.

'And the Germany man, Missee Cari. Does he have bride price? Next wedding, I think.'

'I hope so,' she replied. 'Living under his father's roof, after all. Since the fire. It would be the scandal of Hunter Street if I didn't marry him in the end.'

Some of the guests were dancing, Cookie singing and playing. A tune they all seemed to know. About a little brown jug. Nesta dancing with her brother.

'And you two,' said Miss Cari, 'have you thought about children?'

Amos smiled. The Wolof had told him they would have to face this question. Others he had known at the swimming cavern. Children of mixed marriages, as Tuohey called them. The difficulties for such children in this Liverpool place.

'Yes, children,' he replied. 'Many children. And we have no fear for them. Because the sister of their mother is great fighting woman.'

He saw her turn away, but she said nothing. And then Mister Quilliam had returned to join them.

'A pleasant way to end a difficult year,' he said to them, his plate now brimming with Cookie's finest. 'You think things will ever be the same again, Miss Maddox? Mister Gartee?'

Amos had heard the Wolof's lecture often enough. Still strikes in this Liverpool place. Coal carters. Shipbuilders across the big river. He supposed it might take many years for the city's workers, its men and its women, to find the justice they all sought. But he knew that, one day, they would reach that place. Or very near, perhaps. They already had this coming together. National Transport Workers' Federation, they named it. And Amos was part of it. Amos and Skipper Coleman. King Billy. Jocota. All the rest. One big union, he thought.

'A difficult year, indeed,' said Missee Coconut Palm. 'But just look how far we've travelled.'

'And this fine fellow,' said the solicitor, turning to Amos. 'What d'you think of him? Newspapers. Coroner's Court. What next, d'you think?'

A journalist – this was a fine word to learn – had come to the hospital after Missee Coconut Palm took him there. After his confession, of course. It happened that this journalist fellow wished to report in his *Daily Post* about the fire. Some person had told him about Amos. And it happened, also, this was the same man who had written in his *Daily Post* about the Kru seamen and their strike at the Harrington Dock. March and April. It had been from these writings that Missee Nesta – *Mrs* Nesta now – had first learned about his Kru brothers, had kept every mention of them. And afterwards, in May and in June.

Anyway, this journalist fellow had found him at the hospital and wanted to know the story.

'I was passing,' Amos had told him. 'I see flames down a long place. Run to help. Inside, two men. One on fire. All burn away. Other, I pull outside.'

'I heard,' said the journalist fellow, 'he'd been tied to a chair – this man you rescued from the flames. Is that true, Mister Gartee?'

So yes, Amos was forced to admit. A chair.

'I save chair also,' Amos had told him, with some pride. The chair, after all was innocent. Not like the devil man.

There had been the headline.

Fire at Hunter Street. Suspicious circumstances.

After the headline, an inquest. The Coroner's Court. The Coroner's Jury. Mister Billal Quilliam again. And now, here was Mister Billal Quilliam at Amos Gartee's wedding.

'You did well, Amos,' the solicitor told him. 'At the inquest.' His mouth was full of the *Poké* Cookie had made. It was good. Raw fish, onions, lettuce, sesame oil, soy sauce, peppers, garlic. Amos had asked Cookie for the recipe.

'Read from your paper,' said Amos. 'Not hard.'

Mister Quilliam had helped him. A simple statement. His friend and benefactor, Miss Nesta Maddox, lived at the house. He had gone to visit.

A white lie, Mister Quilliam had said. Later, the Wolof had explained to him. An acceptable untruth. A phrase, Charles Tuohey said, which went a long way towards explaining English attitudes. White was pure. Always. Play the white man. A white lie generally good. Black, however, symbolised the very worst of things. A black heart for example. Or a black man? Ingrained. Bred in the bone. Foolish, but there it was!

The statement had originally used the words, *"sweetheart, Miss Nesta Maddox"* – but, at Missee Coconut Palm's insistence, those words had been changed. In case, she said, their sister Winifred might see some report of the inquest and misunderstand. Bad enough, Missee Cari had said, when she'd had to confront this Winifred with the loss of the house.

After the white lie, a short description of the rescue. The impossibility of saving that other victim of the fire. Nor could he identify the second victim. After the rescue, he had recognised the man he'd saved to be a cousin of his friend. And this Miss Maddox's sister had confirmed the identity. She had, by then, arrived upon the scene.

There'd been questions, most of which he'd been unable to answer.

Then thanked by the Coroner, praised for his courage.

Missee Coconut Palm had given evidence as well. Yes, her cousin. Mister Priddy. A kind young man, she'd lied – and not a white lie, either, Amos decided. A kind young man and no, she could not even begin to imagine what might have happened.

There'd been statements also. The owners of this funeral place – where the devil man himself had been taken before they put him in the ground. And from the theatre where Amos had gone to watch the Tom Show, where he had seen the devil man sing. It was all very strange.

'I was just saying, Miss Maddox,' the solicitor told Missee Coconut

Palm. 'Mister Gartee did very well at the Coroner's Court. Rum business, yes?'

The Jury's verdicts had been returned. For the man they could not identify: *Died from burn injuries, but no evidence to show how they had been received.* And, for the devil man – because he had so obviously been deliberately tied to the chair: *Wilful murder, by person or persons unknown, but no evidence to confirm the identity of the perpetrator.*

'A mystery,' said Missee Coconut Palm. 'And yes, very well indeed.' She gave Amos one of those smiles. Her half-happy, half-sad smile. The Germany man put his arm around her again.

'Your father,' said Amos. 'You will see him?'

'Just off,' she said. 'But I wouldn't have missed the wedding, Amos – not for the world.'

4.00pm

The ward sister had spoken well of him. Mister Hay. John Hay. From Birkenhead, the sister had explained, as though this, of itself, was a commendation of his abilities as a cardiologist.

Yet she struggled to understand. Still somewhat overwhelmed by the wedding. Jibes from all quarters about when she and Ernst might tie the knot – if ever. Her purest joy at having dear Nesta back in her life. And happy. So happy. Though Cari feared the road ahead would not be smooth for her sister. Then, of course, there'd been Amos Gartee himself. A great fighting woman, he'd called her. But was she?

Finally, her poor tada. Still, at least the Royal had a specialised heart department and Mister Hay was its head.

'Mister Hay,' said Cari. 'The tubes in my father's legs…'

'Southey's Tubes,' he replied. 'To drain dangerous fluids, the swelling and so on. I have conducted an electrocardiograph test. We use such tests to check for atrial fibrillation – irregular heartbeat. Generally speaking, a sign of heart disease. That, combined with your father's chest pains, allows me to suspect he has suffered a Myocardial Infarction. In layman's terms? A heart attack, almost certainly caused by a narrowing of the coronary arteries.'

'He's so weak. Seems not to be getting better.'

Hay, she guessed, was not yet forty. Broad-faced. Amicable enough. But she always imagined senior consultants should be – well, older.

'We're doing all we can, my dear. Rest. A light diet.'

'Nothing else? No other treatment?'

'Some excellent Polish research last year. Don't ask me to repeat their names. But we're still evaluating the results. Too early, just yet.'

'Too early?

'Your father, Miss Maddox, suffered what we call a myocardial infarction. A heart attack, yes. Blockages in one or more of the arteries. A smoker, I gather?'

'Yes, though not to excess. In the printshop he would never allow it.'

'Printshop, you say? Has he always been a printer?'

'He has. Why? Do you think there may be a link? Oh, and some time as a quarryman.'

'Sadly, we still know too little about the subject. But my own investigations have led me to believe – well, particles from chemical fluids, for example. And quarry dust, notoriously dangerous. I like your hat, by the way.'

She was flattered, quite forgot to ask whatever additional questions had been in her mind earlier. She'd made it for the wedding, naturally. Because the others – well, lost in the fire along with all the necessaries. Certainly no room in the Jurks place either, to practise her skills. But Mister Lardner the tailor at number thirteen had provided both space and some of the materials. A picture hat with a Battenburg lace crown. She'd seen it in an image within one of Lardner's copies of *The Queen*.

Everybody had been so kind. Though there was torture in the kindness as well. She wished herself far, far away, yet every day having to witness the ruin of their old home.

She thanked Mister Hay, returned to her tada's bedside. He was awake, his eyes with more spark in them than she'd seen since they brought him in. They were letting her visit more or less whenever she liked. He was failing, but he wouldn't die. She knew he would not. He could not.

It was strange, however. To see him there, so weak and helpless. Like he'd been all those times when she was a girl. Hard times.

'Nesta,' he murmured.

'Told you, Tada. She's back with us.'

'Where?'

'Why, at the house, of course. Hunter Street,' she lied.

All gone. The baby carriage. Blackened and burnt. So many other mementos of Pryce and her mam. Did the babe's ghost still wander the rooms, now empty? Blackened and burnt. Or was he, like her, now homeless?

How many times had she almost wished homelessness upon herself. To spread turbulent wings.

Above the shop I shall no longer dwell,
But rather cast my fate upon the wind.

'Where?' he whispered again.

'You mean where did she go? We'll tell you the whole story when you're better, see.'

'Trial, *cariad*?'

'Mine? Bound over. Nothing more. The union – gave me a solicitor. Good one, as well. But all the others, Tada. *Duw annwyl*, all those poor devils.'

She still had nightmares. The women who'd shared her cell at the court. Prostitutes. Petty thieves. All those cast out by society.

'Sentence of death,' said her tada, and she wondered what was passing through his mind. But then she realised. *Great Expectations* again, perhaps. 'Two-and-thirty men and women,' he went. 'Put before the Judge.'

Yes, Magwitch's trial. He was wandering.

'But they let me go, Tada,' she said. 'So all's well that ends well.'

'Crossroads in our lives, *cariad*. Your mam. When we met, I knew. No other path for me. But Thomas. Wronged that boy, I did.'

'You knew, from the first day he turned up at the house.'

The house. How could she ever tell him about the house? But Tom Priddy – those words he'd whispered in her tada's ear while she was still on the stairs.

'Wronged him, I did. Where is he? Thomas. I should…'

'You know what he's like, Tada. Be here later, I expect. But now, look what I've got for you.'

She'd been back to Dai *Papur*'s after all. She took the ring from her coat pocket, slipped it into those arthritic fingers.

'Mam's wedding ring,' she said. 'Lost it, didn't she?'

Cari wasn't certain he could even see it, but he closed his hand around it, and tears rolled from his eyes.

'Had to borrow one,' he whispered. 'Remember – the wedding? Nerys, *cariad*, get me a glass of water, would you?'

Oh, how she prayed now for God to spare him, to allow her still to play the chief cook, the bottle washer. She remembered the last time he'd asked *her* to fetch him a drink. The night Tom Priddy had come into their lives. But now, it was her mam he was asking. Poor mam.

'Rained it did,' he said, 'when we buried her. But blessed are the dead the rains weep upon.'

She patted his hand and stood from his bedside.

'Get you some water, I will,' she said. 'Straight back, though.'

Cari headed from the ward to the sister's office, knocked on the door.

'Excuse me,' she said, 'my tada's asking for some water.'

The sister looked at her watch. A watch remarkably similar to the one Florrie Thompson-Frere had carried. Somewhere in the ashes, she supposed.

'The jugs will be coming around in ten minutes,' said the sister.

'I think he'd like a drink now.'

'Then you must go and buy some, mustn't you, Miss Maddox? The kiosk, outside the main entrance.'

Be careful, you old witch, thought Cari. Or I shall summon the spirit of Thomas Priddy to teach you a lesson.

Back to the domed crossing hall, the arched Moorish corridor, the wide staircase. And the kiosk. Cold out there, and she buttoned her coat while she waited her turn in the queue. A green bottle of Lyon's mineral water. Well, here was their factory, just across the road in Pembroke Place. She picked up a copy of the *Echo*, as well, dodged back inside the entrance. All the normal notices on the front page, including the current performance at the Rotunda Theatre. Hard not to think again of Tom Priddy.

The marriage certificate had still been in his pocket. Singed but intact. What had he been intending to do with it? No clues. And the

Salvage had found little else. Tada's tea caddy burned to a crisp but the tin liner more or less protecting some of his other papers. Insurance policy. The letter from Mister Watkin-Evans in Carnarvon. Cari had written a reply, naturally. Sad to report that his client, Thomas Priddy, had died in a house fire. The Coroner's Court could provide details.

Apart from the policy and the letter, an envelope bearing the printed words *Last Will and Testament*. No need for this one, thank goodness, she'd thought. And in any case, nothing left!

She turned the *Echo*'s pages, remembered her first conversation with Thomas.

'What business?' she'd asked.

'Family business. Family, girl,' he'd replied.

Family, she thought. Well, he was still with her in one way, at least. She rather feared she'd somehow been infected by his malevolence.

Page Four. Halfway down the third column. There it was, the bold headline.

Suffragettes burn another letterbox.

Fools, she thought. For she had progressed from mere paraffin oil. A device, Ernst had called it. Almost blown off the post box lid. Scrawled the words *Action Not Deeds* in chalk on the pavement. There'd been poor Mister Kaplan and the Carters' Union to think about, each having to forfeit their twenty-five quid sureties. But somehow, she'd felt Tom Priddy guided her hand.

She'd sell the papers still. Of course, she would. Go to the meetings. Even London or further if it was really necessary. But here Cari Maddox would take all the trials, mistakes and disasters of her life, use them to fight her own personal war against them. The powerful and the wealthy. The puppet masters.

So, take my tribulations to the forge,
Shape me a purpose new from out the flames.

A new purpose. And here's to you, Tom Priddy, she thought, as she closed the paper. *Brother* Tom Priddy. Hopefully burning in your own fires of Hell, now and for all eternity.

'Well,' she said out loud, 'everybody dies.'

She could have bitten her own tongue, rushed back to the ward.

'Miss Maddox,' called the sister as Cari passed her office door. 'You could have waited, my dear. Water jugs went around ten minutes ago.'

'But you know what they say about *this* water, sister?' She held up the green bottle. '*Nature's Bulwark Against All Ills.* It says so, on their advertisement. Right outside the Infirmary.'

Yet she would never be able to test its efficacy. For when she returned to her tada's bedside, he was quite dead, slumped on his pillows, mouth hanging open and those previously remarkable eyes now entirely sightless.

She took hold of his dear hand.

Cari knew she should call for one of the nurses. Or that sister. But maybe it could wait. For now.

She felt no real sadness. This would come later, as well. And strange, she thought, the things that go through our heads in the face of death. It would have to be registered, naturally. Yet in what name? Maddox or Priddy.

Naturally, there was guilt. She'd always thought it would be Taffy and his love for Theresa that would cause Tada to have an apoplexy. But no, it had been Cari herself. Her arrest. But at least he'd died knowing she was free. Nesta back among them. They'd each visited over the past week and, she hoped, there would be no regrets.

She sat, immersed in her thoughts, her memories, for some while. Yet before she left, she remembered the words from *Great Expectations*. He would have thought it was appropriate. Pip's words for Magwitch.

'O Lord, be merciful to him a sinner!'

The nursing staff were kind. And Mister Hay also.

'How?' she said. 'A second heart attack? It was so sudden.'

'Miss Maddox,' he told her. 'A heart attack damages the heart muscle. This damage produces a permanent scar. This can become – how should I put this? Electrically unstable. You understand? This instability, in turn, may lead to ventricular fibrillation. Sudden cardiac arrest. He will have felt little or no pain.'

No pain, she recalled when she stood once more outside the hospital's entrance. Cold. She pulled the coat more tightly about her.

The news to be broken. Arrangements to be made. Waugh's? Yes, she supposed it would be appropriate.

After?

She would serve in the memory of those women pushed over the edge of St. George's Plateau on that sultry day back in August. Or the others. Like Bessie Butler. Bessie, who'd stood with them on Bloody Sunday. Bessie, who'd once accused her of being part of the "posh" elite. Bessie, who'd died with two dozen more in the Bibby's explosion, the very day after the Hunter Street fire. Yes, all those women. Enshrine them in new lines of verse. Try to recreate some of the lines she'd lost.

Cari would avoid the pitfall of fanatics for whom the propaganda is more productive than the proof.

She would strike further blows to help them win the vote.

She would carve a path through this new century, this new Liverpool.

> Or learn to eat their cake, as well as cawl,
> Shun lobscouse limitations to my world.

For the rest, she knew time would provide all the answers. Time, and the Lord Jesus.

End

Historical Notes and Acknowledgements

Hunter Street is now no more than a busy dual carriageway, running behind Liverpool's Walker Art Gallery and the Museum, connecting the bottom of Islington with the end of Byrom Street. It carries an endless stream of vehicles heading in one direction, upwards, for the city's eastern suburbs, the M62 motorway, the cathedrals and South Liverpool. Or in the other direction down towards the Mersey Tunnels, Dale Street and the waterfront, as well as towards Bootle, Walton and the north.

But in 1911 it was a more modest though far more interesting thoroughfare. Terraced houses and businesses. A mass of other smaller streets leading off in both directions. Spencer Street, Carter Street and others at the top, where Gerard Gardens would later be built. Christ Church and the Friends Meeting House. Poulterers, tinsmiths, chandlers, saddlers and tailors. Towards the bottom, Mellor's Brewery and Avery Weighing Machines. On one corner with Byrom Street, the Byrom alehouse, known locally as Mad John's. On the other, Lunt's Bakery and the Weights and Measures office. And just next to the office, a printshop.

The printshop was owned by William McCall and, later, by his stepson, John Joseph – who had been brought up with McCall's surname but had, in fact, been born John Joseph Ebsworth. And there my tenuous personal link to the tale ends. Almost.

My maternal great-grandmother, Sarah, married a German sailor named Ernst Jurks. Ernst died in 1912, and though Sarah herself kept the surname for the rest of her life – she died at her home on Great

Mersey Street in 1955 – most of their male offspring changed their name to Kirk from 1914 onwards.

Then, the Welsh connection. The Census records reveal that my paternal grandmother (who died after having given birth to fifteen children) was Frances Davies, born in Denbigh and later emigrated to Liverpool. When I was a kid, one of the local churches, on the corner of Trinity Road, was a Welsh church. And since I had friends just near that part of town, it was a regular part of my young life to hear Welsh spoken on our Bootle streets. Chunks of my childhood were spent happily on the hills of North Wales with my sister Joan and her husband Tony – to both of whom I owe a great deal. But for the past forty years and more I've been living in Wrexham, North Wales, with Ann, with Welsh-speaking friends, and even a Welsh-speaking Polish daughter-in-law. So, the Liverpool Welsh connection is, I think, strong in me.

My final personal link to this yarn? The unions, of course. The National Transport Workers' Federation mentioned in some of the chapters was destined to fall apart within a few years, though many of the individual transport-related unions, as well as some of the newer unions for those men and women labouring in a whole mass of other industries and sweatshops, would come together in 1922 to form Britain's mighty Transport & General Workers' Union.

The T&GWU was extended home and family to me from my own early twenties onwards. It set me on the path – the only one of the various directions in which my life could have taken me – which eventually led me to Ann and the significant other blessings which have filled my years, in addition to those from before we found each other.

And the T&GWU was mighty indeed. Its General Secretary, Ernie Bevin, would serve as Minister of Labour and National Service within Churchill's wartime coalition government. A later General Secretary, Jack Jones – friend, comrade and veteran of the Spanish Civil War – would lead the T&GWU to even greater prominence in the 1970s. I hope this novel, published a hundred years after the union's creation, will serve as my own modest reminder of the part played by trade unions in general, and the T&GWU in particular, in 20th Century social, industrial and political history.

As I said in the beginning, this is a work of fiction but, as always,

I've done my best to keep the fiction within the boundaries of historical veracity, to remain faithful to the historical events giving the story its background.

Intriguing events: the industrial unrest that brought Liverpool "near to revolution" in 1911 and beyond; the battle for women's suffrage, which ignited the city and the country as a whole during the second decade of the Twentieth Century; the many racial and cultural tensions apparent along the Mersey during that same period; and evidence of the build-up to an appalling Great War already there for anybody with eyes to see. Interlinked events, some of them almost too strange to be true, that cried out to be brought to life in the way that, in my humble opinion, historical fiction does so well.

Those events – both on the national scene as well as the incidents in Liverpool – are chronologically as correct as I could make them. Though it's maybe worth specifically saying that to reconstruct the events of Liverpool's Bloody Sunday on 13th August 1911, I mainly used *The State Response to 1911* by Professor Sam Davies (deceased), from Liverpool John Moores University. Many of the eye-witness accounts of the city's Bloody Sunday are either contradictory or partial.

Tom Mann's account, for example, fails to even mention the police and soldiers pouring from within St. George's Hall, something that others say took place during the early stages of the unrest. Similarly, his mention of the Mounted Police reads like he'd been told about this afterwards. The logical conclusion is that this phase of the action took place slightly later, as Sam Davies had suggested, after the police charges over the road in Lord Nelson Street, and just after Tom Mann had finally drawn proceedings to a close and himself left the Plateau. In any case, the novel simply relates the sequence of events as remembered by my (fictional) characters, Cari Maddox, Amos Gartee and Tom Priddy – any of whom may equally have got things slightly out of kilter.

We factually do not know what triggered the police charges on Bloody Sunday and since Ernst Jurks, Sergeant Ladysmith, Nesta Maddox and the rest are all fictional characters, I hope it's obvious that my version is simply a piece of fictional "gap filling" rather than an attempt to historically explain how the trouble all began.

I should also admit to taking a liberty, in the final chapters, with Cari's setting postboxes ablaze. In fact, the first recorded incidence of suffragettes setting fire to postboxes comes a few weeks later, on 15th December 1911, when Emily Wilding Davidson did so, she claimed, entirely on her own responsibility and was sentenced to six months in prison. The WSPU, then still uncertain about the impact of such deeds, gave the incident only the briefest of mentions in *Votes for Women*.

Another liberty? The attack on Amos Gartee. Purely fictional, though the racial tensions were rife enough across Britain in 1911, as illustrated by the anti-Jewish attacks in August that year in South Wales. Or the attacks against the Chinese community in Cardiff during April 1911. And Ron Ramdin talks about similar attacks as a precursor to the 1919 race riots in his book, *The Making of the Black Working Class in Britain*. It seemed to me, therefore, that the attack against Amos was still within the limits of historical veracity.

I first came across the separate – and largely ignored – strike by Elder Dempster's West African Kru seamen maybe twenty years ago in archive copies of Liverpool's *Daily Post* for 16th March and 23rd March 1911. Then again on 23rd May and 22nd June. And a bit of a mystery here since, when I went back to the archives in Liverpool's Central Library, the relevant microfilms for March 1911 were missing. And there no longer seems to be any other copy in existence for the relevant editions. Strange, though we continue to search.

But between the *Post*, the *Echo* and the *Courier*, we can at least piece together some of the threads. On 16th March, one hundred black stokers and trimmers on strike against Elder Dempster, beginning with the crew of the *Mendi*, three weeks earlier. Four other crews had subsequently joined them, protesting about only receiving half the pay of white seamen in similar roles. On 17th March, Kru seamen visited the *Echo* office. Elder Dempster prepared to make some sort of offer if they returned to work but otherwise would take them "free" back to Sierra Leone and replace them with white crews. There's a mention that they'd sought help from the National Sailors' and Firemen's Union, but no indication that any such help was forthcoming – simply a note that they weren't members of the NSFU.

On 21st March, the *Echo* reported an offer by Elder Dempster to increase the black stokers' pay by five shillings per month, though the offer declined and the seamen preferring to be returned to West Africa. Then, on 23rd March, a report that some already taken back to Sierra Leone and sufficient white seamen replacing black crews on the *Zaria*.

On that same date, mention of a large meeting of seamen and dockers at St. Martin's Hall on Scotland Road, Liverpool, with African seamen in attendance and apparently congratulated on their dispute. This meeting also received the news that a more widespread seamen's strike was imminent. But then no further mention for quite some time. My own account of another meeting at St. Martin's Hall on 22nd May is, therefore, an invention. There may, of course, have been other such meetings but, if so, they never received any coverage.

On 19th and 21st June, news of more black sailors on strike from Elder Dempster's *Aro* and, once again, the *Aro*'s crew replaced with white stokers. On 23rd June, a similar story in relation to the *Gando* but an indication that Elder Dempster's black seamen were prepared to settle for concessions – though the details weren't reported. After this, the following week, simply a report that the outcome was positive but, again, no details. I've invented some of the detail about Elder Dempster replacing one crew of black sailors with another, though in practice the Company mostly hired white crews to replace them.

I was therefore keen to tell at least part of the story from the viewpoint of the Kru seamen, though that posed problems of its own, and I've talked about the use of languages in my Author's Note at the start of the book. But my story also finishes with a relatively happy ending, which doesn't properly do justice to the actual experiences of the black community in Liverpool over the ensuing years. The publication *Great War to Race Riots* (Madeline Heneghan and Emy Onoura) and the archives on which it's based show us that, while the 1911 strikes may have led to some temporary improvement in the pay of Elder Dempster's West African seamen, the gains were short-lived. And how, despite the huge contribution and sacrifices of our black community during the First World War, it quickly became a scapegoat for post-war unemployment and a shattered economy. Then, the attempts to "repatriate" African and West Indian seamen who had already settled in the city, as well as the race riots of 1919

– which culminated in the murder of seaman Charles Wotten by a racist mob. They are issues which still resonate in Liverpool and elsewhere to this day.

Most of the fictional characters are not intended to represent anybody in particular, though Charles Tuohey – or Abdul Niasse – was based in part on the real-life James Clarke, born in British Guiana and, having stowed away on a vessel bound for Liverpool, was adopted by an Irish family. He worked on the docks and was also a swimming instructor. He became famous in the city and James Clarke Street, in Liverpool 5, is named in his honour. The character was also partly inspired by another old friend and comrade, Eric Scott Lynch, who initiated the Slavery History Rails in Liverpool, and one of the stalwarts instrumental in establishing the International Slavery Museum in the city.

A mention here for Mary Clarke also, who was indeed one of our first black women footballers, though somewhat overshadowed by her more famous sister Emma.

There are, of course, many other real-life personalities, who make appearances in the plot and I hope I've not been unfair to them, nor to the historical events in which they were a part. My King Billy character, for example, is based on William Henry Jones, forty-three in 1911, from Kirkdale, one of the 1911 strike leaders and, in the following year, destined to become General Secretary of the Merseyside Carters' Union. Amos Gartee's Jocota, is based on Joseph Patrick (Joe) Cotter, born in 1887 and also a 1911 strike leader for the Ships' Stewards, Cooks, Butchers and Bakers Union – though Joe remained an intractable opponent to the employment of non-British workers. Billal Quilliam, not simply the union's solicitor, but also a high official within the Carters' Union itself. The dockers' leader, James Sexton.

This story owes a great deal to my friend and fellow-writer, Lucienne Boyce, who frequently provided mentoring for me on the complexities of the suffrage movement. And my thanks also to Liverpool University History Graduate, Liam Davies – now himself a fine history teacher – who served a short internship as my researcher during the summer of 2017. Liam's report contributed significantly to my wealth of knowledge on some of these topics.

I am indebted as well, naturally, to my personal editor, Nicky Galliers, in London. To Cathy Helms at Avalon Graphics in North Carolina for the cover design. To Julie Witmer at Julie Witmer Custom Map Designs in Ontario for the maps – obviously. To Ann and the many and various beta readers who've been helping me pore over the final drafts.

I particularly want to mention Pauline Vickers here for her massively detailed and astute comments. Also, Professors Philip Thulla and Osman Sankoh in Sierra Leone, as well as Hanna-Ruth Thompson in London, for their patient guidance on the Kru and related language issues. Dylan Hughes was invaluable on Welsh language snippets and reminding me about the Penrhyn Quarry disputes. Thanks to Frank Hont and Nina Davies for their valuable support and to our old friend and comrade Donna Maria Kassim, who caused me to revisit many of the cultural issues with fresh eyes. To Jeremy Hawthorn, retired criminal defence solicitor and prominent historian, for his depth of knowledge around the 1911 Transport Strikes, timelines and related issues. Jeremy has devoted considerable time and energy trying to keep my fiction within those crucial boundaries of historical veracity. And finally, of course, my thanks to Helen Hart and her publishing team at SilverWood Books.

But I hope you've enjoyed the story and, if you want to keep in touch, I send out regular monthly newsletters, as well as always being happy to chat and answer questions. My website is: davidebsworth. com. You can also sign up for the newsletter there. I'm on Facebook, with my David Ebsworth author page, @EbsworthDavid – as well as occasionally Twitter: @EbsworthDavid. And if you liked the books, a short review is always welcome.

Finally, for anybody who'd like to take a closer look at any of main resources I used in writing this tale, you can find a detailed list on my website page for the novel.

Thanks again for taking the time to read all this and best wishes.

David Ebsworth
May 2022

9 781800 422230